## Love, Accidentally

Who doesn't like a U-Haul joke! I really enjoyed reading this book. This is the second book in the "A Mile High City Romance" series, by Rey and Clevenger and once again they show how compatible their writing is. It is also great to see that this is not only a collaboration between writers, but also between publishers. This story runs in parallel with the first book *A Convenient Arrangement*. All in all, this is a happy feel-good book, which I easily recommend. I hope Clevenger and Rey will write a book together again in the future.

-Meike V., *NetGalley*

## Just One Reason

I had a lot of fun reading *Just One Reason*. I enjoy diving into a traditional romance where I know exactly what I'm going to get, and then being delighted with a host of clever details that make the story feel fresh and brand new. This book checked all the boxes on my list of what I want in a good book.

-*The Lesbian Review*

I don't want to spoil things, but I was cheering this couple on and I wasn't disappointed. Communication happens and it is beautiful and sweet, but not without a splash of angst. This book gave me all of the feels and really hit a home run with thoughtful, meaningful dialogue.

-Digby M., *NetGalley*

This is the third installment of the Paradise Romance series. I have gotten so much entertainment out of these books. I love the characters and friend group. That while each story focuses on a new budding relationship, the same characters pop in and we see that they continue to progress in their respective partnerships. There is always so much more depth and satisfaction when the writer can put people through the ringer so that they come out on the other side shiny and happy. Overall, this is another great addition to the Paradise Romance series.

-Bookvark, *NetGalley*

### All the Reasons I Need

One of the reasons I love *Three Reasons to Say Yes* so much is that Clevenger wrote such strong secondary characters in Kate and Mo. I fell for them almost as much as the main characters, so to have them get their own book I was excited. This is a story about two best friends since college that have a ton of chemistry but have never done anything about it. ...If you are looking for a well written, angsty romance, look no further. This is an easy romance for me to recommend. I think with this series, Clevenger is at the top of her writing game and I can't wait to see what she puts out next.

-Lex Kent's Reviews, *goodreads*

This book is the second installment in Clevenger's Paradise Romance series. It's not necessary to read the first book, *Three Reasons to Say Yes*, to enjoy Kate and Mo's story... *All the Reasons I Need* is a thoughtful summer romance full of emotion. It let me imagine myself on a tropical beach, napping in a hammock, and sipping an exotic drink with a little umbrella in it. There's just something about beautiful sunsets and waves crashing on the beach that make falling in love seem easy.

-*The Lesbian Review*

### Three Reasons to Say Yes

This is without a doubt my new favourite Jaime Clevenger novel. Honestly I couldn't put it down from the first chapter. ...All in all this book has the potential to be my book of the year. Truly, books like this don't come around often that suit my reading tastes to a tee.

-*Les Rêveur*

...this one was totally my cup of tea with its charming relationship and family dynamics, great chemistry between two likable protagonists, a very convincing romance, some angst, drama and tension to the right extent and in all the right moments, and some very nice secondary characters. On top of that, the writing is technically very good, with all elements done properly. Sincerely recommended.

-Pin's Reviews, *goodreads*

This was a really easy story to get into. I sank right in and wanted to stay there, because reading about other people on vacation is kind of like taking a mini vacation from the world! It's sweet and lovely, and while it has some angst, it's not going to hurt you. Instead, it's going to take you away from it all so you can come back with a smile on your face.

-*The Lesbian Review*

### Party Favors

This book has one of the best characters ever. Me. Or rather you. It's quite a strange and startling experience at first to be in a book, especially one with as many hot, sexy, beautiful women in it who, incidentally, all seem to want you. But believe me, you'll soon get used to it. ...In a word, this book was FUN. It made me smile, and laugh, and tease my wife. I definitely recommend it to everyone, with the caveat that if you don't like erotica you should probably give it a pass. But not only read it, enjoy it, experience it, also find a friend, or a spouse, or even a book buddy online to talk to about it. Because you'll want to, it's that great.

-*The Lesbian Review*

I've read this book a few times and each time changed my decisions to find new and inviting destinations each time. This is a book you can read time and time again with a different journey. If you're looking for a fun Saturday night read that's sexy and hot as hell then this book is 100% for you! Go buy it now. 5 Stars.

-*Les Rêveur*

The story is told in the second person, present tense, which is ambitious in itself—it takes great skill to make that work and for the reader, who is now the narrator, to really connect to the thoughts and actions that are being attributed to them. Not all of the scenes will turn everyone on, as we all have different tastes, but I am pretty sure there is something for everyone in here. And if you do as you're told and follow the structure the author uses, you can dip into this book as much or as little as you wish. An interesting read with some pretty hot interactions.

*-Rainbow Book Reviews*

# OVER THE MOON WITH YOU

JAIME CLEVENGER

## Books by Jaime Clevenger published by Bella Books

*The Unknown Mile*
*Call Shotgun*
*Love, Accidentally*
*Sign on the Line*
*Whiskey and Oak Leaves*
*Sweet, Sweet Wine*
*Waiting for a Love Song*
*A Fugitive's Kiss*
*Moonstone*
*Party Favors*
*Three Reasons to Say Yes*
*All the Reasons I Need*
*Just One Reason*
*One Weekend in Aspen*

## Published by Spinsters Ink

*All Bets Off*

## About the Author

Jaime Clevenger lives in a little mountain town in Colorado. Most days are spent working as a veterinarian, but time off is well-filled writing, reading, swimming, practicing karate, and goofing off with their wife and kids (both two and four legged). Jaime loves hearing a good story and hopes that if you ever meet, you'll share your favorite. Feel free to embellish the details.

# OVER THE MOON WITH YOU

## JAIME CLEVENGER

BELLA
B O O K S
2022

Bella Books, Inc.
P.O. Box 10543
Tallahassee, FL 32302

Printed in the United States of America on acid-free paper.

First Edition - 2022

Editor: Heather Flournoy
Cover Designer: Kayla Mancuso

ISBN: 978-1-64247-383-4

# Acknowledgment

For many years I avoided writing a story with a veterinarian as a main character mostly because writing is a vacation from my day job, but also because I didn't want someone to assume a vet character was automatically me. The truth is, though, I love being a veterinarian and there are so many stories I could share of the animals and people who have touched my life. At some point, I realized I was being silly trying to keep the writing and the vet life completely separate. That said, this story is in no way about my personal experience as a veterinarian. This story is entirely fictional and while I am in debt to many people (and animals) who helped me become the veterinarian I am today, any characters who seem similar to anyone I know or have worked with is entirely coincidental and certainly not intentional. I sadly don't even know anyone with a houseful of cow knick-knacks! Also, I'm not a large animal vet, but I have a deep respect for those in my profession who are, and I thank you for all you do.

Thank you, Corina, for always listening to my story ideas, for offering the best feedback, and for being willing to read a scene over and over again. You make every one of my books better and you are an amazing life partner. Thank you also to my two kids for understanding when I have a story deadline and being ready with a plot twist! You are both amazing storytellers and I love your creativity.

Thank you to my beta readers, Laina, Charlotte, and Maggie. I appreciate each of you and this story is so much better because of your comments and advice. Thank you, Heather, for being a rockstar editor yet again. I love working with you and look forward to the next time already. Thank you to everyone at Bella for all of your help in making this story shine. And thank you, dear reader. Each time I write a story, I get new best friends (otherwise known as characters) and I love that you want to meet them. I truly hope you enjoy their story.

Finally... Thank you to all of the animals, both large and small, who I have loved and cared for, and who have taught me more than I can express with words.

# CHAPTER ONE

"Wow. Your boobs look fabulous." Leslie pushed up her own breasts and made a face in the mirror behind Seren. "Want to share some of that with me?"

"I wish it worked that way." Seren Winters pulled back her shoulders and tried to appreciate the fact that she now completely filled out a D-cup. Her breasts did look fantastic, even if it was more than she was used to.

"Is it messed up that I feel kind of turned-on staring at my best friend's breasts?" Leslie stuck out her tongue to make it clear she was joking. "How much bigger are they gonna get?"

"You, too, could get pregnant. Turns out, all it takes is one trip to the sperm bank."

"Not everyone gets prego the first time they have contact with sperm, you know."

She did know. At thirty-eight, she'd had more than one doctor tell her to expect multiple attempts and likely IVF. Or at least medications to induce ovulation and six to nine months of trying. Nope. All it took was squirting a little tube of defrosted sperm into her uterus and she was on the fast track to being a mom. The reality of that still managed to thrill and terrify her. "I think that's why I'm freaking out. Everything's happening so fast."

"Which means you get to the good part faster. Having a baby in your arms."

"You're right." She had to keep her mind focused on that. Yes, she was overwhelmed, but if the universe kept smiling on her, in roughly five months she'd get to hold her very own baby. A brand-new person—who she already knew she'd love more than anything else in the world.

"But seriously. Do you think your boobs are just going to keep growing?"

"They can't keep getting bigger, right?" She readjusted herself, but that only seemed to push more cleavage into view. "I'm starting to get intimidated. Maybe I should try a different bathing suit."

"You look amazing in this one."

"I look like a porn star."

"Stop. You don't. Well, not entirely." Leslie sidestepped Seren's swat, laughing as she did. "Anyway, it's not like you're wearing this to work. You're going to water aerobics. The only people you're going to see are a bunch of older ladies—and you know they love big boobs."

"Old ladies love big boobs?"

"Well, when I'm an old lady I know I'll love them."

Seren smiled at Leslie. "You're the best." She dropped her shoulders a moment later. "Some days I feel like an old lady already."

"We're in our thirties. We're barely middle aged."

"This"—Seren tapped her belly—"at thirty-eight, is a geriatric pregnancy." The bump wasn't yet visible in her work clothes, but the cut of the swimsuit seemed to broadcast her truth. She'd also seen the ultrasound images with the cute little glob of cells, and there was no doubt her body was changing. It still made her heart race to think about. Again, thrilling...and also terrifying.

"You're gorgeous. And I'm not just saying that because you're my best friend and you're standing here looking uncomfortable in a bathing suit while everyone else is fully clothed."

"Thanks." Seren rolled her eyes.

"It's the truth. At fifteen weeks pregnant, my best friend is a total hottie. You've got that pregnancy glow thing going on."

"Whatever. We both know you're the hottie." Seren did appreciate the compliment though. She was already self-conscious about her body changing, and parading around in a bathing suit took things to a whole different level. "But, just so you know, I love having a best friend who always says the right thing. And who will go shopping with me at the drop of a hat."

"Always. You know how I feel about shopping."

"I didn't expect that the first thing I'd need from the maternity store would be a bathing suit." Stretchy leggings had become her favorite fashion now that she couldn't fasten her other pants and she'd simply switched to wearing more of her loose longer knit shirts. No one at work knew. Yet. She'd promised herself to tell everyone yesterday at the monthly meeting, but she'd lost her nerve at the last minute. As excited as she was, she couldn't shake the worry that any little misstep of fate could rip the future she'd dreamed about right out of her hands.

For as long as she could remember, she'd wanted to be a mom. The time to start a family had never seemed right, though, and then all of a sudden, it'd felt like time had run out. It hadn't, clearly. And she wanted to simply be thankful that she'd gone for it and that so far everything was going exactly the way it should. Well, minus all the morning sickness and the ginormous breasts. She tugged at the shoulder straps to see if she could make her cleavage less pronounced, then made a sultry face. "You really think I should buy this one?"

"Hell, yes. We should also talk about safe ways to earn some extra cash on the side with those girls of yours. How do you feel about pole dancing?"

Leslie's joking always got her laughing—no matter what mood she was in. "Only you could say that right now." At least the suit was comfortable. And her boobs did look amazing.

"When's your first class?"

"Tomorrow morning."

"Want moral support? I could skip my morning run…If I hadn't signed up for this damn marathon, I'd switch to a pool workout in a heartbeat."

"I'll be fine. I'm sure I'll have plenty of company in the pool. Everyone's grandma is gonna be there." As long as she didn't get sick, part of her was looking forward to it. She'd had to give up running and her usual gym workout because every time she broke a sweat, she wanted to vomit. Or did vomit. Her doctor had been the one to suggest water aerobics, and she'd read up on all the benefits. It might not be marathon training, but she was looking forward to it. "When I signed up, the guy at the gym said I should come early to get a spot. Apparently the teacher is super popular."

"Maybe after this marathon, I'll switch to water aerobics. Then I'll get to buy myself a sexy bathing suit for the occasion."

"And then we can shake it for the old ladies together?"

Leslie clapped her hands. "Yes!"

"Deal. After your marathon, you join me in water aerobics." Seren glanced at her reflection again. "I miss our morning runs." Truthfully, she also missed being in running shape, and a little part of her worried she wouldn't ever be fit again. That worry was probably ridiculous, but everything was changing. "What if I made the wrong decision? I mean, I know I want a baby, but switching to water aerobics feels like only the beginning. What if everything's different?"

"Hey. You." Leslie reached for Seren's hand and gave it a squeeze. "Being pregnant is temporary. Yeah, some things will change. For one, you'll have a kid. But I know you. After you pop that baby out, you'll be back to running circles around everyone else in no time. Just with a stroller in front of you."

She wanted Leslie to be right. Unfortunately, she couldn't push away the feeling it wouldn't be so simple. She thought of the pros and cons list she'd made before she'd let herself research sperm donors. Big boobs wasn't on the list. Neither was her whole world changing. But she pictured the sidebar note that was only one word long—"baby"—and knew she hadn't made a mistake.

No matter the cost, there was nothing she wanted more in life. She took a deep breath and rocked her head side to side. "I think I can get used to myself with big boobs."

"Plenty of people could get used to your big boobs."

Seren laughed. "Again, only you would say that right now. Let me change out of this suit and then let's get dinner. I'm starving."

"Think that baby would let you eat spicy food? I feel like Mexican."

"I could probably handle tortilla soup. With a side of plain rice." Everyone said her appetite would bounce back in the second trimester, and she was counting the days. She was even kind of looking forward to the wacky cravings.

"Tortilla soup sounds perfect. Now go change before some porn star walks into this place and gets jealous of your look."

A year ago, she'd have thought that a porn star browsing a maternity store in Davis was as ridiculous as her signing up for water aerobics. But now nothing seemed all that unbelievable. The last year had changed everything.

Before she started cataloging all of the changes in a mental loss/gain chart, she stepped into the changing stall and pulled the curtain behind her. Despite feeling like she had no idea what life would throw at her next, she got through every day tolerably well. Especially if she ignored the question about how long she could work before the baby came, the worries about finances, and the stress about her living situation.

At least she wasn't stressed about being single. In fact, she didn't even want to meet someone now—even if her boobs, not to mention her rising libido, seemed to suggest otherwise. A girlfriend would only complicate things. Thankfully someone had invented vibrators and, really, what more did she need?

# CHAPTER TWO

Paige Dannenberg had ignored the last two phone calls. Whoever wanted to get ahold of her was insistent, however, and the third call came only two minutes after the others. She finished tying the last suture, yanked off her bloody gloves, and reached into her back pocket, muttering, "This better be important."

The number was one she didn't recognize, and between a chorus of moos and the rumble of a passing tractor, it was hard to hear the voice on the other end of the line.

"Mom? Is that you?" Paige plugged her opposite ear with her free hand as she strained to hear. She could now tell it was her mom, calling from someone else's phone, but still couldn't understand what she was saying. She motioned for her vet student intern to gather up the surgery supplies and circled to the far side of her truck. "Can you say that again?"

"I said I broke my ass!"

Paige pulled the phone away from her ear. Beatrice Dannenberg had resorted to yelling right as the noise of the tractor cut out. "Do you mean your tailbone?"

"The doctor called it a cock something or other."

At another time that line might be funny. "Coccyx. What happened?"

"Oh, you know how Charlie is always chasing Squirrel. I'm waiting for an X-ray. My phone shattered. I'm on Vickie's cell."

Talking to her mom was always like unraveling a knotted necklace. "Where are you? Urgent care?"

Heavy Mom sigh. "Yes."

"And Charlie was chasing Squirrel and somehow you fell?"

Another heavy sigh. "Yes."

Squirrel was Paige's cat. Charlie was her mom's toy poodle. They hated each other. Passionately.

"One minute I was making tea and the next Charlie was barking his fool head off and Squirrel was up on the refrigerator. Vickie's worried I broke my hip. I told her I wouldn't be walking if I broke a hip."

True, but tile floors were unforgiving. And at sixty-eight, Beatrice was not made of rubber. A wave of guilt hit Paige's chest. When she'd moved in with her mom, she'd only planned on it being a few weeks. Four months later she still hadn't found a place to buy. And her three cats were driving Charlie wild. Well, mostly it was Squirrel.

She ran her hand through her tousled hair and caught a stench of her own body odor mingled with cow shit. Which basically described her day. "Let's hope it's only a broken tailbone."

"Oh, I'm sure that's all it is. But we'll probably be here all night anyway."

Paige eyed the time. Normally she was done with her day by six, but she'd been called last minute to check out a 4-H heifer who'd managed to eat two yards of wire. "As soon as I'm finished with this last appointment, I'll head over to urgent care so Vickie can go home."

"Are you busy next Friday?"

"Why?" There was no point in hiding her suspicious tone. Beatrice Dannenberg was always scheming something.

"Vickie's niece might be gay."

"Mom, we've been through this. I'm not looking to date anyone." How were they having this conversation now?

"She's single and there haven't been any boyfriends. Not recently anyway."

"I don't want to be set up." Especially not with someone who only "might" be gay. "Remember the last time?" Paige cringed, thinking of the dinner party her mom had organized to set her up with the daughter of her mom's hairdresser—all without telling Paige what she was up to until the moment the woman arrived. Things got more awkward when the woman admitted she wasn't single.

Her mom's matchmaking attempts were only one reason Paige was ready to have her own space. "Tell Vickie I'll be there in an hour. I'll grab dinner for us." Her mom's favorite comfort food was easy: fast-food fried chicken. "Anything else I can do?" She'd pick up flowers too—on Squirrel's behalf.

"I need someone to teach my water aerobics class tomorrow."

"Water aerobics? I have no idea how to—"

"You'll be fine," Bea interrupted. "I'll give you the tape and write down all the moves."

"There's gotta be someone else you can ask. What about Vickie?"

"Vickie?" Beatrice laughed. She said something to Vickie that Paige couldn't quite understand, and more laughter followed.

Vickie was pushing ninety, but she at least took the water aerobics class. "Or someone else from the class?"

"There's no one else. If you can't do it, I'll do it. Even if I have to lie on the side of the pool."

"Never mind. I'll do it." It's not like she had other plans. Besides, she owed her mom.

* * *

Squirrel hopped into Paige's lap, settled in, and began purring as she seemingly contemplated the women in Lycra bouncing around on the screen. Paige scratched her neck. "You know, it's your fault I can't stay home with you and enjoy this Saturday morning."

The purring got louder, as if Squirrel understood perfectly and had no intention of feeling guilty.

"You really don't care, do you? Lazy Saturdays are my favorite and now I have to give that up to teach water aerobics. Because you had to tease the dog."

More purring.

"Then again, I also like chill Fridays and that didn't happen either." She'd ended up spending two hours at urgent care after sending Vickie home. By the time she got her mom home and settled, she was too tired to do anything more than collapse in bed. Without the shower that really had needed to happen.

Beatrice appeared in the kitchen doorway. "If you'd acted at all interested in those nurses, I could have gotten you a date last night and you'd have someone besides your cat to talk to."

"I still can't believe you asked those nurses if they were single."

"They were both attractive and you obviously weren't going to ask. I don't see the problem."

Paige resisted a groan. Barely. "They were working, Mom. When I'm working, I'm focused. I don't want someone asking me if I'd like to go out to dinner with them. Or with their daughter."

"Lots of women want to date a doctor."

"I'm a veterinarian. Women who are interested in dating a doctor are looking for someone who makes a lot more money than me. And those women aren't my type. By the way, should you be up walking? You're probably only feeling better because of the Percocet."

Beatrice ignored her, heading for a refill of her coffee, and Paige turned her attention back to her laptop. She'd watched ten different online tutorials for water aerobics but wasn't convinced yet that she could pull off teaching. She knew her mom couldn't— the urgent care doc had made Bea promise to take it easy for the weekend, and based on how stiff she was moving, the Percocet was only barely helping. But there had to be someone else more qualified.

"You're sure you've asked everyone else you can think of to teach this class?"

"There's no one else. It's either you or me."

Paige wanted to argue that there had to be someone else but held back the words. Aside from not wanting her mom to push it, she felt guilty since it was Squirrel who'd caused all the trouble. Well, Charlie was partly to blame, but there was no reasoning with a spoiled poodle.

Speak of the devil, Charlie appeared. Bea cooed as she set down a platter of treats.

"I did feed him breakfast, you know."

"He needs his treats." After Charlie had inhaled the treats, Bea came over to the table, bracing her side as she moved. She squinted at the screen and tsked. "You can't learn how to teach water aerobics from that."

"I don't have another option. I could have brought more coffee to your room so you wouldn't have to get out of bed."

"Oh, I'm not up just for the coffee. I'm checking up on you."

"You worried I'd forget about teaching the class?"

Beatrice patted her arm. "That's the least of my worries."

"What are your other worries?"

Bea shuffled out of the kitchen without answering.

Paige eyed Squirrel. "How hard can it be to teach water aerobics?" When the cat met her gaze, studying her as if contemplating her abilities, she wondered if maybe she did talk to her cats more because she didn't have a girlfriend. But cats were easier to talk to. Not to mention easier to keep happy.

She picked up her notebook again, reading over the list of moves she'd written out along with the plan. Seeing it all organized on paper made her simultaneously confident and sick to her stomach. She'd never been able to dance and had zero rhythm. Knowing this, she'd settled on a march as her go-to steps and figured she'd spice it up from there swinging her hands around like the YouTube videos.

Bea reappeared, lugging a bulky boom box that looked straight from 1985. She set the boom box on the table. "The play button is a little sticky. You gotta jab it." She jammed her thumb on one of the buttons on the tape player. Nothing happened of course because it wasn't plugged in.

"I can figure out how to get a cassette to play, Mom. Why are you using a mixtape for your music anyway?"

"Don't sound so judgy. If it ain't broke..." Bea stopped and pursed her lips. "That expression is less funny when you've got a broken ass."

"Glad to see you didn't lose your sense of humor."

"The pain meds work." Bea went over to the junk drawer and pulled out a pen and a notepad. She hummed as she started to draw a picture of what was clearly a swimming pool with a little stick figure standing to one side.

"Is that supposed to be me?"

Bea nodded but continued working on the sketch.

"I feel like I've got a little more muscle than that stick guy." No smile from Mom. "I don't think I need the mixtape. I found some workout music that I can stream from my phone. If I hook it up to my alarm clock speakers, I can use that."

"Won't be loud enough." Bea still didn't look up from her notepad. She'd started drawing something behind the stick figure and her brow furrowed as she concentrated. "Besides, everyone loves the Saturday tape. People are going to expect it."

Paige didn't want to imagine what songs she'd hear on the Saturday tape. Splashing to the oldies? Her mom continued working on the sketch, and curiosity got the better of her. She scooted Squirrel out of her lap and went over for a closer look. "I'm guessing that's a supply cabinet with the pool noodles and weights? You know I did research how to teach a water aerobics class…"

Her mother added a diagram of something else along the far side of the pool.

"What's that?"

"The location of the emergency phone and the AED Defibrillator. In case someone has a heart attack. You do know CPR, right?" Her mother looked up from the notepad. "On people, I mean."

Paige opened and closed her mouth. "I took a class. Once." Was it college?

"Well, let's hope no one tries to die today."

*Shit.* How likely was a cardiac arrest during water aerobics? "Maybe this is a bad idea."

Her mom looked Paige up and down, then nodded. "It's a terrible idea. But the other option is me teaching class."

She'd hoped her mom would add some meaningless platitude like, *"Oh, you'll be fine. This is easy as pie."* But no.

"I'll call Rita. She's CPR certified. As long as she's there, you'll be fine."

"Could this Rita teach?"

Mom laughed. "Definitely not." She laughed again. "Rita? Oh, she'd be worse than Vickie."

"If it's too hard for Rita and Vickie, why are you sending me? I've never even taken a water aerobics class. Or any aerobics class for that matter."

"You don't mind embarrassing yourself, sweetie. It's one of your best traits."

Paige was still processing whether her mom's words were actually a compliment or not when she was handed the notepad.

"Don't get too close to the edge of the pool."

"You worried I'm going to fall in?"

"You'd be surprised how easy it is to lose track of where you're standing. Especially when you're dancing."

Paige bit the edge of her lip. "I wasn't planning on dancing. I was thinking I'd focus on marching." Thank god it'd be a pool full of old ladies. They'd go easy on her. Right? "And I learned some arm moves." She demonstrated, punching the air in front of her and then swinging her arms side to side. "Does it look I'm doing it right?"

Beatrice pursed her lips, then nodded unconvincingly. "It'll do. Now, what are you going to wear?"

Paige looked down at the sweatshirt and shorts she'd picked out that morning. "This?"

Bea grimaced. "What are you wearing underneath the sweatshirt?"

Technically, she had a tank top and a sports bra on underneath, but she had no intention of losing the hoodie. "I don't really think the clothes are gonna be the problem. It's the rest of it."

"You'll rise to the occasion. You always do. I know how you used to like dancing at the gay bars. This will be the same thing—only at a pool."

"Mom, when I said I was going out dancing, not a lot of dancing happened."

Bea put both hands on Paige's shoulders. Several inches shorter, she still managed a formidable stare. "You can do anything you put your mind to. Just don't stand too close to the edge."

"I'm not going to fall in the pool."

"Then you'll be fine." Beatrice let go. "And, if you survive, you can teach for me on Sunday too."

"Lucky me."

# CHAPTER THREE

Seren's usual gym didn't have a pool. That was a good enough reason to switch over to Aqua Fitness Zone. The other reason, however, was that she had clients at her old gym and wanted a break from being recognized in the locker room.

One step into Aqua Fitness and she knew the change would also mean working out with less stress. Nearly everyone in the place was older and less muscley. Plus, the club centered around the pool, with only a small room of weights and another slightly larger room of treadmills and bikes. The locker room didn't look as if it'd been updated since the seventies but Seren had no problem with that. Less froofy amenities meant less froofy people.

She changed into her suit, tossed her things into an empty locker, and followed the signs to the pool. The guy on the phone who'd recommended she come early must have given everyone the same advice. The pool was already packed. Everyone had pink pool noodles and fluorescent purple dumbbells, but the marked bins for the items were empty. She looked around for where extras might be, and before she could ask, a woman with an impressive gray beehive pointed to a door marked Storage.

"Saturday's always a full class, honey. You gotta come early. Everyone loves Miss Bea."

"Yes, yes, we do," echoed several swimmers.

Laughing and happy chatter followed. The group all clearly knew each other. They'd also, Seren noticed, gotten the memo to wear water shoes. She looked down at her bare feet, toes newly polished, and hoped it wouldn't be a problem going commando, as it were.

Nervous that class was about to start and not wanting to be the holdup, although she didn't see any sign of an instructor, she hurried over to the storage closet. Yellow noodles spilled out as soon as she opened the door. She picked one, trying not to worry about the fact that she'd be the odd one out with the only wrong-colored noodle, and then dug through the closet until she found a set of purple dumbbells. Once she'd scooted all the noodles back into the closet, she slammed the door only to have it catch on a noodle. One second later, they all spilled out again. She looked down at her feet, noodles scattered everywhere, but did not risk a glance around to see if anyone was watching. Hopefully not.

"You got this," she murmured, jamming all the noodles in a second time. Bracing one hand on the stack, she swung the door closed. The latch clicked and she exhaled. No escapees. At least she'd accomplished that hurdle. Was it more pathetic that she now celebrated small successes, or a sign her general anxiety was improving? She bent to scoop up her chosen noodle and weights, turned around, and walked right into some guy in a hoodie.

At the same moment she recognized that the person she'd bumped into wasn't a guy but a very attractive queer woman—if her gaydar was working anymore—she realized the woman was stumbling backward to the pool.

"Watch out!" Seren lunged forward to grab her. Between the woman's flailing arms and her pool noodle, the only thing she accomplished was adding forward energy to the slow-motion fall. The splash was impressively loud, echoing in the enclosed space.

Seren stared, not breathing, as a flurry of seniors coalesced on the spot where the woman had landed. *Shit, shit, shit.* She'd pushed a total stranger into the pool. What if the woman hit her head and drowned? Did she need to be rescued? With the splashing and everyone talking at once, she couldn't tell what was happening under the water. She finally took a breath when the woman's head surfaced.

"I'm so sorry." She rushed the words, but the woman showed no sign of hearing her. The noise of everyone asking if she was okay overwhelmed her apology.

The woman tried to make her way over to the stairs but the crowd around her slowed her movement. It was a sight to see—more than a dozen older ladies all surrounding one dyke. Under other circumstances, it might have been funny.

The "are you okays?" made an awful cacophony, and despite the woman's nodding, the questions didn't stop. She plodded her way through the water, drenched clothes, drenched hair, and a dour expression on her face. But she didn't look mad. Weirdly, she also didn't seem all that surprised. More, she looked resigned to her fate.

Everyone who hadn't witnessed the actual fall—push—was trying to figure out what had happened while those who had seen it were talking over each other to tell the story. The woman slopped her way up the stairs and Seren hurried over.

"I'm so sorry. I didn't see you and then suddenly you were falling."

It was a pitiable excuse, but the woman gave her a curt nod and then began peeling layers of clothing off. Shoes first, then socks, then her sweatshirt. Seren half wondered if she'd keep stripping all the way down to her underwear, but when she got to the wet tank top, she tugged the bottom edge and shook her head. The white cotton clung to her body exposing a dark sports bra she had on underneath. And the rest of her? Broad shoulders, well-muscled arms, and toned legs below dripping gym shorts.

Seren swallowed. *Fuck.* Why did she have to push a hot dyke into the pool? Of all people?

Beehive Lady stepped forward with a towel extended. "That was quite a splash. Here you go."

The woman nodded her thanks and started drying her face.

Why hadn't she thought to hand the woman a towel? Instead, she'd simply stood there with her pool noodle, numbly transfixed by the strip show. God, how embarrassing. She didn't think it could get any worse, but then the woman looked up. Amber-brown eyes framed in dark lashes locked on to her. She didn't look away, and

Seren went from being mortified at what she'd done to inexplicably turned-on. Not a little turned-on either. But aroused to the point where heat flooded her body and she had to shift her legs closer together to admonish the pulse at her center.

"I really am sorry."

"It's okay. I'm kind of a klutz." The woman gave a half-smile that made her look more adorable than sexy. Although the clingy wet tank top was doing a bang-up job keeping the sexy vibe going.

"You're not a klutz. I pushed you into the pool."

"I was standing in the wrong spot." She finished toweling off her head—leaving the short dark brown waves more tousled than dry—and returned the towel to Beehive Lady.

"Bea did tell me I should remind you to stay back from the edge. I thought she was being dramatic." Beehive Lady shook her head. "By the way, I'm Rita."

"I'm Paige. But you knew that." Paige exhaled. "My mom said you were CPR certified?"

"I am, and I thought I'd have to test my skills when you divebombed Leann." Rita set her hand on Paige's shoulder. "Wasn't sure which one of you I was going to be rescuing."

Seren hadn't even noticed that there was someone near where Paige had fallen. Clearly, she'd been too focused on Paige.

Rita continued, "That was some stumble."

Paige glanced down at the puddle under her feet. "As surprising as this may sound, that was not the first time I've fallen into a pool."

"Your mom sent me three texts this morning—two of which said: 'make sure Paige doesn't get too close to the edge.' I wondered why."

"It really wasn't your fault," Seren interrupted. "I turned right into you."

"Yeah...But..."

Rita pursed her lips as Paige stammered. For some reason, Paige looked guilty. Seren didn't know what to make of it and quickly added, "You would have been fine but then my pool noodle smacked you."

Paige shook her head. "I wasn't paying attention to where I was standing."

"But I pushed you." Why did Paige think this was somehow her fault?

"After she took one look at you and stopped thinking." Rita pushed her own bosom up, accentuating the line of matronly cleavage and winked. "Weapons of mind control."

Paige turned the same color as the safety telephone on the wall behind her. Crimson. And only then did Seren put the whole picture together. Paige had been checking her out. Well, her boobs, anyway. And then she'd pushed Paige—accidentally of course. Talk about instant karma. Still, she felt bad for her part in the mess. Even if maybe there was a little pride mixed in.

"I'm still sorry I pushed you."

"Well, now you know it wasn't completely your fault."

Rita cleared her throat. "So, gals, are we having class today?"

"Right." Paige sighed. "I have to teach."

"You're the teacher?" Seren wanted to take back the words, or at least change her tone of surprise, when Paige gave a shy shrug.

"Usually my mom runs this class, but she broke her tailbone last night. No one else could sub for her." Paige went over to a boom box and pressed the play button, and as soon as the music started, she straightened and met Seren's gaze. "Wish me luck."

Since she looked like she was about to walk the plank to her death, Seren said the words she didn't truly believe: "I'm sure you're gonna be great."

# CHAPTER FOUR

Considering her mom's playlist started with "Baby Got Back" and half the class hollered at her to stick out her butt, things could have gone worse. Paige wasn't certain how many times she blushed—over the hooting from a few of the older ladies when certain songs came up and when she'd accidentally glanced at the left side of the pool.

The left side was where the woman with the yellow pool noodle was and, god, she was beautiful. Like, brain-zappingly beautiful. Wavy blond hair done up in a loose ponytail with wisps falling all around her face, sculpted features, and arresting gray-blue eyes. Paige had felt those eyes size her up. How did she measure? She could only guess after she'd been found guilty of checking out the woman's breasts like some creepy old dude. But, damn, the woman had amazing curves.

In her defense, Paige wished she could say, she'd been distracted rehearsing the routine she'd planned in her head, and then directly in front of her she'd been stopped by a perfect bent-over butt. She'd tried to shake herself out of the trance, but one second later the woman turned and—holy smokes, did she have nice boobs. If only

Rita hadn't called her out on it. At least there was minimal chance she'd ever see the woman again. Unless she came to tomorrow's class.

Paige groaned when she remembered she had to teach again tomorrow. She'd been awkward as shit, stiff-armed, and only managed to pull off the marching, but everyone thanked her afterward. Including yellow pool noodle woman. If Paige had been smooth, she would have met her eyes at least. But she'd pretended to be busy with unhooking the boom box and only murmured, "You're welcome."

Smooth was definitely not her. Not today anyway. She tugged on her wet socks and then laced her wet tennis shoes. Each step made a squelching sound. When she picked up her sopping sweatshirt and wrung it out, she managed to get half the water on her shoes.

At least she'd worked up a sweat leading the class through all the moves and her tank top was half dry. Her shorts and her underwear, unfortunately, were not. Since she had nothing dry to change into anyway, she bypassed the locker room and headed out to the parking lot.

"Hey."

Paige stopped. Yellow pool noodle woman was standing next to her truck. She'd switched out the sexy bathing suit for an equally attractive flowery sundress. Big sunglasses gave her a movie star look. A very sexy movie star.

"I'm Seren. You might remember me because I pushed you into the pool?"

Yellow pool noodle lady—Seren—had waited to talk to her? It didn't seem possible, but… "I do remember." Paige's smile widened. She probably looked like a doofus, still half wet and grinning like a hyena, but she couldn't help it. "You don't have to say sorry again. I'm fine."

"Oh, I wasn't waiting to say sorry. Although I am." Seren pointed to a silver Subaru. "That's my car. Some asshole truck driver pinned me in. I'm waiting for the guy at the front desk to figure out whose truck it is so they can move it."

Paige glanced at her truck and then at the Subaru. So much for thinking the attraction went both ways. "You can't get in?"

"Not on the driver's side. Well, not without dinging asshole's truck. And I'm too close to that wall on the passenger side."

Paige eyed the landscape retaining wall that Seren pointed to and then the white parking lines. The Subaru was in a tiny parking spot. Unfortunately, she'd made the spot even smaller by parking over the line on her side. "I'm the asshole truck driver."

"This is your truck?"

She wished it weren't true, but neither of them was going anywhere until she pulled out. "I'm usually very good at parking my beast, but I was a little stressed this morning. Give me a sec and I'll get out of your way."

"I'm sorry I called you an asshole." Seren's eyebrows bunched together. "It's a big truck and it's probably hard to find parking spots for it."

"No, it's fine. I took up more than my fair share of space."

"You're a veterinarian?"

Paige nodded. It wasn't hard to guess her occupation. Her truck bed was outfitted to carry all of her supplies, and a veterinary caduceus was stamped on the back. Not only that, she had a bumper sticker for the vet school. But Seren had asked like she was genuinely surprised. "In case you're worried, I'm a way better vet than I am water aerobics instructor."

"I thought you did a good job—especially considering you've never done it before. Of course, it was also my first class, so what do I know?"

"You could have stopped at the first part."

"True. But I wouldn't want you to get a big head."

Seren's flirty look made her feel heady. Wait, were they flirting?

"The ladies in the locker room mentioned there's a Sunday class. Is your mom going to be back to teach that, or will it be you?"

"It'll be me again. I think my mom tweaked her back too when she broke her tailbone. She's on a lot of pain meds, but I know she won't be feeling good enough to teach tomorrow."

"That's terrible." Seren shook her head. "The part about your mom. Not you teaching."

"Well, class was pretty terrible today." Paige couldn't deny it. "Rita made me swear to have more footwork next time. She said she'd march me right into the pool otherwise."

Seren grinned. "You weren't terrible. Really."

"I'm pretty sure that I was. But. I promise I'll be better tomorrow."

"In that case, I promise I'll be in class tomorrow."

The promise packed a punch when it was followed up by a perfect smile. Paige managed a nod and a "see you then" as she fumbled for her keys. She could hardly feel her legs as she floated over to her truck. It wasn't as if she hadn't ever flirted with women—but it'd been a long time and Seren was in a whole different category of pretty. She unlocked the door and settled into the driver's seat, her cheeks aching from the ridiculously huge grin on her face. She wanted to sit in her truck and enjoy the moment. Then she remembered Seren wasn't going anywhere until she did.

She backed out, watching her mirrors like a hawk. When she pulled past Seren, she lifted a hand. Seren's head tilted and a little smile lifted her lips.

"Well, damn." As unbelievable as it was, she couldn't wait to teach water aerobics again.

# CHAPTER FIVE

Seren didn't pull out of her parking spot at Aqua Fitness after Paige left. At first it was because she wasn't in a rush to let go of all the happy feelings dancing in her chest, but then it was because she was quickly aware that she needed to eat. She rolled down all the windows and got out the box of granola bars.

*What a morning.*

She'd felt properly sexy for the first time in ages. She smiled again at the way Paige had looked at her when she'd pulled past in her truck. She hadn't realized how much she'd missed someone looking at her like that. But now that the adrenaline had ebbed and her blood sugar plummeted, the wave of nausea made her worry she'd have to puke out the side of her car. Classy.

Hoping to stay ahead of it, she stuffed the bar into her mouth. Eating to stop herself from vomiting was her new reality. Sadly, she'd vomited so many times in the last two months that she had all the logistics worked out along with a case of granola bars for the car, one for work, and more snack packs in her purse than a mom with a toddler.

Surprisingly, she hadn't felt nauseous once in water aerobics. Of course she'd been so distracted during class she hadn't realized that fact until after. And the distraction was all Paige's fault.

She pictured Paige marching on the side of the pool and a fresh smile strained her cheeks. Then she pictured Paige punching the air, not at all in time to Bruno Mars's "Uptown Funk," but adorable nonetheless for how hard she was trying. And finally, she pictured Paige's sheepish wave. She smiled again at that. No two ways about it, Paige was into her. When was the last time she'd randomly met someone attractive who was also into her? No awkward setup, no weeks of working out details online for a first meet. Just a chance connection.

Unfortunately, the timing was absolute crap. She sighed, staring at the half-eaten granola bar. She had no business even thinking about liking someone at the moment. It wasn't only the baby that made sure she ate every two hours. Okay, it was mostly the baby. But there was also the problem of not knowing where she'd be living after she sold her mom's house. Nor when that would happen. On top of that, were the uncertainties about her job. She had to figure out a plan to drop the news about the pregnancy. But as an independent contractor, nothing felt guaranteed. Would they hold a place for her after she went out on maternity leave?

She thought again of Paige and the rest faded into the background. "She's so damn hot."

Her phone buzzed, and she answered when she saw Leslie's name. "How'd you know I needed to talk to someone?"

"Anyone would do, huh?" Leslie pretended to be hurt.

"Anyone named Leslie Brandt."

"What would you say if I told you I swung by Café Venus and picked us up two iced lattes?"

"I'd say I'd like to kiss you."

Leslie laughed. "I know I'm not your type, but thanks for the compliment. Are you home?"

"No. I'm sitting in the parking lot at Aqua Fitness trying to swallow a granola bar before I vomit."

"Oh, honey. Water aerobics was a bust too?"

"No. It was great. I made it all the way through class. I think I might even be sore tomorrow." She couldn't help wondering if

Paige was the type who'd make a lover sore. Not that she had any business thinking about that. "I only started to feel sick after class. Someone parked too close to my car and I couldn't get in. Had to wait for them to move their truck and my blood sugar dropped in the meantime."

"I hate people who can't park in the lines. Total assholes."

"This one is more clueless than asshole. Well, I don't know if clueless is right. She's kind of head-in-the-clouds smart."

"Wait, you know her?"

"I may have pushed her into the pool."

Leslie made a snorting sound that devolved into coughing.

"Are you okay?"

"You made me snort my latte up my nose. I can't believe you pushed someone into the pool. Was it an old lady?"

"No. Our age, I think."

"And she was in the water aerobics class?"

"She was sort of the instructor."

"Sort of? Okay, hang up and drive home. I'll meet you there. I want the whole story."

Leslie was sitting on the front step when Seren got home. She held up one of the two cups she was holding. "I can't believe you pushed someone into the pool."

"It wasn't completely my fault. Really I blame my pool noodle."

Leslie raised a questioning eyebrow. "Is that a sex reference?"

"I kind of wish it were." Seren unlocked the front door and then waited for Leslie to follow her in. "Why are you looking at me funny?"

"Give me a minute. I'm processing. Did you push some hottie into the pool?"

"I may have helped her in the direction she was falling."

Leslie laughed.

"But she was definitely checking me out."

Leslie whistled and held out her hand for a high-five. Despite her embarrassment, Seren clapped it.

"Would it be crazy if I Googled her?" If Leslie hadn't been there, she would have done it without a second thought, but admitting her plan aloud made her hesitate. "Is that too weird?"

"Not too weird for you."

Seren rolled her eyes. "Thanks."

"I'll even help. I want to see who's got you all swoony."

"Maybe it's a bad idea. Not the looking up part but…I'm fifteen weeks pregnant and *now* I find some hot single dyke who's maybe interested in me?"

"First off, getting to know someone is harmless. Second, if you aren't going for this woman, I might. How big was her truck?"

Seren narrowed her gaze.

"Kidding! You know I'd never do that to you. And that proved you really are into her."

"I barely know her."

"Well, let's get to know her better." Leslie waggled her eyebrows. "But we need snacks."

"On it." Seren took a sip of the iced latte and moaned her approval. She headed to the kitchen, pointing to the laptop on the coffee table as she passed. "Want to start sleuthing while I get us food? All I know is her first name—Paige. And she's a veterinarian."

Leslie picked up the laptop and settled in at the kitchen counter. "You said she was our age, right? You sure she's single?"

"She flirted like she was single."

Leslie raised one finger. "Ali flirted with other women all the time. Not being single doesn't stop some women."

"Well, she wasn't wearing a ring. And she seemed nothing like Ali." Leslie's ex-fiancée, Ali, was a world-class flirt as well as a classic narcissist.

"Nothing like Ali moves her to the top of my list."

The other thing she wouldn't tell Leslie but that gave her some comfort was that Paige either didn't have much practice flirting or she'd been off her game—maybe because someone had pushed her into the pool and then gave her a hard time for her parking job. Regardless, she'd seemed sincere. And a little awkward. Definitely not the type who could keep a secret girlfriend.

"Think she works at the vet school?"

"No idea. The truck did have a vet school bumper sticker. Grilled cheese okay with you?"

Leslie nodded over her latte and Seren got out a block of cheddar. "I really shouldn't be thinking about dating someone." She paused, her knife balanced over the cheddar. "It's like the universe wants to mess with me, you know? I've been single—and looking—for the past two years. Then I finally started dating that woman in New York and before we even had sex, she broke up with me. And now this."

"Hold up. New York chick broke up with you because you moved here and she didn't want to do long distance."

"Well, yes, but—"

"And the reason you're single now is because you're picky."

Seren waved her butter knife. "My point is, *now* I find some hot dyke who I'm into and seems perfect, when I'm four months pregnant?"

"You know you can have sex when you're pregnant, right?"

"But I can't start a serious relationship."

"You need to change your rule about only having sex in serious relationships." Leslie continued before Seren could reiterate her reasons for the rule, "You can't ignore the universe. This is how things always work for you. Ahem, Serendipity. Good things fall in your lap. Just not exactly when you expect."

It was true. Good things mostly only happened at random. Blame her mom for the namesake and fate for having a little joke at her expense. "Googling this woman doesn't make me a stalker, right?"

"You're not the one doing it. I am." Leslie studied something on the screen. "But I'm gonna need more details than her first name. Physical description?"

Seren closed her eyes, pulling up Paige's image in her mind. "She's got gorgeous hair. Kind of an auburn brown. It's short, but you can tell it's really thick."

"Are you over there imagining running your hands through her hair?"

Seren's eyes snapped open. "I can't picture someone unless my eyes are closed."

Leslie grinned, clearly not believing her. "Okay, fine. Short brown hair. What else?"

Seren turned back to the grilled cheese project. "Her eyes were this amazing amber color. Or maybe they were hazel? With long dark lashes. And when she looks at you, she really looks at you. Like, sees into your soul."

"So, some shade of brown eyes and you orgasmed when she looked at you. Got it. Short? Tall?"

"About my height. Well, maybe a little taller…"

Leslie narrowed her eyes. "Any distinctive features?"

"She has amazing calf muscles. And really nice arms."

Leslie laughed. "I never knew how bad you were at describing people. Did she flirt before or after you dunked her?"

"After. Why?"

Leslie was busy typing. "Hotness scale?"

"Off the charts." Seren dropped a pat of butter in the pan and watched it sizzle. "Well, objectively, she's maybe not everyone's type. And she's kind of quiet. Not exactly shy, but you could tell she felt awkward after I pushed her into the pool. Who wouldn't though, right? Then she stripped in front of everyone, and when she started class it was one hundred percent clear she'd never taught water aerobics. But she had everyone laughing and she was trying her best—which was pretty terrible." Seren smiled as she remembered Paige's clapping and marching. Completely offbeat. "She only taught class to help out her mom. That says something, right?"

"Back up. She stripped?"

"Not completely. But the wet tank top didn't leave a lot to the imagination." Seren met Leslie's gaze. "That's why I don't think she's actually shy. I bet she'd open up in the right circumstances. She seemed really approachable."

"Approachable? Like every other stripper? Can we go back to the wet tank top part?"

"She didn't really strip. But I did enjoy the show. Would've been even better if I wasn't feeling so embarrassed."

Leslie grumbled about missing the fun and then turned her attention back to the laptop. "I'm not finding any Paige listed under local veterinarians. Should I check the strip clubs?"

"How many vets can there be?"

"You do realize we live in a town with a vet school, right? Between the vet students and all the professors—maybe six or seven hundred? Not to mention the veterinarians who don't work for the university. We need more info."

"I think she works with livestock. She had a cow bumper sticker."

Leslie's hand paused over the keyboard. "She's a cow vet?"

"I don't know for sure but…Why are you looking at me like that?"

Leslie motioned to the cow figurines cluttering the shelf where her laptop had been sitting, then pointed to the teapot on the stove and the cow-shaped salt and pepper shakers and lastly to the leaping cow printed on the dish towel Seren was currently using to dry her hands. None of the cow-themed objects were hers. Her mom was the cow knickknack collector.

"So?"

"Come on. A cow vet? This is definitely your mom at work."

"You think my mom reached down from heaven and made sure a cow vet parked next to my Subaru?" It was completely ridiculous.

"That is one hundred percent her style and you know it. No way is it a coincidence."

"Leslie, my mom could do a lot, and I'm sure she's rocking it in heaven—but setting me up with women on Earth?"

"Don't underestimate your mom."

Seren wanted to laugh off Leslie's words, but a familiar pressure settled on her chest. She glanced down at the dish towel still in her hands. "I never underestimated my mom." Which was why it had been such a surprise that the cancer had moved so fast. "I thought for sure she'd be able to kick it. Or at least blow through those timelines they gave her." She hung the cow dish towel from the hook by the sink.

"I'm sorry, sweetie. I shouldn't have brought her up."

"Don't apologize. I don't want to stop thinking about her." She sniffed. "And I'm making progress not bawling whenever I do think of her. That's good, right?"

"She could've picked out this cow vet. You never know how it works up there."

Seren smiled. She wasn't a religious person, exactly, but she'd thought a lot more about heaven since her mom's passing. She'd done a lot more thinking about life in general, and what she was doing with hers.

The benefit of still living in her mom's house was that she had memories everywhere. It also meant she felt the pain of missing her more often. At the funeral she'd told everyone that she'd only planned to stay in the house long enough to get it ready to sell. She figured that meant a few months. But she'd barely made a dent in sorting through her mom's things, and she still had all the items on the list that needed fixing in the old house.

When she looked over at Leslie again, her focus was on the laptop. She had no time to be thinking about dating, but her mind didn't seem to care about that detail. "Still nothing?"

"We might have to resort to Facebook and Instagram. Maybe we have friends in common with someone named Paige? Davis isn't that big of a town." Leslie sighed. "Or maybe I can find a list of cow vets on the vet school's website."

Seren finished grilling the first sandwich and set it on a plate. She went over to where Leslie was sitting and placed it in front of her, then glanced at the image on the laptop screen. "Wait, I think that's her."

Leslie squinted at the image. "Which her?"

The image of someone who looked like Paige standing next to a cow had already been replaced by three students circled around a microscope.

"Not that picture. The last one. Can you make the computer go back one image?"

Leslie shook her head. "We have to wait for the pictures to cycle through."

In a moment, the cow image came up again. Seren tapped the screen. "That's her." Between the coveralls and the muddy boots and her expression of concentration, Paige was all that and then some. Seren couldn't help smiling.

"The woman with her arm up the cow's butt is your hottie?"

# CHAPTER SIX

The song titles on the mixtape labeled "Sunday" were smudged and mostly illegible, but Paige could decipher a few of them. Including "Survivor" by Destiny's Child and "Confident" by Demi Lovato. "Old Town Road" by Lil Nas X was a happy surprise as well. "Hey, I actually like some of these. How'd you get these new songs on a mixtape?"

"Are you asking because you're surprised I know current music, or because mixtape technology evades you?"

"A little of both."

"I'll let you in on a secret—none of that is actually all that new."

"Thanks for making me feel old, Mom." Paige refilled the water bottle she'd emptied on her ride and promptly drained half of it. She always looked forward to her long Sunday bike rides, but she'd cut short this morning's forty miles to have time to shower and change. And, instead of the usual decompressing from the week, she'd spent nearly all of the ride fantasizing about magically becoming a world-class water aerobics instructor. Not that she'd admit to anyone that she wanted to impress a certain woman with an aerobics routine. "Do you have someone lined up to teach Tuesday's class?"

"Yeah. This gal right here." Beatrice jammed her thumb at her chest.

"I meant what's the backup plan?"

"I don't need a backup plan." She opened the fridge, not moving much better than yesterday. "We're out of eggs."

"And bread." Paige hated shopping but knew she'd need to be the one to do it this week. "If you give me your list, I'll swing by the Co-op on my way home."

Bea shook her head. "The last time we tried you doing the shopping I asked for spinach and you brought home kale."

Honest mistake. She'd been in a hurry.

"And instead of cottage cheese you bought yogurt."

"That wasn't an accident. Cottage cheese is gross. Besides, you only said you wanted something to go with your morning fruit."

Charlie, who'd been snoring in one of his dog beds under the table, suddenly barked. Nutters sauntered past the kitchen doorway right as Charlie shot between Paige's legs. Nutters wasn't as much of a hisser as his sister, Squirrel, but he was good at showdowns, even being three-legged. He turned to square off with Charlie, popping the poodle right on the nose, and then hopped up on the back of the couch just out of reach. Charlie didn't stop barking until Bea got the treat jar.

"Why can't you ignore those kitties?" Bea shook her head as Charlie danced in front of her.

"In his defense, Nutters was taunting him." Paige usually sided with her cats, but the squabbles seemed to be increasing lately and most of the time, it wasn't Charlie that started it. Given her mom's fall, she knew something needed to change. "We all knew Charlie didn't like cats when I moved in. Me and the cats living here was supposed to be short term."

Bea waved off her concerns and tossed Charlie another biscuit. Instead of gulping it down like he had the first one, he paraded off to the couch to show Nutters. As if to prove how unimpressed he was, Nutters rolled back on his butt and licked his crotch. Even three-legged, he had no problem showing off.

"I'm hoping to meet with a realtor this week. Maybe he'll have something that's actually in my price range." Paige sighed. "I could keep the cats in my room until I move out?"

"Three cats in one room? Don't be silly."

"I don't want you to get tripped again and break something more important."

"More important than my tush?" Bea started to shake her butt and then froze, reaching for the counter as she stayed crouched over.

Paige stood quickly, grasping her mom's free hand. "Another back spasm?"

Bea nodded, cursing under her breath.

"Let's get you back to bed."

Although she complained about it, Bea let Paige lead her back to her room. Mouse, the oldest and sweetest of Paige's three black cats, was curled up at the foot of the bed and Bea seemed pleased with the company. "You stay here. I'll get you coffee and come up with something for breakfast."

"You don't need to be fussing with me. You have to get ready for water aerobics."

There was no chance she was going to woo Seren with her moves despite all her fantasies, but she didn't want to show up without a shower. "I have time to get you food."

Paige headed back to the kitchen and started the coffee brewing while she ran through the items in the pantry. The options were limited. Once she'd convinced herself that it was either oatmeal or cottage cheese, she knew the grocery store trip had to happen today—along with laundry, cleaning the house, and finishing Friday's records.

She returned to her mom's bedroom with a mug of coffee and a bowl of oatmeal. Mouse was still curled up sleeping and didn't budge when Paige sat down on the edge of the bed.

"A couple of the older ladies told me water aerobics is the only thing they look forward to. They really missed you yesterday."

"I teach a good class." Beatrice puffed at the compliment.

"About Tuesday's class…could you ask one of the other instructors to be on call for you?" Considering her long to-do list, it was silly to even worry about who'd be teaching come Tuesday. Worst case scenario, the classes would be canceled. Still, she felt responsible.

"Paige, if I'm not better by Tuesday, will you be able to teach?"

"I mean the other real instructors." Which her mom clearly knew. "There are other people who do this, right? I'm not even CPR certified."

"You do fine bringing animals back from the dead. I'm sure you could figure out what to do with a person."

"Thanks for the vote of confidence, but I'm still not certified." She'd probably be able to figure it out, but she didn't like breaking the rules. "Will Rita be there today?"

"She texted this morning and promised she'd be there. She also mentioned there was a woman you had your eye on in class yesterday. A water aerobics virgin."

"Virgin? She said that?"

Beatrice sniffed. "She also called her a busty blonde."

Paige hadn't mentioned how class had started yesterday or the fact that she'd fallen into the pool. She half figured that the gossip mill would get the news to her mom before she even got home, but she hadn't brought it up. Now she wondered how much her mom already knew.

"Want to talk about it?" Beatrice's eyes twinkled as she raised her coffee mug to her lips.

"Nope." It wasn't like her mom wouldn't be supportive. The problem was she'd more likely meddle to move things along faster—things that realistically weren't going to move at all.

"Fine, keep your secrets. But I wouldn't mind if one positive thing came from me breaking my ass. And heaven knows you could stand to get laid."

"Laid, Mom, seriously?"

"Is there a new word for it?"

Paige shook her head. The last thing she wanted to discuss with her mom was sex. "Seren seemed nice, but nothing's going to happen."

"You got her name?"

She wasn't sure if her mom's surprise was a compliment or not.

"Now all you have to do is ask her out. Let's hope she doesn't dunk you again before you get to that part."

Paige opened and closed her mouth.

"I'm not saying there's anything wrong with getting wet," Bea continued, adding an eyebrow waggle. "Do you have a plan for how you're going to ask her out?"

"I'm not going to ask her out." Although she had considered it for at least ten of the miles on her bike ride that morning. Then she'd reminded herself of her promise to not let anything distract from the plan of buying a farm and getting settled on her own. Dating Seren—if she even said yes—would be a huge distraction.

"Planning on becoming a nun?"

"Can you imagine me as a nun?" Paige laughed. "You know I'm trying to focus on getting a farm. I don't want any distractions."

"And you not wanting any distractions has absolutely nothing to do with that disaster of a relationship you had with Miranda?"

"That was over a year ago. I'm happily single now."

"You're happier when you're with someone. When was the last time you had sex?"

"Not answering that." Paige stood as her mom started listing the benefits of a healthy sex life. "Gosh, look at the time. I don't want to be late."

"Fine. Don't listen to me. But at least promise to talk to this woman."

Paige shook her head. "Try to rest."

"If you won't talk to her today, I'll have to overdo it so you'll have to teach Tuesday's class."

Sadly, Paige knew that wasn't an idle threat. "Bye, Mom. Rest up."

# CHAPTER SEVEN

Seren had hoped to arrive early enough to say hello to Paige and then stake out a spot on the right side of the pool. She'd noticed Paige had faced that direction for most of yesterday's class and this time she wanted to make sure she could see. Truthfully, she also wouldn't mind being seen.

Unfortunately, at ten minutes before the hour the pool was already filled with a boisterous crowd. Apparently, it was someone's birthday. All the purple noodles were taken—again—as was the space on the right side of the pool. Even more of a bummer was that Beehive Lady—Rita—and another lady with impressive white curls wouldn't give Paige a moment alone.

Seren picked out a yellow noodle and carefully closed the storage door. She headed for the stairs, repeating the mantra, *I'm not going to fantasize about my water aerobics instructor.* If her dreams last night had been any indication, she'd need more than a mantra.

"Hey." Paige's hand brushed hers. "Sorry. I tried waving to get your attention, but I don't think you saw me."

Her touch was hardly more than a graze, but it sent electricity racing through Seren. Damn hormones.

"Someone parked right next to your car in that same spot I was in yesterday, and you're pinned in again. Those spots are really narrow. Hopefully they'll be gone by the time class is over, but if not, I'll talk to the front desk about having them move."

"I appreciate that."

Paige nodded. "And it's good seeing you here." She seemed nervous as she added the last part, which made Seren smile.

"You too. I woke up thinking about this. This class." She hugged her arms across her chest, wishing she could tamp down her own nervous energy and the hormones that had her nipples rock-hard. It was easier flirting fully dressed.

"Hopefully today will be a better class." Paige glanced at the notebook she was holding and then at the pool already full of students. "After yesterday I wouldn't have blamed anyone for not coming back."

"Well, I promised to be here and I'm not someone who breaks promises." She also couldn't remember the last time she'd looked forward to a workout as much.

"I guess I should get class started, then."

"If you wait too long, someone might push you into the pool again."

Paige laughed. "Are you planning on it?"

Seren lifted a shoulder, not committing, and Paige laughed again. She held Seren's gaze for a moment longer, then headed over to the stereo.

Seren blew out a breath. It was silly being all swoony and filled with happy butterflies flirting at thirty-eight, but here she was. And maybe it was good for her. If nothing more came of it, having someone new and fun in her dreams was nice.

Two of the women from yesterday's class waved her over to their spot, and as she swam past Rita, she heard her say, "Good. You came back."

A wave of belonging swept over her as several others recognized her from the day before and smiled. Weird, considering it was only her second time, but nice, too.

Paige clapped her hands together. "Okay, everybody. I know you're ready to see the new moves I practiced, but—"

"New moves? Which direction are you going to fall into the pool today?"

Seren didn't know who'd asked, but everyone, including Paige, laughed.

"As long as no one pushes me, I think I'll stay right here. On dry ground." Paige's gaze briefly met Seren's. "Ready? We're starting with marching."

Rita groaned loudly, but that only seemed to bolster Paige's confidence. She was definitely different today. Her moves were still a little stilted and there was no chance she'd make it as a dancer, but she added kicks to the marching and new upper arm exercises as well. Clearly she'd practiced as promised, and by the time she started the cool-down stretches, Seren felt like she'd had a more-than-decent workout.

At the end of class, Paige read a birthday announcement. Someone named Gloria—Seren gathered this was the woman with the white curls—had turned ninety on Friday and Rita was hosting a brunch for her. Everyone was invited.

"That means you, too, sweetie." Rita angled her head at Seren. "We may look like a bunch of old broads, but we know how to have a good time."

The woman getting out of the pool ahead of Rita added, "As long as enjoying an array of casseroles is your definition of a good time."

"I love a good casserole." At the moment, any casserole sounded better than a granola bar.

"You and half of the Midwest," Rita deadpanned. "We're setting up on the lawn next to the parking lot. In the shady area." She lowered her voice and added, "I've convinced Paige to join us too. We needed someone with muscles to help us set up the tables."

Rita winked and Seren knew that no help was needed. These women could do just fine on their own. "I'd be happy to help too."

"Thought as much." Rita's conspiring look spoke volumes. "After we change, I'll show both of you where the storage shed is. They have to keep the tables and chairs locked up or they'll walk away. The food is in coolers, and we'll need help with that too."

"Of course." She wondered if Paige had any idea what she was in for. Heck, she wondered if she had any idea either. Leslie's words came to mind: *Getting to know someone is harmless.* That's all she was planning on, right?

# CHAPTER EIGHT

Paige knew Rita was up to something when she asked for help setting up the tables. She was even more convinced when Rita claimed no one else would be able to carry the tables back. That of course meant she'd have to stay for the party. As soon as Rita asked Seren to grab the chairs—conveniently stored with the folding tables in a shed behind the fitness club—and tossed a not-so-subtle wink back at Paige, it hit her. Rita was clearly working as a clandestine agent for her mom's matchmaking plans.

Worse, she had a feeling Seren knew something was up. She considered warning her, but saying, *"I think we're being set up"* would only make things more awkward.

"I can get the chairs and the tables. You don't have to help."

Seren tilted her head. "I'm pretty sure Rita will march me right back here if I show up on the lawn empty-handed. Besides, I feel better helping since I didn't bring anything for the party."

"Did you see all the coolers they brought? They could feed fifty more people easy. You definitely didn't need to bring any food." Paige unlocked the storage shed. "But I get it. I always feel better helping too."

The shed was jammed with what looked like broken equipment in various states of repair, and it took a minute to localize the folding chairs and tables. Paige passed Seren one of the chairs.

"So water aerobics isn't the only thing we have in common."

Paige cocked her head. "There's something else?"

"Helping. We both feel better helping."

"Oh. Right. That might be all we have in common." But the fact that Seren was thinking of things had to be a good sign. She hefted two tables and backed out of the shed.

"I'd bet we voted for the same president last election. And who knows? We might have the same birthday."

"Okay, I'll bite. September fourteenth."

"Never mind. You're right. We have nothing else in common."

Paige laughed. She started toward the lawn area with the tables as soon as Seren had collected two folding chairs. "I feel like it's not fair with you knowing my birthday and me not knowing yours."

"December thirty-first. And, no, my parents weren't trying for the tax break."

"Just a happy coincidence?"

Seren paused midstride and looked right at Paige. Sunlight seemed to catch and hold her in place, her blue-gray eyes suddenly more blue and the gold strands shining in her hair. For a moment, Paige forgot to breathe as she stared. Seren raised a hand to shield the rays but still held Paige's gaze.

"Did I say the wrong thing?"

"No." Seren seemed to consider adding more but then began walking. After a handful of steps, she paused again. "My mom used to say that all the time: just a happy coincidence. She joked that she named me Serendipity because 'Happy Coincidence' wouldn't fit on the birth certificate."

"I take it you weren't planned?"

"Definitely not. No one calls me Serendipity, though. It's just Seren."

"Do happy coincidences happen a lot when you're around? I mean, I feel like it was a happy coincidence that we met." Paige set down the tables, wondering when Seren didn't respond if she'd overplayed her hand. "Only because we wouldn't have probably met in the real world. If my mom hadn't broken her tailbone and she was teaching instead, well…Anyway, it feels like we met by happy chance."

"I don't know how happy you were when I pushed you into the pool."

"Good point. In the moment, I wasn't happy. But you felt bad, and I didn't want to make you feel worse, so I pretended everything was fine. Which meant I forgot to be nervous about... well, everything. And I feel like we might become friends now, so it all worked out." Paige glanced at Seren. She was focused on setting up her chair. Or maybe trying to avoid the conversation? "Am I reading this wrong?"

"You're not reading it wrong." Seren looked down at the chair she'd set up and then back at Paige. Her smile seemed a little forced. "I'm overthinking something." Paige wanted to ask what she was overthinking, but Seren continued, "I feel like we could be friends too. Are you usually nervous? You seem pretty confident."

"When I'm doing something I know how to do? Sure. Teaching water aerobics? Not exactly. Talking to women?" Paige hesitated. "I have my moments." Here she was, not holding back again. But she didn't feel nervous now. More like a happy excitement. "I can be awkward, especially if I'm really into someone."

"I get that. That's why crushes are the worst."

"For real." Paige grinned, relaxing more. "Crushes are right up there with first dates on things I'd be happy skipping in life."

"Nothing fun happens on the first date. They're like job interviews."

"Exactly."

Seren beamed back at Paige. "Check it out—two more things we have in common. We should keep a list."

"Because maybe we're secretly soulmates?" Paige grinned.

"Two souls thrown together by chance." Seren swept her arms out dramatically.

"Otherwise known as my mom's broken tailbone."

Seren affected an announcer voice as she added, "Will they overcome the obstacles in their way—"

"Are the obstacles the pool noodles? Or the women who push you into the pool?"

Seren clapped her hand over her mouth as she laughed. Paige laughed too, not caring that more than a handful of ladies from the pool were staring their direction. It felt good to be ridiculous and laugh and not care.

"Thanks for letting me be a drama nerd there for a hot minute." Seren's eyes still sparkled with the laughter. "Apparently I needed it."

"Anytime." When Seren held her gaze a moment longer, Paige was ready to ask her out then and there. Except…could she ask when they'd both just admitted to hating first dates?

"We should probably get more chairs."

"Right." Now wasn't the time to ask, but she was almost certain Seren would say yes when she did.

Two more trips to the storage shed and they had enough chairs for everyone. Food magically appeared along with pitchers of lemonade—one clearly labeled "spiked." As everyone gathered round, Paige snapped a picture of Rita and the birthday girl, Gloria. She texted the image to her mom, knowing how much she'd be wishing she could have come. She got a text back of an emoji with a tongue sticking out and a string of curses about broken tailbones.

"Texting your girlfriend?"

Paige looked up from her phone. "My mom, actually. I know she'd love to be here. These folks mean the world to her. And she hates missing a party."

"Ah."

"No girlfriend for me." Paige pocketed her phone. "I mean, to be clear, I've had girlfriends. But I'm single at the moment."

"Do you like being single?"

"Sometimes. I wouldn't mind having a girlfriend, but I'm happier now than when I was with my ex."

"Same. Some nights I do miss having company, though. Especially in this town where there's no nightlife. I kind of bore myself after a while."

Paige nodded. "There are definitely nights when I wish I was more exciting."

"Me too. I mean, I'm sure you're plenty exciting. I only meant that I wished—" Seren stopped and shook her head. "You're smiling like you're enjoying watching me work my way out of this hole."

"A little?"

Seren laughed.

"You two better get over to the food table and fill up a plate," Rita said. "Otherwise, you've got about thirty seconds before you have a dozen offended seniors on your hands."

As much as Paige wanted to continue the conversation, there was a bustle of activity around the food table and then the only two empty seats weren't together. Folks lingered even after they'd eaten, and soon Paige began to worry Seren would leave before they had more time to talk. When an empty chair opened up next to Seren, Paige debated only a moment before moving seats. She was rewarded with a wide smile from Seren but then felt a punch of nervousness as she realized how eager she probably looked scurrying over.

And she should have thought about something to say. "Which one of the casseroles was your favorite?" Ideally something better than that.

Seren rocked her head side to side. "I don't ordinarily like to pick favorites, but this cheesy potato really hit the spot." She scooped up the last bite with her spork. "Mm. Delish."

"That's my mom's favorite too."

"But not yours? No hoping we have that in common, huh?"

"Don't tell anyone here," Paige said, lowering her voice. "But I don't actually like casseroles."

"Not any casserole?"

"I don't like creamy sauces. Or mayonnaise. I don't even like cheese. Sacrilege, I know."

Seren shifted back in her seat. "We might not be soulmates after all. How do you feel about ice cream?"

"I love ice cream."

"Well, you're not a complete lost cause."

"Thank you?"

"You're welcome." Seren set her plate down at her feet and reached for her lemonade. "What are your plans for the rest of the day?"

"I'm thinking of taking a drive and looking at some open houses. I was supposed to meet up with a realtor, but they canceled on me." Not exactly exciting plans. "I don't think he was the right realtor for me anyway. I tried telling him the type of place I'm looking for and he sent me links to those new McMansions out east."

"Not what you're looking for?"

"Not at all. I want some land. I don't care much about the house, but I'm hoping to find a place with a barn and some acreage. At a minimum I want room for a few of my own cows. And at least two sheep. I'll have chickens and dogs and cats of course. I've always liked pigs—but they're probably more work than I need, you know?"

"Um…no. I don't know. How much work are pigs?"

"A lot."

"Noted. I keep forgetting you're a veterinarian. So, basically, you want your own farm?"

"I do. The problem is, I'd like some place not too far from town since my mom's getting older." Paige stretched out her legs, eyeing her sneakers. "I probably won't find the perfect spot, but I can't stop myself from looking. And dreaming. And saving up all my pennies that the student loan people don't take."

"I love it when people go for their dreams." Seren studied her for a moment. "My friend Leslie is a realtor. She knows this area better than anyone—she's lived in Davis her whole life. I bet if anyone could find what you're describing it'd be her, and I guarantee she won't sell you on a McMansion. Want me to text her?"

"That'd be great." Paige watched as Seren got up and went over to where she'd left her purse. She pulled out her phone and came back to her seat. "You don't have to do it now."

"She'd kill me if I didn't jump on you. It. This." Seren shook her head and then said, "You, as a possible client."

"Got it." Paige didn't laugh, as much as she wanted to. The blush and the embarrassment on Seren's face were enough. "It's nice when I'm not the only one putting my foot in my mouth."

"You're welcome. But don't get used to it. I don't plan on making it a habit." Seren's eye roll was subtle. "Anyway, if you buy something with her, she'll probably bring me a casserole. Which means this is mutually beneficial. What's your number? I'll send you her contact info."

# CHAPTER NINE

Mutually beneficial. The words ran through Seren's head again after she listened to Leslie's voice mail. She'd called to say that she was on her way over with a cheesecake after having spent the afternoon showing Paige some properties. Seren had missed the call only because she'd been up in her mother's old room sorting through boxes.

The cheesecake was sweet but completely unnecessary. When she'd given Paige Leslie's contact info, her only thought had been helping Paige. If Leslie got some business out of the deal, all the better. But shouldn't it be the other way around? Shouldn't she have been thinking about wanting to help Leslie out first considering they'd been friends for going on two decades? She might never see Paige again.

The front door banged open and Leslie's voice rang out. "Tell me you're hungry for cheesecake because I do not want to eat this whole thing alone." She came into the kitchen where Seren had dumped a box of her mother's paperwork out on the table. "But I will. And it won't be pretty."

Seren smiled. "No way could you eat an entire cheesecake."

"Dare me?"

"No. I'll get two forks." She got up from the table and motioned to the piles of papers. "Feel free to push those back in the box to make room. I haven't gotten far going through them anyway. And still no sign of any will." Her mother had said she'd left a will, but in the midst of everything Seren hadn't thought to ask her where it was specifically. The time had simply gone too fast, and most of the last month had been spent going back and forth to the hospital.

"It really would make selling this place easier if you could find it, but I'm sure there's a way around it. You don't have any siblings, and you said your mom doesn't have any other next of kin, right?"

Seren nodded. "It'll be fine. I'll find it eventually, I'm sure. But going through all of her stuff feels never-ending. I swear she saved every picture I drew from preschool on."

"She loved you. Can't blame her—you are pretty great. But also, it's only been six months. It's okay to take your time going through everything."

Seren motioned to her belly. "This cute little alien argues otherwise."

"You sure you couldn't stay here?"

"I don't want to make my mom's room into the nursery. It doesn't feel right. And the bills for this place have me tapped out."

"Any new thoughts on where you want to move?"

Seren lifted a shoulder. "You know me. I have better luck if I don't try planning too far in advance." In other words, she couldn't decide.

Leslie gave her a sympathetic smile. "Well, I'm selfishly happy you're taking your time. But if you decide you actually love Davis and want to stay, I know of a cute townhouse right downtown that's coming up soon. You could sell this house and almost buy that one in cash."

"I'll think about it...Good thing I've got your number memorized."

"In the meantime, can we binge on cheesecake?"

"Yes, please."

Seren handed Leslie a fork. They didn't bother with plates. She dug in on one side of the cheesecake and gestured for Leslie to take the other half. Fortunately, it was one of the bakery's mini cakes and neither of them would get truly sick if they did manage to polish the whole thing off in one go.

After several bites, Leslie leaned back in her seat. "Can we talk about Paige now?"

Seren felt her cheeks color immediately.

"Judging from your blush, that's a yes. I'll start: She's a hell of lot sexier when her arm isn't up a cow's ass."

Seren nearly choked on her bite of cheesecake. She sputtered and reached for her water glass, all while shaking her head.

Leslie continued, "And—good news—she says she rarely does that anymore. Something about her old job. Also, she wears really long gloves."

"You asked her?"

Leslie nodded. "I mean, it's gross, but I also had this perverse curiosity. You know what I mean?"

"No. I don't."

Leslie shrugged. "Anyway, she does it to check for a baby. I guess it's an easy way to tell if a cow's pregnant." She took another bite of the cheesecake. "Is it messed up that we're having this conversation while eating cheesecake?"

Seren considered the bite on her own fork. "Maybe? I'm glad I got to pee on a stick and no one stuck their arm up my ass."

"You and me both. But. Aside from the whole cow-butt thing, I like her. You're right—she's quiet at first but opens up quick. She told me all about this farm she wants to have. She's got a couple grade-school teacher friends, and the hope is for part of the farm to be a student learning thing." Leslie paused. "She's got a lot of plans. And it's all really sweet. Almost too wholesome, but it works for her somehow. Anyway, I'm hooked."

"Hooked on Paige? Or on the idea of a teaching farm?"

"Both? I think she's perfect for you."

"I know I wanted to look her up last time and maybe I do have a little crush but..." She stopped, thinking of how she'd told Paige she hated crushes and how she definitely didn't hate the feelings she had around Paige. "I can't date anyone right now."

Leslie waved off Seren's words. "Do you know her two favorite animals? Cows and cats."

"You asked?"

"How could I not ask a vet their favorite animal?" Undaunted, Leslie continued, "She makes me want to get another cat."

Seren laughed. "You already have five cats."

"I'm completely a crazy cat lady. I own that. But I'm also ninety percent sure I have room for another kitten." Leslie's eyebrows danced. "What's one more, really?"

"Six cats."

"Paige has three cats. All black. If you moved in together, you'd have four between the two of you—and all black. I feel like it's meant to be."

Seren shook her head. "You're leaping quite a bit ahead." She also couldn't help wondering where her cat, Cymbal, was at the moment. Probably roaming the back alleys looking for trouble. He always showed up at bedtime, but she worried until he made that late-night appearance.

"Did she tell you that she was born here?"

"No, but we didn't have a whole lot of time to talk." She tamped down the building annoyance that Leslie seemed to know more about Paige than she did.

"She moved away before high school. I didn't ask when exactly or how old she was to find out there was any chance we all would have been in school at the same time." Leslie got up to get herself a glass of sparkling water from the fridge. "But. She came back to town for vet school. After she graduated, she decided to stay—because clearly Davis is the best town ever and everyone should stay."

Leslie added the last bit only because she knew Seren's feelings on Davis. She'd complained plenty. "Did she like any of the houses you showed her?"

"I could tell nothing really spoke to her. Know anyone looking to sell a farm? She doesn't care about the house part, but good luck getting a loan without a house."

"I don't know if they're looking to sell or not, but you could reach out to the Landrys."

Leslie's brow furrowed. "Why does that name sound familiar?"

"Mrs. Landry was our high school music teacher."

"Right!"

"Before that, I took piano lessons at her house. She and my mom were friends." She pushed away a nudge of guilt for not getting in touch after her mom had passed. "They have a little farm outside of town. I don't know how much land, but there's a barn and a couple corrals."

"That sounds perfect. You think they want to sell?"

Seren lifted a shoulder. "Mrs. Landry was in her seventies when we were in high school. One of her kids might have taken over the place or they could have already sold, but if not…"

"It's worth a phone call. Any chance you have their number?"

"I'm sure I have it somewhere. Or at least an address. My mom always sent them Christmas cards." Seren felt a heaviness press on her chest. She took a slow steadying breath. "I should have called them when Mom passed. They weren't close, but she knew them for years. There were just so many people to tell."

"You can't give yourself a hard time about that. You called so many people—and your mom's church must have told a hundred others. I didn't even know that place could hold that many people. Plus, her obituary was in the paper."

Seren nodded. Tears filled her eyes at the memory of the service. She clenched her jaw and looked up at the ceiling fan to hold them at bay. In truth, that whole week was a fuzzy blur. She'd spent most of it sobbing and arguing with God about things being unfair.

Leslie set her hand on Seren's. "I still think of all those sweet things you said about her at the service. She would have said your love alone was more than enough."

Seren rubbed away her tears and met Leslie's gaze. "I don't think I would have held it together without you being there." She clasped Leslie's hand briefly, then got up and went over to the cabinet where her mom had stored her address book. She thumbed through the book until she got to the L's. "Bingo. Address and phone number."

There was no guarantee the Landrys still lived there, but if they did, and if they wanted to sell—which was a lot of ifs—it'd be nice knowing she'd had even a small hand in helping Paige find a place.

Leslie screenshotted the entry for the Landrys. "Awesome."

"Thanks for working with Paige." Seren glanced at the address book and then at Leslie's phone where she was typing away a note about the Landrys. "Maybe this will work out."

"Here's hoping…" Leslie's voice trailed as she scanned her phone for details on the address. "I always want to make people happy, but making a hot butch happy? Extra nice."

"I'd be okay if you dated her."

Leslie's gaze shot up from her screen. "We talked about this already. You know I wouldn't even flirt with the woman my bestie has a crush on."

"But your bestie is pregnant and has no business dating."

"Pregnancy is temporary."

"I know, and it's also only step one of all the ways life is going to change. Dating feels possible now, but in five months? No way. Where will I even be living?" She looked around the kitchen at all of her mom's things and shook her head. "I went into this wanting to be a single mom and I still think it's the right choice. And dating when everything else in my life is all up in the air is a bad call."

Leslie set down her phone and grasped Seren's shoulders. "Hon, you know I fully support you having this baby on your own. If anyone could rock being a single mom, it's you. And we'll figure out where you're moving to once you get your mom's place ready to sell. But. There's nothing wrong with you having a little fun on the side."

When Seren didn't respond, Leslie added, "Who knows if you'll even like her after a first date? I know how much you hate first dates."

"She hates first dates too."

Leslie tilted her head. "Then skip right to a second date."

"Leslie, I'm going to have a baby. I don't need a new relationship when that happens."

"Break up with her before the baby gets here." Leslie shrugged like it was the easiest thing.

Seren shook her head. "She hasn't asked me out anyway."

"She will."

Seren bit the edge of her lip. She could argue nothing was certain, but deep down she knew Leslie was right. So, what was she going to say?

Once she'd made up her mind to have a baby on her own, the decision had felt so right she couldn't wait to go through with it. Whenever she'd wanted anything in life, she'd gone for it alone. A baby wouldn't be any different. She'd joined a "Single-Mothers-By-Choice" online group and everything she read only confirmed her decision. Having a baby was the most important thing and she needed to focus on that.

But she liked Paige. A lot. And the idea of turning down the chance to get to know her better made her feel sick. Yet even considering the idea of dating seemed to fly in the face of her plan to focus on herself for the next five months as she prepared for a baby.

"What if you never meet someone like Paige again?"

*What if.*

# CHAPTER TEN

"Hey. There's a gorgeous woman out front asking if my associate vet is single."

Paige looked up, startled from her daydream. "What?"

"Thought that'd get your attention." Jen grinned. "I'm lying about the gorgeous woman, but saying, 'Hi, hello, how are you?' wasn't working."

"You said something to me earlier?"

Jen laughed. "Yes." She hefted Leo's car seat onto her desk and sank into the chair opposite Paige's. Her six-month-old, Leo, snoozed on with his bright orange Tigger at his side.

"Leo let you sleep in this morning?"

"No. He woke up at one, three, and five a.m. Then decided to sleep in. I think it's a teething thing." Jen stifled a yawn. She looked exhausted but still meticulously put together. Paige wondered how she pulled it off.

Then again, Jen was used to pulling off the impossible and acting like it was no big deal. Only one of the reasons Paige admired her. She was a black woman in a profession that was more white than nearly any other, a damn good vet, and had successfully managed her own business for ten years while maintaining a happy marriage. How she did it all was a mystery. What was more, she had the uncanny ability to make any outfit, including scrubs, look stylish.

"How was Monday?" Jen asked. "I saw the numbers. You were busy."

"I was. But I like being busy." They traded off who got a three-day weekend, and in this case she'd been happy to work, hoping the distraction of a hectic Monday would stop her from thinking about Seren. That hadn't been the case.

"And I see you survived water aerobics."

"Two classes down, another two weeks to go."

"Another two weeks?"

Paige nodded. "My mom had an appointment with her primary care doc yesterday. He's insisting she take two weeks off all exercise—including teaching." She'd surprised even herself by immediately volunteering to keep teaching. The next class was tonight and she was hoping Seren would be there.

"I thought you were crazy with those long bike rides of yours, but...teaching water aerobics?"

"I like it." She didn't want to admit that she might have an ulterior motive to keep teaching.

"Well, you're good at surprising me."

"Like that time I showed up asking for a job unannounced?"

Jen rocked her head side to side. "That was no surprise. I knew you wouldn't last working with Miranda."

"Everyone knew it except me." Working with her girlfriend had been a bad idea from the start. When they broke up, things got even worse.

Leo stirred, and at the first plaintive cry, Jen groaned. "Not again." She glanced at the clock above the doorway. "Paul's been working nights these last three days. I wanted to give him a break this morning."

Paul was Jen's husband and the kind of dad that carried equal parenting weight. They'd both adjusted their schedules so Leo wasn't in day care, but that meant lots of mornings with parent switches.

When Leo cried again, Paige stood and went over to him. His smile was impossible to resist—then again, she hadn't been up with him three times in the middle of the night. She scooped him up and kissed his head. Nothing like snuggling a warm, pudgy-cheeked baby.

"Thank you," Jen murmured. "What were you daydreaming about earlier anyway? You find another farm that's out of your price range?"

More than once Jen had caught her daydreaming about Zillow properties. This time she'd been daydreaming about Seren. Definite improvement. "I can't find anything with more than a quarter acre in my price range. At least, nothing close."

Leo fidgeted in her arms, clearly wanting to get down and crawl. Paige snagged Tigger out of the carrier and bounced him and Leo in her arms. "You know your mama doesn't think a vet clinic is the place for you to lick the floors." They'd had the conversation before. Leo didn't seem to care.

"You could buy something out of your price range and go into massive debt like the rest of us. Who cares about money, anyway?"

"The student loan folks who expect a check from me each month?"

"Exactly." Jen made a face like she'd sucked on a lemon. "Who wants to be like them?"

Leo chose that moment to fart, loudly, and both Jen and Paige laughed. Which made Leo laugh too.

"So, do we need to talk about rearranging your schedule for this water aerobics moonlighting you're doing?" Jen asked, turning to wake up her computer.

"Already done. I moved a handful of my afternoon appointments to the lunch hour and I'll come in early to see the others."

"Perfect. Have I mentioned that you're my favorite associate?"

"Seeing as how I'm you're only associate…"

"Whatever. If I had ten more, you'd still be my favorite and you know it." Jen glanced at her watch and then Leo. "Mind entertaining him while I run to the breakroom? I'm gonna need a whole pot of coffee to get through today."

"Go for it."

Once Jen had gone, Paige settled in at her desk with Leo on her lap. He was easily entertained with pens and she gave him two—one for each hand—before opening her laptop. She scanned over the record she'd been working on before the daydream about asking Seren out on a date. She managed to finish her exam findings on the 4-H lamb that wasn't thriving from yesterday, handed Leo a calculator when he tired of pens, and then got distracted again wondering what Seren might be doing at the moment. She'd only realized that morning that she had no clue what Seren did for work.

Could she text her and ask? Although Seren had been the one to send the first text, that had only been to forward Leslie's contact info. Would Seren think it weird if she texted her to chat? She'd resisted yesterday—only because she worried what Seren would think if she messaged her too soon.

She chewed on the inside of her cheek for a moment. She didn't actually have time to chat, but she started a message before she could talk herself out of it: *Thank you for hooking me up with Leslie. I think she's perfect for me. And she didn't bring up that development out east even once. No McMansions!*

Seren's response took only a moment but was briefer than Paige had hoped: *You're welcome.*

Probably she was busy at work—doing whatever she did. Paige wished she'd asked Seren more about herself. Partly she hadn't wanted to come across as nosy. Seren was clearly pregnant—the maternity-style bathing suit had been the first clue, but then she'd overheard Seren at the casserole table say that she'd switched to water aerobics for the duration of her pregnancy. And although she was friendly and outgoing, Paige got the sense that she didn't open up easy.

Maybe Seren liked someone who was more forward? More direct?

*I'm teaching water aerobics for the next two weeks. Figured I should warn people.*

Paige tapped on her phone case waiting for a response. Seconds ticked by and Leo bored of the calculator. She handed him the stapler but when he tried to gnaw on it, she exchanged it for her stethoscope. The last thing she wanted was to explain to Jen that she'd let her kid swallow staples—or worse, staple his lip.

*Does that mean your mom's worse?*

Paige taped the screen. *Not worse but not better. Will you be in class tonight?*

She glanced at her phone again and Seren's text blinked on the screen: *Definitely. I'm hooked.*

*Good. Looking forward to seeing you!* Maybe an exclamation point was too much but Paige hit send a moment later. She stared at her phone, wondering if it was the right time to propose a date. If she got turned down, it would make the next two weeks awkward. But if she didn't ask, Seren might assume she wasn't interested.

She quickly tapped out: *Any chance you'd be up for dinner after?* Her heart raced in her chest as she debated whether to hit send.

"Do you think it's a mistake asking her out now?" she asked Leo, but he was distracted still with the stethoscope. And not yet verbal.

"Asking who out?" Jen stood in the doorway, her coffee in hand and her eyebrows up in her hairline. "Are you crushing on someone and didn't tell me?"

"No. Sort of?" She shook her head. "Would it be weird to get asked out by your water aerobics instructor?"

Jen laughed. "Now I get why you like water aerobics so much."

Paige scrunched up her face. "It'd be weird, right?"

"Well...since you're the teacher for the moment...yeah, probably. Sorry. That's not the answer you want to hear, is it?"

Leo threw the stethoscope he'd been teething on across the room and lunged for Paige's phone. When Paige tried to wrest it from his hands, suddenly worrying he'd hit send, Jen intervened.

"Come here, little mister."

After Jen and Leo left the office to set up his playpen, Paige stared at the text waiting to be sent. Another round of second-guessing and she deleted what she'd typed. As soon as the words disappeared, she heard her mom groaning in her head about how she was never going to get the lesbian wedding she wanted to host.

She didn't want to get married, but she did want to do everything right with Seren. If that meant biding her time, she could be patient. "But I'm not good at being patient." That was an understatement. Still, she could wait one week and then ask.

# CHAPTER ELEVEN

*Water aerobics tonight.* Seren smiled again as her brain happily reminded her that when she finished kneading this last client's tense right trapezius, she'd be off her throbbing legs and in warm water dancing around with the spicy seniors. That's what Rita and her friends affectionately called each other, and Seren agreed that "spicy" was a perfect description.

Although she'd only been taking water aerobics for a little over a week, she felt like she'd known the women for years. They'd dubbed her a "junior spicy" and included her in all of their spicy talk. Which was ear burning to be sure. Leslie had been right— at least with regards to this group of seniors—big breasts were a favorite topic. Along with big other things. Their commentaries in the locker room about the benefits of size had made Seren laugh so hard she snorted more than once.

But what really got her hustling from work straight to Aqua Fitness—and got her out of bed early on the weekend—was the promise of seeing Paige and casually exchanging, "How was your day?"

Paige still hadn't asked her out, though there was plenty of casual flirting. It felt good. And easy. And while part of her worried about her budding feelings, the rest of her maintained she should simply enjoy the attraction until a decision on dating had to be made. More than once Seren was sure the question was on the tip of her tongue and as much as she wanted it, she still hadn't decided whether she could say yes. She had, however, practiced what she might say: *I'd love to go out with you, but we'll need to break up by October.* The other option was less appealing: *I want to, but life's too complicated right now.*

They rarely had many chances to talk alone for more than a moment anyway. Someone was always interrupting when they chatted poolside before or after class, and the number of pet-related questions Paige fielded was staggering. Seren tried not to get annoyed—for Paige's sake if nothing else—but Paige always seemed happy to help. Whether it was not having an opportunity to ask, or if Paige was waiting for her, Seren couldn't tell for sure. Maybe waiting was the right thing. Except time was what she didn't have a lot of.

She shook her head and returned her focus to the woman on her table. "How's that shoulder feel now?"

"Mm. Better."

She stopped kneading and spread her hands, relaxing the traps as well as the other muscles she'd worked. Her thoughts zipped back to Paige. She'd see her in less than an hour.

"Your hands are unbelievable."

The woman's muffled words made her refocus. She was used to compliments and good tips as well, but it was still a pleasure to hear. Especially since her attention had been a little divided this time. "All part of the job."

"You should definitely keep this job," the woman murmured.

Thinking of how long she could keep working brought up a whole different set of problems. She tried to contain her sigh. Her savings account wouldn't last long if she had to go out on maternity leave early. Managing her finances, finding her mom's will, and selling the house was what she should be focused on. Not what to do about her water aerobics teacher. She glanced at the clock and realized she'd gone five minutes over.

"Oops, looks like I went over our time. That shoulder of yours needed a little extra TLC."

The woman groggily agreed.

"I'll give you a minute to dress, and meet you in the lobby." She wanted to add, "Please don't fall asleep," because she really didn't have time for that but hoped her upbeat tone would convey the message.

As soon as she stepped out of the room, she felt woozy. She went to the small office she shared with the two other therapists and found her purse with that snack she'd promised her stomach earlier. Her morning sickness had improved so much since she'd hit the second trimester that she sometimes forgot she still needed to eat every two hours. She stared down the granola bar she'd brought, more disappointed than usual that she had to swallow yet another dry mass of nuts and chocolate.

"It's this or nothing," she grudgingly reminded herself. She'd had no time for a lunch break, and if she took time to pick up dinner, she'd miss water aerobics. Her phone buzzed as she bit into the bar.

Leslie: *Just left the Landrys. Holy shit the property is perfect for Paige. And they want to sell.*

*That's great!*

Leslie: *Right? I'm so excited. Think she'll be at water aerobics?*

*She should be unless her mom magically got better.* Seren didn't even know the lady, but she hoped that hadn't happened. Paige had said she'd be teaching for two weeks, and Seren wanted all of that time with her.

Leslie: *Am I allowed to place a bet on her asking you out tonight?*

Seren bit the edge of her lip. She started typing then deleted, then retyped the original message even if she hated it was true. *I still don't think I should date anyone.*

Leslie: *Everyone can use a little fling.*

A long moment passed and Seren set her phone down. She thought of the Landry ranch and then of Paige possibly buying it. A mess of emotions caught her off guard. Possibilities she was already regretting not going for. It was ridiculous—Paige hadn't even asked her out. Her phone buzzed with a new text and she quickly picked it back up again.

Leslie: *Mr. Landry mentioned he'd heard about your mom and wanted me to pass on condolences. Said his wife was sick and they couldn't go to the funeral.*

*I'm glad they knew at least.* A weight lifted at the same time as her chest felt tight thinking of the funeral again. She thought then of the Landry ranch that had always seemed like an oasis apart from the rest of the world. *I should go see them.*

Leslie: *They'd appreciate it.* A moment later, Leslie texted again: *Speaking of shoulds. If Paige asks, I really think you should say yes. What do you have to lose?*

Seren didn't respond. What could she say? That she'd gone back and forth on dating in general, and dating Paige specifically, so many times that she had a new pros/cons list on her fridge? She finished her granola bar and headed out to the lobby. If she wanted to make it on time for class, she had to ignore her stomach's complaint that one little bar wasn't enough.

# CHAPTER TWELVE

"Our favorite busty blonde has arrived."

Rita winked at Seren after her too-loud announcement. Fortunately, the only others in the locker room were Helen and Vickie. Paige never changed in the locker room. Seren wondered how she had time to get out of her vet gear and shower. For the night classes, she always arrived with hair still wet and like she was out of breath from running.

"Happy to see you here tonight," Helen said, patting Seren's arm. "I needed something sweet to rest my eyes on."

"I think that's Paige's line." Rita chortled at her own joke.

"The question, as always, is will our Paige be able to keep her eyes off of the busty blonde long enough to keep her underpants dry?"

That was Vickie. She was as much of a troublemaker as Rita and cackled now when Seren shook her head. "You all are too much."

"You should see us after a round of gin and tonics." Rita's beehive somehow stayed perfectly in place even when she made her boobs do a little shudder dance. She laughed and added, "Don't tell anyone, but I might have started drinking at five."

"You didn't drive here, did you?" Helen tsked.

"Jack dropped me off." Jack was her husband—Rita talked plenty about his package but Seren didn't know anything else about the man. "I only had one drink anyway. Enough to get me loose so I'll have moves like Seren."

Everyone laughed at this. Including Seren.

Seren hung her purse in the locker and took off her shoes. She was excited about seeing Paige, as usual, but a little nervous with Leslie's comments running through her mind.

"So. I heard you're a masseuse." Rita gave Seren a look like she'd found out some dark little secret.

"I think they liked to be called massage therapists," Helen corrected.

"True. And yes." So much for flying under the radar.

"Frances said you fixed her back," Rita continued. "She said you were magic."

"Magic, huh?" She didn't mind the compliment, of course, but the name Frances didn't ring any bells. And even if she forgot a name, she rarely forgot a face. "I didn't realize anyone in class was a client of mine."

"Frances doesn't like water aerobics." Rita motioned to her hair and added, "Doesn't like to get her hairdo wet. She spotted you in the locker room on Sunday and said something to Pam. Who told Gloria."

"And Gloria told you?" Seren wasn't surprised at the gossip chain, but a little part of her couldn't help worrying. She'd mostly simply enjoyed how the other women all shared stories and talked about each other. It hadn't occurred to her that anything said in water aerobics might get back to her work.

"No, Trudy told me. I think I was the last to find out. Hope our busty blonde wasn't trying to hide her true identity. When's the baby due?"

"October." Seren finished tugging on her swimsuit, wondering if maybe water aerobics had been a mistake from the beginning. Not only all the rollercoaster feelings she'd had with Paige. She'd clearly walked right into the epicenter of the town's grapevine. The last thing she needed was work finding out about her pregnancy as a rumor. "I haven't told my work yet."

"They don't know you're pregnant?" Rita's gaze zipped to Seren's belly.

"I'm better at hiding it when I'm not wearing a bathing suit." A maternity bathing suit at that.

Rita pursed her lips. "I wouldn't hide it too much longer if I were you."

Seren felt an uneasy wave roll through her. When she lived in New York she'd built up enough clients to work on her own, but moving home, and thinking it'd only be temporary, she'd joined up with two other therapists—a married couple who had purchased a new space and wanted to grow their clientele. That's exactly what had happened, and quickly. She'd promised to work with them for the year, and telling them she was going to have to cut that short for a maternity leave wasn't going to go over well. She would still tell them, of course. She was only waiting for the best time to do so. Now she had to hope the rumor mill news wouldn't reach them first.

Two other women came into the locker room and she gave the excuse of wanting to make room for them as she hurried out. She pushed open the door to the pool—with maybe more force than was needed—and nearly smacked into Paige.

Paige did a quick half spin out of the way, her gaze shooting to the water. On reflex, Seren reached for her. Wrapping her hand around Paige's muscular forearm, while locking eyes, was not a good plan if she wanted to keep thinking straight. It did, however, make her libido happy. As heat rushed up her neck, she let go and murmured an apology.

"Don't worry. I'm fine. You didn't push me in this time." Paige smiled. "Besides, I was clearly standing in the wrong place. They painted those red lines for dumbasses like me."

Seren wanted to simply stand there and enjoy the tingly feeling still running through her body from their brief contact, but she realized Paige was expecting her to say something. She glanced down at the red lines around her feet. "It is a bad design. Who makes a door that swings out when there's a pool four feet away?"

"Probably someone who likes pushing people into the pool. Maybe you know them?"

"Very funny." Seren smiled back at Paige. "Anyway. Hi."

"Hi. We should probably not be standing here talking."

"You don't want to get pushed into the pool together?" She chided herself when Paige gave her a knowing look. Without a word, she said plenty: *I know you're into me and I'm into you.* Seren swallowed, fighting back a fresh surge of arousal. She stepped away from the door, and then because she had a good excuse, she reached for Paige and tugged her out of the red-lined area.

She let go quickly, but touching Paige did exactly what she'd expected. Made her hot all over and aching for more. Before she'd gotten her bearings, the door to the locker room swung open and Rita came out followed by two other women.

"That was close." Paige grinned. "Thanks for saving me. I'd better set up." She glanced at the boom box positioned on the bench and then back at Seren. "Any chance we could talk after class?"

"Sure." Seren felt her heartbeat thumping in her throat. This had to be it. Would she really turn Paige down if she asked?

The question still swirled in her head as she waded into the water, smiling back at the smiling faces around her. She tried to respond to the "Hi, how are you?" chatter but her attention was still on Paige. Paige, leaning down to start the music. Damn, she had nice calves. Paige, clapping her hands to get the class's attention. Then Paige looking right at her as she winked and said something about nearly getting pushed into the pool again.

The ladies around Seren laughed and patted her shoulders affectionately. She looked back at Paige and shook her head. *If only…*

Before her fantasies could get far, Paige started marching and Seren fell into step. For the first time all day, when she breathed out, she felt truly relaxed. As much as she would have doubted it even a month ago, she loved water aerobics and realized she'd found her jam. Yes, Paige being the instructor helped more than a little. But she also loved simply being in warm water, surrounded by chatty happy women, with eighties music playing in the background. All stress slipped away.

Paige had clearly upped her game, and by the end of class, Seren was out of breath from working hard to keep up. She'd never thought of water aerobics as a real workout, but tonight proved her wrong. Though lately simply getting through the day pregnant was sometimes a workout. She floated over to the stairs, hungrier than ever and dimly aware she couldn't completely feel her legs. At least her ankles no longer ached.

"You okay?"

Seren looked up at the sound of Paige's voice. The others had already cleared the pool and she realized now she was the last to get out. "I think I'm fine. A little…dizzy."

Paige's brow furrowed. She kicked off her shoes, clearly ready to get into the pool to help Seren.

Seren held up her hand. "I've got it." She grabbed the guardrail, wobbling only a little, and made her way out of the water. As soon as she let go of the rail and straightened up, she wanted to sink right back into the water. Despite knowing Paige's eyes were on her, and wanting to pretend everything was fine, she couldn't. Her legs wouldn't stay steady. When the room pitched, she reached for the rail. Paige caught her first.

She heard the concern in Paige's voice, but her words jumbled together. *Shit.* Vomiting was very likely in her near future.

Paige led her over to the bench by the storage cabinet and she sank down.

"What do you need?"

She dropped her head into her hands and then leaned half over. "I'm gonna be sick."

"Don't move."

Seren registered Paige leaving and then a moment later she was back at her side. She set a trash can down. "Sorry, but this is the best I can do."

"Thanks." Vomiting into a trash can in front of Paige was going to suck.

"You're shivering. I'm going to put a towel on you. Is that okay?"

Numbly, Seren nodded. She hadn't noticed that she was shivering, which was a problem all by itself, but the rush that went through her as Paige's hands grazed her naked skin was a much bigger problem. Paige finished wrapping the towel over her shoulders, managing to get it adjusted without jarring her.

She swallowed back the taste of bile, knowing that fighting it was usually a lost cause. Someone asked Paige if they should call for help. Seren didn't look up. Didn't recognize the voice. She heard the conversation the way she would in a dream. *Dammit.* She hated looking sick. Or weak. And if she passed out, Paige would be the one to catch her. That was not how she wanted things to go.

"You okay if I step away for a minute?"

"Um..." She didn't want Paige to leave but felt ridiculous saying so.

"Never mind. I'll have Claia get the soda."

Claia. Another one of the spicy seniors. Seren recognized the older woman's grumbly but reassuring voice as she promised Paige she'd be back in a flash.

"Thank you, Claia," Seren mumbled.

"She's already gone. Claia's a quick one." Paige squatted down so Seren didn't have to look up to meet her eyes. "I probably shouldn't have spoken for you earlier. Do you think we need to call you an ambulance, or will soda and a minute to sit here help?"

"That's all I need. I think I'm already feeling a little better." She wasn't making any fast moves, but at least the room wasn't swirling. "I don't really like needing help."

"No one does. But we all need it sometimes."

"In the real world, I'm usually the one helping."

"Rita told me you're a massage therapist. That's what I wanted to ask you about—I want to set up an appointment for my mom."

Paige had only wanted to ask that? Seren tried to push away the disappointment. Considering she wasn't sure if she'd say yes to any date offer, it was silly to feel sad about not getting one. Particularly now. "I'd be happy to get her on my schedule."

"We can talk about it later, obviously. She won't set something like that up for herself, but I know she could use it. She also doesn't like being the one who needs help."

Seren sighed. "I probably need to get over that. I'm sixteen weeks pregnant." She wasn't sure why she'd added the last part. Because that was why she couldn't date anyone?

"It was either Sprite or Powerade." Claia handed the soda to Seren. She turned to Paige and asked, "Want me to stay with her?"

Before Paige could answer, Seren said, "Thank you for the soda, Claia. I'll be fine in a minute. I think Paige can handle babysitting me."

Claia patted her shoulder gently and then murmured something to Paige. Oh, there'd be talk in the locker room for sure. Seren wished she could be there to defend herself. She was not someone who threw themselves at women. Ever.

After a minute, Paige took the soda from Seren, popped it open, and handed it back. "It works better if you sip it rather than just hold it."

Seren didn't pipe up with any comment about how Paige shouldn't try to tell her what to do unless they were in bed. As much as she wanted to. The strangest part of all of it was that she was okay with Paige taking care of her. That never happened. Ever. She took a sip and tried not to think too hard about how it was nice that Paige was standing next to her even though she might vomit any minute.

What a mess. She forced down another small sip, then took a deep breath. "Being pregnant kind of sucks."

"So I've heard." Paige sat down on the bench. Not close enough to touch, but closer. "Growing a baby inside you is kind of awesome, though."

"Yeah. It is." Seren took another sip. "I wish I felt awesome. I'm sorry I…"

"Don't be sorry about anything."

Seren looked down at her soda. She didn't usually like Sprite, but at the moment it tasted amazing. And there was no denying it was helping.

"Do you date much?" Seren wasn't sure it was a good question to ask, all things considered, but she couldn't help her curiosity. Besides, she didn't have anything to lose as far as her image at the moment.

"Not much. Why?"

"You seem like someone who would be married already."

"At my age, you mean?" Paige laughed.

"No—I'm not saying—I didn't mean—"

"It's okay. I don't feel like I'm old. Even if I am." Paige shrugged. After a moment she added, "I'm not opposed to it or anything, but I don't think marriage is for me."

"Why not?"

"Having a contract for love seems kind of counterintuitive. I think if you love someone, you stay with them. If things get hard, you try to work it out—if you think the relationship is worth it overall. I wouldn't want someone to stay with me only because we'd signed a document."

Huh. Not the answer she expected. "I feel like I should say that there's legal benefits to being married and it's important that queer people have the same benefits for their relationships. But…the truth is I agree with you. I'd rather know someone was staying with me because it's what they wanted to do. And that they loved me."

"Exactly."

"That doesn't mean two people can't be happy in a long-term committed relationship."

"Right. But who needs a contract?"

"Okay, let me try this again. Why are you single?"

"Want to ask my ex?" Paige shook her head. "Never mind. I'd rather you didn't. Someday, I'd like to be in a relationship that felt like it might last. And if it happens, great. If not? I've got other life goals and plenty of friends."

"How old are you?"

"Ancient. Thirty-seven."

"Hey, now. I'm thirty-eight."

Paige's eyes went wide. "I was joking about the ancient thing. I thought you were younger, but—"

"Yeah, try and talk your way out of this one." Seren laughed.

Paige shook her head, laughing now too.

"It's refreshing talking to someone who's not thinking about marriage or looking for a long-term partner."

"You mean at our age?" Paige's smile lingered on her lips, making her more attractive than ever. "I should probably admit my ex and I almost got married."

"What happened?"

Paige hesitated answering, and Seren quickly said, "It's none of my business."

Paige's gaze fell to Seren's belly for a brief moment before meeting her eyes. "We were trying to start a family. It took a lot of money and it was a lot of stress and, well, we worked together, too, so everything felt hard all the time. After a year trying and her never getting pregnant, she wanted me to try. But we were having all these other problems and I wanted to focus on fixing our relationship first. Then one day at work she admitted she wasn't in love with me, and that was that."

"Oh. Damn."

"In the end it was a good thing. I started over at a new clinic, which I love, and I'm way happier overall."

Seren wanted to ask if Paige wanted kids still, but the question stalled on her lips. She didn't want to co-parent and yet she wanted to know Paige's answer. Why? Because she couldn't date someone who hated the idea of kids?

"Are you sorry you asked?"

"Not at all. Thanks for telling me. Most people aren't so honest." Paige lifted a shoulder. "I'm maybe not telling you all the ways I can be annoying in a relationship."

Seren smiled. "It's good to keep some secrets."

"Are you feeling better? Your cheeks have a little more color."

"I am. Thanks." Seren took another sip of the soda. The nausea was definitely ebbing, though by the way her stomach churned, she knew she needed more calories. "I don't think I ate enough today."

"Me neither. I was rushing from one appointment to the next and then skipped dinner to get here on time. About halfway through class, this image of a BLT came into my head." Paige's eyes closed for a beat. "Mm. Now I'm thinking about it again."

Paige looked entirely too sexy when she closed her eyes and moaned. "I'm sorry if you missed out on a BLT because of me."

"Oh, I won't miss out. Café Ernesto's open late. I'm going straight there." Paige added, "I realize bacon isn't for everyone, but if you like it and you've never had a Café Ernesto BLT, you don't know how much better your life could be."

At the mention of bacon, Seren's stomach rumbled. "Bacon might not be for everyone, but it definitely is for me. I love a good BLT. In fact, now it sounds like the best thing ever."

"No pressure, but you could join me if you like. I'd love the company."

Was Paige asking her out? Or was she only being friendly? She literally couldn't remember a time when she'd felt less attractive. Still, she wanted to say yes. She glanced down at her damp bathing suit. "I need to change. Are you okay waiting?"

"Sure."

She took one last sip of her soda and Paige held out her hand. Instead of handing off the soda, as she realized Paige was expecting, she took Paige's hand. Paige didn't say anything as she helped her to her feet.

"Do you want me to follow you into the locker room in case you get dizzy again?"

Considering the thoughts that had run through her head for the past week, ungracefully peeling off her wet bathing suit in front of Paige would be even more embarrassing than nearly fainting on her. "I'll be fine. Meet you in the lobby in ten minutes?"

Paige glanced at her watch. "Ten minutes."

"Let me guess—you're coming to check on me if I'm not out in eleven minutes?" She'd meant it as a joke, but one look at Paige and she realized she was serious.

"I promise I won't look anywhere that would get me in trouble with Rita. See you in ten minutes."

Before Seren had a chance to respond, Paige pushed open the door leading to the lobby. Seren exhaled. She'd gone from shivering in her wet suit to blazing hot.

"I don't think I can be responsible for my decisions around her." But no way was she turning back.

# CHAPTER THIRTEEN

After a week sweating how to ask Seren out, she'd done it with possibly the least amount of class. *So much for making her swoon with a grand first date.* Instead, BLTs at a cheap café and they were driving separately. Still, Seren had said yes—even after she'd brought up her baggage with her ex, Miranda.

She couldn't stop smiling. What a dork she was. But Seren had said yes! Gone was all the conversation in her brain about focusing on work and the goal of buying a ranch. Why had she insisted she couldn't date while working toward those other goals anyway? Because she hadn't met anyone like Seren.

They passed Fifth Street and she wondered which part of town Seren lived in. Leslie had mentioned that she and Seren had been friends in high school and rekindled the friendship when Seren moved back home. Paige got the feeling that Seren hadn't been back long. She wondered what had brought her back. Something else Leslie had said made her wonder if Seren was planning on staying. How many questions could she ask on a first date without making it like a job interview?

Two spots were available right in front of the restaurant and Paige parked behind Seren. She waited for Seren to get out but when a minute passed, she went over to check on her. The driver's side door opened but Seren didn't get out. "Feeling dizzy again?"

"A little." Seren didn't look like she wanted any help, however. With a sigh, she held up a granola bar wrapper. "I had to take a bite of this on the way. It's my second granola bar for the day. I'm starting to hate peanuts. And chocolate."

"I can't imagine hating chocolate."

"You'd hate it if you only ate it when you were about to vomit." Seren swung her legs out and stood. "You sure you want to go out to dinner with a slightly nauseous, not-sure-I-can-manage-a-conversation, pregnant woman?"

"One hundred percent sure."

Seren gave her a wry smile. "I wonder about your judgment."

Inside, they had their pick of tables. The place was more of a breakfast and lunch spot and the waitress motioned for them to sit wherever they wanted as she continued to chat with a young woman sitting by herself.

Paige snagged two menus as they passed the front counter and followed Seren's lead over to a spot in the far corner. Seren motioned to the sign for the bathroom. "I never thought I'd pick tables based on proximity to the bathroom."

"Do you have to pee a lot already?"

"Yes. I also vomit a lot." Seren shook her head. "I'm sorry. That's gross. And we're about to have dinner. It's gotten better, really. The vomiting part. Everyone said it would second trimester, and they were right." She sank into her seat and quickly opened the menu as if she wanted to hide behind it.

"I can do gross. Doesn't bother me at all. Try to gross me out. I dare you."

Seren lowered her menu, a half-smile on her lips. "Honestly, I'd rather not. I have to remember I'm talking to the person who puts their arm up a cow's butt."

"Exactly. Wait." Possibly Seren was using the example as a theoretical thing but what were the chances she'd bring up the same thing Leslie had? "Were you talking to Leslie about gross things vets do or something? She asked me why a vet would put their arm up a cow's butt."

"There's a picture of you on the vet school's website. Leslie helped me look you up online." A blush hit Seren's cheeks with the last bit.

Paige wanted to be happy that Seren had looked her up, but she couldn't ignore the realization that one picture had likely sunk her chances. "You probably think I'm completely disgusting, but I'm stuck on the fact that you looked me up. Do I want to ask why?"

"I wasn't trying to be a stalker or anything, but you did start that first class by stripping."

"Stripping?" Paige grinned. "Stripping is an overstatement. I took off my wet sweatshirt."

"And underneath was a wet tank top."

Paige face-palmed.

"I couldn't help but look you up."

"And I thought I was embarrassed about you seeing that picture of me with the cow."

Seren laughed. "You shouldn't be embarrassed. You've got a very nice body. And now I'm going to hide behind this menu." She held the menu up and laughed again when Paige tried to peek around it.

Paige gave up and sank back in her seat. "That picture of me with the cow really didn't gross you out?"

"I liked the coverall look but I did have some questions." Seren lowered the menu enough to wink.

Paige rolled her eyes in response. But she didn't mean it. Inside, she was busy doing leaps of joy.

"I didn't even realize your arm was in a cow when I first looked at the picture. Leslie pointed that pearl out."

"I'll have to thank her the next time I see her."

Seren lowered the menu completely. "I wasn't going to tell you about looking you up online. But only because I felt sheepish about it—not because of what I found."

"I wish you'd found a picture of me cuddling a baby lamb or better yet wrangling a bull into a squeeze shoot."

"No one can really choose what people find out about them online."

"True. If I looked you up online, would I find some embarrassing pictures too?"

"Nothing like yours. But maybe don't go looking too hard." Seren raised an eyebrow and Paige laughed. "So, no one came up with a urine test to tell if a cow is pregnant?"

"There's a urine test. You can pull blood too. Or do an ultrasound." Paige held up her hand. "But this is cheaper and faster. Especially if you've got a big herd."

"I'm glad I'm not a cow."

"For the record, I rarely do preg checks anymore. Farm calls are only about a third of my practice and I mostly work with backyard farmers or 4-H kids. The rest of the time I'm in the clinic seeing cats and dogs. Also, I'd like to point out I'm not the one who started this gross conversation. I'm usually the one who gets blamed, but this was all you."

Seren laughed. "I accept that blame. But I'm a massage therapist. I touch naked people all day long. I can do gross too."

"Some people are way more gross than cows."

The waitress appeared at their table. If she'd overheard, she was good at hiding it. She grabbed the pencil stuck behind her ear and a pad of paper from the front of her apron. "Hi. I'm Holly. Are you two ready to order?"

"I think so." Paige looked over at Seren. "Want to go first?"

"I'll have the BLT, please."

The waitress nodded. "With avocado?"

"Definitely. Avocado is the best part of being back in California. People here understand avocado goes on everything."

The waitress agreed and then looked in Paige's direction.

"I'll have the same."

The waitress smiled as she pocketed her pad of paper. "You two are easy. Drinks?"

"Water would be great."

Seren nodded in agreement and the waitress was gone and back a minute later with two waters. Once she'd gone again, Paige considered the questions she'd thought of on the drive over. "Leslie said you two went to high school together. How was Davis High?"

"Not awful in retrospect." Seren lifted a shoulder. "But back then I thought I was too cool for this town. We moved here from Seattle—before that we'd lived in LA. Davis felt like a boring tomato patch in comparison."

"Tomatoes do grow really well here."

Seren tilted her head. "I've since come to appreciate that fact, but back then I took one look at all the tomato fields and told my mom she'd ruined my life moving us here." She scrunched up her face. "I was maybe a little dramatic. It was seventh grade. By ninth grade I was convinced I needed to live in New York. Or any big city. My mom told me I didn't know how good I had it."

"Was she right?"

Seren hesitated. "Davis is nothing like New York, but it wasn't nearly as bad as I made it out to be."

"Not a ringing endorsement."

"Well, no. Davis is...Davis. Leslie said you lived here as a kid too?"

"Only until third grade. Then my dad got a job transfer and we moved to Nevada. Phoenix, Arizona, after that. And I thought Davis was hot in the summer."

"Davis is hot in the summer."

Paige shook her head. "Not like Phoenix."

"Why'd you come back to Davis?"

"That was going to be my next question for you."

"Beat you to it." Seren smiled.

"Okay, but after I answer it's your turn." She paused, thinking of all the ways she could explain how much she'd wanted to be in Davis to someone who'd described it as a tomato patch. "Going to vet school was always my dream. And Davis has the best vet school. When I got my letter saying I'd been accepted, I felt like I'd won the life lottery."

"The vet school is pretty cool. Even if it is in Davis."

"In my mind, this place was basically heaven."

Seren looked dubious. "Davis is heaven?"

"I'm telling you, summers in Phoenix are hell. As soon as I saw the vet school acceptance letter I started whooping."

"You don't seem like the whooping type." Seren grinned.

"I'm not, really, but I did then." More than whoop. She'd been on a high for weeks after the letter arrived. "I was over the moon. For real. I wanted to come back to Davis and go to vet school more than anything. I didn't think I'd stay here forever though. Once I graduated, I figured I'd take a job somewhere else. But one thing led to another, and I never left. Even convinced my mom to move back here. Then she got into water aerobics and no way will she leave now."

"Water aerobics is kind of addicting. But it might be that I have a good teacher."

Paige scratched her head. "I don't think it's that." She knew she was barely making it as a water aerobics teacher, but the look in Seren's eyes made her feel all buzzy inside. "Your turn. What took you away and what brought you back?"

Seren blew out a breath. "You sure you want to know?"

"Definitely." As much as she'd complained about first dates, Paige had to admit she was enjoying herself this time. Instead of feeling like a job interview, chatting with Seren felt like catching up with an old friend.

"I moved away for college and thought I'd never come back. Not to live, anyway. I didn't love it here as a kid and I did everything I could not to come back. For the last ten years I even bought my mom plane tickets every Thanksgiving and Christmas so she'd come to me instead of the other way around."

"Wow, you really hate Davis."

Seren gave a half-shrug. "My teenage self hated it here." She glanced down at her folded hands, seemingly reluctant to go on. "Growing up, it was just Mom and me. After my father left, she never remarried. Never had any other kids either. When she got her cancer diagnosis, I wanted to be here for her. I knew she was going to need help…Everyone said it would probably be a year-long process with all the treatments, but, well, it didn't work out that way." She fanned out her hands like that was the end of it.

"How's your mom's health now?"

"She passed away six weeks after I moved home. About five months ago."

"Oh, shit. I'm sorry. I didn't realize—"

"It's okay. It sucked but it is what it is now." Seren took a long moment before she went on. "The cancer was already a lot further along than we realized initially." Tears glistened in her eyes. "After I lost her, I had kind of a midlife crisis. I didn't know where my life should go next. I'd planned to be here until my mom got better, you know, and then suddenly that all changed. Other than Leslie, the only thing here for me was memories of my mom. And my mom's house, which I need to sell because I can barely afford the payments now—let alone once I have a baby and I'm not working as much. And my job was only supposed to be a temporary thing but...ugh." She rubbed her eyes and then cleared her throat. "I'm sorry. You asked a simple question and I go and lay all that on you."

Paige reached across the table to touch Seren's hand. "I asked because I wanted to know. Thanks for telling me. That's a lot on your shoulders."

Seren exhaled. "Hence the midlife crisis. Everyone around me seemed to have this clear life plan. Even Leslie, who'd always been my go-to bohemian, was engaged—and I had no clue what I was doing. It's one thing to not have a compass when you're twenty-three but thirty-eight?" She shook her head. "I did a bunch of soul-searching and it hit me that the only thing I really wanted was to be a mom. Like my mom."

"So, you got pregnant."

"On the very first try." She looked toward the kitchen when a rattle of plates interrupted the relative quiet. "Leslie's fiancée told me it was a good thing I never had sex with men given how eager my ovaries were."

"Leslie has a fiancée?"

"Not anymore. The engagement got called off. It's a long story and she'd kill me if I told you. It has to do with her job. She's a kick-ass realtor but she makes questionable choices when it comes to women. And this woman may have been her boss."

"Oh."

"Yeah."

Paige shifted back in her seat. After a moment she said, "I'm sorry about your mom and your midlife crisis. But a little part of me is happy you decided to stay in Davis."

"I don't know how long I'll stay. I'm getting my mom's house ready to sell and then, well, then I don't know. I can't imagine what life will be like after the baby comes. I keep trying to picture it, but I can't." She unfolded the napkin next to her plate and then immediately refolded it. "I don't even know if I'll be a good mom."

"You'll be amazing."

"How do you know?"

"I can tell. You're gonna rock it."

Seren sniffed. "Well, I'm not so sure, but thanks for the vote of confidence."

The waitress appeared at their table. "We're out of the potato salad that usually goes with the BLTs. Any chance I can replace that with fries?"

"Sure." Paige answered first without thinking but then quickly looked over at Seren. "Is that okay for you?"

Seren nodded and the waitress zipped off once more. After a moment, Seren reached for her water and met Paige's gaze. "You're used to being in charge, aren't you?"

Paige didn't know what Seren wanted her to say. She was used to it, of course, but had answering for them both been a misstep that she ought to apologize for?

"I didn't mean to stump you with that. And you don't have to answer. I actually already know."

"I am used to being in charge, but I can definitely tone it down a bit."

"Don't. It's kind of refreshing, actually. I've had to make a lot of hard decisions and I'm feeling kind of done." Seren looked around the restaurant and then back at Paige. "I needed this tonight. I never go out anymore. Even just with friends. Leslie and I always get takeout and eat at home."

*Just with friends.* Did that mean this wasn't a first date?

Seren continued, "How long have you lived with your mom?"

Paige pushed away the question of whether they were on a first date or not. "Four months now. Only planned on it being a few weeks. It's worked out *okay*. Her dog and my cats don't get along, and Mom and I get on each other's nerves. I really thought I'd find something to buy sooner than this."

"You don't seem like the type to get on anyone's nerves."

"I have my moments. We all do, right?"

"True story." Seren pursed her lips. "I'm diabolical when it comes to laundry. It drove my ex nuts. I have to sort everything. Everything."

Paige laughed. "Not the worst trait."

"Oh, I have others."

Before Paige could ask for more, their waitress reappeared.

"Two BLTs with avocado and side of fries."

They fell to eating, with Paige's thoughts hopping between all the questions she had about Seren and whether or not she should simply ask if they were on a date.

"These fries are delicious."

Paige looked up from her BLT and nodded. Seren dipped a fry in ketchup and bit it in half. "You're agreeing but you haven't even tried them."

"I'm distracted by this BLT."

"These fries might be even better."

"Not possible."

"You haven't tried them yet. You don't know what you're missing."

Paige grinned. "One could argue that about a lot of things."

Seren narrowed her eyes. "That was smooth."

Paige laughed as Seren shook her head in mock disapproval. Definitely first-date territory.

Seren dipped another fry in ketchup but then hesitated. "I'm eating too fast."

"Feeling sick?"

"Pretty much the story of my life right now. I'm hungry all the time, but if I eat too fast it comes right back. That's gross. I'm sorry."

"Remember, you're eating with a vet. You can't gross me out."

"I feel like that's a dare." Seren half-smiled. "I don't usually talk about this kind of bodily stuff. Especially at dinner."

"We could try to be proper." Paige reached for her napkin, still on the table, unfolded it, and placed it on her lap, then straightened in her seat. "Better?"

"No." This time Seren smiled all the way. "This might sound weird, but I like that I can be myself around you. If this were a first date, I'd be all full of nerves. With you, I feel totally relaxed. I mean, I'm still embarrassed talking about vomiting but…you know what I mean."

"I do." Paige forced a smile. For once, she truly wished she were on a first date. Just when she knew for sure that she wasn't. She reached for her water glass and held it up to Seren. "Cheers to not-first dates."

Seren clinked her glass. "Cheers."

# CHAPTER FOURTEEN

Seren's gaze flicked to her rearview mirror and confirmed the truck was still tailing her. Paige's truck. When Paige had asked if it'd be okay to follow her home, Seren's initial reaction was to hope that meant the evening would close with a good-night kiss. Of course, it didn't make sense to hope for that considering she'd told Paige they weren't on a date.

She could tell Paige had been disappointed. She'd been disappointed too. The whole evening had been one big hurricane of emotions. She'd gone from certain she could date Paige, knowing full well it couldn't last, to sick to her stomach at the fact that she wasn't being transparent. Which was why when the moment came, she decided not dating at all was the right thing to do. Unfortunately, her body kept sending signals like "doesn't Paige smell good?" and "don't you want to lean in to her?"

God, did she.

The traffic light turned red and she slowed to a stop. Could she propose a fling after telling Paige they weren't on a date? If she did, could she really stick to it? Breaking up in October sounded a lot better than not dating at all, but would Paige understand?

She glanced down at the swell of her belly. No doubt about it, the baby was growing. Her OB had promised she'd get to see another ultrasound image at her next appointment, and she wanted to be simply excited about the changes she'd see. With Paige in the picture, though, she couldn't help but wish for time to slow. She wanted a few more months to figure things out.

Paige had surreptitiously paid the dinner bill while she was in the bathroom. When she'd realized that, she'd considered saying they should split it, but Paige had spoken up first—apologizing for taking the liberty of paying and adding that the waitress was trying to close out the cash register for the night. Seren had volunteered to pay next time and silently cheered that she'd ensured there would be a next time. Friends went out to dinner, right?

But she didn't want to simply be friends.

When the light turned green, she again glanced at Paige's truck. Even if part of her wished she were the kind of person to have a fling, and that Paige was coming to her place to get hot and heavy, a bigger part of her appreciated that Paige was following her home to make sure she was okay. At another point in her life, she might have been uncomfortable with the way Paige paid attention to her. Or maybe if Paige was someone else. But nothing about Paige watching out for her made her uncomfortable.

The only thing making her uncomfortable was how much she wanted Paige to jump her. Well, that and the fact that she'd talked about morning sickness during dinner. She'd admitted to vomiting almost daily for the last two months. Instead of being grossed out, Paige had made her laugh about it, which was some kind of superpower. Later, when Paige had turned the conversation over to how cows couldn't vomit and listed some of the weird things she'd removed from cows who probably wished they could have vomited, Seren wanted to hug her.

Mostly, though, she wanted to do a lot more than hug. The way Paige held her gaze made her feel beyond sexy and stirred up all kinds of desires. What she'd give to be the type of person who could ask Paige straight-up for a Netflix and chill night.

She turned down her street and watched in her mirror until Paige's truck made the turn as well. When she pulled into her driveway, Paige slowed and parked on the street. After a moment, the truck's lights flickered off.

Her heart thumped in her chest as she watched Paige hop out of the truck. Her thoughts had swung from one decision to the other all night and she still didn't know what to do. She held her breath as she watched Paige in the rearview mirror coming up the sidewalk toward her car. Maybe Leslie was right. Maybe she needed to try a fling before she decided it wasn't for her. She could be honest with Paige and deal with the aftermath to her own psyche later.

Before she could open the car door, Paige did. Paige stepped to one side and then pursed her lips. "Should I have not done that?"

"Well, I can open doors myself, but I've given you every reason to think I'm not able to tonight." Seren held out her hand. "I also can get out of my car all by myself, but since you're standing there…"

Paige's expression shifted as she clasped Seren's hand. The flash of desire in her eyes came on quick. Hot and unsteadying. Seren's breath caught as she felt the same pulse through her when Paige easily pulled her up. Paige's physical strength wasn't something she'd considered before, but feeling even a touch of it, along with being only inches away from her, had every part of her begging to feel more.

She could have gotten out of the car without any trouble. But she'd wanted an excuse to touch Paige, plain and simple. And now that their hands were locked, she was dizzy all over again. At least this time she wasn't thinking about vomiting. What she did feel was more worrying.

Paige bumped the door closed with her hip. She turned to Seren, held her gaze for a beat, and then loosened her grip. Too soon their entwined fingers released.

"Thanks for dinner. That BLT hit the spot. And it was even nicer spending time with you." She shook her head. "That sounds dorky."

"I know what you mean." Paige jammed her hands in her pockets. "Also, I agree. Tonight was nice."

She hit the lock button and then leaned against the car. One look at Paige and she knew that if she hadn't screwed everything up, they'd be kissing now. She also knew she owed Paige an explanation at least.

Paige glanced over her shoulder at Seren's house and then back at her car. "I was going to make sure you got inside, but I think you probably can handle it from here."

"I can. But before you go, I need to tell you something."

Paige waited, an expectant look on her face.

Seren blew out a breath. "I can't start a new relationship right now. Everything feels too complicated. I don't know how long I'll even be in Davis, and I have no idea what my life is going to be like after the baby comes. There's so many unknowns and—"

"I get it." Paige bit the edge of her lip. "I totally just interrupted you. Sorry. Go on."

Seren had more reasons for why dating wouldn't work, but now she didn't want to finish the list. "If I were going to date anyone, it'd be you. And I feel like I'm making a mistake I'm going to regret turning you down." A moment later she hastily added, "Not that you technically asked."

"I've been waiting to ask. Wanted to avoid the whole awkward first date thing but I couldn't think of a way until tonight." Paige met Seren's gaze. "I'm not going anywhere if you change your mind. Or…if you decide you want to try something casual."

Seren wanted to ask for parameters on casual, but her attention shifted to a car slowing in front of her driveway.

"Isn't that Leslie's car?" Paige asked.

"Yeah, but I'm not sure why she's here."

Leslie got out and looked from Seren to Paige. "I'm clearly interrupting something." She mouthed an apology to Seren and then said, "Had to make sure you were okay. Now that I know you are, I'm leaving."

"Wait. Why wouldn't I be okay?"

"I've been calling you for the past three hours. And texting. You always respond."

"I must have silenced my phone." Seren reached for her purse. She rummaged through it for as long as it took to confirm she was in fact phone-less. "My phone's not in here." She pushed her sunglasses case out of the way along with her lipstick and a few pens from work. "My wallet isn't in here either. Shit. I left both of them in my swim bag." She stopped and looked up at Paige. "Do you remember if I had my swim bag when I came out of the locker room?"

"You had a towel and your keys in your hand. I don't think you had anything else."

*Dammit.* She always left her purse in her car and threw her wallet and phone in her swim bag. Why she'd grabbed her keys but not everything else could only be explained by the fact that she was distractedly hungry. And thinking about Paige.

"Maybe someone put it in lost and found for you." Paige checked her watch. "The gym closes at nine, but someone is usually there for a while after cleaning up. And I've got my mom's key and her code to get in. I can go check."

"No, no, it's fine. I can call tomorrow."

"Do you have a house phone?"

Paige's question made her realize how much she wasn't thinking at all. "No." She'd canceled the landline shortly after her mother passed. Answering spam calls for her mom was simply too hard.

"Let me go back to the gym and check lost and found. I know what your swim bag looks like. Should everything be in that bag?"

"I hope so?" Seren shook her head. "You really don't have to do this for me. I can drive over there in the morning."

Leslie touched Seren's arm. "Let her do it. What if something happens and you can't call anyone?"

Before Seren could argue that she could manage one night without a phone, Paige turned to Leslie to confirm she'd call her number as soon as she located the bag. A moment later, Paige was heading back to her truck.

"She's got a nice butt," Leslie murmured.

Seren groaned. Not because Leslie was wrong but because she was most definitely right.

"Don't tell me you aren't thinking the same thing."

Seren watched Paige get into her truck before turning to Leslie. "I can't tell you how much I want to wrap my hands around her ass."

Leslie laughed. "Didn't we have a whole conversation about you two not dating?"

"Yeah. I need advice."

# CHAPTER FIFTEEN

"I feel like I should have placed some money on you two hooking up." Leslie followed Seren inside, dropping her purse on the coffee table.

"We haven't hooked up. We weren't even on a real date. We went out to dinner because I nearly fainted on her from low blood sugar. She wanted to make sure I got home. Tea?"

"Sure. Nothing with caffeine, though. It's late."

It was late but Seren felt wired. Which was all Paige's fault.

"If that was only a safety check, you're telling me that she had no plan to kiss you?"

"I think she had plans for a kiss before I told her we couldn't date."

"You didn't."

"I did." Seren headed to the kitchen. "Peppermint okay?"

"You know you're a middle-aged lesbian when peppermint tea is your standby."

"So that's a yes?"

Leslie laughed. "Peppermint would be lovely."

Seren filled the teapot and turned on the burner. "Were you really only coming over to check on me because you couldn't reach me?"

"You had me worried." Leslie leaned against the counter. "And to think you were out with that hottie and completely distracted. You, who always has her phone and her wallet and freaks out if you don't know where those things are."

"I don't freak out."

Leslie pointedly arched an eyebrow.

"Okay, I only freak out a little bit." She was relieved something was being done to find her things—and that she didn't need to panic. *Yet.* "Mind if I change while the water's heating up?"

"Go right ahead. Pick out something sexy in case Paige comes back."

Seren rolled her eyes but she'd truthfully already considered it. She got to her room and found Cymbal curled up on her bed. He looked up and began purring before she even stooped to pet him.

"You and I need to talk," she said, scratching under his chin. "You've been spending too many nights out and I've been worrying about you." He rolled onto his back, tempting her with the sleek black hair on his exposed belly. She gave him one stroke, knowing more would get him wanting to wrestle, and then cleared her throat. "Since you're here, want to help me pick out what to wear?"

Cymbal dutifully followed her over to the dresser. He checked every drawer she opened but got bored and went back to the bed. "You're really not the most helpful roommate." She sighed and considered her options. As much as she wanted to go with the impulse to wear something nicer than her usual loungewear, she reached for sweatpants and a loose pajama shirt. It was the best for everyone involved if she didn't try and dress in anything sexy.

When she returned to the kitchen, Leslie was already pouring the hot water over the tea bags. She handed a mug to Seren and then motioned to the table. "Sit. You've gotta be exhausted. This is late for you."

"It's late for Paige too. She told me she starts appointments at seven a.m. I feel bad I sent her looking for my stuff…She probably hasn't even gotten to the gym yet. The aquatics center is across town."

"Trust me, she's happy doing this for you." Leslie held her mug up to her nose. "I do know of a very good way you can repay her."

Despite sex being on Seren's mind pretty much nonstop since they'd finished dinner, she couldn't believe Leslie would suggest it. "I'm not going to sleep with her just because she went looking for my lost wallet and phone."

Leslie took one look at Seren and started laughing. "That's not what I meant. At all. But I love that sex is the first thing you think of."

"What did you mean?"

"I can't wait to say 'told you so' when you two hook up." Leslie smirked. "What I meant was you helping at the showing of the Landry property."

"Oh. Why would you need my help?"

"Mrs. Landry's got dementia. Mr. Landry can't take care of her on his own." Leslie paused. "I think things are advancing quickly."

Seren felt a wave of guilt. And then worry for the Landrys. "I should have checked in on them."

"Well, that's where the favor for Paige comes in."

"I'm not following."

"Everyone in the family is convinced it's time for assisted living. Even Mrs. Landry on days when she's more coherent. But on days where she isn't coherent, Mr. Landry is afraid she's going to have a bad spell if a stranger shows up to look at the house. I was thinking maybe we could time it with a visit from you."

"I get it. Sure. I'd love to help." Seren pictured the Landry ranch again. "Their barn and all those corrals really would be perfect for Paige. At least from what she's said she was looking for."

"You called it," Leslie agreed. "I told Mr. Landry that I think I have the perfect client. He wants to meet Paige himself—his concern is finding someone who'll take care of not only the house but the animals still on the property. They've got a little wiener dog they're keeping but there's a couple barn cats and an old horse he's insisting can't be moved."

"I don't think that'd be a deal breaker for Paige." But as much as the ranch seemed to be exactly what Paige had said she wanted, she couldn't quite imagine Paige living in the Landrys' house. Maybe it was the flowery wallpaper in the kitchen and the gold lamé in the living room. Along with shag carpet. Hopefully they'd made some upgrades to the house in the last twenty years. "You tell me when and I'll be happy to visit with Mrs. Landry while you show Paige around."

Leslie pressed her hands together. "I hope it all works."

Leslie's phone rang and she held it up to show Paige's name on the screen. "Oh, look. It's your knight in a white pickup truck."

The bubbling excitement that came at the sight of Paige's name was ridiculous. God, she had it bad.

Leslie answered. A moment later, she was nodding and smiling. "Great. Thanks, Paige. See you in a bit." She ended the call and looked at Seren. "You sure you don't want to change into some lingerie?"

"What she'd say?"

"She's on her way back with your swim bag. Wallet and phone are in it. You left your bag in a closed—but unlocked—locker."

"I swear I'd leave my head somewhere if it wasn't attached. Lately I'm so distracted."

"Because of the baby you're growing or because of Paige?"

"Yes." Seren set her tea on the table and leaned back in the chair. She closed her eyes. "She said she's up for keeping things casual."

"Like no commitment?"

Seren nodded. "I think that's what she means."

"Why don't you sound happy? That'd be perfect."

Seren met Leslie's gaze. "I don't know if it would work. I like her a lot already. Something tells me having sex with her isn't going to make me like her less."

"Maybe she's got some annoying habits you'll discover. Like being amazing in bed."

Seren stuck out her tongue. "Thanks for being a supportive friend."

Leslie hadn't left by the time Paige got back with the swim bag. The two of them chatted about schedules and properties and then Paige admitted to having to work early. The next thing Seren knew, she was walking both of them to the door. She wanted to ask Paige to stay but decided it'd be awkward unless she came right out and said what she wanted to talk about. Which would be even more awkward.

After they'd gone, she headed to the bathroom, contemplating how exhausted she looked in the mirror's reflection and then the outfit she was wearing. *Loungewear.* Definitely not what she'd pick to impress someone on a first date, but she'd been comfortable in it with Paige.

She shook her head and brushed her teeth. Gone were the days when she wore anything sexy to bed, but as she padded to her room she wondered if Paige would be into lingerie. The question rekindled the smolder of arousal she'd felt for the last few hours. She went to her closet and found the oversized purse she'd loved in college that now only stored her sex toys.

She had two vibrators. One was a fancy wand with way too many settings. The other was a bullet vibe and about the length of her index finger. The bullet vibe alone did the trick more often than not, but tonight she wanted something more. She considered the wand for a moment but then dug back into the purse and sorted through the rest of the toys she'd acquired. She pulled out all the dildos she'd purchased in the last year, wondering if it was a sign if she couldn't even buy a dildo that felt exactly right. The medium-sized dildo vibrated but the angle wasn't quite right. The smallest one was usually too small, but she'd liked the texturing along the shaft. The third, and largest, was a deep burgundy and the most intriguing, but it'd been too big for her on the occasions she'd tried it. Tonight, though, her clit twitched at the sight of it.

"What the hell. If I'm doing this, I might as well go all the way."

She set all three dildos and the bullet vibe on her nightstand, feeling a bit like Goldilocks. "Here's hoping one's just right." She smiled wryly, not caring if it was ridiculous to have a nightstand crowded with sex toys.

More than toys, tonight she longed to have company. Not company in general but Paige specifically. She pictured Paige helping her out of the car and her chest ached all over again at how the universe seemed to be messing with her. Paige really seemed perfect. What if she was?

She shook away the question and lit a candle. Mazzy Star wasn't someone she listened too often, but she picked it tonight, wanting the slow, relaxing rhythm. She pushed down the covers and settled on her back.

When she spread her legs and looked down at herself, her growing belly caught her attention. She'd never been skinny, but she'd learned to like her curves. One time her ex had called her "Marilyn Monroe sexy" as she'd traced over her breasts and hips. In that moment, she'd felt so desired she'd let go of the hang-up of feeling like she always needed to lose fifteen pounds. But she wasn't sure how she felt now about having a belly that meant none of her pants fit. Still, when Paige looked at her, she felt sexier than ever. She ran her hand over the bump and stopped at the triangle of hair between her legs. Trimming was getting tricky, and she knew it'd get worse with more belly in the way. But what was the point of waxing unless she wanted someone to see her naked?

She tried the smallest dildo first, sliding it in and immediately imagining Paige holding the other end. Problematic? Yes. But she didn't care.

A few strokes with the small dildo and she knew it wouldn't be enough. She reached for the next size up—the swirled blue-and-pink tie-dye dildo that had the advantage of also vibrating. The wider girth felt good in her hand, and when she stroked it in, her body hummed happily in response. After a handful of thrusts, she pressed the button to start the vibrations.

Slowly, she eased the vibrating shaft all the way in. Not only was it wider than the first dildo, it was longer and a good bit of the shaft stuck out of her. She wiggled her hips, knowing she looked ridiculous. Thank god Paige couldn't see her now, desperately trying to scratch the itch she'd given her. Except, she had a feeling Paige wouldn't mind knowing what she did to her.

She'd never masturbated with anyone else in the room, but she closed her eyes now and pictured Paige sitting at the edge of the bed, asking if she wanted some help. *Yes.* She pulled the dildo out again and set the vibrating tip on her clit, holding it in place until she was writhing to have it inside again. She drove it in hard then, enjoying how her body clenched around it. The image of Paige holding the other end of the dildo flashed in her mind.

She gulped down her surprise as her body responded to the fantasy. Fantasizing about someone she knew hadn't happened before. She'd always pictured nameless, unidentifiable people. But when she pushed up her hips, not only could she see Paige, she could almost feel Paige's hands on her. When she dropped back down, it was Paige pushing her to the mattress.

She increased the speed of the strokes, the dildo sliding in and out of her slickness. As good as it felt, there was still no hint of a climax. Frustration got the better of her and she tossed the second dildo aside. Sometimes masturbating was like tickling—she simply couldn't do it to herself. But tonight she wasn't giving up. She needed to get off and it was all Paige's fault.

At her first OB-GYN appointment after the positive pregnancy test, her doctor had mentioned that sex was okay—as if she needed the reminder that she *could* get laid if only she could find someone. But her hormones were only lukewarm about the idea of sex that first month. Weeks passed and she'd gotten to the fire-hot stage of horniness she'd been told some women felt. She'd sent an email to the nurse helpline asking if toys were okay. Thankfully, she'd been given a green light. Still, her arousal had never been at this level.

Impatiently, she grabbed the last dildo. As she coated the tip with lube, she wished Paige was the one doing it. Then when she poised the tip between her legs, knowing it was too big but wanting it anyway, she imagined Paige wearing it.

She swallowed, pushed her hips forward, and let the dildo part her slit. The bulbed head met the rim of her vault and went no farther. She bounced her hips on the mattress, bucking as she tried to take it inside. The shaft wouldn't budge. She pushed harder, wanting it more than ever. Her effort was rewarded with a centimeter of progress.

"Fuck me." She sighed, eyeing the burgundy dildo between her legs and wishing she didn't have something that tempting in her house if it didn't fit. It was like a gorgeous dress that would look amazing on someone else. She licked her finger and coated her folds with spit, rejuvenating the lube, then tried again. No luck. The length of the dildo stuck out of her like a popsicle she couldn't have.

"Come on." She pushed again, felt her body strain, and then flopped back on her pillow. It was no use.

If only she had help. She'd let Paige fuck her with anything at the moment. She pictured Paige's hand guiding the dildo and her body opening up to take the length of it. She lifted her hips and pushed the base.

It didn't happen quickly, but under the steady pressure the resistance ebbed. She felt a delicious spasm as the bulb slipped past her rim. When she eased the shaft all the way inside, a warmth spread out from her center. A delicious calm filled her, and she gave up trying to fight back the fantasy of Paige fucking her.

*"You like that, don't you?"* She heard Paige's husky voice in her head and her arousal shot up.

*God, yes.* She tried to stroke the burgundy dildo, but her center was clenching too much around the shaft. The weight of it, the fullness, was what she wanted but she needed more still. She reached for the bullet vibe.

As soon as she cozied the vibrator up to her clit, her hips jerked involuntarily. Her hand banged against the hunk of silicone wedged inside her and her vault clenched. It was almost painful but that turned her on all the more.

"Oh, yeah."

She breathed out and started rhythmically pumping her hips. She pushed one palm against the base, and that was Paige, pushing it deeper into her. She felt it move another centimeter and her clit responded with a tremor.

"Fuck."

Every part of her felt good and tingly. Like tinder about to blaze. She licked her lips, closed her eyes again, and Paige came right to mind. Paige, sitting astride her hips, gripping the dildo.

*"You want more?"*

She nodded her head. Sweat beaded on her brow and her breath came in pants but she increased the pace of her pumping hips. The promise of a climax rose inside her as one song melted into another. The vibrator played on like a backup singer to Mazzy Star's smooth alto.

"I'm so close," she moaned.

*"I know you are," Paige said.*

Her fantasy had taken over completely. It was Paige stroking the too-big dildo that was exactly right tonight. In and out, she stroked. Paige was pushing her almost too far, but she wanted it anyway.

*"Come for me."*

Another stroke and the orgasm hit. She stiffened, her legs clenching hard on the dildo. The wave rolled through her, and she shivered despite the heat. A moment later she went limp. Aftershocks came, one following the other till she felt dizzy and weak, but all she could think of was Paige. Paige's arms around her. Paige caressing her cheek. Then Paige kissing her lips.

# CHAPTER SIXTEEN

Even after a full morning of barn calls, Paige was still replaying her non-date with Seren in her head. So much had felt so right. She'd thought they were on the same wavelength and really connecting up until the moment Seren had said she was glad they weren't on a date. That had hit like a punch. Even if she understood Seren's reasons and partly agreed, she'd gone to bed thinking of all the possible ways they could date without committing—which led to a very nice fantasy. But she'd woken up that morning wishing that Seren would change her mind and consider a relationship.

When her phone rang in the middle of a pitstop for tacos, she hoped it'd be Seren and had to mask her disappointment answering Leslie's call. "Hey."

"Ready for your good news?" Without waiting for a response, Leslie continued, "You know that property I mentioned last night? I got the owners to agree to a private showing. It's a little smaller than what you'd said you were ideally hoping for, but I'm ninety percent sure you'll like it anyway. And I think it'll be in your budget."

"What's the price?"

"We haven't decided on one yet. They wanted to meet you first."

Deciding on a price after meeting a buyer couldn't be standard protocol. Did the "we" part mean that Leslie knew the sellers?

"I'm sure you've got questions, but let me tell you the good parts first. Four-stall barn plus a storage shed. Two arenas. Three raised garden beds and a fruit tree orchard behind the house. Only five acres, but it's all fenced. Want to hear about the house?"

Probably she should care about the house, but a four-stall barn and five fenced acres was enough to make her ready to sign her life away to the bank. "How far from town are we talking?" If the property was anywhere near her budget, it'd likely be a long haul getting to work.

"I clocked it when I was driving out there this morning. Nine miles."

"Wow. That's perfect. You really think their price will be in my budget?" She'd shown Leslie her preapproval paperwork from the bank. No secrets with realtors.

"I can't guarantee anything yet. I'm hoping once they meet you, they're going to want to make this work. It's an emotional sale."

"What do you mean by emotional?" Maybe someone had died in the house? That might deter others, but it wasn't a dealbreaker for her. Still, she could already imagine her mom going on about ghosts and séances.

"Emotional might not be the best word. Complicated? The property is owned by an older couple—actually, Seren knows them. The mister wants to sell, but the missus has memory problems. Some days she understands and agrees that they need to move out, other days she's sure it's 1985 and everyone's on their way over for Thanksgiving dinner."

Paige's mind was still turning over the connection to Seren when her order number came over the loudspeaker. "Hold on a minute, Leslie." She grabbed her tacos and headed outside. The sun shone on another perfectly clear Davis day. Not too hot, not too windy. Exactly how early spring always was, and in her mind, few places could compete. If she could find a ranch—even if it was smaller than the ten acres she'd hoped for—close enough to her mom and work, she was willing to do anything to get it.

"Leslie, I'm not in a rush. If this couple needs more time to be ready to sell, I don't mind."

"They don't need more time. What they need is finessing. I talked to one of their adult children this morning. He's in his sixties himself. All the siblings want the place sold and the parents moved to an assisted-living facility with memory care services for his mom. But he says his dad won't leave unless he is sure the place will be taken care of. There's a few animals that will be part of the deal."

"Animals I can handle."

"That's why I want them to meet you. Any chance you're free this evening?"

After the barn calls that morning, a C-section on a bulldog when she was supposed to be eating her tacos, and an afternoon jam-packed with sick cats and dogs, she ought to be exhausted. But as soon as Leslie pulled up to the clinic and Paige realized Seren was in the passenger seat, she didn't feel tired at all. She did, however, wish she'd had time to shower.

Seren opened the front passenger door and smiled. "Nice scrubs."

"I didn't have time to go home and change." Paige glanced down at herself, guessing she'd find evidence of the last patient of her day—Saint Bernard hair got everywhere. Yep, she was hairy, all right. At least she'd changed out of her boots and coveralls after vaccinating the sheep.

"No, I meant it. You look good in them." Seren gestured to the front seat she'd vacated. "You get to sit up front. I'm only tagging along to visit with the Landrys. They're old family friends."

"The Landrys are the family that own the property?"

Seren nodded. "Mrs. Landry has dementia and Leslie thought it might be less stressful if I kept her company while you check out the place."

Leslie leaned across the car's console. "We'll explain more on the way. I told Seren this was her way of repaying you for fetching her wallet and phone last night."

"Oh, that was nothing."

Seren shook her head. "It wasn't nothing. And thank you. It's silly to worry about going even one night without a phone, but I probably wouldn't have slept."

Seren's sincere tone made it seem like a much bigger deal than it'd been. If she could make her happy that easy… Paige cut her train of thought short. Nothing could happen. "It's not silly. You live alone and you weren't feeling well. Totally reasonable to want a phone handy. I would have given you mine for the night if I hadn't found yours."

Leslie cleared her throat. "Not to rush you two, but I promised the Landrys we'd be there by seven."

For the first five minutes of the drive, Leslie detailed what she knew about the property and the surrounding area. Paige tried to focus, fighting the impulse to climb into the back seat with Seren.

"You're going to love the barn. I don't even like barns and I like this one. It's old school. Red with white trim. Super cute. Did I mention there's two arenas?"

Paige nodded. When she turned to look out the window, she caught Seren's profile in her peripheral vision. She was staring out at the passing view—plowed fields waiting for a first spring planting, more gold than brown as the sun leaned low on the horizon.

Was Seren thinking about the scenery? Or only lost in thought? She'd said the Landrys had been family friends which likely meant a tie to her mother. Paige recalled how her face had clouded at only a brief mention of her mother's passing. Hopefully this visit wouldn't make her feel worse.

"And there's plenty of room for you to add on another barn if four stalls isn't enough for what you need."

Leslie's words pulled Paige's attention back. *Right.* She was here to look at a potential property—not think about Seren.

She glanced out the window again. The plowed fields had been replaced by fields of green alfalfa lining either side of the two-lane road. From the looks of it, the alfalfa was about ready for a first cut. The green wouldn't last long. Still, it was a gorgeous sight.

*Not a bad view for driving home from work.* She couldn't get her hopes up yet, but she'd been doing exactly that since Leslie's lunchtime call. All the open space they passed made her long even more for a spot to call her own. With five acres, she could finally get cows.

Soon Leslie turned off the main road onto a gravel drive. Beyond the green fields, distant mountains made a blue ridge on the horizon. "This really isn't too far from town."

"No, but this gravel road goes for a ways. And it could use a little TLC."

From the back seat, Seren spoke up. "I forgot how beautiful it is out here. I haven't been here since I stopped taking piano lessons with Mrs. Landry." She paused, seemingly thinking. "Feels like forever ago. And yet not."

Leslie slowed over a dip in the road. She was right. The road could use some TLC along with a fresh load of gravel.

"When Seren mentioned the Landrys I couldn't remember why the name sounded familiar." Leslie glanced over her shoulder at Seren and smiled. "Mrs. Landry taught a garage band class that we both took in high school."

"Garage band? That was a class?"

"Special elective," Leslie said. "And super popular. Mrs. Landry was a hoot. I remember thinking she was an old lady then. Twenty years ago. Seren, how old do you think she is now?"

"She's probably in her nineties. Her and Mr. Landry celebrated their seventy-fifth wedding anniversary at my mom's church a year ago. When my mom told me, I tried to do the math." She laughed. "'Old' is what I came up with."

Leslie nodded. "And this house, Paige, looks about as old."

"I'm okay with an older place. As long as it comes with a barn."

"It's all about the barn?" Leslie smiled. "I like having an easy client." She slowed as the car lurched into a dip in the road. "And I'm hoping you weren't looking for a pristine driveway either."

"This road used to be in better shape," Seren said. "But I do remember the potholes even when I used to ride my bike out here."

"Do you still play piano?" Paige knew she should be thinking about the condition of the road and how much fresh gravel would cost. At the moment, though, she was more curious about Seren.

"I can still knock out a few songs. But my heart was never really into being a concert pianist like my mom hoped. I wanted to be a rock star. So did Leslie."

"It's true," Leslie said. "Though Seren had all the talent."

"You had talent too. Along with terrible stage fright."

Leslie sighed. "Also true." She glanced away from the road long enough to stick out her tongue at Seren. "Be careful what you tell my client. I know plenty of juicy secrets about you too. Remember the name of our first band?"

"You two had a band together?"

Leslie nodded. "I played the guitar and another friend of ours was the vocalist. Seren alternated between keyboard and drums."

"You play the drums?" Paige looked back at Seren. "That's awesome."

"Used to play." Seren shook her head in Leslie's direction. "It's been years now."

"She got recruited to play with the G Street Girls. She switched between keyboard and the drums." Leslie glanced over her shoulder and asked Seren, "How long did you play with them?"

Seren waved off the question, clearly not happy with the spotlight on her.

"Anyway," Leslie continued. "In high school she was a backup drummer for anyone touring through the Pubster."

"In high school?"

Before Seren could confirm, Leslie said, "In case you couldn't tell, Seren's one of those cool kids who's good at like a million things."

"You can stop talking about me now." Seren made a face at Leslie, earning her a blow-kiss and a laugh.

Paige pictured Seren behind a drum set. Seren with a pair of drumsticks banging out a rhythm was about the sexiest thing she could imagine. She had about a dozen questions she wanted to ask as follow-up but before she could, Leslie reached across her to point out a red barn.

"There's your barn. I'm guessing you'd like to check that out first?"

The barn was even better than she'd hoped for—bigger than she'd imagined and in better condition. Plus, it came complete with an apple tree on one side and a white fenced-in corral. "Yes, please."

Seren hopped out first as soon as Leslie parked. "While you two check out the barn and everything, I'm going to go chat with Mrs. Landry."

Paige fought back a wave of disappointment. She wanted to see everything with Seren. And talk to her about her plans. Okay, dreams. The fact that Seren knew the family selling the property and wanted to come visit them made the "meant-to-be" feeling impossible to ignore.

# CHAPTER SEVENTEEN

After they'd toured the barn, complete with one old gray mare who Leslie thought was twenty-five but looked closer to thirty, and two black barn cats who were starved for chin scratches, Paige was ready to make an offer. Yes, every surface was in sore need of a fresh coat of paint. All of the fences needed repairing. And weeds had entirely taken over the arena. But each of the four stalls had separate paddocks and there was a turnout area in addition to a main riding arena. Plus, there was plenty of room for hay in the barn and rafter space for more storage in addition to a tool shed.

Paige stopped under a cherry tree laden with blossoms and then looked back at the barn. "I'll take it."

"You haven't seen the house yet."

"It's the location I want and it's nicer than I was ready to hope for. I also have a sweet spot for black cats. Can we write up an offer tonight?"

"As your realtor, I'm going to insist you look inside the house. You have to know what you're getting yourself into—all of it. You can't sleep in the barn."

"You clearly don't know me that well."

Leslie tilted her head. "Okay, let me rephrase. If you ever intend to have any company stay with you—and I think you might already have someone in mind—you're going to want a bed, right?"

Paige felt the blush hit her cheeks. She apparently wasn't hiding her attraction to Seren. "Um..."

"Exactly. So, we're going inside and checking out the house. Besides, I promised Mr. Landry we'd stay for a bit to chat." Leslie headed for the single-level brick rancher without looking over her shoulder to see if Paige was coming too.

Leslie knocked on the front door right as Paige caught up. "Did you talk to the family about ballpark numbers? I know what the bank qualified me for but I'm nervous about going much above that."

"Like I said, they haven't decided on a price. They wanted to meet you first."

It was a long moment before the door opened and Paige had time to go from nervous to excited and back to nervous. An elderly woman stood in the entryway, half leaned over a walker. She scowled as she looked from Leslie to Paige. "We don't want a newspaper subscription."

"Hello, Mrs. Landry. It's me, Leslie. Is Seren in there with you?"

"Seren?" Mrs. Landry shook her head. The annoyed look turned to confusion. "Who's Seren?"

Leslie pursed her lips and leaned to one side, clearly trying to see if she could spot Seren. The interior of the house was dark, with every window covered in heavy drapes.

Leslie pushed on. "Mrs. Landry, I'm here with the veterinarian I was telling you about." She gestured to Paige. "Remember we talked about her coming over to see the place?"

"Hi." Paige raised her hand. "You have a beautiful property here. I'm in love with your barn."

"You're in love with what?"

"The barn." By the angry expression forming on Mrs. Landry's face, Paige realized it wasn't a question of not being able to hear. She had no idea why Paige was there or what she was talking about.

Mrs. Landry turned to Leslie. "Why would he be in love with a barn?"

"She's a veterinarian, Mrs. Landry." Leslie shot an apologetic look at Paige before continuing, "I guess veterinarians really like barns."

"My husband isn't home. You'll have to come back another time." Mrs. Landry promptly closed the door.

Leslie made an O-shape with her mouth. "I promise I did tell her we were coming this evening. I set it all up yesterday with Mr. Landry and even dropped off a note and some flowers this morning hoping that would help."

"I think I confused things saying I was in love with the barn. Where do you think Seren is?"

"Good question."

The door opened again, and an elderly bald man stood in front of them with a platter of cookies. Someone was playing the piano and notes of a song Paige recognized but couldn't name filtered out.

"Leslie. There you are!" Considering the man's short stature, his booming voice was a surprise. "I had a little mishap with an oven mitt and Seren insisted on bandaging me up." He motioned with the bandaged hand. "But there's nothing wrong with the cookies."

The piano music stopped for a moment and Paige heard Seren's voice followed by Mrs. Landry's. She couldn't see much past the circle of light in the front hall and wondered where the piano might be.

"You didn't have to make cookies," Leslie said. "I didn't want you to go to any work today."

"Oh, cookies are no work. Besides, Carol likes them." Mr. Landry turned to Paige. "Judging from your outfit, I gather you're the veterinarian."

"I am." Paige brushed a fluff of Saint Bernard hair from the front of her scrubs. "And I promise I cleaned up after my farm calls this morning but—"

"Don't worry," Mr. Landry said. "You take care of animals, you get hair on you. Not to mention other things. That's life around here too. I won't sniff to see if you stink."

Paige laughed. "Thanks. You've got a beautiful place, sir."

"We sure like it." He glanced behind him when the piano music started again. "It's nice hearing that old thing play again." He lowered his voice and added, "Some days my wife's mind's a little clearer than others. Today's not been so good."

An old dachshund hobbled up behind Mr. Landry. Paige couldn't help noticing the dog favoring the right hind leg. "Who's this?" She dropped down on one knee at the friendly wag and was rewarded with a hand lick. "You're not much of a guard dog, are you?"

"That's our Bella. Sweetest dog you'll ever meet. We had her mother too. You should have seen that one." Mr. Landry chuckled. "Would've taken off two of your fingers by now."

Bella sidled up closer to Paige, tail wagging faster when Paige patted her head. "That's dachshunds for you. Either the sweetest or…"

"Or not," Mr. Landry finished. He chuckled again. "We've had our share of both. Bella here, though, is special. She seems to know she has to take care of my wife. Always at Carol's side. Never even goes outside except twice a day to do her business and then hurries back in." He paused, brow furrowing as he studied the dog. "But she hasn't been feeling like herself these past couple days."

"Mind if I take a look at her foot? I think something's hurting her." In truth, she'd already ran her hand up and down the leg. At Mr. Landry's nod, she lifted the dog's paw. It wasn't hard to find the problem. One of her toenails was so overgrown the tip was embedded in the paw pad. Two of the other nails on the opposite paw were close to the same fate. "Any chance you have a dog toenail trimmer handy?"

"Sure do. But my hands shake too much to trim anyone's nails. You think that's the problem?"

"One way to find out."

Mr. Landry led the way to the kitchen, briefly passing through the living room where Seren was sitting next to Mrs. Landry at a piano bench. Seren was busy playing but looked up long enough to catch Paige looking at her. She smiled and Paige had to fight the impulse to stay in the living room. She knew she couldn't focus on Seren, but it was hard thinking of anything else.

It didn't take long to trim Bella's nails, and Paige decided the dog was in fact the sweetest dachshund alive when she licked her hands after. As soon as she set her back on the ground, Bella excitedly circled her feet with only a hint of lingering pain.

"Well, you fixed her!" Mr. Landry beamed.

"Maybe. If she comes up lame again, bring her to my clinic and I'll give her a better once-over. And maybe you could bring her once a month for a free nail trim?"

"If you're offering, I'm buying." Mr. Landry clapped Paige's shoulder. "I like your prices, but you'll go out of business that way."

"I stay plenty busy with paying customers. I can throw in a free nail trim for a sweet dog."

After a yip in agreement, Bella raced back to the living room. Paige wanted to do the same, but Mr. Landry announced he'd be happy to show her the rest of the house.

Fortunately, the bedrooms weren't quite as dark as the entryway or the living room where Seren was still playing. Paige had to remind herself that it wasn't a recording but Seren herself playing. No wonder she'd been recruited. Paige also had to remind herself that she wasn't there to think about Seren.

After Mr. Landry's tour, Leslie walked Paige back to the kitchen with the excuse of wanting to check measurements on something. She glanced around at the dark brown cabinets and darker brown linoleum—even the refrigerator was brown—folded her arms, and leveled her gaze on Paige. "What are you thinking?"

Seren's playing reverberated in her mind. She loved hearing piano music, especially jazz piano, and Seren sounded like a professional. "Well…" She eyed the brown stove top and the brown microwave hanging above it. Both had to be from the eighties. She tried to imagine the kitchen as her own but couldn't quite picture it. Laughter echoed down the hallway and her thoughts got distracted again by how much she wanted to be in the same room as Seren.

"It'd be a lot of work to update."

"Yeah, it would." The place did have character. Just not character that fit her.

"Maybe you could start remodeling one room and leave the others closed off? I don't know why anyone ever liked shag carpet. And the colors in those bedrooms…" Leslie shook her head. She eyed the wide split in the linoleum below Paige's feet. "Are you handy with tools?"

"If you mean a pair of forceps and a scalpel? Yes."

"How about a screwdriver and a crowbar?"

"Much less so." Paige lifted a shoulder. "But five acres, all fenced, with a four-stall barn?"

"You're ready to write up an offer."

Paige smiled. "Yep."

# CHAPTER EIGHTEEN

Taking on a thirty-one-year-old gray mare with special dietary needs and two flighty barn cats with fleas sounded daunting. Add to that five acres of land that needed care and a three-bedroom ranch house in sore need of updating? Seren couldn't imagine wanting that big of a project. Except she was imagining it.

In fact, she'd spent most of the evening imagining it. The mare's name was Nellie and Mr. Landry promised she was as sweet as their dog, Bella. Bella could come to the new retirement community; the horse and the cats couldn't. Already Seren was ready to give the mare a good brushing and get flea meds on the cats. But she knew next to nothing about horses save what she'd gathered as an eleven-year-old who'd gone to a summer horse camp. Plus, the barn cats had never been named. So of course she'd pitched names to Paige.

Paige was nearly bouncing in her seat as they'd left the ranch and Seren couldn't remember the last time she'd felt so happy for someone else. As Paige described all the animals she wanted to get and her plans for the barn, Seren was swept up in her enthusiasm. Still, she managed to tease Paige about it, which only earned her a wide smile and: "But have you seen a newborn calf? And baby chicks? Oh, and lambs?"

Paige didn't seem at all perturbed by the amount of updating the house would need. Which maybe was the reason Seren was picturing how it might look with the carpet stripped out, a few walls knocked out, the kitchen gutted, and the walls painted. Adding up all the possible expenses in her head was impossible not to do as well.

After Leslie had dropped Paige at her clinic, she took Seren home. Leslie suggested drinks and dinner, but Seren begged out. It'd been a long day. And yet for the hour she'd been home, she hadn't exactly relaxed. She'd made a salad, gone through the pile of bills waiting to be paid, and then fallen down a rabbit hole with an Internet search for ways to update old ranch houses.

The Landry property felt like a part of her childhood. Sitting next to Mrs. Landry on the piano bench had brought back a rush of memories. The conversation about playing keyboard and drums with the G Street Girls also had her thinking. All through junior high and high school, she'd been attached to an instrument. She was on the piano while her mom made dinner, on the drums when she ought to be working on homework, and playing on the keyboard with headphones when she was supposed to be asleep.

Even in college her instruments got more action than any girlfriend or boyfriend could have—she hadn't even dated until her senior year. Late bloomer was what her mom called her. She remembered being embarrassed and mad about the title but there was no escaping it. Well, music had been her escape. After college, though, she'd slowly stopped playing. Not all at once, but inch by inch other things took up her time.

She sat down at the piano bench now and eyed the picture of her mom. "Is this old thing in tune?"

She played a scale and then shifted back on the bench. "Huh. Not half bad." She glanced at her mom's picture again. "What do you want to hear, Mom?"

As much as she'd hated her mom's teasing about her being a late bloomer, she wouldn't mind hearing it now. Even better, she'd love to hear her mom sing again. So many times she'd played on stage with her mom watching in the audience, but she'd loved the nights when her mom had sung along as she'd played in the living room.

Memories flooded her mind and tears burned her eyes, but she made two fists and then stretched her fingers. One of Mozart's concertos, a piece her mom loved but could never remember the number of, came to mind and the old piano rumbled to life. Strange that she'd gone so many years without playing hardly a note yet her mind remembered it all. After Mozart, another song spilled out. Her fingers flew over the keys just as they'd done earlier that evening, songs coming one after the other, as if she were staring right at the sheet music. She had to take breaks to rub her fingers, but she couldn't rest long before another tune nudged her on. Her old endurance was gone but the music wasn't. Along with the songs, all her old hopes and dreams came back too.

One of those hopes, or maybe dreams, was finding someone like Paige. Someone who looked at her in a way that seemed to say, "I pick you." Someone who smiled in a way that said, "You make me happy just the way you are."

Paige had watched her playing piano with Mrs. Landry, and the look in her eyes made Seren feel like a spotlight was shining right on her. Which was both amazing and frightening. In that moment, Seren had wanted to earn that spotlight more than ever. She wanted to give Paige every reason to pick her.

But what about the pros and cons list that ruled out dating? And what about the perfect future where she focused on her baby?

She glanced at the rise of her belly and rubbed the spot above her navel. Some women could feel the baby kick by now. She'd read about it. A kick would be nice. Something beyond big boobs and a tummy that looked like she had gas would make the pregnancy more real. Maybe then she'd stop second-guessing her decision about dating Paige.

Her cell phone rang, and she headed to the couch where she'd left it, half planning on teasing Leslie for checking up on her only an hour after she'd dropped her off. Instead of Leslie, it was Paige calling.

"Hello?"

"Is this a bad time?"

"No, it's a good time."

"You sounded surprised."

"Um…" Well, she was surprised. But in a good way. Before she could say as much, a ruckus of barking interrupted her. Seren smiled as she heard Paige say, "Inside voices, please." More barking followed.

Paige sighed. "Maybe I should have waited to call you until I got home."

"Where are you?"

"At work. I didn't know if it would be too late to call by the time I got home." Paige paused. "We didn't really get to chat much earlier. I thought about texting, but honestly my hands are tired of typing. I'm almost through the stack of records from today, but then I've got emails to answer."

Seren settled in on the sofa, a smile straining her cheeks. It was silly to be happy simply because Paige wanted to talk to her. But it was nice hearing Paige's voice. "Do you sing?"

"Only when I'm alone. Why?"

"You've got a nice voice." Seren felt herself edging toward flirting. She didn't want to fight it and didn't want to think about what it meant.

"I can't really hold a tune, but thank you."

A loud crash sounded on Paige's end followed by a round of excited barking. "Shit, I'm sorry. Carl just knocked something over." A sound of more crashing followed. Then a howl. "Peabody, get back here!"

"Are you okay? Who's Carl? And Peabody?"

"Can you hold on a minute?"

Seren didn't have time to answer before the line was filled with more barking. Then a distinct howl and more of Paige's "inside voices, please" along with promises for treats if everyone behaved.

"Okay, I'm back now. Sorry about that. Carl—our hospital cat—knocked my water glass over. Peabody was lying on my feet and got wet. Peabody's one of our boarders. He's a grumpy basset hound with an amazing howl."

"I heard." Seren wouldn't have described the howl as amazing, though it was impressively loud.

"Carl's being a punk because I have another one of our other boarders—Malti, this cute little Yorkie—on my lap instead of him. Carl doesn't really like dogs."

"But he's the hospital cat? I'm guessing he has to deal with a lot of dogs."

"Oh, he does. He usually keeps them in their place but it's hard to boss around a Yorkie."

Seren pictured the scene: Paige still in her scrubs in a vet office with cats and dogs crowded all around her. Like so much about Paige, it was pretty much perfect. "Are you often at work this late?"

"No. Well, sometimes. The spur-of-the-moment house-hunting kind of threw off my schedule."

"Oh, right. So, you really want to buy the place?"

"I do. Which is scary." Paige blew out a breath. "That's actually why I called you. I know Leslie said that the Landrys need to sell, but I don't want to push anyone out of their house. Since they're your old family friends, I thought you'd tell it to me straight. Do you think they need more time?"

"I don't. I think they're past ready, actually. Before you and Leslie came in, I was talking to Mr. Landry about it. He can't keep up with taking care of his wife, and he's got health issues himself. He's ninety-four, she's ninety-three. His kids are pressuring him to sell, and he wants a break from all the work. Honestly, I don't think he ever expected a veterinarian would want to buy the property. That part alone has him ready to move. He was worried leaving the animals to anyone who wouldn't take care of them. I think you won him over with Bella."

"He seems like a cool old dude."

"He is. Once upon a time he was kind of a surrogate grandpa for me."

"So, you wouldn't feel weird if I bought their place?"

"Not weird at all." Especially now that she'd seen the Landrys and realized how much they needed to get into a place where they could both have more help. Besides, she knew Paige would love the ranch as much as they had.

"Then I guess I'm ready to plunge myself into more debt." Paige chuckled. "What are you doing tonight?"

"Nothing exciting." Seren smiled at the casualness of the question and how she didn't mind telling the truth. Something about Paige was just easy. And dating was never easy for her. Then again, they had seen each other almost daily for the past week and weren't technically dating. "I made myself dinner, paid some bills... then I decided to see if my mom's piano was out of tune."

"Is it?"

"No. It sounds perfect. She must have had someone tune it before I moved back." Tears came again at that realization. She hadn't played for her mom at all those last six weeks.

"I loved listening to you play tonight. You're really good."

Seren swiped tears away before they fell. "Thank you. I've been kicking myself for being out of practice."

"You used to be even better, huh?"

"Yes." She felt like a pendulum, one minute about to cry over another memory of her mom and the next high as a kite flirting with Paige. It felt dangerously good to flirt. She pulled a throw blanket out from where it was folded on the shelf of the end table and cuddled up.

"I wish I could have seen you playing the drums with the G Street Girls."

"There's a clip online somewhere."

"Really?"

The excitement in Paige's voice made her smile. "If you want it bad enough, I bet you could find it."

"Nothing I could say or do to get you to send it to me, is there?"

"Nope." She settled back on the sofa as Paige laughed. A warmth filled her. She wasn't sure if it was because of talking to Paige or the image of the leaping cow printed on the throw blanket or how they seemed to go together. "This is probably weird to say, but I'm cuddling with one of my mom's old cow blankets and I think you'd like it."

"The blanket? Because I like cows?" Paige laughed again. "Honestly, I probably would. But I'm a sucker for anything with kitties or puppies on it too."

"My mom was obsessed with cows. All of our dish towels growing up had cows embroidered on them. And the teapot in the kitchen is a cow. When the water boils, the cowbell rings."

"I love that."

"Yeah, it's cute and also really obnoxious." Seren glanced around the room at all the cow knickknacks she'd yet to box up. "It used to annoy me that our house was filled with cow stuff. Now it only makes me see my mom everywhere." She didn't want to cry, but the urge caught her again. She was a mess tonight. After a few breaths, she got hold of the emotion and continued, "My mom's friends and all of our relatives knew they could give my mom anything with a cow on it. You would not believe all the cow trinkets they sell. I've cleared out a bunch, but there's only so many cow things Goodwill wants."

"Don't give away the cow blanket."

Seren's first response was to ask if Paige wanted it, but mostly she was surprised by the intensity of Paige's words. "Okay. I won't."

"I mean, you can do whatever you want but…one day you're gonna want a mom hug and the cow blanket will be there waiting for you."

Seren pulled the blanket tighter around her and let the tears finally course down her cheeks.

Paige continued, "My dad died a few years ago. I helped my mom go through his stuff—a lot of it went straight to Goodwill—but I kept one of his old jackets and his harmonica. The jacket smells a little bit like smelt. Okay, a lot."

"Smelt? Like the fish?"

"Yeah. It stinks."

Seren found herself laughing despite the tears.

"But I don't care. Sometimes I put on the jacket and play a note or two on his harmonica. It's like he's sitting right next to me and we're back at Lake Berryessa waiting for some trout to bite the line."

Seren clenched her jaw, trying to stop the tears, but more pushed at her eyes. She knew Paige was waiting for her to say something, but she couldn't.

After a long moment, Paige said, "I think I made you cry. I'm sorry."

Seren took a shaky breath and then forced herself to talk. "Don't be. I just don't really want to break down on you."

"Do you want company?" A second later Paige added, "I'm only saying that as a friend. I'm not trying to cross any lines."

Yes, she wanted Paige to come over. She also wanted to cross all the lines. But mostly she wanted to wrap her arms around Paige. And to have Paige hold her close. She didn't want to be a tearful mess around her, though. She wanted to be someone Paige desired. Not someone she'd need to take care of.

"I'm gonna take that long pause as a no. And apologize for overstepping."

"You didn't overstep. But…it's late." Definitely a cop-out answer, even if it was after her bedtime.

Paige didn't say anything for a long moment, and Seren wondered if she'd messed up everything. Again. She squeezed the bridge of her nose. "I'm feeling conflicted."

"I'm not really sure what you mean by that."

That was fair. She didn't know either.

Paige continued, "It's okay to tell me that I need to give you some space. Maybe trying to be friends would be complicated."

"Actually, I was thinking the opposite." Fuck. Seren closed her eyes. She did know what she wanted, and it wasn't to push Paige to the curb before they'd even had a chance. "What are you doing tomorrow night?"

"Teaching water aerobics."

"Right. I knew that." She pressed her hand to her head. Could she really do this? Then again, how could she not? "What I meant was, what are you doing after?"

"I don't have any plans."

"Want to come over for dinner?" She quickly added, "I owe you a meal. Not only did you pay for the BLTs, you had to deal with me talking about vomiting."

"You don't owe me anything. If you're asking me over because you want to make me dinner, and hang out, that's a different thing."

"I want to hang out."

"As friends?"

"No." There. She'd said it. She took a deep breath and plunged on. "I'm asking you over because I think it's a mistake not giving us a chance. I need to be honest with you, though. I'm pretty sure you met me at the worst possible time."

"But you want to date anyway?"

"I want to try."

She heard Paige's muffled cheer—*"Yes"*—and Seren's smile widened so much her cheeks hurt. How was it that in the same phone call she'd gone from crying one minute to stupid happy the next?

"It might not go well. And I might need to take things slow."

"I got that part," Paige said. "We'll keep it casual. If things don't work out, then we stop."

Was it really that easy? Seren hoped so.

# CHAPTER NINETEEN

Sparkling apple cider didn't seem like enough to bring, but flowers would be trying too hard. Unless flowers were the appropriate choice? Paige stood in front of a display of bouquets weighing the decision. She had class to teach in a half hour. No time for waffling. The sunflower and purple daisy arrangement looked happy. Then again, the one with roses and lilies was nice too. Roses did seem more date-like. Paige reached for the roses and then stopped. What if Seren had a cat? Not knowing, lilies were risky. Maybe bringing any flowers would be coming on too strong?

"This is ridiculous." Paige checked the time again. She was down to twenty-eight minutes before the hour. "Sunflowers it is."

She'd hoped for a chance to chat with Seren before class but hit two stoplights wrong and watched as the minutes ticked away. By the time she got to the pool, Seren was already in the water—as were nearly twenty others. It was the biggest turnout she'd had so far, and she kicked herself for not looking over her lesson plan ahead of time.

She also had no idea what to expect with the music. Her mom had insisted on sending her with a cassette tape that ominously only said "Spicy Thursdays" on the label. As soon as she popped it into the player, Justin Timberlake's "SexyBack" drew cheers from the crowd.

Paige turned to face the class, taking a deep breath. Seren met her gaze and smiled. She returned the smile and then called out, "Who's ready to bring sexy back?"

A chorus of hoots and whistles came from the spicy seniors, and she started in on her failsafe marching steps, swinging her arms in time.

"You're supposed to slap your tush every time that fellow says sexy," a woman in the front said. "That's what Bea always does."

Paige looked over at her and shook her head. "Yeah, not happening."

"If you've got it, flaunt it," someone else said. That got plenty of laughs.

"Fine. How's this?" Paige did a one-eighty hop and jiggled her butt. Someone whooped and more laughter followed. When she turned around again, she saw only the backs of most of the students and realized they'd followed her move. Everyone except Seren. No way was she impressing anyone with water aerobics moves. But she wasn't embarrassed either. And Seren's smile only bolstered her confidence more.

"All right, everyone turn back to the front."

"We're bringing sexy back," Rita crooned.

The others laughed and Paige couldn't help but sing the next two lines. For the rest of the hour, Rita kept the class laughing with comments about the relative sexiness of water aerobics. Paige didn't mind that the students were only half paying attention to her directions. In fact, she was the most distracted of all. She caught herself staring right at Seren more than once, her gaze tracing the line of Seren's swimsuit to the dip between her breasts.

When the last song on the tape ended, Seren was one of the first out of the pool. She brushed by Paige, promising to hurry before disappearing into the locker room. Paige cleaned up her things, surprised that for once no one hung around after class to chat or ask questions about their pets. Thanking the universe, she headed to the lobby to meet Seren.

"I hear someone's having dinner with a certain busty blonde tonight."

Paige froze, caught in Rita's piercing gaze.

Rita clicked her tongue. "I'm going out on a limb and wagering this isn't a friendly thank-you dinner like Seren insisted."

Paige pursed her lips. What would Seren want her to say?

"I hear you found her wallet and phone?"

"Yeah, she forgot her swim bag here after class on Tuesday."

"I see. And you gallantly delivered those items right to her doorstep?"

"I did but—"

"And this dinner is payback?"

"Um…" She'd done nothing wrong, but Rita's questioning had her palms sweating. Before she thought of an answer, Rita stepped forward and patted her cheek.

"To think your poor mother believes you have no idea how to get yourself a woman. Enjoy your evening."

Seren stepped into the lobby and Rita glanced between them knowingly. Without a word, Rita waved and was out the door. Paige blew out a breath.

"Everything okay?"

"Yeah. Rita was…" Should she say that Rita had seen right through the "thank-you dinner" line and knew tonight was a date?

"Did you know she's a retired detective? Professional interrogator."

Paige chuckled. "Didn't know that, but I'm not surprised at all."

"I wasn't either. She's got a sixth sense when it comes to anyone trying to hide anything. I wasn't trying to keep our date a secret, but I didn't plan on telling the entire locker room either."

Paige grinned. "It's fine by me."

"Good thing, because the spicy ladies are gonna spread this story fast." Fortunately, Seren didn't seem to mind. She hefted her swim bag. "I made sure I had everything. Want to follow me? Probably easier than leaving one of our cars here."

Although Paige had briefly seen the inside of Seren's house on Tuesday, she hadn't noticed all of the cows. In addition to a front doormat with a cow, the door knocker was also a cow. But that wasn't where the cow decor stopped. Throw pillows, wall hangings, and even picture frames were all adorned with cows. "Your mom was really into cows."

Seren looked from the entryway where they stood to the living room adjoining it. "You don't want to know how many cow knickknacks I cleared out trying to clean up for tonight."

"You didn't have to clean up on my account."

Seren narrowed her eyes. "Would you not have cleaned up your place for me?"

"Well…"

"Exactly." Seren set down her swim bag. "Thank you for bringing Martinelli's. Don't tell anyone, but I've always liked it better than champagne."

Paige glanced down at the bottle. "Me too. Bubbles without the headache."

"But, sadly, no happy buzz." Seren tapped her belly. "This little one is changing lots of things in my world already." In a loose blouse, the baby bump so obvious in a bathing suit was entirely concealed.

"Getting buzzed is overrated."

"You sure you don't mind? I might have some white wine I could chill. I finished the last of the red the night before I went in for the IUI." She bit the edge of her lip. "That was probably too much information."

"I promise I'm fine with Martinelli's. That's why I brought it."

"Right. Okay." Seren nodded, as if convincing herself.

Something was off. Did Rita and the other spicy ladies knowing about their date bother Seren more than she'd let on? She glanced down at the bouquet. "Should I not have brought flowers?"

"No. I mean, yes." Seren shook her head. "I'm being weird. Ignore me. I like flowers."

Paige smiled. "Okay. Do you have a vase?"

"Yes." Seren returned the smile, but it seemed a little strained. "Come in." She motioned Paige into the living room area.

The house didn't exactly fit what Paige knew of Seren, but it wasn't entirely wrong either. It felt homey, the sofa and recliner more comfortable than stylish and the walls cluttered with everything from pictures to cow ornaments to quilts. Everything was clean and tidy, but Paige wondered how Seren would decorate it on her own.

Seren led the way to the kitchen. She opened the door to a cupboard and then paused. "I should have asked—do you have any allergies?"

"None that I've found so far."

"Good. We're having my mother's old recipe of minestrone and salad." She glanced at the bouquet Paige was holding and then reached for a vase. "You're sweet to bring flowers. Do you mind putting them in water while I heat up the soup?"

The kitchen continued the cow theme both subtly and overtly. The floor was black-and-white tile. The dishrags were embroidered with cows. Even the vase had a cow silhouette etched into the glass.

While Seren set a pot on the stove and fussed with something in the fridge, Paige arranged the flowers. She wasn't a pro, but the daisies and the sunflowers were forgiving. "I almost went for the bouquet with lilies, but I didn't know if you have a cat or not."

"I do. But he's rarely around when I have anyone over. He's black and good at shadow hiding."

"I love black cats. I've got three." Paige glanced around, hoping she'd spot Seren's. Instead, she only saw more cow decorations. It was like they popped out of the woodwork the longer she was in the room. "I'm thinking your mom was more of a cow person than a cat person."

"That'd be a yes." She laughed softly. "She loved baby cows most of all. A few years ago, we took a drive out to the coast and stopped along the way at this field with all these Jersey cows. The babies were out so we decided to have a picnic right on the side of the highway. It was amazing watching them. My mom talked about it for months after." She handed Paige a plate of sliced cheese and a breadboard with a baguette. "Mind setting these on the table?"

Paige set down the bread and cheese, and Seren brought over two steaming bowls of minestrone. "That smells good."

"It's my favorite of my mom's recipes." Seren smiled. "I'm hoping I pulled it off. Bon appétit."

Paige had a sense that Seren's need to eat was more urgent than her wanting to talk, so she focused on the soup. In no time, the soup as well as the bread and the cheese disappeared between them.

"That was delicious."

"My mom's version was better. I shouldn't have left out the sausage…" Seren looked between their empty bowls. "But it wasn't bad. Would you like more?"

"I'm good. Thank you. And thank you for having me." Paige lifted her glass and held it up to clink against Seren's.

Seren started to raise her glass but set it down a moment later. "I forgot the salad." She moved to get up, but Paige touched her hand.

"This was plenty of food. You can get it if you want, but I don't need it."

Seren started to nod and then stood anyway. "I can set it out if we want to have it later."

"You really don't have to."

Seren sucked in a breath as if about to say something, then gave a slight headshake and headed to the fridge. Focusing on the food earlier had seemed to make sense—especially given their last dinner conversation about her getting sick if she didn't eat when she was hungry—but there was clearly something else bothering her.

"It's hardly a meal with only soup and bread." Seren set the salad bowl on the table and then looked over at Paige. "You don't have to eat salad if you don't want to."

Paige lifted a shoulder. "We should all probably eat more greens, right?"

"That's what my grandma used to say when she served green jelly." Seren shook her head. "I'm feeling a little ridiculous right now."

"What's wrong?"

Seren sank down in her chair. "Other than me?"

"There's nothing wrong with you." She was ready to give Seren a list of all the right things, in fact.

Seren took a deep breath and looked around the kitchen for a moment. "I've haven't had anyone over here. Other than Leslie, I mean. This house doesn't feel like my space. It's my mom's still. And those flowers are beautiful. But I haven't had any around since my mom's funeral."

"Oh. Shit. I didn't think about that."

"Don't feel bad. I like them. Really."

Despite what Seren said, she wished she'd skipped the flowers. Now Seren being uncomfortable earlier made sense. "I'm sorry."

Seren shook her head. "Please don't be. The flowers just made me think…I've spent so much time in this house missing her. But now it feels like I'm moving on. And I feel bad because I want to." She clenched her jaw. When she continued, her voice was lighter.

"This is also the first time I've used the new bowls. I got tired of seeing a smiling cow every time I finished eating my food."

"I wouldn't mind a smiling cow bowl."

"Why am I not surprised?"

Seren made a little crooked smile that seemed to show how much she was trying to keep the conversation going while fighting back her emotions. Paige wanted to say it was okay not to hold back, but she knew, too, the expense of giving in to those unexpected moments of grief. She was the first to admit that sometimes it was better to hold the flood at bay for a while.

After a moment, she met Paige's gaze. "Years of the same cow face staring up at you from an empty cereal bowl and you might want something new."

"I doubt it."

Seren ran her finger along the brim of her empty soup bowl. "The other thing is I was feeling a little nervous about this dinner in particular."

Paige waited for her to go on, but instead of explaining more Seren simply left it at that. "Let me guess, you were worried I'd start talking about cows' digestive systems again?"

Seren pushed Paige's shoulder, a playful smirk transforming her face.

Humor had definitely been the right call. But now she wished Seren would touch her again. They'd only been joking around, and yet the contact had felt entirely too good. "Can I ask you something that's been on my mind since yesterday?"

Seren nodded.

"Do you still have a drum set?"

"No."

"Damn."

"Were you hoping for a performance?"

"Maybe," Paige admitted. "Drummers are so sexy. And you playing the drums is pretty much the hottest thing I can think of."

"I have a feeling you've got me confused with Mary Stuart Masterson from *Some Kind of Wonderful*." She lifted an eyebrow. "Harboring an old crush?"

"No. But blondes are my type."

Seren laughed. "Okay. You earned one point for that comment. Sorry I can't play for you."

"Would you if you had a drum set here?"

Seren considered it. "If you asked nicely. But I haven't played for years. I'm sure I'd be terrible. My mom gave my drums away to one of the neighbor kids a few years ago…" Her voice trailed. "I found a picture and a news clipping my mom had saved from when I was playing with the G Street Girls. I swear it feels like that was a different lifetime."

"Do you still have that picture?"

Seren opened her mouth, and Paige knew the answer was yes.

"Can I see it?"

Seren hesitated again. "Only to prove not all drummers are sexy."

"I'm gonna be the one who's right." Paige laughed when Seren rolled her eyes. "Do you think you'd ever get back into it?"

"Drumming? Maybe. I miss it sometimes. It's an incredibly good way to zone out and de-stress."

"Plus, drummers are cool. And sexy."

Seren shook her head. "I've had my cool moments. Now I'm a massage therapist whose main excitement for the day comes when I take my first sip of morning coffee—which is now decaf."

Paige grinned at Seren's grumpy tone. "Are you saying life in Davis isn't exciting?"

"That's an understatement." Seren brushed off Paige's mock surprise. "Although I did have to go to the police department last month and that was pretty thrilling."

"Decided on a life of crime to spice things up?"

Seren's "as-if" response was full of lighthearted snark. "Someone stole my bike."

"Oh, that sucks."

"Right? I never thought anyone would want my bike. It was a piece of crap, but I loved that cushy cruiser seat." She sighed. "Anyway, in case you were wondering, there's been a rash of bike thefts this past month."

"That's how you know you live in an exciting town."

Seren shook her head, and Paige wondered how long she'd stay in Davis. There was no comparing the thrill of a big city, but there was a lot to love about Davis. She stopped herself from saying as much. Barely. She'd agreed to keep things casual. That meant there was no reason to plan for a future with them living in the same town. Unless Seren changed her mind about the casual part.

# CHAPTER TWENTY

After the dishes were cleared, they headed to the cow-bedecked living room. Seren pulled out a photo album and pointed Paige to the sofa. "I'm not going to let you look at all of these pictures because I was an awkward teenager and I'm embarrassed, but I did promise you this."

She sat down a foot away from Paige, thumbed through the pages, and then paused. "Oh, god. Why'd I tell you I had a picture?"

"Let me see." Paige leaned close. Before she'd focused on the picture, she caught a whiff of Seren's perfume. Something sweet like vanilla or coconut and vaguely flowery. She had to fight the impulse to shift closer.

"That's Margo at the mic and that's Ronni playing the guitar. The G Street Girls."

"And that's you?" Paige touched the cellophane over the image of a teenage Seren behind a drum set. "You're adorable."

"I didn't think so back then. I had acne and I was awkward." She shook her head. "I tried to joke a lot, but I never knew if people were laughing at me or with me. I do miss that drum set."

Paige tried to block out the building warmth in her body. She longed to close the distance between them but knew she couldn't rush things.

"Anyway. That was pretty much the end of my performing days." Seren started to close the album but when Paige reached for it, she let her take it. "Don't look at the other pictures, okay?"

"Okay." Paige studied the teen behind the drums again. Seren's hair was shorter in the shot—not quite as short as Mary Stuart Masterson's in *Some Kind of Wonderful*—but a shaggy wild cut. Dark eyeliner and goth style makeup completed the image. She didn't look tough, though she seemed to be trying for that. The sweetness in her features was impossible to cover up.

"Your haircut's cute here but I like how you wear it now a little longer." That wasn't all Paige liked better about the Seren sitting next to her. She'd filled out in the best ways, and while teenage Seren had a lost sort of expression as if she were waiting for direction or something to happen, thirty-something Seren wasn't waiting anymore. Paige set the album on the coffee table. "Do you miss performing?"

"Sometimes. I used to go watch other bands perform and I'd imagine myself up on stage. I rarely even go out anymore."

"What bands have you seen?"

"You sure you want to ask me that? I might keep you here for the rest of the night talking music."

"Wouldn't be the worst thing."

The look Seren gave in response made Paige long to do more than talk. But a moment later Seren cleared her throat. "Maybe we should start with our favorite musicians."

"Okay."

Seren seemed to know Paige needed help focusing. She started listing bands she'd seen and then quizzed Paige on her music tastes. Soon Seren went to get her phone, saying she had a moral responsibility to introduce Paige to a musician she'd never heard of. When Seren returned to the sofa, she settled in closer and they took turns picking out favorite songs and watching the respective music videos on the phone. Seren apologized once for the sound quality, but Paige insisted it was perfect. The little screen also made sitting close a necessity.

At first it was distracting being close enough to enjoy Seren's scent. Definitely coconut and vanilla. And it was impossible not to notice when Seren laughed at one of the lead singer's open-mouthed expressions and her knee bumped Paige's. Even more impossible ignoring when Seren shifted closer to show Enya's full name spelled out on the screen. But song after song followed, and Paige felt herself relax even with Seren's leg pressed against hers. It was a distracted sort of relaxed, to be sure. A warm, comfortable-yet-wanting-more, happy feeling.

If Seren hadn't been holding the phone between them, Paige would have reached for her hand. That desire, and the longing to feel more of Seren without clothes between them, lit up her body. Right when she wasn't certain she could hold out longer, she looked over and noticed Seren fighting back a yawn.

Paige shifted over an inch, separating the contact of her leg with Seren's. She glanced at her watch. "I should go. It's late."

Seren scrunched up her face. "Not for normal people."

"Are you saying I'm weird?" Paige teased.

"Not you. Me."

"You're not weird. At all." Paige stopped herself from saying more. She stood up and stretched, aware that her body might have reasons for wanting to stay up late but also was quite ready to find a bed. Unfortunately, it wouldn't be Seren's tonight.

Instead of stopping at the front door to say goodbye, Seren walked Paige all the way to her truck. She looked up at the night sky.

"Penny for your thoughts?" Paige asked.

"I was thinking about how I feel like I'm in the right place for once."

"For once?"

Seren nodded. "Tonight made me feel that way. I haven't felt it for a long while."

"I am getting better at the whole water aerobics thing."

"Don't get too cocky. You have room for more improvement." Seren winked. "And you know I wasn't talking about that part."

Paige eyed her truck and then glanced back at Seren. "You still feeling okay about us trying this dating thing?"

"I am. I've told myself to relax and not think too far in advance. I really like being around you."

"In that case, are you busy Saturday afternoon?"

Seren smiled. "Well, I take this awesome water aerobics class…"

"I meant after class. Would you be up for another date?"

"I would." Seren tilted her head. "Why do you have a look on your face like you're scheming something mysterious?"

Paige laughed. "Because I might be."

"Do I get a hint?"

Paige considered telling Seren her idea. She'd been thinking about it since she saw the picture of Seren with the band, but she wasn't sure she could swing all the details. "Not yet."

"Hmm. Mysterious. Now I'm extra curious. What if someone asks what I'm doing on Saturday night?"

"You can tell them you're doing something mysterious with your water aerobics instructor."

Seren laughed again. "I can't wait."

Electricity shot through Paige when Seren reached for her hand. She entwined their fingers and looked up to meet her gaze.

"We probably shouldn't go too fast, right?"

Paige didn't answer. It was Seren's decision to make and from the look in her eyes, she knew that.

"Right…" Seren's voice trailed. In a whisper she added, "I want to anyway."

Paige was still trying to figure out what to say in response when Seren stepped forward and brushed a soft kiss against her cheek. It only lasted a moment, but Seren's lips were smooth and perfect.

When Seren stepped back and let go of Paige's hand, she seemed as off-balance as Paige felt. Mostly it was the sensation of sharing the same space, the scent and sound of someone only inches away, and then the sudden absence. Paige ached to kiss her lips.

"Anyway," Seren murmured. "Now you know."

"It's going to be hard waiting until Saturday."

Seren's coy smile was everything Paige wanted. "You'll manage. I'm the one who doesn't even know what we're doing for our date. Night, Paige."

"Good night, Seren."

Seren turned and walked up the path to the house and Paige brushed her fingertip over the spot she'd kissed. The floaty feeling that had swept her up as soon as Seren had leaned closed filled her again. When Seren reached the front door, she looked over her shoulder and raised her hand. Paige waved back. A second later, Seren disappeared inside.

# CHAPTER TWENTY-ONE

"Sixteen weeks. How are you feeling now that the first trimester is officially over?" Dr. Bueller looked from her laptop screen to Seren. "Excited? Nervous? Still nauseous?"

"All the above." Seren exhaled. Since everything with her mom and a month spent in and out of the hospital every day, she was nervous around doctors now. Despite how nice Dr. Bueller seemed, she couldn't help wishing she wasn't alone at these visits. "Well, the nausea has gotten better, actually."

"Good. Then my job today is only to make sure you and your baby are staying healthy." Dr. Bueller smiled, helping to break the tension. "The last time we talked, you mentioned you'd had to stop going to the gym. Did you try the water aerobics class we talked about?"

Seren nodded.

"How's that going?"

"Great. I think I've been less stressed overall because of it." At the last appointment she'd gotten a lecture about her borderline-high blood pressure and then another about being at increased risk for gestational diabetes because of her age. Neither of which had helped her stress level.

"That's exactly what I was hoping for." Dr. Bueller clicked a few buttons on her computer, clearly distracted. "And, good news, normal blood pressure today." She stood up from her desk and went over to put on a pair of exam gloves. Seren instantly thought of Paige examining cows and nearly laughed. These gloves were much shorter, of course. Thank god nothing was going up her butt.

"Something funny?" Dr. Bueller asked, her lips upturning.

"Oh, no. I mean, not really." Paige was the one doctor she didn't feel nervous around. All things considered, that was a good thing. "I have a friend who's a cow vet and she mentioned how she determined a cow was pregnant."

Dr. Bueller smiled. "I've seen a lot of techniques. Lucky for you, I'm only going to feel your belly and then listen to your heart and the baby's heart." She directed Seren to lie back on the table and shifted the exam gown up on Seren's chest. After a little poking and prodding, mixed in with a few nods, she motioned for Seren to sit up. "Everything's perfect. Are you taking folate supplements or one of the prenatal vitamins?"

Seren nodded. She hadn't forgotten a single dose, though she'd vomited more than a handful of the horse pills back up again. At the thought of horse pills, her mind went right back to Paige. True, she hadn't had many free minutes since their date that didn't include thoughts of Paige. Wondering what she was doing. Wondering if she'd had as good a time as Seren had. Wondering about the plan for tomorrow. And then worrying how it was that they were dating despite her best attempts at not doing so.

Dr. Bueller had taken off her gloves and was tapping away on her laptop. "We did the genetic screening with the blood sample at your twelve-week visit and checked that nuchal translucency… which was all great." She squinted at the screen then tapped away again. "But I wanted Shonda to take a quick peek at a few other things today."

"Shonda?"

Dr. Bueller looked up from her laptop. "My ultrasound tech. I can't recall if you wanted to know the baby's gender."

"Um…" The argument about not being able to identify gender based on parts came to mind. Dr. Bueller probably didn't care but she wanted to mention it anyway. Unfortunately, she wasn't certain she could confidently spout off any queer theory at the moment. Did she want to know the baby's parts or not? She hadn't anticipated needing to answer the question yet.

"Not sure?" Before she could answer, Dr. Bueller said, "Don't worry. I'm only verifying your baby's size today because either you're having a very big baby, we have your delivery date wrong, or the measurement was off last time. I'm sure it was the latter."

Seren wanted to ask her to slow down, but there was no getting a word in edgewise. How big a baby?

Dr. Bueller continued, "We typically recommend the anatomy ultrasound to check important details like the baby's heart at twenty weeks, so you'll have time to decide on knowing the gender. At sixteen weeks, we can often see what's going on between the legs, though, and I don't want to ruin any surprise."

"Um, okay." Seren's mind was swimming. She'd thought the last time was stressful when Dr. Bueller had gone through all the possible genetic diseases in twenty seconds flat. But now she was stuck on the question of whether or not she was going to have a huge baby. She wished someone was with her. Someone calm who'd be able to translate everything. Someone like Paige.

"I'll mark down that you don't want to know gender for now, so Shonda doesn't reveal anything." Dr. Bueller stepped out into the hallway and called for one of her nurses. She popped her head back into Seren's room and continued, "I've got a delivery I need to get to, but Shonda will take care of you. And if there's any problems, we'll talk."

When a moment turned to five minutes, then ten, and then fifteen, Seren went from pacing to fidgeting. She fished her phone out of her purse wondering if Paige would think she was ridiculous if she called. She hoped to find a text from Paige about Saturday but there was only a note from one of the other massage therapists about taking a new client on Monday. She quickly tapped out a reply and then considered texting Paige. While she was debating what to say, her phone rang. Leslie.

"Hey lady. Are you busy?"

Seren glanced down at the hospital gown. "Not exactly. I'm waiting to see another blurry picture of my little alien. And trying not to freak out."

"I forgot that was today! Excited?"

"My baby might be huge. Or else there was a measurement error last time."

"Hmm. Did the doctor seem concerned?"

"No?"

"Then I wouldn't worry."

Too late. The anxiety had started as soon as she'd woken that morning and remembered her appointment. Now it'd only gotten worse.

"Big babies are cute. Big fat cheeks. I can't wait to squish your big baby. Can you hurry up and bake that thing?"

"I'm really hoping it won't be too big."

"You've always had great hips. You'll be fine. What's a little more stretch?"

She wasn't ready to think about the stretching part.

"Want me to meet you at the doctor's office? We can scream together if they tell you you're gonna have a twelve pounder."

"Leslie! Seriously?" She laughed despite herself. "You're the worst."

"I'll be an amazing babysitter and you know it."

"I do." And as much as she loved Leslie and valued their friendship, she hadn't asked her to come to the last appointment when they'd done the genetic screening because having her in the room if she got bad news would only add more stress. And although Leslie had already volunteered to be her partner-in-crime when it was time to deliver, she worried that Leslie would amp up her anxiety. At least she had five months before she had to decide on that. "I'm not sure how much longer before they come to get me for the ultrasound. Were you calling for a reason?"

"I'm meeting Paige later to sign our offer letter for the Landry property. I wanted to ask how your date last night went before I headed over to her clinic."

"Give me a second to regroup here. I'm half naked and thinking about giant babies." Seren pulled her gown closer around her.

"I'd like to point out that you didn't give me a hard time for calling it a date. So. How was it?"

Thinking about Paige was probably a good distraction. She closed her eyes, imagining the moment she decided to kiss her. She'd chickened out at the last second and pecked her cheek instead. "Honestly, it was nice. Paige is…chill."

"Chill?"

Seren had come up with several other adjectives, but the one she found the most appealing at the moment was that. "I know there's other things I could say. She's sweet and easy to talk to. I kind of wish she were the type to simply jump me, but I told her I might need to take things slow and I think she took that to heart."

"Tell her it's commitment you have an issue with—not sex. Or drop some hints that you're extra horny now that you're prego."

Seren covered her face with her free hand. "You know more about me than a best friend should. I did try telling her last night that I didn't want to take things *too* slow."

"Drop more hints. Or I can."

"Don't you dare."

Leslie laughed. "Fine, be that way. I'm betting you two are fire in bed when it finally happens. The way she looks at you—oh, lord. I wouldn't mind someone looking at me like they wanted me spread out on the kitchen table for dinner."

"Leslie, I'm still in the exam room." And despite no one being able to overhear the phone call, she knew she was blushing.

"You know it's true. That woman doesn't have a poker face. I'm sure she wouldn't mind taking your—"

"Okay, stop. I'm not gonna lie. I want the sex. The problem is all the reasons on my list for not dating are still true. And you know I don't often fall for people, but when I do…"

"You fall hard. I know. This time you have to try not doing that. Or maybe it'll magically work out."

Seren wondered what working out would mean in this case. She eyed the fetal size chart on the exam room wall opposite the table. At sixteen weeks, the fetus was supposed to be the size of an apple. How big was hers? Clearly it was already affecting her in little and big ways. Speaking of, was she supposed to pee before the ultrasound? Her bladder wished she'd thought to ask. But now that the nausea had seemed to improve, lately she'd go an hour or even two without thinking about the pregnancy. Maybe that was why dating seemed doable when it didn't last week?

"Do you think it's fair for me to date Paige and not tell her directly that I'm planning on breaking up before the baby comes?"

"I think she knows what she's getting into. She's smart. And if you don't break up, think of how many rescue cats you could have in that Landry barn."

"So many." Seren smiled. "We could be a home for all the black stray cats."

"Exactly. What I've been wondering is how you two haven't met until now. You're like two stars destined to collide."

"I think if stars collided they'd explode."

"Details. So, can I tell her how much my best friend wants to get laid when I see her this afternoon? I can write it on a little slip of notebook paper and pretend we're back in high school."

"Like you said—she's smart. I think she'll figure it out. Or maybe I'll tell her myself."

Leslie cheered.

The door opened and a black woman in pink scrubs smiled at Seren over her clipboard. "Serendipity? I'm Shonda. By the way, love your name. Ready to follow me across the hall and we'll take a peek at your baby?"

She nodded at Shonda and reminded herself to breathe. "Leslie, I gotta go. The nurse is here for the ultrasound."

"Bye, hon. And don't worry. Your baby's gonna be perfect."

# CHAPTER TWENTY-TWO

"I feel like I'm signing my life away." Paige flipped to the next sheet of the contract.

"It's always nerve-racking the first time." Leslie pointed to the next spot for Paige to initial. "But if all goes well, you'll have your very own little farm."

Between worrying about the bank financing and all the fine print she was skipping over, she wasn't ready to think about actually owning the place yet. And after a long day of work, it was hard to do anything more than nod at everything Leslie said about the offer terms.

"Ordinarily I do this all electronically, but the Landrys don't want to use a computer so we're going old school." Leslie pointed to the next line for Paige to initial. "Now usually I recommend a thirty-day close, but I don't want to make the Landrys nervous."

"Me neither. And I'm not in a rush."

"Good. I've written up the offer with a forty-five-day close. I'll let them know you're flexible on that. You said you had a few more documents to get to the loan officer?"

"I've got to close an account with money my dad left me. That's most of my down payment."

Leslie nodded. "Sorry about your father."

"Thank you." Paige swallowed, trying to focus on the last line Leslie pointed out for her to sign. It'd been three years since her dad had passed, long enough that she wasn't caught off guard by emotion. Still, tears stung her eyes. He'd love the ranch—especially the old mare, Nellie, and the barn cats. He'd been as much of an animal lover as she was, though he'd never understood why she liked farm animals more than house pets. She thought of Mr. Landry then and hoped he was truly ready to leave. "I don't mind giving them longer than forty-five days. If they need more time—"

"Mr. Landry is ready to have more help with his wife. If you want this property, we need to move on it."

"I definitely want it." A week ago, she'd never have expected all the stars to align so perfectly that a place like the Landrys' ranch would even be available so close to town—let alone in her budget. Well, the budget part wasn't a done deal yet. Her fingers and toes were crossed the Landrys would take her offer.

Leslie sorted all the sheets into an ordered stack and Paige settled back in her seat. "So, what happens next?"

"I'm meeting with the Landrys at seven thirty." Leslie glanced at her watch. "That was when his eldest daughter could do a video conference and Mr. Landry wanted her input. I'll go through our offer and they'll have until Monday morning to respond."

"Monday?" Paige wasn't sure she could wait that long. As much as it was true that she didn't want to push the Landrys out, she hated having to wait all through the weekend to know what her future held.

"You said you didn't want to pressure them. I made the window a little wider than usual."

"I don't want to pressure them…" Paige picked up the pen and clicked it. "I'm just not very good at being patient. Once I figure out what I want, it's hard to slow down and wait for it."

"That's funny. I have another friend with that same problem." Leslie winked. "She mentioned you have plans tomorrow and also that she can't wait."

"Seren said that?"

Leslie reached across the table and set her hand on Paige's. "In case you're wondering, yes, she likes you."

"I mean I thought she liked me but…it's been a little up and down."

Leslie's sympathetic look only helped marginally. "I don't think she knows what to do with you. She really wasn't looking to date anyone."

Leslie seemed to be saying "Don't get your hopes up," but Paige worried it was too late for that. The problem was, she wanted to imagine that her future included someone else. Someone like Seren. Even if she knew better than to let her heart race ahead, she could easily picture Seren living with her on the ranch.

Leslie continued, "I think you're exactly what she needs. You've just got bad timing."

"I could wait for her. Maybe after the baby comes and her life is a little more settled?"

"Do you really think you can wait that long? Even if you could, do you want to?"

Paige left Leslie's office with the question of waiting still on her mind. She knew she could wait, but no, she didn't want to. She didn't even want to wait until their date tomorrow to talk to her. She brought Seren's number up on her phone even before she got to her truck.

Seren answered on the first ring. Did that mean she didn't want to wait either?

"Hey. How are you?"

"I'm good. Wasn't expecting you to call, but I will say that I was thinking about you. Guess what? I'm not going to have a ginormous baby."

"Um, okay. That's good news, right?"

"Right. I wasn't really worried but then I was…because who wants to birth a giant?"

Paige laughed.

"TMI?" Seren laughed too. "Anyway, the baby is perfectly average."

"Sometimes being average is the best thing."

"Exactly." Seren exhaled. "I'm sure you wanted to have this conversation, didn't you?"

"I'm here for any conversation you want to have." Could she admit that she didn't have a reason to call and only wanted to hear Seren's voice? "Did you get any pictures?"

"I did. Only one, but I've stared at it off and on for the past hour. I'm convinced that my baby may be average size but above average on the cuteness scale."

"Well, that's a given. Have you seen the mom?" Hopefully that wasn't too much. She quickly added, "Can you text me the picture? I'd love to see."

"Really?"

"Unless that's too personal?"

"No—but I don't want to impose my baby excitement."

"Impose away. I love baby animals. Even baby humans."

Seren laughed. "Okay. I'm sending it now. I don't want to know the baby's sex so if you can tell, don't say anything."

"I doubt I'll be able to tell." Paige's phone chimed when the picture was received. She lowered her phone and squinted at the ultrasound image. She couldn't help smiling. Babies got her every time, but knowing that this one was growing in Seren made it all the more exciting. She raised the phone back to her ear. "You're right. This baby's high on the cuteness scale. I love that little high five they're giving you. Those fingers are adorable."

"I know. I'm worried I'm already too attached."

"That's not a bad thing."

"Apparently they give you more pictures at the next visit. This was a quick thing to check the size and the placenta."

Seren had brushed over the subject of getting attached so Paige decided not to push it. "Usually calf ultrasounds are my favorite, but this human giving you a high five might win on best pictures."

"Calf ultrasounds? You do that? Oh, my mom would have loved that."

Considering how important Seren's mom was to her, Paige was sad not being able to have known her. She glanced at the ultrasound picture and felt a pang realizing Seren's baby would never know their grandma.

"What are you up to tonight?" Seren asked. "Working late again?"

"Not tonight. I left early to meet with Leslie to sign the offer on the Landry property."

"Oh, right. She told me she was going over the paperwork with you. Congrats."

"They might not accept, but I'm pretty excited." Now that she had Seren on the line, she realized she wanted to share the news with her more than anyone else.

"I'm excited for you. I've always loved that ranch. It's a perfect spot. But. I may be slightly more excited about our date tomorrow."

"Honestly, I am too." Hopefully Seren would enjoy what she had planned. "Speaking of, I should probably hang up. I've gotta run to the store or my plan won't work at all. See you tomorrow at three?"

"You can't drop a hint like that and then hang up. I've got questions."

"Sorry. Can't answer questions. I'm counting on the element of surprise." She also didn't want to disappoint if she couldn't pull it off. "Thanks again for that picture of your cute baby. Made my day." Actually, hearing Seren's voice had been all that it took.

# CHAPTER TWENTY-THREE

"What are you frowning about? Sea level rise? Those lines are gonna stick, you know."

"What lines?"

Bea jabbed her between the eyes.

"Ow. Why'd you poke me?"

"You're going to have the same wrinkles as your father."

Paige rubbed the spot. "Did you used to poke Dad too?"

"No. That's why he got so many wrinkles."

Bea handed her the day's mixtape—"Saturday Special." "This sounds ominous," she murmured, popping the tape in the stereo. She didn't need to read the smudged titles to know she was going to be embarrassed on her mom's first day back teaching. Bea had insisted she needed Paige to drive her to the pool and then insisted she needed backup teaching. She clearly had an ulterior motive. Bea wanted to meet Seren.

Paige wished there was some way she could avoid it, for her and Seren's sake, but that wasn't the only reason she was wearing her dad's worry lines. Even though Leslie had told her not to expect an answer on her offer until Monday, she'd hoped to hear something after Leslie's meeting with the Landrys. Was she within range? If not, could she take on a second job and offer more? She bounced between pondering those questions and wondering if the date she'd planned with Seren was a terrible idea. Before the date, though, she had to get through water aerobics.

"Is Ms. Tatas always late?"

"You know her name's Seren. Please don't say anything about her boobs in front of her." Paige glanced at the locker room door, willing it to open and reveal Seren and simultaneously hoping she'd skip today's class.

"Someone's touchy."

"I'm not touchy. Women don't need to be objectified by other women."

Bea rolled her eyes. The locker room door opened but it was Rita, not Seren, who came out. It was thanks to Rita that her mom knew about the planned date that afternoon.

"How much do you know about Ms. Tatas anyway?" Bea asked. "She's a pregnant masseuse—could be carrying anyone's baby."

Claia came out of the locker room next. Along with Helen. Paige lowered her voice and said, "She used an anonymous sperm donor." That part Leslie had told her. "And she conceived with IUI." That part Seren had mentioned herself. "Any other questions?" If she didn't put everything out there, her mom's supposing would get out of hand.

"IUI?"

"Intrauterine. Meaning she got pregnant in a doctor's office." Paige looked at the clock. "Are you starting class, or am I?"

Before Bea could answer, Rita waded up to the edge of the pool. "Where's Seren? You didn't break up with her already, did you?"

Claia and Helen exchanged a worried glance, and then a dozen pair of eyes all pivoted to Paige. "I don't know where she is, but we aren't even officially a couple. This is a casual thing."

"Casual thing? What's that?" Claia looked at Rita who shrugged.

"Something new-fangled," Helen said. "Like swingers, probably."

Claia's brow furrowed. "What's swingers?"

"No, no." Paige held up her hands. "Not like swingers. We're just not serious yet."

"Why not?"

Paige couldn't tell who'd asked the first "why not" nor who asked next, but she wanted to duck her head when the question bounced around the pool. "She's probably only running late."

The music started and Bea clapped her hands together. "Let's make enough noise that we get Ms. Tatas out here!"

It was some relief Seren wasn't there to hear what was said next. A lot of it was teasing Paige about how she thought Seren was sexy, but when the "spicy" ladies got talking, things got crass quick. Still, where was she?

It wasn't until class ended that Paige had time to check her phone. No message from Seren. She decided on a simple text: *Checking in. Everyone missed you in class.*

Seren's response was immediate: *Literally just woke up. Slept for thirteen hours. Right through my alarm. Was trying to decide how to apologize about missing class.*

*Do you feel okay?*

*Like a rock star.* Rock star face emoji. *But I'm sorry I missed water aerobics.*

*My mom was teaching. You missed an interrogation.* Paige wondered if that was admitting too much. Yes, she was thirty-seven years old, and, yes, her mom would still grill any potential girlfriend.

*Sorry anyway. Wanted to see you. Now I have to wait until this afternoon.*

*Still on for our date?*

*YES!!*

Paige knew she was grinning like an idiot as she read Seren's words over again. Fortunately, all the spicy seniors were in the locker room changing and her mom was chatting with them.

Her smile didn't leave her face for the next several hours. When she'd pulled up to the gray and white house with Seren's Subaru parked out front, however, she'd gone from stupid happy to cautiously optimistic to worrying the entire afternoon would be a big fail. Maybe Seren would prefer something fancy instead. Or something simple like dinner and a movie. She eyed her reflection in the rearview mirror, noticing the lines her mom had poked earlier.

"She either likes Davis nerds or she doesn't."

She got out of her truck, unstrapped the bikes, and then walked up to the front porch. The sight of the smiling cow restored some of her confidence. She raised the knocker and stepped back to wait.

"I'm back here." Seren's face peeked over the side fence. "I forgot to water the flowers. I'll be done in a minute if you want to join me."

Paige let herself in through the gate. She had to remind herself to breathe when she caught sight of Seren leaning over a planter full of petunias and marigolds. Her outfit probably would qualify as casual—a pair of blue capris and a white button-down blouse with a tank top underneath. But Paige's libido argued otherwise. All the buttons on the blouse were undone and the tank top gaped low enough to show off cleavage. The spicy seniors' comments came to mind, and she fought down a blush.

"I've been running through possible ideas for where you're taking me on this date. I have to admit not knowing your plan has made my day more exciting."

"You might think it's silly."

"Mini-golf?"

"No. Although that might have been a better idea."

"I'm sure your plan is better than mini-golf. I've got a terrible swing." Seren moved the hose over to a planter box with what appeared to be lettuce and tomato starts. The yard wasn't big, but it was tidy with a cute patio set—complete with cow-patterned cushions—and a grill that seemed to be in good condition. Perfect for summer evenings.

"Are you taking me to a restaurant where you pick your own food and then cook it?"

"Because it's only three in the afternoon?" Paige smiled. "No."

"The time is what's made it tricky to guess. What do people do in Davis at three in the afternoon?" Seren waited as if expecting Paige would volunteer the answer. After a moment, she shook her head. "You are a really good surprise-keeper. Okay. How about an early concert in the park?"

"I'm sure people in Davis do that."

"You're impossible. Will you at least tell me if I guess it right?"

"Maybe."

Seren narrowed her eyes. "I didn't peg you for a tease."

"I'm not a tease."

"Mm-hmm. But you like me not knowing what you have in store for me. I think that says something about you." Seren gave Paige a look that was more sexy than scolding. She wanted to be a tease if it earned her more of those looks. Seren turned off the water at the spigot and turned to face her. "Okay. I'm ready. For whatever."

"Riding a bike doesn't make you want to vomit, does it?"

Seren folded her arms. "No. Which is also why I was so mad when my bike got stolen. But I don't have a backup."

"I found you one."

"You found me a bike?"

Paige nodded.

"I could have borrowed one if—"

"This one needed a home. And we needed two bikes for our afternoon adventure. Just don't get your hopes up too high." She pushed open the gate and Seren followed her to the front yard. "Rita roped me into helping her clean out that storage shed at the pool last weekend." Paige stopped in front of the red cruiser leaning up against her old road bike. She had two other road bikes at home she'd considered giving to Seren, but when she'd spotted the cruiser she knew it'd be a better fit.

"This bike got dumped at the fitness center years ago. Rita called the police station to make sure it hadn't been reported missing, and, well, it's yours if you want it." Paige looked from Seren to the bike, realizing that if Seren hated the bike, she might not say so. "I replaced the seat with an extra cushy one and put new tubes in the tires. Thought I was going to have to replace the chain too, but a little oil goes a long way."

She couldn't read Seren's expression, but she didn't seem exactly excited. "I know it's old and probably not that great of a bike and I'll totally understand if you don't want it—"

Seren touched Paige's arm to stop her. "I want it. It's exactly like my old bike only red instead of green. And the seat looks even more cushy."

"Am I reading you wrong, then? Cause you look a little sad."

"I'm not sad." Seren shook her head and forced a smile. "I'm maybe a little overwhelmed that you found me a bike and fixed it all up for me. For a date. It's really sweet. No one's done something like that for me in a long time."

"Yeah, you still look a little sad."

Seren bumped her shoulder against Paige's. "Stop. I'm not. I'm…" She took a deep breath and met Paige's gaze. "I'm maybe a little uncomfortable. A bike is a lot. And I'm sure it was a lot of work, not to mention you spent money fixing it up."

"I'm a whiz fixing bikes. It's kind of my thing. And we're actually helping the gym by getting this thing out of their storage shed. I only had to pay for the seat and that was cheap." Paige hoped that'd be enough to convince Seren, but she still seemed on the fence. "Would it make any difference if I told you that I was actually doing this for me?"

Seren's brow furrowed. "How is getting me a bike helping you?"

"You can't really enjoy this town without a bike. And I don't expect you'll love Davis after today, but I'm hoping you'll at least agree there's a few cool things about the town."

"Still not following."

"Our date may involve a bike ride to the highlights of Davis."

Seren laughed. "The highlights of Davis? That's a thing?"

"It is today." Paige grinned. "I'm going to take you to all my favorite places to convince you that Davis is better than a tomato patch."

"Who'd call this town a tomato patch?" Seren winked. A moment later she added, "You think you can make me like Davis?"

"I'm gonna try. It is, after all, in my best interest if you decide to hang around for a while."

Seren shook her head.

"Do you blame me for trying?"

"I'm blaming you right now for making me feel all sorts of things."

"Good things?"

Seren didn't answer, stepping up to the bike instead and running her hand over the handlebars. "It's really pretty."

"Want to take her for a spin?"

Seren smiled over her shoulder at Paige. "I do. And I can't wait to see the highlights of Davis. I love that you want to convince me this town is cool."

Paige wanted to kiss Seren then. In the middle of the afternoon on the side of the street where anyone could see, she wanted to wrap her arms around her and pull her close. Her lips ached to press against Seren's, and she wondered what their first time would be like. A tentative getting-to-know-you sort of kiss? Or would Seren want her to go for more?

Seren got on the cruiser and shifted her position on the seat. "You got me a very cushy seat."

"Like it?"

"I love it."

Seren pedaled off the sidewalk and circled the empty street before coming back to where Paige was waiting. "Don't tell my old bike, but this one is way nicer. So, where are we going first?"

No kiss yet, but things were going in the right direction.

# CHAPTER TWENTY-FOUR

Spring in Davis didn't disappoint—seventy degrees and sunny. Riding alongside Paige was no disappointment either. Fortunately, she didn't have to pay attention to where they were going. With Paige leading, she let herself relax and enjoy things like the way Paige kept looking in her direction. Along with the sexy way Paige's forearm muscles tensed and shifted as she gripped the handlebars.

"First stop—the bookstore. Because any town with an independent bookstore is automatically cool." Paige parked her bike and pulled out a chain lock. "I didn't get you a bike lock. We'll have to chain ours together."

Seren sidled her cruiser up to Paige's, not at all upset to watch her new bike get chained to Paige's. Paige tugged off her helmet. "Ready?"

Browsing with Paige was nice. They chatted about books and Seren almost decided on picking up the newest N.K. Jemisin novel when Paige held up an "I Heart Davis" magnet. With a wink, she headed to the checkout counter. As soon as they stepped out of the store, she handed the bag with the magnet to Seren.

"What am I going to do with a Davis magnet?"

"By the end of today, you're gonna want to put that on your fridge where you can see it all the time." Paige grinned. "Next stop, the Co-op. It might not be exactly cool, but they make good sandwiches."

Seren rocked her head side to side. "I don't know. I think the Co-op is kind of cool—in an overpriced, patchouli-scented vegan hipster kind of way."

Coolness was hard to measure, Seren decided, as they walked down the aisles of the Co-op. Maybe Davis was cooler than she gave it credit for. When she'd moved away for college, her impressions of the town were all tied with being an unhappy teenager who hadn't really found her way in the world. Sure, she had her music, but aside from Leslie she didn't have friends. And unlike Leslie, who'd bopped from boyfriend to boyfriend throughout high school, she hadn't dated.

After college she'd spent so much energy bashing the town, and avoiding coming back, that she hadn't really considered the good parts. Then when she had finally come back, of course, everything had gotten worse in her life. Until, well, recently.

"You okay?"

Without realizing it, she'd stopped walking. Paige studied her from across a display of strawberries.

"I'm good." She held up the wrapped sandwiches they'd selected from the deli counter. "Fantasizing about eating these."

Paige squinted at her. "That was your happy fantasizing face?"

"Not exactly. Was I making a weird expression?"

Paige bit the edge of her lip. "A little, yeah. But I'm not going to push it if you don't want to say what you were thinking. Strawberries?"

Seren dropped her chin. "I don't want you to think I'm some big-city snob because I don't like Davis."

Paige didn't respond, clearly waiting for her to go on. She took a deep breath and let it out slow, glancing around at the produce. Her gaze settled on the avocados, all stacked up in a perfect green pyramid.

"When I was a teenager, I had this whole life plan. I was going to make it as a musician, and if that didn't work, I was going to travel the world and live in all the big cities. My life was going to be a big, exciting adventure. I just knew it. And no way would I end up living in my hometown. It'd be Paris or London or...New Orleans."

Paige nodded but again didn't say anything. Seren knew she had to go on. "I didn't want to come back because if I did, it'd mean that I never had that exciting life. Then, when I did move back to take care of my mom, the woman I'd been dating in New York decided she didn't want to do long distance."

She considered adding it was a new relationship and they hadn't even had sex yet, but she wondered if then she should admit that most of the time she waited a month or more before sleeping with someone.

"Anyway. I was so consumed with everything going on with my mom that I told myself I didn't care. But it made me hate this town even more—which I know doesn't make sense. Then my mom got so sick so fast and everything sucked and it was somehow worse because..." Her voice trailed. She swallowed and met Paige's gaze. "Because I was back in Davis. Maybe this town is cool. Maybe I'm the one who's not."

Paige reached out her hand and Seren clasped it. "Probably it doesn't change anything, but I'm just getting to know you and I already think you're the coolest person I've ever met."

"I think you might be biased." But it helped hearing Paige's vote all the same. She motioned to the strawberries. "By the way, I fucking love strawberries."

"Me too." Paige's closed-lip smile conveyed a lot. "Should we blame Davis?"

"Fucking Davis. Making me love strawberries."

Paige laughed. She didn't let go of Seren's hand as she reached for a basket.

After they left the Co-op, Paige led them down G Street. Seren figured Paige would head toward the park for a picnic, but instead she pulled up to the Pubster. The pub served lunch as well as dinner, but it was closed for three hours in between. The fact that it served food was how she'd been allowed in underage. Seren was about to mention the hours when Paige pointed to the side door.

"We're supposed to knock there." She glanced at her watch. "Hopefully the guy I talked to will be here."

"Why are we here when they're closed?"

Paige gave a noncommittal sort of shrug. "You'll see."

Seren didn't recognize the guy who answered their knock. He mentioned he'd recently taken over as manager as he introduced himself as Mathias. "Heard you used to perform here back in the day," he said over his shoulder as he switched on the lights.

"Way back when." Twenty years was a long time, but when Mathias led them past the bar and pointed to the stage, one look at the drum set and the gap didn't seem so long at all.

"You've got a half hour before I've gotta open up the place." Mathias handed her a pair of drumsticks. "These are an old pair of mine. I don't play often anymore. Have fun."

She wanted to admit that she didn't play either anymore, but Mathias headed to the back room before she could gather her thoughts.

"You don't have to play if you don't want to," Paige said. "But I thought it might be fun for you. And I'd love to hear."

She sucked in a breath, then eyed the drumsticks in her hands. "This is not what I was expecting." Still, she couldn't just stand there holding the drumsticks. Not with a drum set so close. "Remember, I haven't played in a long time."

"Don't worry. I've got low expectations." Paige coughed and under her breath added, "Mary Stuart Masterson."

Seren laughed and pushed her shoulder. She pointed with the drumsticks to one of the chairs. "Sit down over here where I can't see you. I'll be embarrassed if I know you're watching me."

Maybe she should have been embarrassed, but as soon as she settled in on the throne, the snare drum in front of her and a pedal underfoot, worries about what Paige would think and how long it'd been since she'd played all slipped away. She started a simple rhythm and quickly fell into the beat. Time slipped away as she moved into a more complicated set. At some point, the spotlights came on, but she didn't look up from the drums. She let herself be carried away so much that she jumped when Mathias stepped on stage, apologizing about having to cut her off.

After thanking Mathias and handing over the drumsticks, she turned to see Paige waiting exactly where she'd told her to sit. She walked over to the table. "I have no idea how you knew what I needed before I did, but thank you."

"That was truly my pleasure. You're amazing." Paige stood. "Ready to go see the next cool spot in this town that really isn't big enough for you?"

"I don't actually think it's too small anymore. Remember, it's me, not the town."

"But you're still not convinced it's cool, right? Because I want to keep going with this tour."

Seren smiled. "I'm not ready to put up the 'I Heart Davis' magnet yet." She was ready, however, to wrap her arms around Paige. Fighting that temptation wasn't easy, but Mathias was waiting for them at the back door.

# CHAPTER TWENTY-FIVE

It wasn't until they passed Central Park and angled south that Seren suspected Paige's plan. "Picnic in the arboretum?"

Paige glanced over her shoulder, maneuvering around a car. "Unless you hate trees."

"I love trees, and I've always loved the arboretum. I haven't been in a long time."

"It's my favorite spot in Davis. And definitely cool." Paige winked and then turned her attention back to snaking through the pedestrians and car traffic.

As soon as they turned their bikes onto the arboretum path, the noise of the town faded abruptly. Car sounds and the racket of people were replaced with birds chirping and a whispery light breeze lifting leaves. The path followed a creek lined with trees of all types and bushes in full blossom. As they made their way deeper into the arboretum, sunlight glistening on the water and branches arching overhead, it seemed they'd entered a different world. Seren felt her shoulders relax. She exhaled and then breathed in deeply. *Okay, some things about Davis are nice.*

Paige turned her bike across one of the bridges and Seren followed, realizing how much she didn't care where they went. When was the last time she hadn't planned anything at all for a whole afternoon? It was freeing and a pleasure she hadn't enjoyed in way too long.

Aside from a rumbling in her stomach, and thoughts of the sandwiches and strawberries they'd bought, she didn't want anything else from the day. Well, there was one other thing she wanted. Since Paige had shown up at her house that afternoon, looking sexier than ever in perfectly fitting cargo pants and a sky-blue T-shirt that showed off her form, she'd wanted a kiss.

Paige hopped off her bike when they reached the old wooden gazebo. Seren leaned her cruiser against a tree and then slowly turned in a circle, trying to take it all in. The gazebo, the trees, the spring-green lawn sloping down to the creek. "It's like time's stopped here. I remember coming here with my mom once. I was too old to feed the ducks, but she insisted I wasn't. We had the best time." Instead of making her sad, the memory only made her happy to have come back to the spot.

Paige smiled. "I love that."

"I don't think it's changed at all."

"Trees change a lot slower than us," Paige said. She'd brought a backpack and she opened it now, pulling out a blanket, plates, napkins, and two bottles of water. She handed one of the bottles to Seren.

"What else do you have hiding in there?"

"Chocolate chip cookies. I'd like to say I made them myself but they're from Rita. Payment for helping clean out that shed."

"She gave you cookies and a bike?"

"You wouldn't believe how many spiders there were in that place." Paige shuddered.

"Are you scared of spiders?"

"Not really. But I'm not a fan."

As soon as Paige turned to set up the picnic blanket, Seren reached over and touched her neck. Paige jumped at the light stroke, then spun around to face Seren. She laughed as she swiped at her neck. "I don't know what you just did but it felt exactly like a spider."

"Thought you weren't scared of spiders." Seren raised an eyebrow.

Her smile widened and Seren ached to kiss her. Again, she hesitated, and again she lost her chance. Paige stepped back and held out one end of the picnic blanket. "For that move, I'm making you help."

"If you ever need someone to move a spider for you, call me up. I happen to like them."

"I'll get you on speed dial."

Once they'd set out the food, they sat down with a view of the creek and Seren stretched out her legs. Maybe it was the sound of the creek or watching the ducks glide past. Or maybe it was the company. Whatever it was, she was happier and more relaxed than she'd been in a long time. "This is nice. A bike ride was a good idea."

"You like your new ride?"

"I love it." She'd glanced over at the red cruiser. Not only did the new bike have a smoother ride, it came with a basket. Big upgrade. "I know it was free, but you did all the work fixing it up and my conscience is nagging me about a way to repay you."

"You definitely don't have to pay me back, but I understand the conscience thing. I'll happily accept another dinner invite as payment."

"You're that easy, huh?"

"Before I moved in with my mom, I'd do all sorts of things to get people to cook for me."

"What sort of things?" Paige blushed at the innuendo in her tone and Seren added, "Those sort of things, huh?"

"No. I've never had sex with anyone for food. Although I'm not saying it's a terrible idea, depending on the person—and what they cook."

Seren laughed. "You could probably get a lot of offers for that trade if you advertise in the right places."

"I think I'd need to have some legit skills if I do that sort of thing for a business venture. And probably a better wardrobe."

"I can't speak to your skills, but you wearing that tank top you had on when I pushed you into the pool along with those cargo pants would be enough for most interested parties." Seren hadn't meant to look at Paige's crotch, but she did. A warmth immediately shot up to her cheeks.

"My ex told me to never wear cargo pants on a date. But we agreed to disagree on a lot of things."

"I had an ex like that." Seren nearly asked about Paige's ex but then stopped herself. Everyone had history. Still, she wanted to know Paige's and if she'd measure up to her exes. It was a messed-up thought, but she couldn't help it. She glanced at the sandwich she'd unwrapped. Paige's past didn't matter if this was really only a fling.

"Sorry about bringing up exes," Paige said. "I did tell you that I'm the worst with dinner conversations, right? If I don't bring up something gross, I take the conversation to other off-limits topics."

"I'm fine talking about exes. People act like it's taboo to have been in love with anyone else when you meet someone new, but it'd be weird if we hadn't at our *ancient* age. Besides, I brought up my dating history first." Seren sighed. "Remember when I broke down at the Co-op?"

"That wasn't a breakdown. That was you being honest. I appreciated it, by the way." Paige unwrapped her sandwich and took a bite. She chewed for a moment, then swallowed and said, "I am wondering what the hell your ex was thinking not wanting to keep her hands on you, though."

"We could talk about it if you want. I'll answer any questions. But I promise my exes aren't the most interesting thing about me."

"Huh. Well played. Now I want to ask what's something interesting about you, but I've already got a long list. I'm starting to wonder why anyone as cool as you would hang out with a nerd like me."

"Don't sell yourself short. I mean, you do teach water aerobics. Besides, everyone likes nerds."

"Not sure that's scientifically proven," Paige joked. She took another bite of her sandwich and shifted back on one elbow, looking across the creek at the far shore where a line of ducks was waddling up the bank. "I get why you don't like this town, and I guess I don't blame you, but I'm wondering...where do you want to go from here? Back to New York? Or are you ready for somewhere new?"

Seren turned the question over in her mind. God knows it wasn't the first time. "I was already thinking about leaving New

York when my mom got sick. For a while I considered moving to LA. My mom and I lived there for a few years when I was in grade school, and one of my friends from New York started up a spa there. He wants another massage therapist. I also considered Miami because I've got connections there too. Miami would be an unknown but that could be exciting. The problem is, now that I'm going to have a kid, I'm not sure if unknown and exciting is what I want."

"Could you stay in your mom's house?"

"Money's going to be tight soon." She glanced down at her belly. "My mom took out a second loan on the house when she got sick. She had to pay for a lot of medical bills…Anyway, I'll stay for a while. But I don't know how long."

Paige nodded, seeming to understand what she meant. *Don't get too attached.* She needed to remind herself to do the same.

"You have convinced me that this town does have a few things going for it. And some cool people. One in particular." When Paige met her gaze, Seren wondered if she had any chance not getting attached. To downplay her admission a little, she added, "I used to think the vet school was the coolest part. I mean, how many towns have a vet school?"

"In the US? I think we're up to thirty."

"See? That's not many. And you went to the best one, right? Automatically makes you cool." Seren bumped Paige's shoulder. Her body seemed to wake up at the contact, and when Paige shifted closer, letting their legs touch, she wondered how much longer she'd have to wait to feel Paige's hands on her. She tried to remember what they'd been talking about. Vet school. Right.

"When I was in high school, we took a tour of the college campus." Seren paused as a flock of geese soared overhead, honking loudly. After they'd passed, she continued, "I remember seeing a group of vet students heading into the hospital and thinking how cool they must be. I always wondered what that hospital was like on the inside. The tour didn't include that part. I imagined those vet students in little exam rooms learning how to talk to their patients." She smiled and looked over at Paige. "That happens, right?"

"That's the first class you take. Everyone uses Dr. Dolittle's textbook."

"I knew it!" She laughed. "And I pictured this line of dogs and cats and horses all waiting their turn. No people, just animals, all chatting about their problems while they waited." She shook her head, feeling ridiculous for admitting her daydream. "Anyway. I do think the vet school is another cool thing about Davis."

"Want me to give you a tour of the hospital? It should be pretty quiet on a Saturday night and we're only five minutes away."

"Oh, no, I couldn't ask you to do that."

"Why not? How many other chances are you going to get to walk into a teaching hospital and see where veterinarians learn to talk to their patients?"

"Probably none."

"Then you should take me up on my offer."

"This isn't going to mess up your other plans for us?"

"Plans can be changed." Paige took another bite of her sandwich and murmured her approval. She held it out to Seren. "Want to try mine?"

Something about the way Paige offered made Seren not want to say no. She took a bite of the sandwich, savoring the chicken-pesto-provolone combination, and then handed over hers. Paige tried the turkey and avocado—with extra avocado—and nodded in approval.

"You really do like to add avocado to everything, don't you?"

"Best part of being back in Davis." As often as she'd said it, she knew it wasn't true. There were many things she missed about New York and there was no comparing the energy and opportunities of a big city to a place like Davis. But a lot of things made her happy here. And there was no one like Paige anywhere else she'd been. If only she could let go of all the reasons she didn't want to stay.

After the sandwiches, they polished off Rita's cookies. Paige texted a friend who worked in the vet hospital, confirmed he was working, and then nodded to Seren. "Okay, we got a tour guide for the small animal part of the hospital. If you want to see the large animal barn too, I can get us in there no problem. I recommend we avoid the equine barn because you do not want to make horse people annoyed."

"I'll be happy if I only see one vet talking pig latin."

Paige grinned. "In that case, ets-lay o-gay."

Seren laughed. "'Let's go' in pig latin?"

"You seem surprised. Forget I was a nerd?"

"I keep forgetting and you keep reminding me." Once more she wanted to close the distance to Paige's lips. Before she made her move, Paige stood and started packing up their things.

# CHAPTER TWENTY-SIX

The bike ride from the arboretum to the vet school's hospital only took five minutes. Paige's friend Dr. Adrian met them out front. He led them from the main entrance through the waiting area, past exam rooms to the hospital wards. Paige was right—the place was quiet on a Saturday night. They chatted with a vet student helping a dog walk with a new splint and then peeked in on a cat that was a patient of Adrian's and eating well for the first time in weeks, before checking out the surgery suites and the ICU.

"Was it what you expected?" Paige asked as they stepped outside.

"It's bigger inside than I thought. Less stressful than a people hospital but not that different I guess."

"Wait till you see the large animal side of things." Paige led the way across the path from the small animal building toward a pair of long beige-colored barns.

A horse neighed and then came a racket of hooves pounding against something hard. Seren glanced at the first barn. "Let me guess, that's the equine barn we aren't touring?"

"Was it the neigh that gave it away?"

Seren smiled. "I'm a quick one."

"I like that about you." Paige held open the door to the second barn. She pointed to a line of boots. "We're gonna take off our shoes and borrow some boots."

"Whoever owns these won't mind?"

Paige had already started unlacing her shoes. "I got friends in the right places."

"Right here, actually." A woman in tan coveralls had come around a corner. She looked from Seren to Paige. "Thought I heard your voice, Dannenberg. Then I said to myself, 'Now why the fuck would someone that smart come to my barn on a Saturday night?'"

Paige straightened. "Seren, this is Connie—Dr. Morrison. Dr. Morrison's head of the large animal barn. Connie, Seren."

Connie didn't offer to shake hands. Instead, she gave Seren a curt nod and muttered something like "Welcome to my night of dystopia." Except the last word didn't quite sound like dystopia.

No introduction was needed to guess Connie was in charge. She had a no-nonsense confidence and seemed like the type who didn't get ruffled by anything. Still, she seemed surprised by Paige's presence. And Paige clearly hadn't expected to see her.

"How'd you end up working on a Saturday night?" Paige asked.

"A damn stomach bug took out my two residents."

Maybe Seren was imagining it, but she sensed more familiarity between Paige and Connie than a work friendship would suggest. And maybe a little guarded animosity. Or competition? As soon as she realized Connie was giving her another critical look, she guessed she was Paige's ex.

Well, Paige had good taste. Apart from the confidence thing, and a tough edge that was equally intimidating and appealing, she had a fit build, subtly graying brown hair pulled back in a low ponytail, and an angular face with faint lines at the corners of her eyes and on her forehead. Probably ten years separated them, but Seren could well guess how someone even a lot younger might fall for a woman like Connie.

Connie retrieved a vial of something from a cabinet opposite the row of boots and then looked back at Seren and Paige, now both booted up. "So, to what do I owe this surprise visit?"

"I'm giving Seren a tour. She's always wanted to see the vet school's hospital."

"Hmm."

Seren smiled, trying not to melt with Connie's piercing blue eyes on her.

"Don't suppose either of you want to work tonight? I've got a heifer who delivered one calf but won't push out the second, a goat who needs a C-section, and a vaginal prolapse on a ewe that I think's gone septic. Oh, and apparently there's a neurologic alpaca on the way."

"I'm a massage therapist." Seren cringed as the sentence repeated in her head. Why had she spoken up?

"I'll take that as a no thank you. Although the heifer could use a massage."

Paige cleared her throat. "If you really need help, I could probably—"

Connie held up her hand. "I'll be fine." She looked back at Seren. "I'd like to say Paige is generally better at coming up with ideas for dates than a tour of the Large Animal Teaching Hospital. But…"

"I asked her to show me around," Seren said.

"If you want an extra exciting tour, you can feed the Holstein calf that's out there crying. No one's had time to do any feedings and he could use some colostrum." She glanced at her wristwatch. "His mama's still trying to get his twin out. I'm hoping a little oxytocin gets things moving."

"We'd be happy to feed the calf." Paige glanced at Seren. "I mean, if it's okay with you?"

"For real?" Seren couldn't hold back her excitement. Who could say no to feeding a newborn calf?

"For real." Connie chuckled. "The calf's in a stall in the middle bay. You won't be able to miss him. There's only one Holstein bull-calf here tonight. For now." She looked at Paige as she added, "I'm gonna assume I don't need to tell you where to find the bottles of colostrum. Or the nipples."

Paige's eye roll was subtle but definitely happened. "I know my way around."

"Always did."

The innuendo wasn't lost on Seren, but when she looked over at Paige, she couldn't see that it bothered her. Seren had no doubt now that Connie was Paige's ex. The question was if there was any residual baggage.

After Connie left, Paige turned to Seren. "For the record, this is not what I had in mind for tonight. You sure you're okay helping out here?"

"Yes. But one question. When you say it wasn't what you had in mind, do you mean the running into an ex-girlfriend part or the chance to feed a baby cow?"

Paige scratched her head. "Both?"

"You should have included feeding baby cows in your original plan. Talk about cool."

"Not gonna argue there." Paige went over to the same cabinet Connie had opened earlier and got out a bottle and a rubber nipple. Then she opened a fridge and filled the bottle with something that looked like heavy cream. "Are you letting me off the hook about the ex-girlfriend part?"

"Would you tell me if there's anything I need to worry about?"

"I'd tell you. And there's not." Paige paused, seemingly contemplating the bottle in her hands. "It's been years since we dated. I was twenty-eight when we met. I made a lot of mistakes and things didn't end well. Mostly because I was immature and dumb. We didn't talk for a few years. Then after my breakup with Miranda, Connie became my stand-in therapist. She was always better than me about talking through things. In fact, she had no trouble telling me all the ways I'd fucked up." She shrugged. "We've been good since."

"Is Miranda the ex who wanted kids?"

Paige nodded and Seren decided to leave it at that, reminding herself that everyone had history. When they headed into the main part of the barn, the smell of manure got stronger, especially as they passed an area Paige called the treatment bay. For some reason, though, Seren's stomach didn't complain at the smell.

One vet student, a pretty twenty-something who clearly had worked with Paige, stopped to chat but then was called away by another vet student working with a sad-looking goat. The second student also recognized Paige and waved.

"Did you used to work here? Everyone seems to know you."

"I work with a lot of the vet students. Once a week I have a student intern with me on farm calls. It gives them a chance for more of the real-world experience." Paige seemed to hesitate and then added, "I was a senior vet student when I met Connie. Not that it matters, but we didn't date until after I graduated."

"You don't have to explain. It's okay."

Paige stopped in front of a stall and said, "You're being extra nice about me taking you on a date and running into one of my exes."

Seren laughed. "I'm in a good mood."

"On a different note, here's the part of our tour where we both get to ooh and ahh." Paige pointed to the stall.

Seren looked past Paige. A black-and-white-splotched calf was curled up on the hay, head resting on folded legs and eyes closed. "Oh, my god." She reached out and clutched Paige's arm. "He's adorable. You can't let me take him home. No matter what I say."

# CHAPTER TWENTY-SEVEN

Seren was beautiful. No two ways about it. But seeing her look at the bull-calf, a smile stretched from cheek to cheek, Paige's heart tripped over itself.

"I seriously don't think I've seen anything that cute. Ever." Seren held up her phone, snapping a picture of the riot of black and white that was a curled-up baby Holstein.

"Wait till he takes a bottle from you." Paige pushed open the stall door. At the creak of the hinge, the calf opened his eyes. Seren gasped and Paige couldn't help but chuckle.

Connie likely hadn't had time to give the calf more than a cursory once-over, so Paige gave him a quick exam, and then, noticing that Seren hesitated outside the little 4x4 stall, waved her in. "You know you want to snuggle a baby bull."

"I do." She came into the stall, her gaze not leaving the calf. "He's so small. I thought he'd be bigger. Maybe I shouldn't feed him? I'm really not trained in…well, cow."

Paige resisted laughing. Seren was completely serious. "You're gonna be fine."

"Do I hold my hand out like when you meet a dog?"

Before Paige could say that wasn't necessary, Seren had dropped down on her knees and stretched out her hand. The calf took one sniff and then his tongue slicked across her hand. Instead of being grossed out, like Paige half expected, Seren looked over at her and said, "I could die right now."

The calf continued nosing Seren's hand, trying to suckle on her fingers and getting oohs and ahhs from Seren. He got up on his stumbly legs, pushed her shoulder, then took a nose-dive right into her lap. "Oh, love, are you okay?" Seren cooed to the calf like a parent over a baby and then wrapped him up in a hug.

Paige reached into her back pocket and pulled out her phone. She caught a picture right as Seren kissed the calf's white-starred forehead. "Want to feed your little monster?"

"Monster?"

Paige grinned. "He looks small now. But just wait."

Seren looked at the bottle of colostrum, then down at the calf and bit the edge of her lip. "You're gonna have to give me a little more direction."

"I promise it's not rocket science. You really can't screw it up with calves. Pretty much, you stick the nipple in their mouth and they take it from there."

"Too bad women aren't that easy."

Paige laughed, and when she looked over at Seren, she laughed harder. Seren's hand was over her mouth like she'd obviously surprised herself.

"I can't believe I just said that. Out loud."

"Me neither. Though I'll be the first to say I agree."

"Thanks." Seren looked from the bottle to the calf snoozing next to her feet. "I'm not sure why I'm so nervous. Can I watch you do it first?"

Barely resisting another quip filled with innuendo, Paige took the bottle, held it in front of the calf, and then after he'd had a good sniff stuck her thumb in the side of the calf's mouth and a second later replaced her thumb with the nipple. The calf immediately started suckling. As soon as he got a taste of the sweet colostrum, he pushed into the bottle as if that would get the milk flowing faster. "A little hungry, are you?" Paige let him get a good gulp in before taking the bottle away.

She passed the bottle to Seren. "All right. You have a go."

Seren took a deep breath. She offered the bottle to the bull-calf, and when he didn't open his mouth, she gave Paige a worried look. "Maybe he had enough?"

"Not possible." Paige stood up and came to the other side of the calf closest to Seren. When she kneeled next to her, she was acutely aware of how much she'd been waiting for a moment exactly like this. Well, except for the fact that they were in a stall with a calf. She tried to focus. "Okay, remember, you gotta get the nipple right in his mouth."

"Got it." Seren tried pushing the nipple into the calf's mouth but instead of opening for it, he nosed around the bottle to lick her hand. "I'm gonna need more help."

Paige leaned around Seren and stuck her finger in the bull-calf's mouth. "As soon as I pull out my finger, stick in the nipple. One, two, and go."

Seren quickly jabbed the nipple in at the same moment Paige's finger came out. "You forgot three."

"I knew you were ready." Paige grinned—not that Seren was looking at her. She only had eyes for the calf now.

"It's working!" Seren's smile could not get any bigger. "He's the smartest cow ever. Isn't he? I mean look at him."

"He's brilliant."

Seren glanced over her shoulder. "Are you teasing me?"

"Maybe a little. Taking a bottle isn't the litmus test for calf intelligence."

Seren leaned down and kissed the calf's head. "Don't listen to her. You're brilliant."

"I think he only caught on so quick because the person feeding him that bottle is a natural."

"Nice save. Can he have the whole bottle?"

"It's all for him."

Seren was quiet for a minute, and the sounds of the calf chugging away claimed center stage. After a while, Seren looked up at Paige. Tears glistened in her eyes. "Thank you for this." She didn't say anything more, but the look was enough to get Paige's heart bounding all over again. Seren glanced back at the calf. "This is the best date ever. No joke."

"I'm glad you're having an okay time."

"Okay?" Seren patted the calf's white tuft of hair between his ears. "When I get home, I'm putting my damn 'I Heart Davis' magnet on my refrigerator."

Paige leaned close to the calf. "Did you hear that? Seren thinks the Davis nightlife is as exciting as New York City."

"I don't know if I'd go that far."

"Where in New York City can you go on a bike ride to a place where you can feed a newborn calf at eight o'clock on a Saturday night?"

"Nowhere. New York City is really missing out." Seren grinned. "Also, I seriously underestimated your determination to prove this town is cool."

"Hey, Paige." Ty's voice interrupted. "Connie sent me to get you. Another dystocia came in and she's got her hands full. The cow that had this bull-calf isn't looking so good. No movement on the other fetus she's carrying. Connie's wondering if you can step in."

Paige looked from Ty to Seren. "Would you be okay if I leave you here for a minute?"

"Go. His mama needs you." Seren's eyes were moist again. She looped her arm around the bull-calf and added, "Your mama's gonna be fine. Don't you worry."

Ty shot Paige a worried look that seemed to say, "Don't make any promises." Paige took a deep breath and stood. She glanced down at Seren cuddling the calf. "I'll be right back."

Unfortunately, after getting a better history on the cow, she knew "right back" wouldn't be so quick.

"She's looking worse than she did an hour ago," Ty said. "I don't think she's gonna make it without us throwing all-in, and even then it'll be dicey. But we got approval to try."

Paige glanced down at her cargo pants and T-shirt. It wasn't like she was dressed nicely—she'd gone for comfortable attire for a bike ride—but checking on a distressed cow definitely could get messy. "I'm gonna throw on a pair of coveralls first."

"Good call. I'll meet you in the treatment bay."

As she changed into a pair of Connie's old coveralls, she wondered at the irony of the evening. Helping out her ex-girlfriend while on a date had to be against some basic dating rules. She wanted to explain to Seren that Connie didn't usually work Saturdays, but that would only make things more awkward. All things considered, it really hadn't been weird having Seren meet Connie. Still, she didn't want to leave Seren alone for long.

"This is her?" Paige blew out a breath when Ty nodded. One look at the poor animal, lying on her side and laboring for every breath, and she wondered if euthanasia wouldn't be the kindest thing. But then she thought of Seren cuddling the bull-calf.

"We gotta get her up."

"Right. How you want to do that?" Ty didn't look hopeful.

Ty was Connie's rock star vet tech. Everyone liked working with them because they usually had a "we can do anything" attitude. Not this time, apparently.

"Any chance whoever brought this cow is still here? And did they look like they could be of any use?"

Ty nodded. "An old ranch hand from the MacMillan farm brought her in. I think he's out in the truck waiting. Want me to get him to see if he'll give us a hand?"

"Yes, please."

The guy from the MacMillan ranch was gruff but not unreasonable. He took one look at the cow and shook his head. "I could call my boss if you want. Might be the kindest thing to put her down?"

Paige couldn't argue with his assessment, even if he'd phrased it as a question, but she didn't want to give up that easy. "Let's try to get her on her feet first. I want to give her a good once-over and then check on the calf before I make any recommendation."

Chances weren't good that the calf still in the cow would be alive, but Paige made a silent wish to the universe anyway. Even more than wanting a healthy calf, she wanted the mama cow to make it through. It wasn't only that she didn't want to explain to Seren that the mom of the baby she'd fed and cuddled hadn't survived. She hated not being able to save an animal—especially one that should have a good chance.

With some work, all three of them encouraging the tired cow, they managed to get her standing. She gave a deep sigh once she was in the squeeze shoot and then met Paige's gaze. Her dark brown eyes seemed to ask for help. Paige's chest tightened. She wanted nothing more than to do exactly that.

As she did her exam, listening to the cow's chest and then checking gut sounds, the ranch hand mentioned labor had started early that morning. Paige didn't push him on why they'd waited to bring her in. Probably it wasn't his call to make. She tried to push statistics out of her mind but knew time wasn't on the cow's side— or hers, since they were in this together now.

The cow shuddered and started to lower herself. "Keep her standing," Paige said, motioning for Ty to assist on one side and the ranch hand to take the other. "I'm gonna check on the calf."

She hurried to glove up, mentally focusing on finding a live calf. Probably it didn't help, but it was force of habit. Connie had been the one to train her into that—*Always believe you can help until you find out that you can't.*

She was up to her forearm in the cow when Seren appeared in the doorway to the treatment stall. Seren stared open-mouthed at the scene, and Paige could only wonder what she was thinking. Probably she didn't want to know. Seeing someone with their arm in a cow could in no way be sexy. That thought flew from her mind, however, when she felt the calf suckle her index finger.

"Baby's alive."

"No shit?" Ty cheered. "Let's get 'em out."

Paige palpated for a moment longer. One of the calf's legs was forward in front of her nose where it should be, but the other leg was jammed backward. They'd tried to shoulder through the narrow opening but were now officially stuck. "I gotta move the calf. Ty, keep the cow on her feet."

Paige pushed the calf back, then reached for the second leg. It took some maneuvering, but soon both legs were forward, and the calf was in the right position.

"Got it." Paige pulled out. "Now, we only need one good contraction."

As soon as she said that the cow dropped down. Getting her up a second time took a lot more encouragement than the first, and once she was standing, she didn't seem at all interested in trying to push out a calf.

"She's exhausted," Paige said. Stating the obvious had never felt so depressing. "We're gonna have to pull the calf."

Ty gave a quick nod and went to get the ropes. Paige risked a glance over at where Seren had been standing. She was still there, one hand on her chest, the other clutched in a fist of worry. She met Paige's gaze and mouthed, "Poor mama."

"Heads up." Ty tossed the ropes to Paige.

For the next several minutes, all of Paige's focus was on the calf. Once she had a rope looped around each of the calf's front legs, she handed one line to Ty and took the other herself. "Pull on three. One, two—"

As soon as the ropes went taut, the cow gave a half-hearted push. It might have been half-hearted, but it was enough. The calf shot out. Paige caught her, stumbled back, and the next instant was on her butt with a wet calf in her lap. Ty took one look at her and bust out laughing. The MacMillan ranch hand snickered as well but did a better job covering it.

"Fuck, that hurt." Her butt didn't hurt as much as her pride, however. How many times had she pulled a calf and not once fallen on her ass?

"Oh, my god. That was amazing." Seren dropped to her knees next to Paige. "Are you okay? You have a baby cow on you."

Paige glanced at the calf. "I do."

"You forgot about three again," Seren teased. "It goes one, two, three."

"I should learn how to count."

"Something tells me you have many other useful skills. I can't believe I got to see you do that. Seriously amazing. Can I touch this one?"

Paige nodded. As soon as Seren caressed the calf's wet head, her eyes watered. "This one's even cuter than JJ." Her voice sounded choked, and when Paige loved over at her, she saw tears in her eyes.

"You named the other calf JJ?"

"I know it's silly. He'll probably get a new name when his owners take him, but I wanted to call him something for now."

Paige didn't want to tell her that calves didn't get names. They got numbered ear tags.

"Is this one a girl or a boy?"

Ty reached down and lifted the calf off of Paige. "Girl." They unceremoniously plopped the calf back on Paige's belly. Paige groaned with the sudden weight and Ty chuckled with a wicked grin. "You missed me, didn't you?"

"Not even a little." That was a lie, and Ty knew it. They chuckled, then sobered a moment later when Connie appeared in the stall.

"Sitting down on the job?"

Paige lifted a shoulder. "I got the calf out."

"I noticed. Good job." The usual bite wasn't in Connie's tone, and Paige realized then how exhausted she looked. Knowing how much she hated asking for help, Paige guessed she'd been working herself to the bone—and likely worried about more than one animal surviving—before sending Ty to ask her to step in.

The cow lowered herself and Connie went right to her. The work wasn't done yet. Paige shifted the calf off her lap. "Mind taking this one for a minute? I have to take care of the mom."

Seren looked unsure, but before Paige could say more, Connie spoke up. "I'll take the case from here." She patted the cow's shoulder. "But I won't stop you two from cleaning that calf up and getting her fed."

Settling the second calf into a stall across from her brother took longer than it should have. All the new calf wanted to do was snooze in Seren's arms like a big puppy dog. Paige worried about her until she finally latched onto the nipple and sucked down a full bottle of colostrum.

"I can't remember the last time I've been this happy sitting around doing nothing," Seren said. She glanced from one calf to the other and sighed.

"Not a bad gig even if it's not that exciting, huh?"

Seren met Paige's gaze. "Sometimes we're wrong about what we think is exciting."

"We should probably let them sleep." Paige stood, brushing straw from her hands. She'd already taken off the coveralls and washed as thoroughly as she could, but she still needed a shower. And to toss everything she was wearing into the laundry.

"You think they'll be okay alone?" Seren was clearly reluctant to leave. "They don't have anyone looking after them."

"They'll be fine. I promise." Fortunately, the mama cow had a good prognosis as well. They'd gotten the news from Ty that the cow was looking good and Connie had moved on to another dystocia. Paige felt guilty not helping more until she reminded herself that she'd quit a job for reasons exactly like tonight. She was on a date, and work-life balance was important.

"I suppose I can't buy two calves."

"Well, you could. Theoretically. But where would you keep them?"

"I've got a guest room."

Paige chuckled. "They're gonna get big quick. And you can't potty train a calf."

"Details." She sighed and kissed April's lightning-strike blaze. The heifer-calf she called April and she'd named the bull-calf JJ for June and July—her mother's two favorite months, she'd told Paige. Seren had gushed about both of their markings but especially April's lightning blaze until Paige finally agreed that April was cuter than most calves. Probably it was the same with babies—that all of them were cute but that the ones you took care of seemed the cutest.

After Seren had scooted April off her lap and settled her on the straw, she held out her hand to Paige. "I got a little stiff down here."

Paige helped her up, and as soon as Seren was standing next to her, the desire to kiss her was overwhelming. Before she could ask, Seren said, "You really think that whoever owns these calves wants to keep them?"

"I do."

"Okay. Fine."

Seren's thoughts might not be on kissing, but it was adorable how much she'd fallen for the calves. "They'd probably sell for the right price, though. And if I already had a farm and a place for you to keep them, I'd completely support you in offering way too much money for these two."

"Can you hurry up and get a farm, please?"

Paige laughed.

"I'm serious."

"I know you are. And I love it. When I first met you, I didn't figure you'd be the sort of woman who'd be okay spending an evening in a barn."

"Clearly you misjudged. Watching you deliver April was amazing."

"Not too gross?"

"Gross wasn't even on the list. If you want, I could tell you all the words I've come up with tonight to describe you. Starting with sexy as fuck."

"Technically that's three words."

"Davis nerd is also on the list." Seren eye's sparkled mischievously, but when her gaze flicked to Paige's lips, there was no doubt she was thinking of a kiss as well.

"You two still here?" Ty stopped in front of the stall. They had their arms full with towels, buckets, and other supplies. "In case you're looking to spend all night in the large animal clinic, I hear there's another dystocia case on the way."

"Definitely time for us to leave," Paige said.

"I'm kidding. But I probably just tempted fate." Ty shook their head. "Nice seeing you again, Paige. And nice meeting you, Seren. Whenever you want some time with calves, you know where to come."

After Ty left, Paige knew the moment to try for a kiss had passed. It also seemed a little late for a fun bike ride home. "How would you feel if we leave our bikes here and I call us a Lyft?"

"That would make it a lot easier to sneak home with a calf."

Paige grinned. "If I get the Landrys' place, you can help me pick out my first set of calves. And name them as well."

Seren leaned close and kissed her cheek. "Best offer ever."

Another cheek kiss. Was Seren trying to tell her something?

# CHAPTER TWENTY-EIGHT

Riding bikes home in the dark wouldn't have been a problem. Hell, she'd grown up in Davis and won dares riding with no hands and her eyes closed. But she didn't mind Paige thinking she needed a break. Not when it meant sitting in the back seat of the Lyft driver's Prius, close enough to feel how much Paige wanted to reach for her. Paige's hand had brushed her leg as they'd first buckled in, and for the next ten minutes Paige kept her fingers laced together so tight that Seren almost teased her about it. She didn't, however, because her own need was threatening to short-circuit her brain.

If only it was simply a physical need. Unfortunately, it was more than that. She couldn't stop herself from listing all the ways Paige was exactly who she'd always wanted. Worse, she was letting her mind leap to scenarios of co-parenting cows and kids. And remodeling the Landry ranch.

Paige stayed quiet on the drive and even after paying the driver. Seren wondered if it was too late to ask Paige in as they walked up the steps to her porch. She didn't want the night to end, but Paige seemed tired. If nothing else, she wanted a kiss. She'd make the first move if she had to. Wondering if she had the courage, she turned to look at Paige and immediately laughed. "Are you smelling yourself?"

Paige grinned sheepishly, still holding the edge of her T-shirt up to her nose. "I know we washed up at the barn, but I think I still smell like cow. That driver looked at us funny as soon as we got into his car."

"We definitely smell like cow. But you caught a flying calf."

"And then I fell on my ass."

"Impressively."

Paige laughed. "Thanks."

They'd stopped at the top step of the porch. Paige looked sexier than ever. Partly it was her short hair, all messed up from wearing a bike helmet and the countless times she'd run her hands through it after, and partly it was how relaxed she looked. Seren realized she didn't look tired so much as relaxed. Maybe she would want to come inside?

"Today was nice," Paige said.

"It was." Did that mean Paige was ready to leave? Seren pushed down her disappointment. "Can I get it on paper that you'll let me name your calves if you get the Landry ranch?"

"Don't trust my word?"

Seren had only been joking, but Paige's question made her realize how much she did trust her. Add it to the list of things she had going for her. "I trust you. But I also really want to name more cows."

"First, I have to get a ranch. How about we agree to sign on it then?"

"Okay, fine." Seren only pretended to be sad by the compromise. She looked over her shoulder at the front door and then back at Paige. As nice as the day was, she felt unsteadied by it all now. Was she ready for the next step? "I want to ask you to come in."

"I'd like to come in." Paige took her hands out of her pockets. "But I feel like maybe there's a *but* that you aren't saying."

She considered admitting the truth—that she didn't usually have sex so soon—but she was horny and really wanted it. They hadn't even kissed and she wanted to strip Paige's clothes off. But what was on her mind even more was how perfect their night had been. And how perfect Paige seemed. And how she was really good at messing up perfect things.

When she didn't answer, Paige said, "It's late. I'd planned on us getting home a lot earlier. I know we're up past your bedtime."

"True." *But you could take me to bed.*

"I'll bring your bike by tomorrow."

"Thanks." Seren clenched her jaw. Yep, she'd screwed things up again. *Dammit.*

"Also. I'm sorry we couldn't bring home a baby cow."

Seren smiled. "I do think I could make room for one. I don't know about two, though, and how would we pick?"

"From experience, I can tell you the mess is a lot more than you bargain for—especially if maybe you let them sleep in the kitchen."

"Meaning you've done that?" Seren smiled. "Good to know I'm not the only one who makes questionable decisions."

"If you don't make at least some questionable decisions, life gets pretty boring. Sometimes I go too far the other direction. I think about everything rationally and weigh all the variables…and then miss out on something I really wanted."

Paige's tone was more serious than suggestive, but when she met Seren's eyes, what she wanted was obvious. Her longing was so palpable that a rush went through Seren.

"Anyway, I should go."

"Can I tell you something?" When Paige only waited for her to go on, she said, "I don't want you to leave even if it is late."

"Thanks for telling me." Paige's hesitation turned to a cocky look that only notched Seren's arousal up more. "Can I tell you something too?"

Seren nodded.

"I'd really like to kiss you."

"I know." Seren laughed a moment later when Paige's mouth dropped open. "You've looked like you wanted to kiss me more than once today."

"At the bookstore. At the grocery store. At the pub. At the arboretum. And definitely at the barn." Paige ticked off each one with the fingers on her hand, then shook her head. "Why did I take you to the place where one of my exes works?"

"It was amazing anyway." Her heart raced with anticipation. She couldn't wait to feel Paige's lips against hers.

Paige stepped forward, closing the distance between them. She didn't move to kiss Seren, though. Instead, she waited, making Seren want her all the more. Seren met Paige's gaze, already breathless. When Paige's hands settled on her hips, she stopped thinking. Her whole body hummed with the light pressure of Paige's fingertips.

"Can I kiss you now?"

Seren nodded. A moment later Paige's lips met hers. The porch disappeared. The sounds of Davis, a dog barking somewhere and crickets calling, a bike whirring past on the street, all slipped away too. Seren moved into the kiss, not holding back the soft moan when their lips parted only to meet again. Paige's hold shifted from her waist to the low of her back, pulling them closer together.

The strength in Paige's body came as no surprise, but how much she wanted to melt into it was unsteadying. Paige moved them a step back and then another until Seren was pressed against the front door. As Paige deepened the kiss, she felt her knees go slack. Paige's grip tightened around her, and every kiss made her hungry for the next.

Each time Paige's lips pressed into hers, she wanted more. She slipped under Paige's jacket and gripped her shirt, enjoying the soft moan that escaped Paige's lips. The warmth and closeness was exactly what she wanted, and confirmation she needed more.

She slid her hand down and found Paige's belt. It wasn't hard undoing the buckle. Or slipping the top button of Paige's pants open. She tugged on the zipper, half amazed Paige wasn't stopping her. When the pants gaped open, giving her access to Paige's underwear, it hit her that they were still on the front porch. In full view of anyone walking by. She pulled her hand back and turned her head to break their kiss. Breathless, and still so turned-on she could hardly think, she managed to murmur, "I'm sorry," before squeezing her eyes closed.

"Hey," Paige said, gently tipping Seren's chin up. "Why are you apologizing?"

"We're on my front porch. I don't live on a quiet street." As if to prove that point, a car alarm beeped nearby. Then came the click of someone's heels on the sidewalk and someone called out, "See ya tomorrow, babe."

Seren pressed her lips together. Fuck. Paige looked sexier than ever half-undressed. And she'd done that. She never wanted someone so desperately that she lost her inhibitions. Until now. Could she blame it all on her hormones?

"We are on your front porch. And that cow"—Paige pointed to the cow door knocker grinning at them with way too many teeth— "is definitely judgy. But also, I like it. I might get one for my own door."

Seren smiled.

"Are you actually sorry?"

Seren shook her head.

"Good, because you sure know how to kiss."

"That was supposed to be a good-night peck. Not a full on make-out session." Still Seren didn't regret it as long as Paige didn't.

"I think I share some of the blame." Paige took a step back and looked down at her undone pants and then up to Seren's eyes. "Have to admit, I wasn't expecting you to get into my pants that fast."

Seren didn't want Paige to leave. It was more than the fact that she was impossibly wet. No vibrator would satisfy what she wanted tonight. She watched as Paige pulled up her zipper and rebuttoned her pants. When Paige started on her belt, Seren couldn't ignore the ache of longing. She reached out and caught Paige's hand, stalling her progress. "Would you like to come in?"

# CHAPTER TWENTY-NINE

It would be a lie to say she hadn't hoped the evening would end with a kiss. But more than that she hadn't expected. After the make-out session on the porch, though, she wasn't surprised that one step into the house, Seren was already helping her out of her jacket.

"I don't want to stop you, but I really could use a shower," Paige said between kisses.

Seren tugged off Paige's T-shirt and kissed her again. She pulled back. "Good news—I have a shower."

"That is good news."

Another kiss. "I'll even take you there." Seren clasped Paige's hand and took a step back, pulling them into the living room. "I should warn you, though. I might get shy. This is not how I usually act on a second date."

"It's hard imagining you shy." They passed the living room and turned down a hallway.

"Yeah, well, you might not have to imagine it." Seren opened the first door on the right. It was a small bathroom—clean and tidy but tight for two people. Paige paused in the doorway as Seren pushed the shower curtain to one side and turned on the water. She looked over her shoulder. "I didn't tell you that to make you pull back."

"I'm not pulling back."

Seren narrowed her eyes. "Hesitating?"

"I'm giving you space to think. If this is faster than you usually take things—"

Seren stepped forward and kissed Paige. She shifted back and said, "I've been trying not to kiss you all day. I can't seem to stop now. And I don't want to go slow."

"Anything else you want to admit?"

"Other than the fact that I'm not letting you shower alone?" Seren smiled. "No." She reached into the shower again to check the water temperature. "Well, I guess I should tell you that you're the first person I've had sex with since I got pregnant."

"Who said anything about sex?"

Seren's eyes darted up, a surprised look on her face. A second later she clearly realized Paige was joking and turned the shower nozzle right at her.

Paige hopped back a step, but it didn't help. Since she'd already lost her shirt, she caught the blast right on her belly. A shriek slipped out, which led to laughing—both from her and Seren. At least the water was warm. "Now that I'm wet…" She tugged her sports bra over her head and then dropped her pants.

"I do seem to remember getting you wet is all it takes to get you to strip."

"So you pushed me into the pool on purpose that first day? Wanted me to take off my clothes, huh?" With a wide smile Paige added, "I like knowing you wanted me the moment you saw me."

"Not completely untrue."

Paige stepped around Seren and into the shower. "Two can play that soaking game."

"You wouldn't." Seren had rehung the shower nozzle and she groaned when Paige reached for it now. She held her hands in front of her face. "You can't spray a pregnant lady."

"Is that a rule?" Paige lowered the nozzle as Seren nodded. "Alright, fine. Then what do I have to do to get you to take off your clothes and join me?"

Seren drew a circle with her finger in the air. "Turn around. I'm not ready to show off my pregnant body quite yet."

With a sigh, Paige turned halfway and averted her gaze. Not peeking was torture, but she wanted to respect Seren's wishes.

"Can I borrow your soap?"

"Yes. And there's shampoo you can use as well."

Paige lathered the soap, scrubbing away any remaining scent of the barn. She rinsed and repeated, then turned her face into the stream, wondering if the long wait meant Seren had changed her mind about joining her. The water didn't relax her. Instead, it felt like a drumroll on her skin amping up her anticipation.

"It's about to get dark," Seren said.

A second later the lights in the bathroom went off. Paige stuck her head out of the shower. "You shower in the dark?"

"I like showering with candles. Helps me relax."

Paige squinted but still couldn't see where Seren was standing. Suddenly a match was struck and Seren's face was outlined as she lit a candle. A moment later the room was filled with a warm glow.

"Nice, right?" Seren briefly met Paige's eyes then placed the candle on a shelf between the sink and the shower. The light bathed Seren's skin in a warm softness that made Paige's breath catch.

"That is nice." No matter how many times she'd seen Seren in a bathing suit, she wasn't prepared for how gorgeous she was naked.

Seren's eyes met hers and she raised one eyebrow. "You weren't supposed to look."

"I was looking at the candle."

"Were you?"

Paige shook her head slowly. "You're so beautiful."

"Close your eyes."

Grudgingly, Paige did as she was told. She heard the rustle of the shower curtain being pushed open and then felt Seren move against her back. "I usually take showers to relax after a long day." This time, no part of her was going to relax until she had Seren.

"Not to get clean?" Seren kissed Paige's shoulder. "You have a very dirty job."

"I do." She sucked in a breath when Seren kissed the nape of her neck.

"Is it weird admitting I liked you smelling like a barn better than my soap?"

Paige turned, unable to wait any longer. She found Seren's lips and arousal gripped her body as Seren moved against her. She deepened the kiss then spun them around, letting Seren have the full stream on her.

"I take it you're in charge now?"

Seren's question had a playful tone, but Paige wondered if she'd come on too strong. "Do you mind?"

"Not at all."

"Good." Paige liked the look she got from Seren in response. When she kissed her again, need surged through her. She tried to hold herself in check, keeping the kisses light, but every time she pulled back, Seren seemed to ask for her lips again.

Desire made her want to rush, but she knew it'd be better taking her time. She reached for the soap and traced Seren's arms with the bar—up one side and down the other. When she repeated the pattern with Seren's legs, she avoided her upper thighs despite the focus of her thoughts. Straightening, she drew a sudsy line with the soap between Seren's breasts. Seren shifted forward right at that moment and Paige fumbled, dropping the bar.

"Did I distract you?"

"You did. And I think you meant to." She wanted to take her time appreciating Seren's curves, tracing her full breasts, and letting her smooth skin slip under her fingertips. But her body didn't want to go slow. "I don't think I can wait till we get out of this shower."

"Wait for what?"

"For you." Paige shifted closer. Seren's nipples brushed her chest, and she couldn't hold in her moan. She grasped Seren's arm above her elbow and pulled their bodies together. The smash of wet skin against skin pushed her past thinking.

Seren kissed Paige's neck. "You feel so good."

"That's my line." Paige ran her hands up from Seren's thighs to her waist. When she caressed her breasts, grazing over perked nipples, Seren inhaled sharply.

"You okay?"

She nodded, swallowing. "My nipples have been sensitive since I got pregnant. Didn't realize how much."

"I'll be gentle."

"Don't be too gentle," Seren said, shifting her hips forward.

Paige got the hint and gave up reining herself back. When she pressed against Seren, they both moaned. Skin, slick and wet, slid under her hand as she stroked up Seren's arm. She slipped behind Seren's neck and pulled her into a kiss.

Seren parted her lips, asking for more. She obliged with another deep kiss and her arousal surged. Kissing wasn't enough. She pulled away from Seren's lips and dropped to her knees.

Fingernails sank into her shoulders as she parted Seren with her tongue. Her taste was everything she wanted.

Seren moaned. Her clit was swollen and hard. Paige licked a circle around it, then braced herself, gripping Seren's butt, and dove deeper. The sound of the water pelting their bodies was no match for the sounds Seren made.

Seren thrust her hips rhythmically, murmuring "don't stop" again and again. She had no intention of stopping. She'd never been so hungry for a woman. Never wanted to make anyone come as much as she did now. She wanted to lavish everything she had on Seren.

Seren's grip on her shoulders tightened and Paige felt her own body tense as if she were the one cresting. The moans grew louder and Seren thrust into her with more force.

"Oh, yes. *Yes.*"

One more stroke of her tongue and Seren's orgasm hit. Paige held her place, tongue still cornering Seren's clit. Seren shuddered, clenching her legs, and satisfaction swept through Paige.

Seren shuddered again, then stumbled back a step. Paige stood up fast, her arms encircling Seren's body. "I've got you."

Seren sank against her, dropping her head onto Paige's shoulder. "Fuck me. Are you good at everything you do?"

"No…This one time I tried to teach water aerobics."

Seren laughed. "Thanks for that reminder."

"Thanks for letting me go down on you. I've been wanting it for a while."

"You've been wanting it?" Seren tilted her head. Her eyelashes were wet and water dripped down her forehead. "I'm not going to tell you how many times I've thought of you as I've touched myself these past two weeks."

Paige swallowed. How could she want her all over again so soon? "You did, huh?"

"Mm. Remember, I'm not telling you."

Paige didn't need the details. Seren, wet and satisfied in her arms, was enough for her to have plenty to think of later. "Think we're clean enough to go to bed?"

"If I say no, would you do what you just did all over again?"

"Happily."

"I wish I could handle it twice, but I can barely stand at the moment." Seren took a shaky breath. "A bed is a good idea."

Paige leaned close and met Seren's lips. Waiting until Seren was ready for more wasn't going to be easy.

Seren pulled back from the kiss. "Will you spend the night?"

Music to her ears.

"I might need you to come back tomorrow night as well."

Paige found Seren's hand and brought it to her lips. She kissed her knuckles lightly. "Whatever you need."

# CHAPTER THIRTY

*Whatever you need.* Seren had to steady herself when Paige kissed her again. They'd been playfully bantering but she'd felt Paige's seriousness in that moment. She considered saying something to lighten things, but she hadn't. Instead, she'd let Paige hold her gaze and everything shifted in that moment. Paige had kissed her as if she knew, as if she could guess how she'd sent Seren into a freefall of emotions with one simple sentence, and that she wasn't going to let the moment pass without claiming her part in it.

It wasn't what Paige had said, though, so much as what she wanted to offer in exchange. Despite how many times she'd told herself she wouldn't date, and then that she'd only keep it casual, she was ready to give Paige anything and everything. And this time she wasn't convinced it was only her hormones talking.

She stepped out of the shower, letting Paige take a moment to rinse off and giving her mind a moment to recalibrate. The flickering candle made her reflection waver in the bathroom mirror, but for the first time in a long time, she liked what she saw. She looked…sexy. Maybe it was only the effects of the orgasm she'd sorely needed. *Afterglow.*

She'd only had sex with three women before Paige—not a lot considering she was thirty-eight. The number of times she'd orgasmed during sex, though, compared to the number of times her lovers had tried to get her off, was completely disproportionate. Basically, she assumed she wouldn't get off and was rarely wrong. But this time she'd known it was going to be different.

As soon as Paige kissed her, she realized that *she* was different with Paige. She'd let Paige kiss her first. And she'd consciously relaxed when Paige held her. Paige made it easy to drop her guard.

Still, she'd figured she wouldn't orgasm the first time. Something in her head always seemed to stop the flow of energy. But with Paige, the brakes that usually came on while having sex didn't get engaged.

One orgasm, of course, didn't mean anything. Maybe Paige wouldn't get her off again. She wrapped a towel around her and set out a clean one for Paige. Maybe she should tell her as much. *Fair warning, but I rarely come so easy.* Or so hard.

The shower stopped and Paige stepped out, flush from the hot water and deliciously naked. With one look, arousal pushed past all other thoughts. Good thing she had no plans of doing anything other than having more sex tonight.

"Everything okay?" Paige asked.

Seren nodded. Think—she told her brain—about something besides how much you want her hands on you again. "Do you want something to drink? Or something to eat?" As soon as she said it, she felt her cheeks get hot. Her question was innocent enough, but with it she'd seemed to acknowledge they had unfinished business that she was eager to get to. At least the candlelight would hide a blush.

"No thanks." Paige rubbed the towel over her skin, missing half the wet spots, then hung it on the shower door. "Don't let me stop you if you want a snack. It's been a while since we ate dinner."

Seren couldn't think of eating. Not now. "I'm good."

"I know you are." Paige stepped forward and wrapped her arms around Seren's waist. "Very good."

Seren had enough composure to roll her eyes though her heart was racing. The towel she'd wrapped around herself blocked Paige's skin from touching hers, but she could feel the pressure of Paige's hands on her hips. She shifted forward, wanting to push herself onto Paige and half desperate at the need in her body. She'd already gotten off. What was wrong with her?

"You were going to show me your bedroom."

"I was."

Paige ran a finger along the top edge of the towel, sending a shiver through Seren. "Then again, we could stay right here…" As her voice trailed, Paige bent her head and kissed Seren's neck.

Seren didn't hold back her moan.

"You saying right here is good?" Paige waited a beat. "I think so too." She loosened the place where the towel had been tucked in, and then as soon as it gaped stepped forward to press herself fully against Seren's body.

Paige's breasts brushed Seren's and their hips thrust together. "Here is nice."

Paige stroked up Seren's side and then slowly made her way down again, kissing her as she did. She pushed Seren back a step until her butt was against the sink, then she kissed her another time, asking her to open up and diving her tongue inside as she moved her hand from Seren's hip to her center. Her fingers brushed over the folds like a promise.

"You want it right here?"

Seren managed a nod.

"I thought so."

She gasped when Paige entered her. To say she was ready was an understatement. Everything Paige had done in the shower had left her trembling to have something inside. And yet it felt even better than she'd imagined.

Paige moved one finger, then two, into her. Slow firm strokes with one hand while she kept the other wrapped around Seren, holding her in place.

Seren felt her body ease open for Paige. She didn't know when she'd started to rock against Paige's hand, but she was—hard and fast, as if that could communicate exactly how much she wanted it. "Oh, god."

Paige increased her speed, spreading Seren more and going deeper with each thrust. She kissed Seren's neck again, then sucked the tip of her earlobe into her mouth. As she let it slip out, she whispered, "I want you to come so hard on me."

"I don't usually orgasm," she said between panting breaths. She loved how hard Paige was working her. "With people I don't know. I don't usually…" She couldn't finish.

"You know me." Paige whispered the words, then grazed Seren's neck with her teeth. When she thrust again, her thumb pressed into Seren's clit.

Her center pulsed with pleasure. "More." She wasn't used to wanting more, to needing to be filled, and she felt almost embarrassed by her desires. But she could feel how much Paige wanted her. Wanted to be fucking her.

Paige kissed her again, murmuring a promise to give her everything she could take, and slid in another finger. When she pumped again, Seren felt a flood rush over. She would have staggered if Paige hadn't been holding her.

But Paige didn't slow down. Her hand drove in and out faster, and all Seren could do was hold on. She was pinned—her backside pushed back against the vanity and her legs spread. She couldn't move even if she'd wanted to. Not that she wanted to do anything that would stop what was happening. She wrapped her arms tighter around Paige, loving the feel of her shoulders and naked back, loving that Paige had taken over completely.

*This. Yes. This.* This was exactly what she wanted. How long had she waited to be fucked like this?

She knew she was going to come. Like the last time, her body clearly had every intention of going all the way. *Why not?* The thought almost made her smile, but she was panting too hard. The climax was definitely coming. She could feel it building every time Paige thrust into her, every time Paige's thumb roughly coursed over her engorged clit.

She bucked harder, sinking down so she could feel more pressure when Paige's fingers dove into her and letting Paige take more of her weight. She loved that Paige could hold her up. That it was nothing to her.

"You like it rough."

Paige wasn't asking. She knew. And that knowing, even more than the fact that she'd said it aloud, pushed Seren's desire into the stratosphere.

"More." Her voice broke on the one word. Could she take more?

Paige drove into her again and she lost all control. She felt the orgasm burst between her legs and then race through her. She squeezed her thighs together, blindly riding the climax, and relying on Paige to keep her standing. Nerves fired from her toes to her fingertips and the rhythmic tightening of her center didn't ease. She wanted to beg Paige not to move her hand, but she couldn't speak. She was spent.

Paige found her lips. Her kiss was like a caress. After her lips, she kissed Seren's cheek, her forehead, then her neck before returning to her lips right as she pulled out her fingers. Seren's clit pulsed and she gripped Paige's shoulders as an aftershock rattled her.

"You're amazing." Paige kissed her again. "How many times will you let me do that to you?"

"That might be all I can handle." *For now.* But Seren knew, as unbelievable as it was, that she'd want Paige again soon.

# CHAPTER THIRTY-ONE

Seren made Paige step out of the bathroom while she peed, suddenly demure. Paige nearly said that she didn't need to be, but she got the feeling they were already in territory that was new for Seren.

She waited in the dark hallway, wondering if they'd gone too far too fast, but then Seren came out and immediately reached for her hand. It was only a few steps from the bathroom to the bedroom, but Paige liked that Seren wanted to stay close.

Energy seemed to reverberate between them when they entered the bedroom. Seren didn't turn on the lights. Instead, she found another candle. It took her a minute to find a match, but Paige's eyes adjusted quickly. Since there were no drapes, a faint light from the night sky gave a quiet calm to the space.

After lighting the candle, Seren set it on the nightstand. She turned down the bedcovers and looked back at Paige. "I'm a little embarrassed that I told you I don't usually orgasm with new people and then came hard two times in a row."

"You came hard, huh?"

"I'm sorry, did you not notice?" Seren's sarcasm was subtle. "I don't think I could have come any harder."

"That sounds like a challenge."

Seren pursed her lips. "I was hoping I'd get a turn with you."

"Hmm. By the way, you're really sexy in a towel. Ever consider wearing that instead of regular clothes?"

"I'll think about it." She exhaled as if trying to let go of whatever was holding her back.

Paige wanted to say something more to reassure but she couldn't think of what. "You know we don't have to—"

"You know how I told you that you were the first person I've had sex with since I got pregnant? Part of me was a little nervous I'd pee on you."

Paige laughed. "Okay. Anything else you want to tell me?"

Seren shook her head but then added, "I've been really horny."

"Worked out well for me."

"It did. But I think even if I weren't pregnant, my body would like how you fuck me."

Paige chuckled. "Thank you. Is there a *but* coming?"

"No buts. I just thought you should know. Well. Also…I had to get tested for STDs before I got pregnant and I was negative for everything."

"I'm negative too." Paige realized she should have volunteered that info earlier and wondered if maybe some of Seren's apprehension came from that. "I got tested a few months after my ex and I broke up and haven't been with anyone since."

"You were waiting to find me." She batted her eyelashes as if to make sure that Paige knew she was mostly joking.

"I was." Paige smiled. "And you might as well know I think you're way sexier than anyone I've ever been with."

"Thank you for telling me that. I didn't need to know, but I like knowing it anyway. Should I ask how many I was up against in this little competition?"

"Do you want to know?"

Seren hesitated, then shook her head. "I'm thinking it's more than three. That's how many people I've been with. And I've never had a fling before—not that this is exactly a fling, but—"

"I know. We can't be serious. I'm going to try not to, but I can't promise I won't get attached. I like you a lot. But no matter what happens, I know we're not making any commitments." She exhaled. "And, yeah, I've slept with more than three women. But in my defense, most of those were flings in college. I had some friends on the soccer team."

Seren raised an eyebrow. "That's your excuse? Soccer?"

"It was a crazy time in my life. There were a lot of... opportunities?" She shook her head. "Anyway. I'd like to say I've matured. Anything else we should tell each other?"

"I think we've covered a lot of ground. I mean, not as much as you did in college."

Paige chuckled at Seren's jab. "I really have matured."

"If I'd known you in college, I probably would have tried for you too." She came over to where Paige stood. "There is one more little thing I need to ask."

"Anything."

"Are you the kind of top who wants to give me rules before I touch you?"

Paige opened and closed her mouth, more surprised by Seren's question than anything else that night. She noticed Seren's lips subtly turn up at the corners. "I don't, I mean I'm not—"

"Are you going to tell me you're not really a top?"

"Well, no. I mean, I am. And I'm not going to tell you I'm not."

"Didn't think so." Seren's knowing smile was sexy as hell.

"I don't have rules. That's what I was going to say."

"You sure about that?"

"Rules make it sound like I'm an asshole." Paige knew she was caught. "Yeah, I like to be the one calling the shots, but I can back down if you want me to. And maybe I do like to be the one getting you off and not the other way around, but..."

"Uh-huh. Toppy." Seren laughed. "I've never had sex with someone quite as toppy as you. I have to admit I like it."

"Toppy, huh?" Paige swallowed when Seren stepped closer.

"If you'll let me, I'd like to make you as satisfied as you made me." She started to reach for Paige but stopped herself. When she met Paige's gaze there was no question that she wanted permission. "But I want to play by your rules."

Arousal roared through Paige. She held her breath as Seren brushed a fingertip over the back of her hand. Seren's touch was so light every nerve seemed to pay attention. She watched Seren's ascent from her hand up her forearm and past her elbow. When Seren reached her biceps, she wondered if she could possibly be any more turned-on by something so subtle as a single slow stroke.

Seren traced Paige's fingers, stopping when she got to the middle finger. "I thought sleeping with you would be a bad idea. Me being pregnant and the timing and all of that. Then I told myself, okay, one time probably won't hurt. Now I want to go through your phone and get rid of every other woman's number so you'll only have me to call when you're horny."

"Go right ahead." Paige sucked in a breath when Seren lightly caressed her forearm. She knew what she was doing with her hands, and Paige couldn't wait to feel them other places.

"I keep thinking of all the things I'd like to do with you...but I'm not sure what you'll let me do."

Paige touched Seren's chin, tilting her face up to kiss her lips. She slid her hand behind Seren's neck, pulling her close. She didn't let up on the kissing as she guided Seren to the bed. They fell back on the mattress, still pressed together. When Paige's thigh brushed Seren's middle she felt her wetness, and the urge to run her fingers through it was hard to ignore. But she wanted to prove that she didn't always have to be the one on top. She rolled onto her back, pulling Seren with her.

Seren shifted between her legs and murmured her approval.

"See, I can be on the bottom too," Paige murmured, pushing up on her elbows to kiss Seren's lips again.

Seren pulled back and laughed. "You literally pulled me on top of you. And put me right between your legs. That move"—she tapped Paige's chest—"is super toppy."

"Super?" Paige grinned. "But if I like you between my legs, and I'm technically not on top. That's not toppy, right?"

"Wrong." Seren shifted, trailing kisses down Paige's chest. She reached Paige's belly, kissed her navel, and then looked up. She held Paige's gaze for a moment, then bent her head and kissed just above Paige's trimmed hair. She looked up again. "You're still toppy. You want to know why?"

Paige swallowed. It took everything to ignore the impulse to push Seren's head between her legs and tell her to lick. "Why?"

"Because right now you want to tell me what to do." Seren brushed another kiss right at Paige's hairline. She turned her head and kissed Paige's right upper thigh. Strands of her hair brushed over Paige's pulsing center. "Doesn't matter where you are," she continued. "Pinning me against the sink in my own bathroom or lying on my bed like you own it." She shifted and kissed Paige's left thigh, then slid her hands under Paige's legs. "You know you're the one in charge." She parted her lips, ready to take Paige into her mouth, but then looked up and met Paige's gaze again. "Are you going to tell me to suck you off or not?"

The phrase alone—so different from "eat you out" but no less crass—made Paige want to say yes, but the way Seren asked the question was what really tipped the scales. Knowing how much Seren wanted to do it made her want to oblige. And the truth was, she'd never wanted it more. She pushed up her hips, bumping into Seren's chin.

"Suck me off."

As soon as Seren's tongue was on her, Paige felt her orgasm banging against the gates. She wouldn't be able to hold it off for long. She threaded her fingers through Seren's loose locks, loving how the gold caught the candlelight. Seren was gorgeous. All of her. But maybe especially her mouth.

Paige heard her own moan as if it belonged to someone else. So full of need. How long had she been turned-on? Hours. Days. Weeks.

She could feel how much Seren wanted to please her. Licking and sucking and showing no sign of slowing down. But she wasn't used to lying on her back not doing anything. Every other time she'd had sex with someone, she hadn't been comfortable not doing *something*. Then again, she'd never felt like anyone wanted to satisfy her quite as much as Seren wanted it. Maybe not doing anything was precisely what she needed to do for Seren.

She tried to relax but found herself thrusting into Seren's mouth. At first it was subtle, but then she noticed her hips setting a rhythm that Seren matched. She caressed the side of Seren's face, outlining her cheek and tracing her jawbone. When she cupped Seren's chin, pushing herself more firmly into Seren's mouth, Seren gulped and then upped her tongue-lashing. The low-level happy buzz turned to a tingly sensation, and Paige realized an orgasm wasn't completely off the table. "Don't stop," she murmured.

Seren's gaze flitted up to hers. God, she was as turned-on by this as Paige was. She dipped her head and sucked Paige into her mouth again. Tongue strokes alternated with kisses and clit-sucking in a dizzying pattern that Paige didn't try to keep up with. Seren's building speed matched her mounting climax.

*Fuck.* She wanted to savor it. She wanted to memorize the sight of Seren, between her legs, her hair cascading everywhere, her arms wrapped around her thighs as if she needed to hold on to her.

Seren didn't slow down when Paige pumped her hips faster. She didn't stop licking either. She seemed to want every drop of cum.

Paige pushed into Seren's mouth again, feeling her control give way. One more thrust and her climax hit. She trembled, tensed, then remembered Seren between her legs. She didn't want to hurt her, but damn... Seren's tongue was still on her clit. Another wave rolled through her and she couldn't fight it.

"Come here." She pulled herself away from Seren's mouth and reached for her.

Seren moved into her arms. She draped her body over Paige's and sighed with obvious satisfaction.

"You're happy with yourself, aren't you?" Paige kissed Seren's cheek lightly. "You should be."

"I wanted to please you."

"Well." Paige was spent and words weren't coming easy. "You succeeded..." The drowsiness was edging on sleep. "I don't think I can move."

"Good. I like you in my bed. Right here." Seren shifted off Paige's chest and then curled against her. "I've been looking for a body pillow."

"Is that what I am?" Paige tried to open her eyes, but her lids were too heavy. She should have warned Seren how quickly she nodded off after sex.

"Do you mind?"

"Mm...mind? Not at all."

Seren's arm wrapped around her chest tighter. One of her legs was draped over both of Paige's, and she nestled her head in the hollow between Paige's neck and her shoulder.

"I'd like to keep you," Seren whispered.

Paige heard the words, but she was so close to sleep. Was she supposed to respond? "Okay. I can do that."

Seren brushed a kiss on her lips. "I love that you're so agreeable. You'd probably agree to anything right now, wouldn't you?"

Anything.

# CHAPTER THIRTY-TWO

As soon as she opened her eyes, Seren realized she was still hugging Paige. She also realized that Paige was wide awake. "I'm sorry. You probably want to move, don't you?" She let go of the viselike grip she'd held on Paige apparently all night and rolled onto her back. For as awake as she'd felt last night, it had been late and her body reminded her that she needed nine hours of sleep now at least.

"You still tired?"

Paige sounded far too awake. Seren didn't open her eyes but she shook her head. Okay, it wasn't completely the truth. She wanted to be awake even. She wanted to offer to make breakfast. Coffee. Of course, she only had decaf.

"An alarm went off. I'm not sure if it's important."

"Oh. Dammit." She'd set the alarm yesterday—after sleeping until ten. She hadn't wanted to miss water aerobics twice. "I didn't want to be late to water aerobics. I've got a crush on the teacher."

"You know my mom's back to teaching, right?"

Seren laughed. "I forgot. I'm sorry the alarm woke you."

"I was already awake." Paige brought Seren's hand up to her lips. Her kiss was gentle.

"I don't want it to be morning, but I really have to pee." She paused. "If I go to the bathroom, will you stay here so I can come right back to this spot?"

Paige smiled. "Yes. Go."

Seren didn't take long, and Paige was indeed exactly where she'd left her. She slipped under the covers, shivered once, then curled against Paige. "I love my new body pillow."

Paige chuckled and wrapped an arm around Seren. They lay together for a few minutes, but Seren could tell Paige wasn't relaxing.

She couldn't exactly keep Paige captive in her bed all day. Probably she had things she wanted to do. "Do you want to get up?"

"No. But I would like to give you a massage."

"I give other people massages."

"Sometimes you could use a massage too, right?"

"Well, yes, but…"

"Would you take one from me then?" Paige waited for her nod. The bed creaked as she moved into position. "On your back. Please."

"You know you don't have to say please."

"I know."

Paige's smile was smug. And sexy. "Fuck. Okay." She shifted from her side to her back, willing herself to relax. When Paige straddled her hips, she tried to ignore a thrum of desire. Ignoring it got a lot harder as Paige's center pressed against hers.

Paige leaned down and kissed her lips lightly. "I'll go slow and you can tell me to stop anytime."

She breathed out as soon as she felt Paige's hands on her shoulders. She should have expected that Paige would have a nice touch, given how thoroughly pleased her body had been last night. But it was still a surprise. Strong, steady pressure that eased over the sensitive spots. She let herself rock into the kneading, moving under Paige's direction. After working on her neck and shoulders, Paige told her to roll over.

"You don't need to give me a full massage. After last night, I feel well taken care of."

"Good. Now roll over. Unless I'm not doing a good job and you want me to stop."

Seren sighed. "You're doing a very good job, but…"

"Then roll over." Paige arched an eyebrow. "Do I need to be more toppy?"

Seren smiled. "No. That was plenty toppy." She rolled onto her belly, pushing her pillow out of the way as she tried to convince herself she could enjoy this pleasure the same as the two orgasms Paige had gifted to her. But even as Paige's hands kneaded up and down her back, she couldn't stop from thinking the roles were usually reversed. How many times had she given a massage to a lover the morning after? "I'm the one who's supposed to give massages."

"You get massages too, right?"

"Well…" Not from her past girlfriends. Or if they ever tried to reciprocate it was always a half-hearted sort of gentle rub. Nothing like the massage Paige was giving her now. "I trade massages with other therapists."

"I'm sure I'm not doing as good a job as they could."

"You're more than decent."

"More than decent, huh?" Paige worked a pressure point on Seren's lower back. "I did take a class once."

"A couples' massage class?"

Paige's hands stalled momentarily before she answered. "Yeah. And now I'm thinking I probably shouldn't have mentioned that."

"With Connie?"

"Someone else." Paige worked her way up either side of Seren's spine then slowly down again. "It was a long time ago. College."

It didn't really matter who Paige had dated, but she was curious anyway. Curious why the past relationships hadn't worked. And curious who had ended things. "Given how good you are with your hands, I'm guessing you were the one to end things and not her."

Paige didn't answer, and Seren knew she'd guessed correctly. She was distracted, though, by Paige's hands. She'd found the tense spots at her hips that Seren always had to stretch. When she felt the release, she shifted to rubbing Seren's legs.

"That woman in college…I still feel bad about our breakup. I told her I had to get good grades. I wanted to get into vet school and I couldn't just have sex all the time."

Seren looked over her shoulder. Paige seemed genuinely sorry at the admission. "She was crushed?"

Paige frowned. "She was. It still bothers me. I mean, I don't think about it all the time but I was an asshole. I thought we had an understanding. I thought we were only fucking around. Her understanding was that we were going to get married."

"Oh."

"Yeah. We were only twenty-two. I figured we were on the same page about things not being serious. Besides, I didn't think I was the marrying type back then either. I certainly wasn't ready to get tied down."

"Metaphorically?"

Paige opened her mouth, clearly surprised, and Seren winked. "Can't blame me for asking. I'd like to know all of your skills and interests."

"I wasn't that adventurous in college. I don't even know what she saw in me."

"I do." Seren met Paige's eyes briefly, her heart unexpectedly racing. She needed to crack a joke to ease the sudden tension, but she couldn't think of anything to say. How was she already getting so attached? "Do you still know her?"

"No. I sent her an apology email a few years ago. She wrote back telling me to go fuck myself." Paige bit the edge of her lip. "So I figure we're on good terms now."

Seren smiled. "Definitely."

"If you want to relax again, I'm not done with your massage."

Seren rested her cheek on the mattress and closed her eyes. She thought of Paige's ex and wondered if the woman was married. Wondered if Paige truly wasn't the marrying type or simply hadn't found someone she wanted to spend her life with. And then her mind skipped to wondering if Paige was the one for her. She chastised her mind a moment later. She wanted to simply enjoy the moment. This moment. Paige's hands on her. Nowhere to be, nothing to do but relax.

Letting out a deep sigh, she finally eased completely into Paige's touch. Minutes passed, and she felt tension she didn't know she had slip away. Except for the nagging realization that she needed to eat soon, falling back asleep could be a very real possibility. She'd like to stay in bed all day. Or at least all morning. She opened her eyes, studying the light coming in through the window.

"I don't want to stop this massage, but if I don't eat a little something right after I wake up, I'll get sick. I've got a granola bar on my nightstand."

Paige's hands stopped. She kissed Seren's shoulder and then shifted away, reaching for the granola bar.

Seren sat up when Paige handed it to her. She stared at the foil-wrapped bar for a moment and then ripped it open. As unappetizing as granola bars were now, vomiting was worse. "I could make us some breakfast after this."

"I'm up for whatever." Paige glanced at the clock. "Actually, I should probably check my messages before I make any promises. I'm on call today." She got out of bed and then looked around the floor as she ran a hand through her tousled hair. She looked sexier than should be legal first thing in the morning.

"Wondering where you left your pants?"

"How'd you know?"

"Cause your phone was in your back pocket. I felt it when I was trying to strip you last night. And you left your pants in the middle of the hallway."

"Don't know why they ended up there." Paige smirked.

"I do." Seren forced down another swallow of granola and chocolate. "I'd really like an omelet. Or at least toast."

"And then after we can come back to bed for other things?"

"I like your one-track mind." Seren reached for her water glass and took a big swig. Even though she'd already peed, she felt the urge again. She got out of bed, snagged her bathrobe, and then briefly kissed Paige as she passed.

The rest of her body wanted more than a kiss. After a good look at Paige in the daylight without any clothes hiding her muscles, she was ready to hand herself over for another good fucking. It was crass but true.

She'd no sooner sat down on the toilet than Cymbal pushed open the bathroom door, his black tail held straight up like a lightning rod. He beelined right to her and rubbed against her leg. His throaty purr made not giving him at least a chin scratch impossible. "Hi, you."

It was little surprising that he was making an appearance despite there being a stranger in the house. When she'd lived in New York, and Chicago too, he'd always hid when she had company, and now since he had a cat door and could come and go as he pleased, she hadn't figured on seeing him.

Paige's footsteps on the other side of the door made Cymbal glance that way but he didn't run to hide. Instead, he headbutted Seren's leg. She finished peeing and wiped, then after washing, reached down to scoop him up. "Is this your way of telling me Paige isn't too scary?"

"Who are you talking to?" Paige asked from the hallway.

Seren toed open the door farther. "Just some guy who wandered in."

Paige smiled. She stepped halfway into the bathroom and then leaned against the doorjamb. "I like your taste in guys. What's his name?"

"This is Cymbal."

"I finally get to meet your cat. He's handsome."

"He is. I love him—when he lets me. When I lived in the city he had to stay inside, but he was born feral and always missed it. Now he comes and goes as he pleases, and I'm sure he doesn't think I own him."

Paige held out her index finger. Instead of trying to push out of Seren's arms to get away from a stranger, he turned his head and sniffed. His purr didn't falter. Paige took a step closer and scratched his cheek. Still, he didn't bolt. "Apparently you pass the Cymbal test."

Paige lifted a shoulder. "Cats like me. Especially black cats."

"I'm still impressed Cymbal likes you." She put him down, wondering if Paige did have a way with cats or if Cymbal was only being social because his food bowl was empty. She washed her hands again. She'd been worried about keeping Cymbal when she got pregnant, but her doctor had told her handwashing was enough to keep from catching any diseases he might pass.

She looked back at Paige, thinking to ask if she'd found her phone. Paige had dropped into a squat and Cymbal strode right up to her. She made a purring meow sound and he gave his characteristic tiny mew in response. Fifteen pounds of solid alley cat power and he had the most unimpressive meow.

"Oh, man, that's adorable." Paige gave him a head-to-tail stroke. "Can you meow again please?"

As if he understood, Cymbal promptly responded with another pathetic but cute cry. When Paige answered, Cymbal pushed against her hand, purring louder than ever.

"You speak cat?"

"Remember? They teach it at the vet school."

Seren smiled. "Right." She meowed to Cymbal all the time, too, but she'd never admitted it to anyone. "I guess I shouldn't be surprised you have a way with cats. You are a vet. But I keep thinking you're a cow vet."

Paige shook her head. "Seventy percent small animal, thirty percent large. That was the deal when I agreed to work at my friend's clinic. I didn't want to give up working with farm animals, but I needed a break. And I missed working with dogs and cats."

Paige pet Cymbal again, then stood. She brushed against Seren as she pointed past her to the toilet. "I gotta pee too."

"Oh, sure." Seren stepped out of the way, her clit twitching at simply the feel of Paige close. *Ridiculous.* Her raging hormones were turning her into a wilting maiden.

She stepped out of the bathroom, giving Paige a moment, and went to check on Cymbal's food bowl. It was half full of kibble, which meant Cymbal had simply wanted attention. And hadn't been scared off. *One more point for Paige.* How many more points could she rack up and still stay in the casual category?

As much as she wanted to go right back to bed for more of the casual fuck part, her stomach was fully awake now. She popped two slices of bread into the toaster and got out some blackberry jam and aged cheddar. It wasn't a high-class breakfast, but she'd happily make Paige a proper meal if she wanted it later.

"I've got some bad news." Paige had her pants on now but still no shirt.

"Do you have to work?"

"Not exactly." She held out her phone for Seren.

Seren quickly read the text message. She tried not to feel let down, but by the time she reached the end, it was unavoidable. Paige's mom had overdone it at the water aerobics class yesterday and couldn't get out of bed now. She needed Paige to teach. Beyond that, she'd gone on a tirade about how much her butt hurt. "Your mom is good with colorful language."

"She is. It's a miracle I don't cuss constantly being raised by her." Paige sighed. "I knew she was pushing too much teaching yesterday. She tweaked her back when she broke her tailbone and I think that's acting up more now."

"I'd be happy to give her a massage. I work with folks who have injuries all the time."

"You sure you want my mom as a client? You haven't met her yet."

"I like to help where I can. You of all people should understand that." Seren smiled to let Paige know she meant the niggling as a compliment. "I think I can handle your mom."

The toast popped, and Seren looked from the toaster to Paige. "I don't want to whine, but I really was looking forward to morning sex." From the text exchange, she knew Paige's plan was to head home, get her mom breakfast, and then head over to the pool to teach water aerobics.

"So was I. Any chance I could get a rain check?"

"There's a very good chance." Seren stepped forward and ran her hand along Paige's belt. "Aside from the sex, I was looking forward to giving you a massage in return for the one you gave me."

"I'll take a rain check on that too. You busy this afternoon?"

"I'd definitely be free for you." The possibility of having an entire afternoon with Paige was enough to get Seren's clit paying attention all over again. Plenty of time for a massage and other things. "I could probably think of a more clever way to ask this, but I'm just going to come right out and say it. Do you own a strap-on?"

Paige's lips turned up ever so slightly. "I do."

The almost smile and cocky look made Seren want to beg Paige to fuck her again before she left. "Maybe you could bring it with you when come back later?"

"I could arrange that. I'm happy to know you like strap-ons."

"I like them but haven't had a lot of…willing partners."

"I'm very willing."

"Good." Her clit pulsed again. "It's going to be hard paying attention in water aerobics knowing what you'll be doing to me after."

"Hard for you?" Paige shook her head. "For the rest of the morning, I'm going to be thinking about one thing." She shifted closer and kissed Seren's lips. "One thing and one thing only."

# CHAPTER THIRTY-THREE

After Paige left, Seren tidied up and showered. She was so distracted thinking of what Paige would bring later that she considered getting out her sex toys for a quick self-love session. But nothing she had was ever quite right, and imagining Paige wearing a strap-on made her own toys seem even more inadequate. Masturbating was nice, but holding the dildo herself wasn't the same as being fucked by someone wearing it. Unfortunately, she could count on one hand the number of times she'd had the experience.

Natalie, who she'd dated in college, had been too nervous to try toys. Then she'd met Deion. Deion liked toys but wanted Seren to be the one wearing the strap-on. She'd tried to get into it but couldn't wrap her head around being the one with a cock. Which was silly since plenty of femmes rocked strap-ons—she'd read all about it. Still, wearing one didn't feel right.

Then came Addie. She'd insisted Seren wouldn't need anything but her tongue. To be fair, she was very good with her tongue. But sometimes Seren wanted more, and Addie hadn't wanted to talk about options. When she'd finally convinced Addie to try it, the night had been, well, unmemorable. They'd tried a few more times, but she'd decided that unless both people were into it, and the giver and receiver roles felt right to them, the idea of strap-on sex was better than the actuality.

Still, she'd asked Paige anyway even if maybe it was too soon to be testing boundaries. Why? Because she wanted strap-on sex more than ever? Even as that answer occurred to her, she knew it wasn't the whole truth. She felt comfortable with Paige. More comfortable even than she'd felt with women she'd known a lot longer. And she'd known instinctively that Paige would be into it.

From Paige's confident answer, Seren got the idea that she'd had plenty of experience. She couldn't wait to find out how experience changed things. Now all she had to do was get through water aerobics and patiently wait for Paige to show up on her doorstep. She nearly laughed. If a fortune teller had told her a month ago that she'd soon be sleeping with a strap-on-wearing water aerobics instructor, she'd have told them they needed to get their crystal ball checked. And yet, here she was.

In her tidying up, she'd found her cell phone and realized the charge had run out. After her shower, she went back to check it and saw a list of text messages from Leslie. Something about important news and wanting to run something by her. Rather than read through all the texts, Seren rang her back. "Hey you. What's up?"

"I thought maybe you lost your phone again."

"Nope. Just died. It's been charging. Everything okay?"

"Better than okay. Did you read my texts? I've been trying to get in touch with Paige since last night. Called her twice but she didn't answer."

"Have you texted her?"

"No. I wanted to tell her the news directly. The Landrys accepted her offer."

"Seriously? Oh, she's gonna be thrilled." Honestly, she was too. *Baby cows.*

"It's weird because she usually gets right back to me. Do you think maybe an emergency came up and she had to work?"

Seren felt a pinch of guilt. "Technically she did work last night."

"You've talked to her?"

"We went on a date."

"Oh, right!"

A very good date. Followed by the most satisfying night she'd had in pretty much ever.

"I'm sorry she had to work. Did your night get cut short then?"

"It's kind of a long story."

"That's all you're going to tell me? Come on, I'm single and bored over here. What'd you two do?"

"She took me on a bike ride."

"I thought your bike got stolen."

"She found me a bike. Someone had trashed it but she fixed it all up. Turns out she's really into bikes." Seren wondered if she should stop there. Leslie was her best friend and she usually told her everything, but she was Paige's realtor. She decided she could share the PG parts. "We had a little picnic and then I convinced her to take me on a tour of the vet school's teaching hospital. Which is how she got pulled in to working. She delivered a calf. It was really messy but also amazing. I got to feed a baby cow. Two of them, actually."

"Okay, that sounds amazing, but more importantly—did you two finally kiss?"

Seren smiled at the memory of the first kiss. And the ones that followed. "Yes."

"Ha! Knew it would happen. Can I place a bet on when you two are sleeping together?"

"Um…"

"You already slept with her? You, who always takes it slow and who's only been with three women, got busy on your second date?"

"It was our third date if you count the time she took me to dinner so I wouldn't vomit." She laughed when Leslie groaned. "You know how horny I've been."

"How was it?"

Seren pressed her hand to her forehead when she felt her center clench at the memory of Paige dropping to her knees in the shower. Maybe things had gone faster than her usual, but she couldn't deny how good it had felt. "Everything I was hoping for." And then some.

"I'm so happy for you. Now, on a related but separate note. Does Paige have any friends you could introduce me to?"

Leslie was mostly joking, but the question gave her pause. She wasn't the type to run a background check on a potential date, but she usually knew more about them before sex was part of the picture. "I don't know her friends." Did Connie count? "I don't even know if she has any siblings. All I really know is that she lives with her mom. And her dad died a few years ago."

"And she's a vet."

"That, and she's definitely slept with more women than I have. Do you think I let things move too fast?" She'd paced from her bedroom to the living room and only stopped when Cymbal threaded between her legs. She reached down to pet him but straightened a moment later. "I feel like I know her but maybe not well enough? I've never slept with anyone who I didn't think would be long term, you know? But there's no way I can think about long term this time."

"Slow down. You're going into one of your worry spirals."

Leslie wasn't wrong. She sank down on the couch. "The problem is I like her."

"That's not a problem, you know. You just need to relax and enjoy this."

"And not get too attached. What if this is all a mistake?" Seren dropped her head back against the cushions. "Fuck. These hormones. If she were here right now, I'd be spreading my legs even while telling myself I'm in too deep already."

"As much as I want to tease you for that, I'm gonna be serious. This with Paige, whatever it is, isn't a mistake. It's what you need. You know how your mom named you Serendipity? Good things happen to you. Usually things you need right at that moment. But then you go out of your way to sabotage yourself and mess it up."

"I wouldn't say that I sabotage—"

"It's not really your fault. At least not completely. The stars align when you aren't paying any attention. Then you freak out and run in the other direction. I'm not going to give you a list, but it's happened over and over again. And you know it."

Seren sighed. Her gaze fell to the picture on the coffee table of her mom giving her a sideways hug. The shot was taken the summer before last. When her mom had no idea she had cancer. They'd gone to Florida for a long weekend. "*Let's take a trip just for fun*," her mother had said—knowing she needed it. If only her mom was still here. "I wish I had more say on when the stars aligned. I want to talk to my mom. I want to tell her I'm pregnant. And tell her I met someone."

"Ah, sweetie. I'm sure she already knows. Remember? She picked Paige out and sent her to you in a white pickup truck."

Seren took a shaky breath and looked up at the ceiling, hoping to hold back the tears.

Leslie continued, "You know how she felt about cows. Why wouldn't she send you a cow vet? Even you have to admit it is kind of her style."

Seren laughed.

"I gotta go. Do me a favor and stop worrying. For once have fun with what the universe gives you."

As soon Leslie ended the call, Seren picked up the framed Florida picture. That day had been so carefree, so happy. "Did you send me Paige, Mom?" She shook her head. It was crazy enough to be true. "If you did, thanks. But please don't pay attention to what we do in the bedroom, okay?"

# CHAPTER THIRTY-FOUR

"How'd that bike work?"

"Great," Paige said, unplugging the stereo. "Thanks again for letting me know it was up for grabs." She hoped Rita didn't want to chat long and tried to drop that hint by hurrying as she stowed her water bottle and notebook in her day pack. "A little elbow grease goes a long way." She smiled and slung her pack over her shoulder. Before she'd gone more than a step, her attention was drawn to the water.

Seren was backing out of the pool and not looking in her direction. It didn't make a difference that they'd seen each other only a few hours ago. Or that she was going to her place later. Paige wanted her now. If only they could slip away to a quiet corner.

But Seren was in the middle of a conversation with Claia. She laughed about something Claia said as stretched out her arm to help the older woman up the stairs.

"She does have a nice butt," Rita said much too loudly. "I thought you were a breast woman, but clearly you appreciate all of her attributes."

"I wasn't checking out her butt. I was—" Technically she had let her gaze linger on Seren's butt. How could she not? Seren was dripping wet and the bathing suit hugged her ass perfectly. Before Paige could figure out an excuse, she saw Seren walking toward them.

"Everything okay?" Seren asked.

"Oh, just cheeky," Rita said, patting Seren's shoulder. She winked at Paige. "Enjoy your afternoon, you two."

As soon as the locker room door closed behind Rita, Seren turned to Paige. "What'd I miss?"

"Rita caught me checking you out. Again."

Seren laughed. "That's Rita. Always working. Should I tell her how much I like you checking me out?"

"You like it, huh?"

"Even more because I know what you'll be doing to me later." Seren's eyes sparkled. "Before I forget, did you talk to Leslie?"

"I did. The Landrys accepted my offer." She'd been thrilled at the news earlier. Now her thoughts were more interested in sex. How much she wanted Seren was almost a problem. "She told me you already know."

When Seren took a deep breath, her cleavage pushed up and it was impossible not to imagine those breasts in her hands. "I hope that's okay."

Focus. "Totally okay."

"So are you excited?"

"I am. I'm also a little distracted."

"By what?" Seren tilted her head, then smiled. "Are you thinking about what you want to do with me later?"

"Maybe. Yes."

Seren laughed. "How about a celebration dinner? I was thinking of making fish tacos."

"Sure. I can come early to help cook."

"You say you want to help, but I think you want to do other things."

Seren's coy look only made Paige hungrier. "I'd help too."

"Mm-hmm." Seren looked behind her, clearly checking to see if anyone was left on the pool deck, then met Paige's gaze. "We seem to be alone. Do you want to take advantage of that?"

Paige didn't wait to close the distance between them. When their lips met, her body's response was immediate. Heat spread through her along with a desire so strong she gripped Seren's towel, aching to pull it off.

"Ahem."

The sound of someone clearing their throat made Paige freeze. She looked past Seren and saw Claia. Sweet, ninety-something Claia, stared back wide-eyed.

Seren took a step back from Paige and forced a smile. "Hi, Claia."

"I thought you might need another Sprite."

"No, no. But thank you for checking on me." Seren glanced back at Paige and murmured, "I should go change."

"When we see each other later, I'll make up for the conversation you're about to have in the locker room."

Seren smiled. "I'm holding you to that promise."

Twenty minutes of debating whether to bring a bag or show up already attired and Paige still hadn't decided. She had, however, gone through all of her sex toys. She'd picked a new dildo—one she'd bought before breaking up with Miranda but never used—and her favorite leather harness. Once she had the o-ring adjusted and the dildo in place, she put it all on and a rush of arousal filled her body as she tightened the straps. She wrapped her hand around the shaft and her hips thrust forward almost subconsciously.

"Damn, I missed this feeling." Relationships were a lot of work, but they came with benefits. It'd been a long year of not having any reason to dress up for anyone.

She pulled her boxers on and then her jeans, spinning the dildo so the head pointed downward and the curve would be less obvious under her clothes. Her jeans were tight to zip, but she wiggled until everything fit and then stood in front of the mirror. She angled side to side, rethinking her impulse to show up already attired. The rise in her jeans was undeniable. She unzipped, dug her hand into her boxers, adjusted herself again, then rezipped her jeans and eyed her reflection. No less obvious. Then again, maybe discreet wasn't the goal.

She'd done the grocery shopping, made sure her mom was set with meals, talked with Leslie about next steps on the ranch, and even fit in a workout around a load of laundry. All that hard work meant now she could play. She hollered goodbye to her mom and grabbed her wallet and keys.

She had to unzip her pants for the drive and made a silent prayer that today would not be the day that the Davis cops were out in force. It wasn't a long drive—Seren only lived ten minutes across town—but she made sure to keep her eye on the speedometer.

When she got to Seren's she took a minute to readjust and zip up before getting out of her truck. It was a gorgeous sunny afternoon. A little warmer even then the day before. Nice enough to sit outside in lawn chairs and enjoy the sunshine.

Paige had only made it a few steps from the curb to the front door when she heard Seren call from the backyard. "Come on back. I'm watering."

Paige pushed open the side gate and looked for Seren. A flagstone path led from the side yard with the planter boxes and flowerpots to the backyard where it turned a corner. A hedge blocked the view beyond. She started down the path but stopped as soon as she'd passed the hedge. Seren was indeed watering plants. Barefoot. And otherwise only wearing a flowy sort of white cotton skirt and a bra. She looked up from her begonias and met Paige's gaze.

"Hey. How are you?"

Paige managed a nod, which wasn't much of an answer. "Good. I'm good."

Seren's lips turned up in a smile. "You sure?"

"I'm sure." Paige walked over. She eyed the early bloomers, thinking she should compliment Seren on her gardening skills. But, damn, did she want to unhook Seren's bra and let those breasts fill her hands.

"I was wearing a blouse earlier." Seren paused to point out a light blue shirt draped over a chaise lounge chair. "But it's such a nice day." She switched the nozzle, stopping the spray of water and set down the hose.

"I like your outfit."

Seren inclined her head and smiled knowingly. She clearly knew the effect she had on Paige and wasn't going to hide it.

"I like yours too." She reached out and touched Paige's collar, ostensibly fixing it, then drew a line down the buttons on Paige's untucked shirt. When Seren got to the last button, she paused for a moment. "I love knowing you're ready to fuck me."

"I thought I was coming over to help make dinner."

"Dressed like this?" Seren's hand slid lower. She traced over the curve in Paige's jeans.

"Jeans and a button-down aren't appropriate for dinner?"

"I'm thinking more about this part." Seren pushed the base of the dildo against Paige, moaning softly. "Been thinking about it for hours. I can't wait to see what you have."

"You could peek. If you want." Yes, they were outside. But Seren's fence was a six-footer and hedges blocked the neighbors on either side. Even better, there was only an empty field to the back.

Seren undid the top button of Paige's jeans, then slid down the zipper and moaned again as she ran one finger over the opening of Paige's boxers. "I didn't know you'd come over wearing it."

"Like the surprise?"

Seren's eyes said everything. Paige closed the distance between them. She wrapped her arms around Seren, bringing her into a full kiss. When Paige shifted her hips forward, she felt Seren shudder.

"I'm so ready for you," Seren murmured.

Knowing how much Seren wanted it, Paige couldn't resist a slow grind as they fell into another kiss.

"Want to go inside?"

Seren pulled back and looked around for a moment, then tilted her chin up, asking for another kiss. "No one can see us here."

Paige loved that answer. She pushed Seren's skirt up and realized only when her hands grazed over naked hips that Seren wasn't wearing underwear. She couldn't hold back her own moan. "No underwear. It's like you were just hanging out in your backyard waiting for someone to show up and fuck you."

"Maybe I was."

She moved from Seren's hips to her butt, cupping the round cheeks she'd admired earlier. It was one thing to look. But this? This was a million times better.

"I want to feel you," Seren said, working at Paige's buttons. As soon as the shirt gaped, she slipped her hands inside. Her touch sent flares through Paige. She grazed over Paige's ribs, then moved to her back, making muscles tingle with anticipation.

Between kisses, Paige reached into her boxers. She spun the dildo in the o-ring. It sprang up, angling right for Seren. When she moved against Seren, she knew the move from first to second base didn't go unnoticed. Seren stroked the shaft and Paige felt a thrill at her clit.

"I can't believe you're going to fuck me right here."

"You want it."

Seren nodded. "So much."

As much as she wanted to thrust her hips forward and push right in, the dildo wasn't small. She wanted it to feel good and she wanted Seren to be ready. Twisting Seren's skirt up in her fist, she dropped to her knees.

Seren was already wet, and her scent made Paige even more turned-on. She bent her head and slid her tongue inside. Seren moaned, gripping her shoulders. Paige worked Seren's clit until she realized how close she was to an orgasm. She pulled back and Seren whimpered.

"Not fair to tease that."

"I want to make it feel even better."

She stood and wrapped one arm around Seren, pulling her into a kiss. When she shifted her hips forward, Seren's hips met hers. The tip of the dildo parted her slit and Seren's chest heaved.

"Fuck." Seren moaned. "That's what I want."

Paige kissed Seren, a full, deep kiss that aroused every part of her. "I want you lying down." She glanced at the patio furniture. Along with the lounge chair, there was a sofa sectional plenty long enough. She grasped Seren's elbow and kissed her again as she moved her toward the sectional.

Seren sank down on the cushions. "I feel like I should be embarrassed being outside, but I'm not. I want you too much to care." She started to reach for Paige and then stopped. "What is it?"

"You're beautiful."

"That's all you have to say?" Seren's lips formed a sultry smile. She shifted up on her elbows. "You wanted me lying down. Here I am. Waiting for you."

"I know. And I like it." Paige pushed Seren's skirt up and out of the way. Seren parted her legs, letting her wetness glisten in the sunlight. The sight was intoxicating. Seren was so wet. So ready. And her need was obvious.

She touched Seren's thigh, caressed her sun-warmed skin, then pushed her legs farther apart. Seren moaned when she settled between her knees. "How slow do you want me to go?"

"Not slow at all."

Desire surged when she looked down at Seren's full breasts and her wet pink center. She clenched her jaw. Had she ever wanted someone more?

"And I might be pregnant, but you don't need to be gentle." Seren hitched up her hips, nudging the dildo. "I should rephrase. I don't want you to be gentle."

"If something hurts—"

"I'll tell you. You focus on the fucking part."

"Deal." Paige drew in a breath, then leaned down to kiss Seren. "I love how much you want this." She sank all the way in with one thrust.

Seren gasped, then cussed, then clutched Paige's forearms. "Oh, that feels good."

"Again?" Paige waited for her nod. She pulled all the way out and gave another deep stroke. Seren moved with her, shifting her grip from Paige's arms to her hips.

"You like that?"

"No." Seren licked her lips. "I love it."

Paige reached down to finger Seren's clit. She waited until Seren was pushing her hips up insistently, bumping her hand and whining with need, before she slid in again.

Seren's unchecked pleasure sounded in her ears. One long loud moan. She didn't pull out again. Instead, she started rhythmically thrusting and Seren moved with her, her cries loud enough that the neighbors had to hear.

The louder Seren was, the headier she felt. The base of the strap-on bounced against her clit, and Seren drove up her arousal with every moan.

"Fuck me. I can't keep up." Seren sagged back against the cushions. "Don't stop. You feel so good." She closed her eyes, and her lips parted.

Paige shifted and kissed her lips, still pumping her hips. She pulled back from the kiss and put her fingertip on Seren's lips. Seren sucked Paige's index finger into her mouth. Her tongue stroked the length of it before she took Paige's middle finger into her mouth as well. She held Paige's wrist and guided her fingers in and out of her lips.

Paige pulled her hand away from Seren's mouth. She'd stopped thrusting to watch Seren take her fingers but now she started again. Sliding in and out, then grinding deep to fill Seren completely. Her own clit pulsed in response. "I want to get you off."

"I probably won't," Seren said, her eyes still closed. "But I don't care. This feels so good."

Paige reached down to find Seren's clit. She rolled it between her fingers, coating it with wetness. "I'm gonna make it feel even better."

Seren nodded, her chin tipped up to the sun and her hard pink nipples on display. "I don't think that's possible."

"Oh, it is." She feathered Seren's clit, then started pumping her hips again. She wanted Seren to come hard so she remembered it. All of it. The sun on her exposed skin, her skirt pushed up above her waist, her legs spread, and being fucked so well she didn't want to move.

Seren's breathing ratcheted up as she wrapped her arms around Paige. Her hips bumped against Paige's, her rhythm getting faster. "Oh. I might come."

"I know you will," Paige murmured. She didn't let up on Seren's clit. She didn't stop with the thrusting either, even as her own body clamored for a climax. Once she was done with Seren, she'd see to her own need.

"Fuck, I'm gonna come." Seren whined the words as if she'd been fighting it.

"Wait for me." It was rare for her to get off by only fucking someone, but Seren had her right on the edge. Her body had never been more aroused.

"I can't. Can't wait." Seren tensed, and then came in a rush. She clutched Paige hard, pushing her hips up to take the full length of the strap-on.

Paige held steady pressure on Seren's clit for as long as she could, but then her own orgasm broke. She bore down on Seren, letting go and sliding into shivers of pleasure.

Seren held her, murmuring her name between kisses on Paige's neck and shoulders, seemingly indiscriminate, anywhere she could reach.

The waves rolled through Paige. Seren felt so good under her, all softness and warmth and sweat. She didn't want to move.

Couldn't move. She couldn't remember ever coming so hard. Minutes passed before she thought to worry that Seren might be uncomfortable.

When she opened her eyes, Seren's were still closed. The sight of her took Paige's breath. *It'd be so easy to fall hopelessly in love.*

Seren looked at her then. "Fuck. That was…so good."

"It was. I'm gonna come out, okay?"

Seren nodded.

As she slowly eased out, she had to push away the desire to fuck Seren all over again. Seren needed kisses, not more fucking. She placed her hand over Seren's slit, feeling a rush of protectiveness.

Seren pushed against her palm, then moaned softly. She'd closed her eyes again and every part of her looked sated. Paige rolled her hand, coating her fingers in Seren's cum. She'd made Seren this way. Wet and spent.

After a moment, she settled on Seren's body, more careful now where she placed her weight. She kissed her lightly, then shifted to the side so the dildo would be out of the way.

Seren sighed. "I could stay here forever. Right here."

"You know how I told you that Davis was basically heaven?"

"Is this when I'm supposed to say that you were right?"

"You can say it now or save it for later."

Seren smiled. "Does that mean I get you again later?"

"You could have me again now if you want."

"I can't handle more. You have no idea how hard I came." Seren reached for Paige's hand and brought it to her lips, kissing it gently. "Will you stay the night?"

"I'll stay as many nights as you want me."

# CHAPTER THIRTY-FIVE

It was a rainy Friday night and Seren was glad she was staying in. With Paige.

A little over three weeks had passed since their first date. Whether that date was over BLTs or minestrone soup was up for debate, but what wasn't in question was how seamlessly their lives had folded together. Seren didn't want to think about the seamless part mostly because she didn't want to tempt fate—which was silly considering she was the one who kept mentioning how nice it was keeping things casual and commitment free.

The only time Paige brought up the casual conversation was to joke about casual Fridays. She'd proposed Friday nights as their special together time—both because it was the time they reconnected after their week apart and because of course they kept things casual. They made dinner together, talked over the week, snuggled on the sofa, and ended the night reconnecting in bed. Seren loved it. Especially the reconnecting in bed part. But how much she loved it was beginning to feel like a problem. How long before they weren't casual? Or was it already serious?

"Dinner was delicious. Again. Thank you." Paige rinsed one of the plates and set it in the dishwasher.

"I'm getting the hang of fish tacos." The second attempt had definitely been an improvement over the first. "Then again, it might have been that perfect avocado."

Paige grinned. "You and avocados. I'm gonna get you an avocado tree one day."

"How about tomorrow?"

"I have to work."

Seren dropped her chin. "I know and I don't like it." She couldn't keep the whine out of her voice. "I've gotten used to having you all weekend."

"I'm only scheduled until two. After that, I'm yours."

Seren pursed her lips. "Can I file a complaint with whoever does your scheduling?"

"That'd be me. I scheduled this a long time ago. Before you."

"There was a time before me?" Seren gasped in mock surprise.

"It was awful. Horrible. Truly." Paige laughed. "I am sorry I have to work tomorrow." She rinsed the cutting board, sighing as she did. "I'd much rather have a lazy day here than go in for the sixth day in a row. I'm beat."

Paige always helped with dinner, but because Seren did more of the cooking and prepping tonight, she'd insisted on cleaning up after. But it was clear she was tired. Seren came up behind her and took the cutting board. "Sit down. I want to clean."

Paige started to object but Seren snagged the sponge. "Sit. You can entertain me with stories of all the cute animals you played with. That's what vets do all day, right?"

Paige rolled her eyes. "Sure. And no pet ever tries to bite or scratch. Or kick."

"Tell me about one cute thing you saw today."

Instead of sitting, Paige leaned against the counter and scratched her head. "Something cute, huh? Well, there was this pug that came in all dressed up in a tuxedo. Even had little shoes with those white flappy things on them."

"Spats?"

"That's it. How'd you know?"

"I know all sorts of things."

"You do." Paige eyed the skillet Seren had used to cook the fish. "I feel bad not doing the cleaning. You do most of the work for our Friday dinners."

"You help too. You help me with so many things around here I'm starting to worry about what I'd do without you." It was more than how Paige helped with things around the house—though that was huge. With her help, Seren had finally gotten the garage and the shed cleaned out, not to mention a dozen other things fixed around the house. But it was also how Paige kept tabs on her while somehow managing to not be clingy or stifling.

They talked on the phone every night and Paige texted every day. She still had Leslie, of course, but she didn't need her as much now, which was lucky because Leslie had started dating someone she'd met online. She always dropped off the radar when she had a new relationship, but Seren couldn't fault her for that. She'd basically done the same since meeting Paige.

"Did you want me to check out that slow drain in the bathroom? I think I could probably fix it."

"Not tonight. Tonight I want you to relax." Because she knew Paige needed more encouragement, she added, "Just to see if it's possible."

Paige exhaled. "I did have a long day. And I started bleeding which always makes everything feel harder."

"I forgot about things like periods." Not really, but only now did it occur to her that in the month she'd been dating Paige, they hadn't skipped sex for that reason yet.

"I guess pregnancy has to have some benefits."

"Aside from the obvious one where you get a baby at the end of it?" Seren smiled. She'd finally told her work she was pregnant. The conversation didn't go over great initially. Although she hadn't been working there long, her boss's main questions were how to manage her clients and how quickly she planned to come back to work after the baby came. She'd given the answer of twelve weeks being her hope for a maternity leave. But where would she be living then? Would she even still be in Davis?

With Paige in the picture, she couldn't imagine living anywhere else, but finances were still a huge looming question. Selling her mom's house and moving somewhere cheaper than Davis would mean she'd be able to afford a maternity leave and childcare after. If she didn't sell, she wasn't sure how she'd manage to pay the bills without an income.

"You seem a little tired yourself," Paige said. "Maybe we could watch a movie?"

Seren finished with the pan she was cleaning and set it on the rack to dry. She toweled off her hands and went over to where Paige stood. "We could watch a movie...I don't want to sound needy, but I like making the most of our Friday nights. I can watch a movie any night you aren't here."

"That doesn't sound needy."

"It might if I admitted to how many times I've wished you could come over during the week." Not that Seren had time through the week either. After work, she came home and started her second job—cleaning out closets, drawers, and sorting through her mom's things. "I want more time for us."

"I'd like that too. I'm just not sure how to make it happen." Paige paused. "What are you doing next Friday at noon? I know it's not that exciting, but you could come with me to sign the papers on my new ranch. I took the afternoon off. We could do something fun together after the signing."

"Fun like going to my next OB appointment? It's not until four, so we could snag lunch between the signing and that." She bit the edge of her lip. "I know it's not exactly fun."

"I'd love to go—if you'd be comfortable with me there. Oh, wait. You said at the twenty-week checkup they check all the anatomy, right?" Paige's eyes lit up. "We'd get to see your baby's heart and all of that?"

Seren nodded, encouraged by Paige's excitement. "It might be boring."

"Are you kidding? I already know it's gonna be the highlight of my week."

Seren narrowed her eyes. "Remember how you're closing on your dream ranch this week?"

"And seeing an ultrasound of your baby will still be the highlight."

The funny thing was, she believed Paige. And as nervous as she'd been about asking, she'd already known what Paige's answer would be. Paige wanted to be at the appointment as much as she wanted her there. But by asking, had she crossed the casual relationship line?

"It's gonna be so cool to see your baby." Paige reached for her hand and squeezed it. "You look worried, but it's gonna be fine."

"I don't like the doctor visits." Not untrue, even if that was only part of what was weighing on her mind. "I always worry they'll find something wrong."

"There won't be anything wrong. I've got a sixth sense about these things."

Trusting a sixth sense might be silly, but trusting Paige wasn't. She breathed out. "Thanks for wanting to go with me. It means a lot." More than Paige could know. "On a different subject, I have an idea for tonight. It's actually something I've been wanting to do for a while."

"Sex?" Paige guessed. "I might be bleeding, but I can rally for the right reason."

Seren kissed Paige's cheek. "Such a martyr. For the record, I'm not always thinking of sex."

"You sure?" Paige waggled her eyebrows.

"Yes." It was true she'd enjoyed Paige's appetite for it, and it was nice being well taken care of in that department. In fact, if they didn't have sex tonight, it'd be the first time they slept together without it. "I think it might be good for us to not have sex tonight."

"In case your hormones change and you're not feeling like me jumping you all the time?"

That Paige had guessed exactly what she was thinking was a little disconcerting, but Seren simply nodded. Her body could change at any moment. Scratch that—it was changing. She'd already had to give up on all her clothes that weren't maternity outfits. Fortunately, her libido hadn't gone anywhere. Still, she knew her desire for sex likely would wane in the third trimester. Everyone said it would.

"I want to do something, but I'm afraid you might be too toppy to let it happen."

Paige cocked her head. "All right, I'm intrigued. What am I too toppy for?"

"Before I tell you, I want to say first that I'm not complaining about what we do in bed."

"But?"

"How often do you let me take care of you?"

"You take care of me in all sorts of ways."

Seren crossed her arms. "How?"

"You...I..."

"I'm not mad. I don't even want things to change. But there is something I want." She'd planned all the way to this point. No, she hadn't planned on the conversation happening tonight, but she knew the time was right. And yet she was still nervous. "I want to give you a massage. We talked about it once at the beginning, but then it never happened, and I want to do that for you. It'd be for me too."

As soon as the words were out of her mouth, emotion mowed down her defenses. She met Paige's gaze, hoping she'd say something. It was ridiculous to feel so shaky and exposed. Giving people massages was literally her livelihood. But this was different. Not because of the massage itself but because of what it would mean. One more step past casual.

Did Paige have any idea how much she wanted this one thing? Did she know what it meant? "If you don't want a massage from me, I understand."

Paige pushed away from the counter and put her hand on Seren's hip. "I'd love a massage. But giving other people massages is what you do all day every day. I don't want you to feel like you're working when you're with me."

"It'd be different with you." Seren felt her body respond to Paige being close. Happy anticipation making her center clench. *Eager much?* But sex wasn't what her head wanted tonight. "It'd be different for me. It wouldn't be like work at all."

"You sure?"

"Yes." She rested her hand on Paige's forearm. The contact grounded her and gave her courage. "I want to take care of you. Will you let me?"

Paige swallowed. She looked up at the ceiling, clearly considering, and then met Seren's gaze. "It's hard when you put it that way."

"I know. That's why I'm asking." Partly she wanted to show Paige what she could do, but it was more than that. She wanted Paige to let her close. Only if that happened could she admit to everything she was feeling.

"Okay." Paige closed the distance between their lips.

Seren gave in to the kiss. A perfect kiss she didn't want to fight that seemed to prove their relationship was about more than sex. She could argue with her feelings all day, but the truth remained. She was falling for Paige. Falling hard.

Paige broke off the kiss and met her gaze. "Letting you be in charge isn't going to be easy for me."

"Good thing you're with a professional." Seren added a wink but her chest was tight. She felt more like a novice than ever.

When they got to the bedroom, Seren lit a candle and turned off the other lights. Paige pulled off her shirt and pushed back the comforter. Without Seren asking, she lay down on her belly, her arms at her side, then looked over her shoulder, a soft smile on her lips, and murmured, "I'm all yours." A moment later Paige closed her eyes, sighing into the pillow that had become hers.

Seren pushed a few strands of Paige's hair away from her face and caressed her cheek. Paige's eyes didn't open. "You're exhausted."

"Mm. Hard day," Paige murmured. "And a long week."

"I'm going to make it better."

Seren steadied her breathing, one long breath in and one long breath out. She rubbed her hands together, exactly like she did at the start of every treatment, but when she looked at Paige again, emotion undid her. The gorgeous woman on her bed wasn't a client but someone she loved. Someone she trusted, who she'd come to depend on, and someone who was trusting her with their heart. She knew it even if Paige didn't say it.

*I love you, you know.*

Did Paige know? She wanted to tell her, but instead she focused on what she knew how to do. Like always, she started with light stroking and some lotion. She studied Paige's body more than she ever had, learning all she could from the taut muscles, the angles and curves.

As Paige relaxed further, she felt for the tense spots, and as she started kneading, she read every twitch. After weeks of having sex and plenty of touching, she thought she knew Paige's body, but tonight it seemed she was discovering her for the first time. And falling in love with every part she touched.

"Your hands are amazing," Paige said. "I know you're a professional and all, but..." Her words were slurred like she was half-asleep. "This is seriously the best massage I've had in my life."

"Thank you."

"I have to tell you something else."

Seren felt the shift in Paige's voice and stilled her hands. "What is it?"

Paige rolled onto her back and looked up at Seren. In the candlelight she seemed more beautiful than ever. "I love you. I know it's too soon and you want this to be casual, but—"

Seren pressed a finger to Paige's lips, stopping her words. "I love you too." She pulled away her hand, her heart hammering in her chest.

"For real?"

"For real."

"I didn't think anything could top that massage." Paige spread her arms. "Come here."

Seren melted into their embrace. Maybe it was too soon. And it definitely made everything more complicated. But saying "I love you" to Paige felt like the most right thing in the world. Knowing Paige felt the same? She couldn't put that feeling into words.

# CHAPTER THIRTY-SIX

"You know it's six thirty. In the morning. On a day you're not even scheduled to be here."

Paige looked up to see Jen's figure in the doorway, complete with Leo in his car seat. Leo strained to reach for her as soon as she met his eyes. "Hey, buddy. Did you wake your mama up early just to come see me?"

"Maybe that was his plan." Jen groaned. "I figured since I was awake, I might as well get some records done."

"Smart people think alike." Paige pointed at her stack. "And, sadly, records don't write themselves." She also wanted to have more time to spend with Seren that weekend, and taking a day off was stressful. The work had to be caught up at some point.

Leo strained against the car seat straps and Jen set down the carrier to lift him out. He immediately reached in Paige's direction. Jen shook her head. "Sure. I take care of you all night, and you want someone new first thing in the morning."

Paige happily scooped Leo from Jen's arms when he reached for her again. Being around Jen and watching her time-manage with Leo had shown the reality of having a kid and a full-time job. But she'd also seen how Jen and her husband shared responsibilities. With two people, it didn't seem impossible.

"You excited to go into massive debt today?" Jen flashed a wicked smile. "When's the housewarming party?"

"I'm not sure I'll have one for a while." Seren had suggested it. Paige hadn't been keen on the idea but warmed to it when Seren offered to help host. "There's so much work I'd like to do on the place before I have people over."

"And all of it will be more expensive, and more work, than you think. Sometimes not owning's worth it."

"Wait, you were the one who encouraged me to buy a place."

"Because I know how much you want your own farm. But it's gonna be a ton of work."

Paige sighed. "And money."

Jen waved her hand. "We're vets. We take on debt like we take on pets."

True, but she'd done her best to pay down her college and vet school loans so that the debt wasn't overwhelming. "Speaking of pets, how's that little pug mix you took home last week?"

Jen grimaced. "Leo loves him."

"You're adopting him, aren't you?" Paige glanced at Leo. "Good job, buddy."

"We already have five dogs," Jen said.

Paige laughed. "As soon as that owner relinquished him, I knew he was going home with you."

"Who relinquishes a thirteen-year-old puggle?" Jen shook her head. "He's best friends with Rufus, and you know everyone else hates Rufus." Rufus was Jen's crusty but sweet Pomeranian.

Paige grinned. "Sucker."

"Whatever. As soon as you get this ranch, you're gonna be as bad as me. Only you'll have too many cats instead of too many dogs."

"And cows." Paige also fully expected to take on too many chickens. "I can't wait."

Jen shook her head and mumbled something about needing coffee. After she'd gone to the breakroom, Paige made herself focus on the records, letting Leo play in her lap with jar of pens.

By nine thirty, she'd finished her calls and the records, despite spending a good amount of that time entertaining Leo, whose babysitter was late picking him up. She had a little over two hours before the signing and decided on a bike ride to try to shake off the nervous energy. After the ride, she showered and called Seren.

"Hey, sexy. How are you?"

"Finished my third client of the morning. I'm ready for a break. Are you on your way over?"

"You sure you want to come to this signing? I don't think it's gonna be very exciting."

"I'm sure. Come get me."

Paige exhaled. It wasn't like she couldn't sign the papers on her own, but she knew she'd be less stressed with Seren there. She was simply happier and more relaxed with her around.

The signing took nearly an hour, and lunch plans turned to picking up an order from Dos Coyotes. In addition to a fixation on avocados, Seren had developed a pregnancy-induced craving for fish tacos and was bent on sampling every restaurant in town to decide on a winner.

"Yours are still better," Paige said, polishing off the last bite of her taco.

"I like this agave-lime slaw. But really, it needs more—"

"Let me guess. Avocado?"

Seren laughed. "Yes. More avocado."

"That's the same thing you've said about the last three fish taco places we've tried."

"They never put in enough avocado." She shook her head like she was mourning something grave. Then looked over at Paige and grinned. "Hey, guess what? You own a ranch."

"I do!" Paige even had the keys in her pocket. After Seren's doctor appointment, they planned to drive over and take a look around—not that Paige hadn't been there twice daily for the last few weeks to take care of Nellie and the barn cats she still had to name.

The Landrys and little Bella had officially moved out. Seren had already been to visit them twice in their new apartment at the memory care facility. The apartment didn't give Mr. Landry or Bella as much room, but Mrs. Landry was getting the extra help she needed. "I'm hoping Mr. Landry doesn't get bored."

Seren lifted a shoulder. "He says he's happy to be on vacation."

"Must feel that way after all the years of work." Paige knew it might feel like too much work at some point, but for now, she couldn't wait to get started on all the projects. "You know what I'm gonna do first?"

"Buy two calves for me? I mean, for you."

Paige smiled. "I'm gonna plant avocado trees. There's already a beehive on the property, so it's perfect. Avocados need bees."

"Before getting any calves—the one thing you most wanted—you're gonna plant trees? There's already an orchard."

"But no avocado trees. If I'm gonna be wooing you with avocados, I gotta get on it."

"Wooing me?" Seren shook her head, laughing. "Too late. I'm wooed. Is that even a word?"

"It is now." Paige leaned across the truck's console and kissed Seren. "Just so you know, there's gonna be more wooing. Prepare yourself."

When Paige started to shift back in her seat, Seren caught the front of her shirt and pulled her close again for another kiss. As soon as they separated, Seren smiled. "You smell like avocado. I want to eat you up."

"You're weird."

"But I'm your weird."

"My weird, huh?" Paige grinned.

"What? Don't want to be stuck with this weird?" Seren held out her hands.

Paige knew she was teasing but she also felt a hint of insecurity. Seren looked like she realized what she'd said and how Paige took it. "I want you to be my weird. And I want to be yours."

Seren reached for a chip and scooped up guacamole on it. She ate the chip and then glanced sideways at Paige. "Are we in trouble here? Do we need to call for an intervention?"

Paige lifted a shoulder. "I think it's nothing we can't handle." She wasn't one hundred percent sure about that, however. The line between casual and serious had gotten blurred as soon as they said, "I love you." At least for her.

By the time they got to the doctor's office, Paige was worrying about other things. Seren had said she had anxiety around medical professionals and that hospitals really got to her, but Paige hadn't expected to look down and see Seren shaking. At first, she'd thought she might be cold, but then she saw sweat beading on her forehead.

After Seren signed in for her appointment, they sat down in the waiting room and Paige reached for her hand. Seren didn't make eye contact, but she clenched her fingers. When the nurse called Seren's name, Paige expected her to let go. She didn't. She held her hand all the way to the restroom. Paige waited for her to come out and then took her hand again.

"I hate peeing in those little cups." Seren scrunched her shoulders up to her ears and then dropped them like she was trying to shake off the tension. "I'm always worried I'm gonna get pee on my hands."

"Pee's sterile. Nothing wrong with a little on your hands. Poop is a different story. That's just plain gross if it gets on your hands."

"Only you would say that." Seren smiled as if she didn't want to but couldn't help it. They followed the nurse down the hallway and Seren bumped Paige's side. "Thanks for being here."

"Highlight of my week." Paige meant it, too.

The doctor didn't have the warmest bedside manner but seemed more than competent. She asked Seren if Paige was her partner and surprisingly Seren nodded. Paige wasn't sure if that was because the complexities of their relationship didn't really matter in the moment or if Seren wanted her in that role. Either way, the doctor let Paige stay during the brief exam and Seren held her hand the whole time.

When the sonographer came to get Seren for the ultrasound, she smiled widely at Paige and introduced herself. Shonda. She added that it was nice to take care of Family. Family with a capital F. That seemed to give Seren permission, and she shifted even closer to Paige, practically hugging her arm as they walked to the dimly lit ultrasound room.

Seren got in the seat and half leaned back, not exactly comfortable looking.

"You okay?"

She nodded, clutching Paige's hand again.

Shonda lifted Seren's gown and started applying ultrasound gel to her belly. When Seren cringed, Shonda said, "I warm it up, but I know it's still a little shock. Ready to see your baby?"

"No." Seren's chin trembled. A tear slipped down her cheek.

"Seren."

She looked up and met Paige's gaze.

"Everything's gonna be fine." Paige brushed away the tear. "Shonda's only gonna take some measurements and the baby's gonna be fine. There's not gonna be any surprises today." She brought Seren's hand up to her lips.

"We ready then?" Shonda asked.

Seren let out a shaky breath and nodded. She closed her eyes as soon as Shonda placed the transducer probe on her belly. "I don't want anything to be wrong. It's all starting to feel real. Like I might get a baby."

"Oh, you're gonna get a baby all right," Shonda said. She moved the transducer probe and the unmistakable image of a fetus popped on the screen.

Paige's breath caught in her chest. It was one thing seeing the little photo on her phone that Seren had sent four weeks ago, one thing knowing she was dating someone who was pregnant and noticing Seren's belly stretch. But this? This was amazing.

"Seren. Your baby's beautiful." Tears pricked Paige's eyes.

"Is it okay?" Seren's voice was barely a whisper.

"Your baby's perfect."

"You sure?"

Paige pointed at the monitor. "See for yourself."

It took some cajoling, but Seren did look. Briefly. "I'm worried if I look something will be wrong."

"Nothing's wrong," Paige continued. "See that little heart lub-dubbing away? Exactly what it's supposed to be doing. See that little baby hand? Perfect." The baby flexed all five fingers a moment later, and Paige brought Seren's hand to her lips for a kiss. "You gotta little show-off. They're trying to show us how perfect all five fingers are." The baby kicked and turned. "And two perfect little legs."

Paige knew Shonda also had a perfect view of what was between the legs. Shonda's lips pursed. Paige hadn't thought she'd be able to tell the parts, but it was undeniable.

"You don't want to know the gender, right?" Shonda asked.

"Right," Seren said. "Don't tell me."

Paige wished she hadn't seen. Now she'd have to keep it a secret that she knew.

"Is everything okay?" Seren asked.

Shonda answered first. "Girl, everything's perfect. All these measurements are on target and I'm not seeing any issues."

Seren breathed out. "Okay, good." She looked over at Paige. "You got tense all of a sudden."

"Sorry." Paige relaxed her shoulders. "I think I'm just realizing that you're having a baby. Like, it's real." That part was true.

"It's a little terrifying. But also amazing."

"Yeah."

When Shonda finished, swiping away the remaining ultrasound gel and directing Seren to dress, Paige stepped out of the room. Seren joined her a moment later and they walked out in silence, Seren again holding tight to her hand.

As soon as they got into Paige's truck, Seren turned to her. "You know the baby's sex, don't you?"

Paige dropped her chin. "I wasn't trying to see, but…yeah."

Seren nodded slowly. "I believed what you said in there. That you'd gotten tense because you were finally realizing that it was all real. Then I realized the other part too."

"Are you mad?"

Seren took a slow breath in and out. "A little. You kind of lied."

"I knew you didn't want to know and so I didn't want to know either. If that makes sense." But now she felt even worse having lied about it. "I'm sorry. Do you want me to tell you?"

"No. I don't think so. It's not your fault that you saw and that you can read ultrasounds. But as a general rule, I'd like you to tell me things."

"Totally fair." Paige met Seren's gaze. "The good news is I'm a terrible liar."

Seren's brow furrowed. "You actually are. Quite horrible."

"You say that like it's a surprise."

"Most people have at least some poker face."

"At least you know when I'm telling you the truth." Paige turned in her seat to face Seren. "I love you. I love that you're having a baby. I love that you let me come today. And I'm sorry I saw something I shouldn't have seen."

"I believe you. I don't care if I'm having a boy or a girl. That's why I don't want to know. I only want a healthy baby." Seren paused. "And a calf. I'd really like a calf as well. I've been doing some serious thinking about it."

Paige laughed. "Want to go check out my new ranch?"

"Yes." Seren leaned over the console and kissed Paige. "Thanks for coming with me today. What are you doing in four weeks at this same time?"

"Coming to your next appointment with you?"

"Great." Seren exhaled. "I'll make it up to you somehow."

"Don't feel like you have to make it up to me at all. I'm happy you want me here."

"I believe you. But I still want to make it up to you. This is going above and beyond casual girlfriend duty. Which do you want—chocolate chip cookies or sex favors?"

"Both." Paige forced a smile. The words *casual girlfriend duty* swirled in her mind.

In four weeks, Seren would be that much closer to having a baby. They hadn't talked about what would happen when the baby did come. Or after. Would they keep dating? Paige hoped so, but she knew Seren wasn't convinced their relationship would weather all the changes. And then there was the question of how long Seren would be staying in Davis. Paige had stopped thinking about all the what-ifs, but now they came slamming back.

This was still a casual thing for Seren.

The reality of that one thought stung more than any other. For all Paige had said about not being the marrying type, and being okay with something not serious, the truth was she'd fallen for Seren. And it didn't take any work at all to imagine how they could spend forever together. If only Seren could see what they had.

# CHAPTER THIRTY-SEVEN

Summer had arrived. Seren was stripped down to a tank top and shorts and still sweating buckets. "Next purchase for this place." Seren waved her paintbrush at Paige. "A new AC unit."

"It's gonna have to wait till next paycheck. In the meantime, you could try painting naked." Paige shot her a hopeful look. She was close to naked herself, wearing only a sports bra and an old pair of board shorts dotted now with paint.

"There are certain places I don't want to be scraping paint off of. My nipples being number one."

"Good point." Paige finished rolling the wall and stepped back, mopping sweat off her brow. Even with all the windows open and the ceiling fan chugging away, the room was still a sauna. "Am I imagining it, or is this wall still pink?"

Seren came over to where Paige stood and pursed her lips. "It's a little pink. But way less magenta."

Paige's shoulders sagged. "I was really hoping this wouldn't need a third coat."

The Landrys had painted each one of the rooms a different color. Paige had joked that they'd wanted the place to look like all the least-used crayons in the box—magenta, chartreuse, mango, burnt sienna, and mustard yellow. She wasn't wrong. Now, though, they'd coated the entire place in a soft cream. Once the newly painted white baseboards were installed and the wood flooring arrived, the change would be amazing. Even simply tearing out the brown shag carpet had done wonders. Paige had also hired someone to knock down a wall between the living room and the kitchen, opening up the front room. Seren had been skeptical at first, but the entryway now felt bright and welcoming as opposed to depressing and dark.

"When are the new windows coming?"

"Next week. And the floors are installed the week after. Then I'm taking a break from all this home improvement crap."

Paige set down her roller and wrapped an arm around Seren's side. Seren wanted to relax into the embrace, but between the heat and the anxious feeling of having too much to do, she only tensed. She kissed Paige lightly and shifted away a step.

"Too hot to cuddle?" Paige guessed.

"After the AC unit, want to buy a pool?"

"Add it to the wish list." Paige sighed. "Thanks for helping with the painting. Now that we're basically professionals, we're gonna do an amazing job edging when we do your mom's place next."

"You know there are more exciting meanings to the word *edging*."

"Maybe, but it's hard to beat a smooth paint line." Paige winked. "Anyway, you're the one who doesn't even want to cuddle."

"I didn't say no to sex."

"Just no to cuddling?" Paige waited for her nod, a half-smile on her lips. "Okay, my misunderstanding. Really, that still leaves a lot of things we could do."

While that was true, now that they were talking about it Seren wasn't sure she was in the mood. Maybe she should try anyway? Since Paige had moved to the ranch, they'd spent more time working on projects than having sex. She'd worried about it but decided the together time they did have made up for it.

Still, she wished there wasn't quite so much to do. All the time at the ranch meant the work to get her mom's house ready to sell had stalled out completely. She'd woken up that morning thinking of her long to-do list. Her car was jam-packed with boxes for the Goodwill, and the clearing out seemed endless.

Paige took Seren's paintbrush from her hand and dropped it in the rinse bucket. "How about we take a break and do some other types of edging?"

"We have too much work to do before your housewarming. And I still need to do so much at my mom's house."

"We'll get everything done. I promise. Next weekend we'll get back to working on projects at your mom's. You can give me a list and I can try to tackle some of them through the week after work."

"I really want a weekend off projects." Preferably with her feet up in the air. She'd hit the point in her pregnancy where she was tired nearly all the time. Twenty-five weeks. A whisper past the six-month mark. She'd been warned that the exhaustion would come and, boy, had it ever.

Each night after work all she managed to do was eat dinner and shower. Often, she fell asleep still wrapped in a towel. Pajamas, apparently, were too much work. On the nights she stayed at her mom's instead of the ranch, Paige dropped by with meals because she was too tired to cook.

No matter how many times she reminded herself that she was busy growing a baby and needed to give herself a break, she worried time was slipping away. She still hadn't found her mom's will and Leslie kept reminding her it was crunch time to get the house on the market.

On top of that, she hadn't decided where she'd move after her mom's place was sold. Should she get an apartment and a year-long lease? Or take whatever money she made on the sale and put it down on a little condo? Either of those options meant she'd stay in Davis for at least a while. Was that what she wanted? Overall, she was happy—happier than she'd been anywhere else, really—though she hated the feeling of things being undecided and not having a clear plan.

"Anyone home? Seren, where are you? I brought ice cream. Seren? Paige?"

"We're back here, Bea," Seren hollered. "Give us a minute. We've been painting."

"Funny how my mom calls your name first and then mine sounds like an addendum," Paige murmured.

It'd become a joke that Bea liked her more than Paige. After the first massage, Beatrice had become her biggest fan. She now was a weekly customer and wasn't shy about telling everyone that Seren was the best thing that had ever happened to her. And Paige. For her part, Paige only seemed amazed that Seren got on so well with her mom.

"She still loves you too."

"I'm not worried." Paige reached for the T-shirt she'd stripped off earlier and tugged it on over her bra. "It's just a little weird dating someone my mom likes so much."

"Maybe you should date more likable people in the future."

Paige looked as if she was about to say something in response, but Bea hollered about forgetting carrots. She'd called Seren that morning asking if she wanted any groceries. Seren had told her not to worry about it, but she'd insisted. "Let's hope she didn't forget avocados."

"You and avocados. If she forgot them, I'll run to the store."

Seren blamed being pregnant and her baby's growing appetite on why she regularly ate an avocado a day. Sometimes two. She worried about weight gain with the added ice cream cravings, but her doctor had assured her she was fine.

Paige only seemed to appreciate Seren's added curves. In fact, the way Paige looked at her when she was naked made Seren wish her libido was as strong as it had been when they'd first met. It wasn't that she didn't want sex now, but often she was simply too tired. When they did get to it, everything still felt amazing and she could tell Paige's desire for her hadn't ebbed. But what would happen if she didn't want it at all? What would that mean for a relationship that was supposed to only be casual?

Beatrice had bought a quart each of five different flavors. Along with avocados, tomatoes from her garden, and a bag of tortilla chips. Seren picked up the avocados, her mouth already watering.

"You're going for the avocados over ice cream?" Paige had snagged the container of rocky road and was already cracking the seal. "I swear that baby of yours needs a direct line."

"Pipe down, you." Beatrice swatted Paige's arm. "Avocados are full of vitamins. A pregnant lady knows what she needs better than anyone else."

"Thank you, Bea." Seren raised an eyebrow at Paige. "You should listen to your mom. She's smart."

Beatrice grumbled about Paige never listening to anyone, then turned to Seren. "Is there anything else that baby wants?"

"No, Bea, but thanks. How's your hip this week?" When she'd broken her tailbone, Bea had also wrenched her hip. That had sent her back into a spasm.

"Better. I'm not even taking those medications. Rita wants to get in with you too. I told her you probably can't take new clients, but she wanted me to ask anyway. Her neck's been giving her a headache."

"I'll give her a call." Seren cut an avocado in half, shook on some salt, and grabbed a spoon.

"I could make you guacamole," Paige said.

"This is faster." Seren spooned a bite into her mouth, savoring the rich nutty taste.

"I'm worried about how much you're working, Seren," Bea said. "You sure you can take on another client?"

"Rita's a friend. And, honestly, I need the money. I want to build up a nest egg so I can afford maternity leave."

Paige looked over at Bea. Something passed between them. Seren nearly asked what she was missing but stopped herself. If it was important, Paige would tell her. But what if she didn't? Something had seemed off earlier that morning, and she felt it again now.

"Well, like I said, pregnant ladies know what's best for them." Bea sniffed. "If you want more customers, say the word. Nearly everyone in water aerobics has some ache or pain you could do your magic on."

Paige shook her head. It was a subtle head shake that Seren would have missed if she weren't watching closely.

"Speaking of..." Beatrice gathered up her purse and keys. "I'm off to check on Claia. She wasn't at water aerobics again this morning."

Seren had noticed Claia's absence as well and had worried about her. Claia lived alone and insisted she was fine taking care of herself, but she was ninety-two. "If there's anything wrong, let me know. I'd be happy to drop by with some soup if she's under the weather."

"I'm hoping she went off to Tahiti and forgot to mention it."
Bea gave Seren a half hug. "Ooh, you're hot." She looked over at
Paige. "You need to get the AC fixed in this place. You've got a
pregnant lady here."

"I'll get on it, Mom."

"Today."

# CHAPTER THIRTY-EIGHT

Seren watched as Paige saluted then thanked her mom for the food delivery. As soon as her mom left, she held up the grocery bag full of avocados. "She definitely likes you better than me."

"At least she lets you share my ice cream."

Paige chuckled, finishing off a bite of rocky road. She put the container in the freezer and then held out the mint chocolate chip. Seren loved that Paige knew it was her favorite and treated it accordingly. "You want a different spoon for this?"

"Nope. Mint chocolate chip goes with avocados." Seren opened the ice cream. It took a little maneuvering, but she managed to get avocado and mint chocolate chip on the same spoonful.

Paige's eyebrows bunched together as she watched her. "I'm trying to be okay with that. Really I am. But I don't think *everything* goes with avocados."

Seren waved her spoon. "Remember what your mom said? Pregnant ladies know what's best."

"I bet I could find you some avocado ice cream at the Co-op. Can't imagine it'd be anywhere else than at the hippy store."

"I'd try that." Seren laughed when Paige groaned.

"You knew I was joking, right?"

"And you know how I feel about avocados." Seren scooped up another bite, this time only the mint ice cream. "Can I ask you something?"

Paige nodded.

They'd talked a lot about not keeping things from each other after the ultrasound appointment, although she'd decided she was okay with Paige knowing the baby's sex. In a way, it was comforting. Paige had reassured her that the baby was fine, and she trusted her completely. But this was different. This time she didn't know what Paige wasn't saying. She'd only felt some space between them and seen the look between Paige and Bea.

"This morning I had a feeling there was something on your mind you weren't mentioning, and now when your mom was here, I got that feeling again." Seren kept her tone light. She didn't think that whatever Paige and her mom had exchanged a glance about was too serious, but the whole keeping-things-from-her thing was definitely not her favorite. "Is there something we should talk about?"

Paige exhaled. "There is something I've been thinking about—about us—but I'm trying to wait to bring it up. I might have mentioned it to my mom. Kind of on accident."

"Tell me. I'm only going to worry until you do. Even if it's something little. I don't really like your mom knowing something about us that I don't know."

"That's fair. I don't like it either." Paige hesitated still. Finally, she took a deep breath and said, "I want you to move in with me."

Seren narrowed her eyes. "You told your mom you were thinking about asking me to move in with you before talking to me about it?"

"No. I mean, not exactly. I accidentally called one of the rooms the baby's room. The one we were painting today."

Seren set the avocado down with the ice cream. Okay, she'd been wrong. This wasn't something little. "What'd your mom say?"

"She asked me when you'd decided to move in. I told her you hadn't." Paige didn't seem to want to continue, but said, "My mom thinks I'm going to push you too fast." She shook her head. "She also said you were the best thing that's ever come into my life and

I was going to screw it up if I backed you into a corner. Which I think, from the look on your face, I may be doing right now."

"Us living together hasn't ever been the plan."

"I know. And right now, this place is a disaster, but once I have it in better shape…" Her voice trailed. After a moment, she straightened. "Once I get it fixed up, I'd love it if you moved in with me. That's why I've been trying to work so much to get it ready. Why I've been working on the house instead of the barn. I want it to be some place you'd like to live."

It wasn't that she hadn't imagined living with Paige. She had—too many times to count. The problem was what it would mean. "Does your mom also know we agreed our relationship wouldn't become serious?"

Paige's jaw clenched. "No."

"That's probably an important detail, right?"

"Maybe. Maybe not. Whatever we call our relationship, you living here makes a lot of sense. For one, we can get your mom's place ready to sell easier if all your stuff is out of it. If you can get it sold before the baby comes, you'll have that money in your savings account if anything unexpected happens."

When Seren didn't respond, Paige continued, "While you're here, you won't need to pay rent or anything, so you can save up that nest egg you were talking about. I can swing all the bills. And you won't have to take on as many massage clients. It's gonna get harder for you to be on your feet all the time, and—"

"Paige, stop." Seren felt blindsided by the whole conversation. Her head spun with too many thoughts. "I can't move in with you."

How had she not seen this coming? A moment later, she corrected herself. She had seen it coming. She'd even added fuel to the idea by saying how much she loved the ranch, how peaceful it was being away from town. The spot was close enough to feel like they weren't isolated but far enough away to feel like there was plenty of room. And the sunsets were gorgeous with no buildings getting in the way. She'd said all of that only last weekend. And Paige had looked at her and smiled. Agreed with her. *Fuck.*

"Why not?"

"For so many reasons. Mostly, I'm six months pregnant. I won't be able to focus on a relationship when the baby comes. And you knew I didn't want this to be anything serious because of that. Me moving in with you is the definition of serious."

"It doesn't have to be. I'm not asking you to marry me. You could have your own room. The baby can have their own room too."

"And you're telling me that you wouldn't help take care of the baby?"

"Well, of course I would."

"Right. We're two months into a relationship. When the baby comes, we'll have known each other for a little over five months. You don't know someone well enough in five months to sign up to co-parent with them."

"Well…What if I didn't help unless you really needed it? I wouldn't make parenting decisions. It'd be all you."

"I don't even want to have this conversation. I'm not ready."

"Okay, fine." Paige dropped her gaze to the brown linoleum. "Forget I brought it up."

"I can't forget you brought it up." A weight pressed down on Seren's chest. "Dammit, Paige."

"I'm sorry. I know it's too soon for us to take our relationship to the next step. But you moving in here makes sense. Even you could agree with that, right?" A moment later Paige added, "You like it here. I know you do. And I'd love coming home to you every night."

"Paige…" God, what could she say?

Paige came over to where Seren stood and reached for her hand. "When I close my eyes and picture a perfect life, it's you here with a baby and us raising calves and chickens and growing avocados. And too many black cats running around."

Seren couldn't help smiling. Cymbal loved life on the ranch and was best friends now with Squirrel, Paige's cat. But liking it here wasn't the point.

"I know you always wanted something more exciting, and this place isn't that, but—"

"I don't want excitement. Not anymore. That was my teenage self wanting…wanting my life to start." Seren shook her head, trying to hold in her emotions. "This place is perfect. I love it here. I really do. But we can't jump in to living together. It'll backfire. I know it."

"How can you be so sure? I've never been with someone where things felt so right. Maybe we don't need to wait."

Seren pulled her hand out of Paige's grip. "You said you weren't the marrying type."

"I'm not talking about marriage. But even if I was, maybe I hadn't met the right person before."

"Very funny."

Paige shook her head. "For the first time I'm thinking about forever."

"Don't do that." Seren squeezed her eyes closed. She hated what she'd said, but she hated that Paige had pushed her to say it more.

Paige was quiet. Waiting for her. What else could she say? She looked around the kitchen. Brown tile counters, brown appliances, brown shutters on the windows. Paige hadn't tackled the kitchen remodel yet. She'd joked that she wanted to wait on that part until Seren moved in. Except clearly it wasn't a joke.

"Fuck, Paige. I wish you hadn't started this conversation."

"If I'd waited two months, do you think you'd have a different response? Then it'd only be one month before the baby was due. You'd say the timing was wrong and you couldn't think about it then." Paige continued after a moment, "What's the worst that could happen?"

Seren immediately pictured the baby booties she'd found with the price tag still on them. And the note from the father she'd never known. "Do you know what's in my car, Paige?"

Paige's expression made it clear she was thrown by the question.

"I was going through my mom's attic last week. She'd saved some of my old baby toys and I found a little shoebox. There was a note from my father with these two little cute pink booties that I'd clearly never worn." She took a shaky breath. "Do you know what the note said? 'To Serendipity—I'll love you forever.' Except he didn't."

"Shit, Seren. I'm sorry."

Seren felt tears sting her eyes, but she fought them back. "My mom and my father were together for eleven months. You can do the math. Two months after I was born, he split. Before I ever fit those booties. He couldn't even love me to my first birthday."

"I wouldn't leave."

"He didn't think he would either."

For a moment, neither of them spoke. Seren felt Paige's eyes on her, but she only stared at the popcorn ceiling until she had control of her tears. When she was sure she could speak without crying, she said, "My mom did fine without him. I did fine too. And those booties are going to the Goodwill where they should have gone thirty-eight years ago. I don't need help raising my baby. I'll figure out the finances part and I've got Leslie if I need anything and about a dozen women from water aerobics already lined up to babysit." Water aerobics. To think this had all started there.

"If I made a promise, I wouldn't leave."

"Dammit, Paige. Stop. I don't want you to make a promise after knowing me for only two months. Think about it. You're amazing and I love spending time with you, but what happens when the honeymoon wears off? What happens when we start fighting over money, or time, or whatever people fight about? Then I'm stuck trying to deal with a co-parent that I never wanted in the first place."

She saw the hurt in Paige's eyes but pushed on. "If I move in with you, you know what'll happen. We both do. Things will be great. And when the baby comes, you'll end up helping. You'll help me raise the baby. But then when our relationship goes sideways, everything will be fucked and messy."

"If. Not when. You're assuming it wouldn't work out. But it might. I'm not your dad. You aren't even giving us a chance here."

"You want to know how to test a relationship and make sure it fails? Throw a baby into the mix when two people haven't even been together for six months."

"If I promised to let you parent, and not get involved, I wouldn't break that promise."

"Like how you promised that this wouldn't be anything serious?" Seren didn't look at Paige then. She knew it was harsh. She knew she'd been as much to blame. But she wouldn't take the words back. Silence stretched, and when she finally looked up, she saw anger for the first time in Paige's eyes.

"I think I just realized something." Paige's voice was calm. Almost steely. "I've been going on the assumption that this relationship has the potential to be great, and this whole time you've planned on it failing."

"I didn't say that."

"You didn't need to."

Seren felt Paige's words like a gut punch.

"I'm sorry, Seren. Whatever happened between your mom and your dad, I'm sorry. You didn't get two parents raising you, and I bet it was hard on your mom. And now you can't trust me."

When Seren started to interrupt, Paige held up her hand. "I'm not done. You're right. Your mom did an amazing job on her own, and I'm sure you'd do the same with your kid. You don't need my help. Maybe, though, you'd like it. Sometimes things work out, you know. Not every relationship fails. Although if one person has already decided it won't work..."

"I never said that."

Paige laughed, but it sounded hollow. "I felt bad bringing this up, and rushing you and everything, but now I'm glad I did. If you don't even want to talk about where our relationship could go, there's no reason for us to keep going."

"Don't say that." Seren swallowed, tears burning her eyes all over again. "I'm not the bad guy here. You're the one who's being unrealistic."

"Unrealistic? Because I think some relationships work? Fuck, Seren. What do you want me to say? That your way of seeing the world is right and mine's wrong and we leave it at that?"

"I'd be fine if you just thought I was someone fun to mess around with." Seren heard the catch in her voice but pressed on. "Someone who doesn't mean anything more than a good time."

"I can't do that." Paige held Seren's gaze. "I love you. It hurts how much I love you."

Seren heard the rawness and the pain in Paige's voice. She saw the truth in her eyes. And she wanted to say one word—*same*. But she didn't. She couldn't. Because no matter how much she loved Paige, the most important thing was still the baby she'd soon have. That had to be her priority. Nothing could get in the way of her focusing on that.

"I met you when I was four months pregnant. A relationship— like what you want—was already off the table. It's not that I'm not in love with you. I am. And it's not that I can't imagine how great it would be us living together. I can. But I want to be a mom. I want it more than anything else. And as soon as this baby comes, that's what I want to focus on."

"Okay. I get it now. Thanks for the explanation."

So damn calm. Why'd she have to be so calm? Seren wanted to throw things and rage, but Paige stood there simply looking sad and resigned. "Fuck."

"Yeah. Well, I guess now we know."

"Now we know what?" When Paige didn't answer, Seren asked the question she didn't want to ask. "Do you want to break up?"

"No. Not at all. Remember the part about me loving you?"

Seren squeezed her eyes shut. "Just because we don't want to break up, doesn't mean it isn't happening."

"I don't want to break up. But I also don't know how we go forward. Do you?"

Seren shook her head. After a moment, Paige touched her arm. Gentle, so fucking gentle. Seren wanted to scream at her and collapse into her arms in the same moment.

"I swear I tried not to get too attached," Paige said quietly.

She couldn't meet Paige's eyes. She knew she'd start crying if she did. Why had she told Paige to tell her what she was thinking? To not keep things from her? Some things were better left unsaid.

Paige waited a beat and then another. After a long minute, she said, "Maybe we need a break. Some time to think. Some space."

She didn't want space. She didn't want time to think. "I want to go back in time and have this conversation never happen."

"Okay. Let's pretend I didn't say anything."

Seren felt nauseous like she hadn't in months. What was she doing having a baby? She couldn't even manage her own life. If only she could close her eyes and open them again and know what to do.

Finally, Paige said, "Maybe we should have sex. That fixes everything, right?"

Paige was joking—trying to break the tension with humor like she always did. But when Seren looked over at her, thinking of telling her that now wasn't the time to joke, she watched a tear course down Paige's cheek.

Paige swiped away the tear and shook her head. "Don't worry. I'm fine. And I'm joking about the sex part. Obviously."

Seren's chest clenched. "I'm sorry." She was sorry. So sorry.

"I'm sorry too."

Seren didn't want to cry, but the tears came anyway.

"Come here." Paige spread her arms and Seren stepped into her embrace. When Paige wrapped her tight, she gave in and sobbed against her shoulder. Her damn perfect shoulders. She wanted to hold those shoulders forever. A long minute passed before Paige's grip lessened.

"I don't want this to be the end."

"Then we'll pretend we didn't have this conversation." Paige kissed her cheek, then her lips.

Seren returned the kiss with a crushing one of her own. After everything, the last thing she should be thinking of was sex. But she slipped her hand under Paige's tank top and desire surged in her.

"I want you." She didn't add the words *one last time*. This couldn't be how they ended. It was only a disagreement. Their first fight. That's all it was, right?

Paige kissed her, then encircled her wrist. She wanted to memorize the familiar feeling, the calluses on Paige's hands that she loved and the confidence in her grip. What if this was the last time? She wanted to memorize how the roughness felt against the smoothness of her wrist. She closed her eyes and let Paige lead.

When they reached the bedroom, bare walls and no furniture save the bed, Paige didn't waste any time helping her out of her clothes. Paige stripped as well, then moved them to the bed.

They tumbled onto the mattress, Paige on top, pinning her, taking kiss after kiss from her lips. Then something seemed to switch in Paige and her rough touch turned painfully sweet. She caressed Seren from the arches of her feet to the soft divots under her ears. One minute her hands had been all force, and the next only lovingly tender. Seren realized she was crying only when Paige kissed away the tears.

Paige moved between her legs. As soon as her tongue lapped against Seren's clit, her orgasm was a foregone conclusion. She wanted to beg Paige to not be so gentle. It was killing her to feel Paige's love in every stroke, every kiss. *Just hate me a little*, she wanted to say. *Fuck me like this doesn't mean anything. Make this easier for both of us*. But no. Paige lifted her hips and took her into her mouth like she was a fine wine. She licked and sucked, pushing Seren to almost hating her for making her feel so good.

"I want you inside." Seren knew Paige heard her, but instead of pushing into her, she continued licking and sucking. Seren realized then that she was going to orgasm with that alone. It wouldn't be as satisfying as having Paige fill her, but maybe that was the intention. Maybe Paige wanted her unsatisfied. It was only fair.

She felt the climax rising, but Paige seemed to sense it as well. Before it broke, she shifted her attentions away from Seren's clit and patterned soft kisses along the inside of her thighs. "Fuck." Seren panted. She needed the release now. She tried to push up into Paige's mouth, but Paige was stronger than her and easily pressed her back on the mattress.

A moment later, Paige's tongue coursed over her clit. She circled and stroked, and the climax built up again. Then, as before, Paige shifted away. Seren cursed again. Paige was doing it intentionally. Keeping her at the point of coming but holding back the orgasm. She'd never had someone edge her before. It was infuriating—and turned her on more than ever.

"Please." Seren's center clenched rhythmically. Begging for Paige. "Please."

Paige shifted up to kiss her lips, then slid into her, filling the place Seren needed her most. They hadn't had sex in over a week, but Seren's body was ready. Paige moved into her easily. Spreading her knees farther, then filling her more.

"More." She needed more of Paige. This couldn't be the end.

One, two, three fingers slid inside. Paige turned her wrist, sending shivers through Seren. She rode in and out, hard and fast. Seren writhed with pleasure until Paige finally had to hold her in place. One hand gripping her as the other drove her to a place of unthinking.

Paige dipped her head again. As soon as her tongue lapped over the swollen clit, almost painful with need, there was no holding back. No way but to give in to what her body wanted.

She cried out with the climax and Paige's name spilled from her lips. Strong arms took her up and she curled against Paige's chest, clenching her legs together as the aftershocks raced through her. She felt weak. Spent from the orgasm. And Paige knew what she needed—to be held in a grip too sure and strong to bother fighting. She didn't want to fight it. She wanted to give herself to Paige.

If only she could.

Soon Paige moved them so they were lying together, side by side, lips almost touching. Their sweat and her cum had made the sheets wet, but they lay on it like a mistake they'd made. Every time Paige breathed out, Seren breathed in. Wanting her desperately all over again. Wanting this not to be the last time.

Minutes passed, and then Paige got out of bed without a word. Without a kiss. Seren felt her leave like a wrenching in her chest. She squeezed her eyes closed and curled up, wishing she could push something into the empty place Paige had left.

Two months ago, she'd been fine. She hadn't wanted anyone to hold her then. Not acutely, anyway. Sure, she'd entertained the idea of someday finding someone, but she hadn't gone looking—because the timing was all wrong and she knew it. Screw the universe for handing her Paige at exactly the wrong fucking time. For letting her love something she couldn't keep.

After a minute, she rolled onto her back and stared at the ceiling, wondering if she should leave, wanting to beg Paige to come back to bed, and hating herself for all of it. There was no pretending that today hadn't happened. Paige was right—they needed a break.

# CHAPTER THIRTY-NINE

Jen leaned back in her chair, studying Paige. "So, did you two break up or not?"

Paige ran a hand through her hair and eyed the computer screen with her half-finished surgery report. It'd been a long day filled with too many sick patients. She knew Jen probably wanted to get home to her family. But she also knew she needed someone to talk to. "No…not yet anyway."

Officially they hadn't broken up. Unofficially, Paige didn't see a path forward. "We had a fight and agreed to take a breather. I think we'd gotten too close too fast. Since I got the ranch, Seren's been over at my place almost every night for weeks now."

Then the fight came, and they'd gone four days without seeing each other. Four days didn't seem long in theory, but it was killing her not knowing how Seren was doing. "I don't know where things are going from here."

"You want to be with her, right?"

"Yes. Definitely." A moment later she added, "If she wants to let me into her life I do. I like her too much to pretend it's not serious."

"But you like her so much that you're willing to break up with her if she doesn't want something serious? Am I getting that right?"

Paige pursed her lips. "When you say it that way—"

"Men are less complicated."

"Doesn't mean relationships with them are any better."

Jen held up one finger, acknowledging her point. "True."

"Anyway, unlike you, I'm not bi."

"Weren't you the one who said everyone was a little bit bi?"

"That was when I was hoping that straight pharmacist would consider dating me." Jen laughed and Paige added, "She had nothing on Seren."

"Are you in love?"

Paige sighed. "For a while now."

"Okay, let's recap. You love her. She loves you?" At Paige's head nod, Jen continued, "And the sex is good?"

Paige nodded. "But she doesn't want a serious relationship and I do."

"Unless you're leaving out some crucial details, I think she's making a mistake."

"Thanks. But you're my friend. You've gotta take my side on this." Then again, Paige had to allow that her own mom hadn't taken her side. Beatrice had sided with Seren. She'd even brought Seren a cheesy potato casserole the night after the fight—and told Paige she was doing it.

Her mom was convinced that once the baby came, Seren would realize she needed help and then they'd move in together and all would be perfect. Would have been perfect had Paige not messed everything up by pushing too fast. But Paige didn't trust that would happen, and more than that, she wanted Seren to choose her, and to choose their relationship. Not instead of being a parent, obviously, but in addition to. And that had nothing to with needing help.

"I asked her to move in because I knew it would make things easier. But when she turned me down, I realized it wasn't that I wanted to be helpful, I wanted to be wanted."

"We all want that," Jen said. "I'm sure she does too."

"Not enough to work on a plan for us going forward."

Jen shifted on her chair and kicked her feet up on her desk. "Maybe this break will be good for you. You look almost as exhausted as someone with a newborn."

"Every moment that I'm not here, I'm working on the house." Or biking. She'd had several long bike rides since the fight, hoping endorphins might blanket out all the negative feelings about the breakup. A moment later, Paige reminded herself that they hadn't broken up. Not yet. "Seren's got it in her head that the baby is going to screw up any chance we have of a relationship. So, why bother trying, you know? Her parents broke up when she was a little baby, and she's convinced we'd follow the same path if we got together now."

"Honestly, the odds aren't in your favor."

"I know." Paige even agreed that it was too soon to discuss moving in together. But she stood by what she'd told Seren. She didn't think the conversation would have been any different if they'd waited.

Which is why she'd wanted some space. Some time to feel less angry about the whole thing. Seren hadn't liked the idea of a break, but she'd agreed. She'd asked Paige how much time she needed, but how long would it take to stop loving someone too much?

"I guess the part I didn't really tell you—that I knew from the beginning—is that she wants to be a single mom."

"Wait till the kid pops out. She's gonna change her tune."

"I don't think so. Being a single mom is important to her. She told me straight-up that she doesn't want a co-parent. She's convinced any relationship would go south and screw things up for the kid. There's no getting around that part."

"And you knew all this going in?"

"I knew she didn't want things to get serious." Paige shook her head. "A little part of me thinks there's still hope. What we have is so good, you know? It's just the kid thing. But I wouldn't have to be a co-parent. I'd let her make all the parenting decisions."

"You want her to move in with you, but you're not going to be involved in parenting the kid? At all?"

"Well, I'd be around and part of the kid's life, but I'd leave the parenting decisions to her."

Jen raised an eyebrow. "She's right. It wouldn't work. Not if you're living together. I'm not saying it couldn't work for someone, but that someone's not you." She held up her hand when Paige started to interrupt. "You're not wrong for wanting what you want, and I still think she's making a mistake not trying to work things out. But, if she's got her heart set on being a single mom, she shouldn't move in with you. You'd become part of her kid's life and you'd be a co-parent. You wouldn't be able to stop yourself from helping. And clearly she knew you well enough to know that too."

"You think there's no hope?"

"I've seen you with Leo. You love kids." Jen inclined her head to Leo's picture pinned above Paige's desk. "You love kids enough to put a picture of mine on your wall."

"Anyone would put up that picture. Look at him snuggling Tigger."

"And you can't help taking care of little things."

Paige sighed. "Maybe you're right. I can't not be who I am. And she wants someone I'm not."

Paige left work feeling more down than she'd been even the day Seren had left. She avoided the house and went straight to the barn. Nellie nickered as Paige mixed up a bucket of what she called Old Horse Ensure, stomping her feet and eager for her dinner. In the month since she'd taken over full care, Nellie's ribs were showing less and she clearly had more energy. Paige hung the bucket on a hook she'd made especially for it, then leaned against the stall rail as Nellie buried her nose in the mash.

She felt something brush against her leg and looked down expecting to see Storm, one of the feral cats the Landrys had left behind. Instead, a sleek gray cat with gorgeous green eyes looked up at her. In one glance, Paige knew she was pregnant. "Hey, stranger. Where you from?"

The cat darted behind a hay bale at the sound of her voice but reappeared a few minutes later when Paige set out cat food for the two residents. Paige tossed a few kibble her direction and they disappeared immediately. Moments later, the cat was diving into the bowl of kibble with as much gusto as Nellie inhaled her mash. Paige watched her eat, wondering again where she'd come from. She was young—probably under a year—and skinny save for her protruding belly.

"You joining the herd?" Paige waited, as if expecting an answer. "Well, gray is pretty close to black, but I'm spaying you after that litter, just so you know. And you're gonna have to tell me where you found a boy, 'cause he's getting clipped too."

Paige's phone rang, startling the newcomer. As she skittered off, Paige reached into her back pocket and answered the call without looking to see who it was. Her mom always called at this time. Once a day, without fail.

"Yep."

"Yep?" Seren laughed softly. Not her usual full laugh, but like she was trying to figure out if the situation was funny or not. Or like she was nervous.

Paige straightened, her mind racing. *Seren.* "Um, hi. I didn't look at the caller ID." She paced in a circle. "Figured it'd be my mom."

"She just left. We had dinner together."

"You had dinner with my mom?"

"And Rita and Leslie. I invited them all over. I was going to ask you too, but I chickened out at the last minute. I thought maybe having other people around would make it easier, but the more I considered having you here and not touching you or talking about everything, the more I knew it'd be a mistake."

"I had a lot of things to finish up at work anyway." Not untrue. Still, she wished she could have been at the dinner.

"I've missed you."

Three words and Paige's throat tightened. "Yeah."

"Yeah?"

Dammit. She sounded like a damn caveman who was butt-hurt. She hated both how much she wanted to tell Seren it was her fault and how she knew it was all hers. "I've missed you too."

"I woke up this morning wondering if we were over or if we we're really only taking a break."

Paige pressed her hand against her eyes and clenched her jaw to hold back the tears. When she'd gotten ahold of the emotion, she swallowed and said, "Me too."

"I want things back the way they were."

Paige wanted to say, "Me too" again, but the words didn't come. Seren's breathing was the only sound on the other line for a long moment as she weighed admitting the truth. "I don't think I can go back to that. I'm not good at pretending."

"Or lying. I like that about you. Anyway, it's not fair for me to ask." Seren sniffed. "I found my mom's will. You won't believe where it was."

"Tell me." They'd gone through so many boxes looking for the damn thing.

"In the top drawer of her nightstand. Along with a list of all her bank accounts and passwords. She also wrote me a letter." Seren's voice broke on the last sentence, and she took a moment before going on. "Why I didn't look there first, I have no clue. She always kept everything important in her nightstand."

"Sometimes we don't think things should be easy."

Seren murmured her agreement. "Also. I've got a cowbell I want to give you."

"Okay."

"I know it's silly, but I think you're gonna love it. And I was wondering if you'd like the door knocker. You know the cow that's out front?"

"I remember the door knocker." She doubted she'd ever forget that cow staring her down after their first kiss.

Seren continued, "Leslie told me I've gotta clear out more of the cow stuff and a bunch of the furniture so the place looks more open. Less cluttered. I've been trying to focus on that so I don't miss you too much. But all I do is think of you anyway."

"I'd like the cow door knocker." Even if it came with memories.

"Mom and you would have gotten along so well it's scary." Seren cleared her throat. "Anyway…"

"Don't throw out her cow quilt. I know you'll want it someday."

"I promised myself I'd save that and the annoying cow teapot when you told me that story about your dad. And his stinky fishing jacket." Seren seemed to wait for Paige to say something. When she didn't, she said, "It's late. I'll let you go."

"Okay. Good night."

Paige expected Seren to say good night and the line to click. When it didn't happen, she sat down on a hay bale and listened to Seren's breathing. Minutes passed. Finally, she had to say the three words that were still true. So true that her chest caved in trying to hold them back. "I love you."

"I love you too." Seren's voice sounded shaky. "That's what I was sitting here thinking but I wasn't going to say it because maybe that's not fair."

"It's fair. You can't help falling in love." Although she really hadn't tried to stop herself from falling for Seren. But it was too late to look back. "I could come to your house and pick up the cowbell tomorrow if you want. After work. We have that list of things I was going to fix over there. You helped me here and I didn't finish helping you."

"I'm not sure it's a good idea for you to come here. For me. I'm sure you'd be fine, but I'm having a hard time with this."

What could she say to that? The gray cat reappeared, threading between Paige's legs. A moment later she hopped up on the hay bale and pushed her head into Paige's side.

"I want you so much I can't think of anything else," Seren said. She wasn't holding back her tears now. "These past few nights have sucked. I lie in bed wishing you were holding me. Wishing I could say the words that you wanted to hear."

Which meant she couldn't. Paige took a deep breath. She didn't want to cause either of them more pain. "I feel like we're stuck. I want to go forward, and it's not right for me to ask you to take that big of a leap. And you want to pretend we're not in as deep as we are."

Seren murmured an agreement.

"You know how I said that I wouldn't have to be a parent? That I'd leave everything to you? I've thought about it a lot, and I don't think I'd be able to do that. I started thinking about being a parent when you sent me that first picture of the ultrasound—when they had to remeasure to make sure you weren't having a huge baby. I was ready to help you raise an Andre the Giant."

Seren half laughed, half choked. "You would, too."

"I would." She sighed. "If you moved in, and our relationship kept going forward, I'd want to be part of the kid's life. I'd want to be involved. And if you didn't let me, I'd be mad at you for keeping that from me. For not letting me help you. I want someone who's willing to share their whole self with me. Not only the parts that feel safe."

"I know."

Another long, quiet minute passed. The gray cat took a tentative step onto Paige's thigh. Paige held still, and a moment later all four legs were in her lap. She scratched under the cat's chin and was rewarded with a loud purr. *If only women were so easy.*

"So, I guess I should say good night. Or do you think we should say goodbye instead?" The words hurt, but she wanted to be done with the pain. She wanted to move on if that's all that was left to be done.

"There's some things you were right about too," Seren said. "I should have taken a minute to think about what you were saying. I didn't. I jumped to a conclusion that wasn't completely fair. You're not my dad. And this relationship isn't my parents'."

Paige couldn't help how fast her heart stood up at attention. Her mind, though, propped up doubts just as fast. "What are you saying?"

"I'm saying I'd like to talk more about what we are. About what we both want. Honestly, I feel sick when I think about not having you in my life. Even if we're only friends."

Paige's stomach turned. *Only friends.*

"If you need more time or more space or more whatever, I get it. But it's killing me not knowing what we're doing."

"I haven't been able to think about anything else either."

"Maybe we could go for a walk? Or go to a coffee shop or something?" Seren's voice was hopeful, but there was a trace of uncertainty in it. Like she worried Paige might not agree.

"A walk sounds nice."

# CHAPTER FORTY

A walk had never felt like such a big deal. Seren stressed about what to wear. About where they should go. About if it'd be too warm—there'd been a heat wave with no days under a hundred for a week. She wondered if she should have suggested Paige come over to her house instead. Most of all, though, she stressed about what she'd say.

She'd talked to Leslie about everything. But she'd also discussed most of the situation with the water aerobics class. Rita and Claia weighed in, as did a dozen others—including Beatrice—which might have been weird but wasn't. Seren had come to feel comfortable with all of them.

At first, everyone agreed it was too soon to move in with Paige. But when she'd admitted she'd never felt happier than she had those months with Paige—nor more miserable in the four days she'd gone without her—everyone said what she felt in her heart: maybe they belonged together. Maybe taking a chance was worth the risk of heartbreak.

On Thursday, the heat wave broke. Rain came, as unexpected in Davis in August as a free lunch. It positively never rained in

August. But it rained. Not a downpour, but enough to make the dirt smell good. And the weather app predicted the high to only hit eighty-five.

Seren fussed in the garden after work, trying to keep herself busy while she waited until seven when she was due to meet Paige. She showered and changed into a blue sundress she'd picked up at the maternity store. Gone were the days of trying to hide her belly. Tomorrow was her twenty-eight-week appointment, and it was undeniable that the baby was growing. She felt kicks regularly now. The first few seemed like miracles, and she'd stopped everything to put her hand on the spot the baby had kicked, hoping for another. Then it became clear the baby was training to be a soccer player.

She decided to bike the ten minutes downtown. Her dress and the belly made it a little awkward, but she managed. She was from Davis, after all. Biking was part of life.

The park was swarming with people and a band was playing. She hadn't worried about not being able to find Paige, but five minutes after parking her bike she was still searching the crowd. Was it a bad sign if they couldn't find each other? It was a silly thing to think, and yet she'd spent the past week considering all the signs that had pointed for or against Paige. She'd dreamed about her every night. In one of the dreams, Paige was holding a baby and she knew it was hers. The baby was laughing, and her heart had filled. But it was only a dream.

Kids darted every which way in a big game of tag. Couples spread out picnic blankets and leaned together listening to the music. She checked her phone. No text, no missed call.

"Hey."

Seren looked up at Paige's voice. She had on a faded blue UC Davis baseball hat that Seren hadn't ever seen her wear, and a pair of shorts and a T-shirt. Casual, and fitting the weather, but for some reason the hat tipped things to sexy. Or maybe that was simply Seren's libido surging up despite everything.

"Hi."

"You look nice. New dress?"

Seren nodded.

"It looks great on you."

Seren wanted a hug. A kiss would be even better. But Paige clearly wasn't making a move to touch her. In fact, she took a step back, gazed around the park, and said, "I forget how busy it is here when they have the Music in the Park nights. Did you want to listen to the band?"

"I'd rather walk. If that's okay with you?"

Paige nodded.

She hadn't really planned where they'd walk, but when she headed east to the rows of shops, it felt right. The noise of the park slipped away after a block, but it was hard to start talking when there was so much to be said.

"It's weird not holding hands," Paige said.

"We could hold hands."

Paige's brow furrowed. "I don't think I'm ready."

Neither was she, despite how much she wanted it.

Paige paused at the corner of the intersection and half turned to face Seren. "I'm friends with a lot of people I've dated. But it takes a while for me to be ready for that."

"You want to be friends?"

"You mentioned it when we talked and, well, I thought you should know that I'd consider it, but I'm gonna need more time."

"You didn't really answer the question."

Paige nodded slowly. "I want to keep you in my life, so I guess I'd take the friend option. If that's the choice."

"Good to know." She glanced at the street as a group of bikers rode past, then at a parked car, anything to stall her from looking at Paige. "I feel the same. Being friends is kind of a last resort." She met Paige's gaze, and the hope in her eyes was unmistakable, but so was the steeliness. Paige was prepared to break up. It was up to her to decide whether they went forward.

"I had a plan for what I wanted to say, and what I wanted to ask, but I'm not sure where to start." She shook her head. "You know I wasn't nervous on our first date, but I am now."

Paige glanced at the store they'd stopped in front of, and Seren realized it was the same bookshop they'd been to on their second date. "Want to go inside?"

"Sure."

Paige opened the door and waited for her. When Seren stepped past, she caught a familiar scent of barn and soap and wanted to turn right into Paige's arms. Instead, she made herself hurry past.

The clerk working the counter looked up and smiled. "Let me know if you want any help finding anything."

"Thanks." Seren forced a smile. *Are there books on navigating a relationship that you'd doomed from the outset but now desperately want to work?*

"Think it's my style?"

Seren turned around. Paige had taken off her Davis hat and replaced it with a court jester hat. There was a rack of them to the left of the door. This time the smile came easy. "You're a dork."

"If I wear this, will it make it easier or harder for you to tell me what you want to say?"

Seren pulled the jester hat off Paige's head, and then because she couldn't resist, ruffled her hair. God, it felt good to touch her.

Paige winked. "Harder?"

"Actually, no." She returned the hat to Paige, then reached for one herself and put it on. "To do it right, we both need to wear one."

"Okay." Paige tugged the hat back on. Her smile barely turned up her lips, but it was there. She walked past Seren toward an aisle of self-help books and picked up the first one. "*The 4-hour Workweek*? This guy's definitely not a vet." She glanced at Seren. "Or a massage therapist."

"No kidding." Seren picked up another. "How about this: *The Subtle Art of Not Giving A Fuck*."

Paige shook her head. "Yeah, that guy's also not a vet. Or a massage therapist. Probably a rich asshole, though."

Seren replaced the book she'd picked up and then reached for another. "*Who Moved My Cheese?* I read this one in high school."

"Really? So did I. Always felt bad for those starving mice. It's kind of a messed-up story."

Seren couldn't help laughing. "Of course you felt bad for the mice. You know, the point is not to starve. The smart mouse goes looking for more cheese."

"Yeah. One finds more cheese while the others starve. It's capitalist bullshit. And who feeds mice cheese, anyway? They should be eating seeds and little insects."

"I don't think that was the author's point." But she loved Paige's commentary.

"I could have missed the point. I often do." Paige picked up another book. "*The Year of Yes*. Okay, now this person might be a vet." She turned it over and read the back. Then she looked up at Seren. "Never mind. It's about saying yes to things like dancing— not taking on more appointments."

Seren took the book, trying to place the author's name. Shonda Rhimes. It clicked a moment later. "I've been wanting to read this."

"You thinking about taking up dancing too?"

"I've been thinking about taking up you." Seren said the words under her breath, but she knew Paige heard by the way her gaze darted to hers. She continued, raising her voice a little, "It's written by the woman who created *Grey's Anatomy* and *Scandal*. Two of my favorite shows."

"Good reason to get the book."

Seren thumbed it open, reading the first line she came to. "'All I have to work with is the truth. But it's *my* truth.' I like that." She flipped the page, scanning the words on the next.

"What's your truth?" Paige asked.

Without looking up from the book, Seren said, "Right now, my truth is I've realized I'm scared to take chances. I don't know where along the line I got to be the person who'd rather not fail than try something risky. But here I am."

Paige didn't say anything, so Seren continued, "I met this woman. In water aerobics of all places. She's amazing. I fell in love with her, but then she asked me to take a chance on us and I turned her down." She took a deep breath, feeling the weight of regret all over again. "The really dumb part is, I wanted what she was offering. I was just scared it might not last."

"Is she cute?"

Seren smiled. "Yes, but she's not your type."

"You had every right to turn me down. I asked you to do something that was a big step. And we weren't ready."

Seren didn't meet Paige's eyes. "Leslie says this is what I do when the universe hands me something on a platter. I run in the other direction even if it's exactly what I want. Something seems too good to be true, too easy, and I think it can't possibly work." She paused, closed the book, and read the title again. "I've always wanted to live on a farm. Always. Used to dream about it when I was a little girl. That and being a mom. My other truth I recently discovered is that I love baby cows."

"They're hard to resist."

"Impossible, actually." She looked up, caught the sight of the red-and-yellow felt hat Paige was wearing, and shook her head at the ridiculousness. The bells on her own hat jingled.

Paige cocked her head. "You think I look silly? You should see yourself."

"How'd you know what I was thinking?"

Paige's smile was still tentative, but her eyes had a familiar spark. She took off her jester hat and then Seren's, combing her fingers through Seren's hair as she did, ostensibly pushing strands back into place. Seren held her breath when Paige didn't pull her hand back. Fingers threaded through her hair and then slipped behind her neck.

*Kiss me.* If she could feel Paige's lips, feel her kiss, she'd know if Paige was willing. Willing to be the one who would catch her if she jumped.

Paige pulled back her hand a moment later. "It's so hard not kissing you."

Seren wanted to push past Paige's wall. She wanted to step forward and show her they didn't need to resist what they both wanted. But she'd given them every reason to resist. She was the one who hadn't wanted to take a chance on them.

Paige looked down at the hats and then walked over to the rack and rehung them. When she came back to Seren, she held out her hand for the book. Instead of replacing it on the shelf, she walked up to the counter and passed it to the clerk along with her credit card. The clerk chatted with Paige, but Seren didn't pay attention to their conversation. Nothing mattered except Paige's answer to her unspoken question.

After a moment, Seren turned and headed outside. She leaned against the building and closed her eyes. All the thoughts racing through her mind made it feel like she was standing next to a six-lane highway. She felt something brush against her arm and opened her eyes. Paige stood in front of her.

"I have my twenty-eight-week checkup tomorrow. Will you go with me?"

Paige nodded.

"Will you be my birth partner?"

"What about Leslie?"

"She's my second choice. You're my first. But if you're not willing—"

"I'm more than willing."

"Good." Seren exhaled. She'd been carrying the weight of the birth partner question for months, and yet she'd known Paige's answer would be yes if only she asked. Now it was done. Paige would be there. "I'm gonna be a disaster. I'm a nervous wreck in hospitals after everything with my mom."

"I'll be with you every minute. You won't be alone." Paige held out her hand and Seren took it. "What you said in there...what does it mean for us now?"

"I guess a lot depends on you. What are you thinking?"

"We're not a sure thing. You're right about that." Paige hesitated. "There's a lot of reasons why it might not work. And maybe if we don't want to get our hearts broken—or if we don't want things to get messy—maybe we should only be friends."

It was the last thing she wanted to hear, but she couldn't argue. "Is being friends what you want?"

"I want a relationship with you. I want all the parts of your life you're willing to share with me."

"What if it's everything?"

Paige straightened. "Are you saying you want to try something serious?"

"It might not work. I'm pretty sure I'll screw things up for us more than once. You'll have to fix things probably and keep me from freaking out, but I know you can do that, which is the only reason we might have a chance. Anyway. I want to try. More than anything else. It's gonna be messy and hard and neither of us are gonna get enough sleep and—"

"And we'll be there for each other."

Paige took a step forward and Seren melted into their kiss. Being gathered up in Paige's arms and reminded of their love was everything she wanted. When Paige started to pull back, Seren pushed away from the wall. She wrapped her arms around Paige's shoulders, going for a kiss of her own. As soon as she parted her lips, Paige deepened the kiss.

On the middle of the sidewalk, in the middle of her hometown, where anyone could see, she claimed Paige as hers. And Paige claimed her right back.

# CHAPTER FORTY-ONE

"I've got to hand it to you, Paige. No way would I be able to keep a secret like that for months." Leslie leaned over the platter of mini quiches and lowered her voice. "You don't have to tell me, but if one of the presents I brought was a blue jumper, would that work?"

"Definitely. Seren loves blue."

Leslie rolled her eyes. "For the baby."

"I'm sure the baby will love blue too. And pink. What baby doesn't like bright colors?"

Leslie plucked up one of the spinach and mushroom quiches and then turned on her heel. "You're impossible," she called over her shoulder.

The baby shower was in full swing. Nearly everyone from water aerobics was there as well as a half dozen of Seren's other friends and a handful of people from her work. It was true—she had plenty of people who were more than willing to help her with the baby if she needed it. There was a page-long list of folks who wanted to be babysitters circulating the room with more names being added. Rita had claimed the second spot, adding that she was infant-CPR certified to secure her position, and Seren had already promised to call her. Bea and Leslie were arguing over who should be in the first spot, and Paige wasn't sure who'd win.

Paige felt arms wrap around her from behind. She turned to face Seren. "Hey. Was wondering where you'd gone."

"I had to pee." Seren leaned forward and pecked Paige's cheek. "Are you surviving this?"

"Are you kidding? I'm having a blast. Baby showers are totally my thing."

"Remember how I always know when you're not being completely truthful?"

"Mini quiche? There's also five different casseroles if you'd like me to dish you up one of those."

Seren laughed and reached for a quiche. She polished it off in two bites then shifted closer to Paige. "The house looks great. It was so much work, but it was worth it."

They'd decided to combine the housewarming party with the baby shower. Aside from all the work, and not really being a fan of baby shower games, Paige had been looking forward to having everyone over. The ranch house finally felt like a home—their home. Seren had finished moving all of her stuff over the week before and her mom's place was officially on the market. Leslie seemed confident it would sell quickly and then there'd be nothing left to do but get ready for a baby.

"Honestly, I am having fun. It's nice seeing our house full of people."

Seren met her gaze and nodded.

"And baby showers might not totally be my thing, but I wouldn't miss this one for the world. But you know what really made our house look good?" Paige held up the dish towel she'd slung over her shoulder. A leaping cow was embroidered on the front. "All your mom's kitchen stuff."

"I can't believe I let you convince me to bring those towels. But I will admit they work here."

"So do the bowls, the plates, the teapot…Oh, and especially that judgy cow door knocker."

Seren laughed again. "If you have to put up with a baby shower, I guess I can live with those cow bowls."

"So, are you having fun?"

"I am." Seren glanced at the living room crowded with people and smiled. "I wish my mom were here. I keep thinking how much she'd love all the women in water aerobics and, well, this."

"I wish she were here too." Paige set down the platter of quiches and wrapped an arm around Seren, pulling her into a hug. They shared a kiss and then she pulled back. "I may have channeled your mom when I went shopping. Can I give you the present that she helped me pick out?" Since everyone else was still busy eating and talking, it seemed like the perfect time.

"Uh-oh."

"You worried?" Paige grinned. She'd planned on buying the crib that Seren wanted but that gift had been claimed by the water aerobics crew who all went in together on it. The other few things on Seren's wish list also got scooped up by the other guests so she'd had to think of something else.

"I'm not worried. Okay, maybe a little." Seren held up her hand, her thumb and forefinger separated by a good three inches to show her level of concern.

Paige retrieved the blue-and-pink-wrapped box from where she'd placed it with the other gifts. Seren took the box and immediately gave it a shake.

"What if it's fragile?"

Seren tilted her head. "I know you and my mom. Neither of you would give me something fragile."

"Good point. Just so you know, this is only part of the gift."

Seren unwrapped the box and pushed past the tissue paper. She lifted the painting up and then turned it round to have a look. "Oh. Paige." Her eyes teared up as she gently touched the swing hanging from the moon. Above the moon, a cow leaped. "Are you sure you had anything to do with this? Because I swear this could've come straight from my mom."

"It was mostly her."

Seren swiped her eyes. "I can't wait to hang it in the baby's room."

"I also put a hold on a rocking chair in the antique store downtown, but I want you to try it out first. There may be a little cow painted on the back of it."

Seren set the painting down and reached for Paige. "Thank you." She pulled her into a big kiss and then added a second little one when Paige started to step back. When she let go, her smile made Paige's chest ache.

"Ahem." Rita cleared her throat. "Did someone announce that it was time to open presents?"

Seren pointed to Paige. "If anyone should get into trouble, it's her."

"Me? I never do anything wrong." Paige's comment was returned with eye rolls from Seren and Rita both.

"I'll make the announcement," Rita said, grumbling only half-heartedly.

As Rita clapped her hands, trying to get everyone's attention, Seren leaned against Paige. Under her breath she said, "I know baby showers aren't your thing, but I can't imagine doing this without you. I can't imagine doing a lot of things without you now."

"Gotten used to me, huh?" Paige slipped her arm around Seren's shoulder and pulled her closer. "Careful, people will think you like having me around."

"I think that secret's out."

# CHAPTER FORTY-TWO

Scheduling an appointment with Dr. Connie Morrison wasn't easy. The receptionist who'd taken her call had tried to convince her to see one of the large animal residents, then seemed completely baffled that she didn't have an animal to bring to the appointment. She'd finally relented when Seren dropped Paige Dannenberg's name and said she wanted to pay for the visit in advance. Technically Paige hadn't referred her—and didn't have any idea Seren was meeting with her ex—but the receptionist didn't need to know that.

Seren got to the barn ten minutes early. She'd tried to dress for the occasion by wearing a loose flannel over one of her pregnancy tops and the muck boots Paige had bought for her to wear around the barn, but she still felt like a city-girl poser. Partly that was because the boots looked new. Paige had insisted she didn't need any help cleaning Nellie's stall and the other stalls in the barn were still empty—save for the barn cats and a dozen chicks. Paige had bought the chicks from a client and Seren had overridden her claim that she didn't need help by saying that yellow fluffs were impossible to resist. While that was true, she also wanted to prove she could handle at least basic farm chores thirty-seven weeks pregnant.

Before Seren could decide if she should knock on the side door Paige had taken her through when they were there last or stand out front by the open stall marked for patients, she spotted the vet tech who'd helped Paige. She couldn't remember their name, unfortunately, but waving, and probably looking completely out of place, got their attention.

"I've got an appointment with Dr. Morrison. Should I wait at the patient entrance even if I don't have a patient?"

The tech squinted at her like they weren't sure what she was asking. "Weren't you here with Dr. Dannenberg a while back? You helped feed those calves, right?"

Seren nodded.

"You can follow me. Dr. Morrison's in her office."

As the tech led the way through the open stall, past a gate, and into the barn, Seren couldn't help taking a deep breath. The smell of fresh hay mingled with cow poop. Pregnancy had given her a strange acuity for scents and while "barn" probably wouldn't be on anyone's top-ten fragrance lists, she couldn't get enough of it now.

The door to the office was open but the tech knocked anyway. When she looked up from her laptop, eyes narrowing on Seren, Connie Morrison looked even more intimidating than the first time.

"Seren Winters?" When Seren nodded, she added, "I saw your name on the schedule this morning and was trying to figure out why it sounded familiar." She motioned for Seren to take a seat, then waved the tech off when they mentioned needing to get back to a patient. "What can I do for you?"

Seren cleared her throat. She'd practiced her opening lines in the car on the way over. "First, thank you for meeting with me. I know you're probably wondering why I'm here."

When Connie only stared at her, Seren decided to get right to the point. "I was wondering if you could help me buy a calf."

Connie arched an eyebrow. "You want a calf? Like as a pet?"

"Well, more as the start of a small herd."

Connie studied Seren for a moment. "Are you and Paige still—"

"Yes. We're together."

"Have you asked her about this? She's got plenty of contacts."

"It's kind of a surprise. For her." Despite the skeptical look Connie was giving her, Seren pushed on. "Do you remember those two calves born here that night Paige and I came for a tour? One of them Paige had to pull out. A little girl cow?"

"A heifer. Yes."

Seren silently chided herself. She knew girl calves were called heifers after all the reading she'd done and hated she'd used the wrong word. "Heifer. Right. Paige mentioned that ranch had good stock—I think that was the word she used. She said when she was ready to get a calf, she planned on contacting them."

"You want to surprise her with a calf from the MacMillan ranch?"

"Exactly." Seren was more than a little surprised that Connie had made the leap that fast.

"Does she have a place to keep a calf?"

"She bought a place with five acres. And there's a barn." Seren didn't know how often Paige and Connie talked, but she clearly hadn't kept her in the loop lately. "She's done a ton of work to get it ready for cows. She keeps saying she'll wait until after the baby comes, but who knows how crazy things will be then." She was rambling now. Should she tell Connie she'd moved in with Paige? Would that make her more likely to help or less?

"I know it might seem like a bad idea to surprise her with this, but she told me I could pick out the first calf and I don't want the baby holding her back from getting started on this." More rambling. "It's her dream to have her own cows."

Connie reached for a pen and then clicked it a few times. "Part of me wants to tell you to let Paige do this on her own. But the other part of me thinks I have no business giving relationship advice."

"I'm here for advice. If you think I shouldn't do it, I'll listen to you. But I know this is something she wants."

Connie nodded.

"I guess I could get her something calves would need like blankets or something instead."

Connie's lips turned up in an almost smile. After a moment, she turned in her chair and tapped her laptop awake. She scrolled through a few screens and then scribbled down a name and number. She tore off the notebook page and handed it to Seren. "This is the main guy over at MacMillan ranch. Drop my name and he'll give you one of his best calves." She paused. "A good heifer won't be cheap, but I know Paige won't want something they're happy to get rid of. And make sure you don't settle for any calf that wasn't fence-weaned. That's important to Paige."

Seren glanced at the paper and the number, then realized she hadn't fully explained what she wanted. "The thing is I don't want just any calf. I'd like the one that Paige delivered."

Connie pursed her lips. "That's gonna be a lot harder. They keep good records, and everyone gets ear-tagged but…you're sure that's what you want?"

"Yes. As long as she'd be weaned by now. I've been reading up on it, and as far as I could tell nearly all dairy calves are weaned by four months and it's been four months since April was born so…" Her voice trailed when she saw Connie's pursed lips. "You're probably thinking I'm silly for feeling sentimental about one calf."

"That goes without saying," Connie continued without a smile to soften the blow. "You're sure this is what Paige wants?"

"I'm sure. Well, ninety percent sure."

Connie clicked her pen again. "Paige wouldn't let me pay her that night she helped me. She really did save my ass. Not to mention that calf." She held out her hand. "Give me back that number. I'll make this call myself."

Connie might be Paige's ex, but Seren now owed her a big favor. Or at least a pie. She insisted that nothing was owed and that she'd only pulled a few strings for Paige, but the fact remained that five hours after their meeting, a truck with a livestock trailer pulled up to the ranch and a guy named Pablo led out not one but two heifer calves. The first was April. Seren had checked the pictures Paige had taken of her feeding April about a hundred times, and she only needed to take one look at the calf to know the markings matched. She had to hold herself back from bounding forward and throwing her arms around the calf. She'd gotten big, but her lightning-strike blaze was identical.

Then she saw the second calf. "Oh! She's big."

Pablo's smile seemed to have a tinge of pride. "Good-looking heifer, no?"

Seren nodded. Bigger was also more intimidating. Connie had convinced her to go for two calves so they'd have each other as friends. Seren had wanted to find JJ, but Connie told her he'd be next to impossible to track down. Bull-calves were sold off quick, apparently. Seren had to push away a worry about what would happen to him and instead focused on Connie's recommendation to get a five-month-old heifer for the second calf so the adjustment would be easier. But now suddenly there were two calves in the driveway and Paige wasn't due home for another hour.

"Want me to get these little ladies into your barn?" Pablo asked.

Seren wanted to hug him for the offer. "Yes, please." She hadn't thought about how to move a calf, but the two girls followed Pablo like well-behaved puppies. Connie had mentioned that the calves got handled a lot on dairy farms—and especially on the MacMillan ranch—but it was a relief to see.

For all the reading she'd done, and as much as she thought she knew what she was doing, aside from one date with newborn calves, she had no experience. Well, that would change starting now. Unless Paige took one look at the two calves and wanted to send them back because of the timing. She only hoped she could convince her.

After Pablo left, Seren went between the two stalls talking to the calves. She introduced Nellie across the way, then explained how during the day they'd all be out in the fenced pasture together. Every night they'd have their separate stalls in the barn, but as she watched the calves nose each other through the slats, she had to agree with Connie's assessment. One calf would have been lonely.

Her cell phone buzzed, and she wasn't surprised to see Paige's text. *Heading home. Do we need anything at the store?*

*We've got avocados. Who needs anything else?*

Predictably, Paige responded with a laughing emoji.

*I've got a surprise. Meet me in the barn.* Seren's heart raced as she hit send. Hopefully Paige wouldn't be upset. At least she could say she'd had an expert's help. She left the calves to check in on the baby chicks. Changing the chicks' water and filling their feeder occupied ten minutes, but when she still couldn't relax, she went over to scratch Nellie's head. The old mare had a knack for calming nerves, and as she leaned into Seren's hand, her charm worked its magic.

"It'll be fine, right? Paige will get over the part about this being bad timing as soon as she sees how cute the girls are, right?"

Nellie's head moved up and down as if she were nodding.

"Thanks. I needed that. Horse counseling should be a thing." Seren picked up a brush and entered Nellie's stall. She'd discovered that she loved grooming the old mare as much as Nellie liked the company, and she couldn't resist braiding the silver mane. "Maybe you'll like having company in the pasture. Wait, do horses like cows?" Another thing she should have researched…

Nellie turned her head, ears twitching as she caught the sound of something. Seren followed the mare's gaze over the paddock gate and heard the sound a second later. Gravel crunching under the wheels of a truck. *Paige.*

"I'll finish your braids later." She gave Nellie a pat and slipped out of the stall. Seren paced from Nellie's stall to the calves' and then back again. When she heard the barn door creak open, her heart rate shot up.

Paige had her usual vet outfit on that she wore in the clinic: blue scrubs paired with her faded gray Carhartt vest. The vest nearly always could stand to be washed but Seren loved her in it. Actually, it wasn't only the vest. She loved the whole package.

"Everything okay?" Paige's brow creased. "You look worried."

"I'm nervous." Seren crossed over to Paige. She took a deep breath as she reached for Paige's hand. "I know you wanted to wait, but—"

A moo interrupted. Paige's gaze shot in the direction of the sound. "No way."

"Yes way."

A wide smile spread across Paige's face. "Tell me that's my surprise."

"One of them." Now Seren was smiling too.

"One?" Paige went over to the first stall and peeked in, then hustled to the next. She glanced back at Seren, looking happier than ever. "I can't believe this."

"I was only hoping to find April, but now we have May too." She paused, biting the edge of her lip.

"May?"

"Since she's five months old and April's four months, well…"

Paige nodded. "I get it. I like the name."

"I know you said I could pick out the first set of calves, but I didn't want to mess up so I enlisted some help. Connie did most of the work, actually."

"Connie helped you?"

"She picked out May. She said if you were finally getting your cows, she wanted to make sure you had the best."

Paige leaned over the stall rails. "This is really April? The same calf I pulled?"

"I quadruple-checked her picture. And they ear-tagged her right away." Seren still wasn't sure Paige was really okay with what she'd done. "I know you wanted to wait until after the baby and everything, but I didn't want you to put your dreams on hold for me."

Paige glanced between Seren and the calves. "You shouldn't have spent your money on this. You're saving up for—"

"I've saved plenty. You pay for nearly everything around here. And this came out of my mom's money anyway." After the sale of her mom's house and all the accounts were settled, she had more than a little cushion. "She would have loved knowing I spent some of her money to buy baby cows."

Paige chuckled but her eyes were wet. She took a deep breath, wiped her eyes, and nodded.

"So what do you think of them?"

"I think they're perfect." Paige came over and wrapped her arms around Seren. "But I have to tell you something. My dream wouldn't be on hold if we'd waited till after you had your baby. It's kind of one big dream now. A ranch with a sweet old mare. A bunch of barn cats. An avocado tree. Chickens. Cows. And one day there's gonna be a little kid running around chasing everything."

"But you like your surprise?"

"I love my surprise."

"Then you're welcome." Seren leaned forward and met Paige's lips. She pulled back and caught the zipper of Paige's vest. "And I love your dream. Even more, I love that you let me be part of it. I don't know how I got so lucky."

"I'm the lucky one. I met this woman named Serendipity." Paige kissed her again. "It's crazy, but things have gone right for me ever since."

"I should remind you that you met someone named Serendipity and immediately got pushed into a pool."

"See? Total luck."

# CHAPTER FORTY-THREE

Paige finished tying the last suture and then dabbed a gauze to absorb a drop of blood. She stepped back from the table and tugged off her gloves. "All done."

All done with the laceration repair, but she still had an afternoon full of appointments. And records. Always there were more records to write. With every day closer to Seren's due date, she'd become more anxious about staying late doing paperwork. Seren's maternity leave had officially started and the baby could come any minute. Knowing Seren was alone at the ranch, even if it wasn't very far from town, made it hard not to be home with her.

She gave the dog one last look over, then nodded to her tech. "I'll be working on records. Let me know if our beagle friend has any issues waking up."

Jen was in the office on a phone call. Paige picked up the half-eaten sandwich she'd left at her desk—the emergency bleeding beagle had interrupted her lunch—and sank into her chair. Her phone buzzed with a text and as soon as she saw the words on the screen, she shot up from her seat. She spun around, pointed to her phone, and mouthed, "It's happening."

"It's happening?" Jen repeated without bothering to cover the phone she was holding. "You sure?"

"Seren's water broke."

"Holy shit. It's happening. Okay. Go."

"I've got that beagle, Brady, just waking up and—"

"Go." Jen pointed to the door. "I'll take care of the beagle and we'll get the afternoon appointments rescheduled. Go."

The twenty-minute drive home took a lot less than the usual twenty minutes. Fortunately, no speed checks were happening at one o'clock on a random Thursday. Paige raced into the house and found Seren half bent over the kitchen table, gripping the wood so tight her knuckles were white.

At the sight of Seren, obviously in pain and obviously in labor, Paige's heart jumped up to her throat. Since the moment they'd met, she'd known this day would come. She hadn't known she'd be a part of it, but Seren being pregnant meant one day a baby would come. And yet it still felt surreal. Like the sky was suddenly under her feet instead of overhead. But more than ever, she had to be calm.

"I'll grab your hospital bag."

Seren managed a nod and Paige hustled to the bedroom. She snagged the blue duffel bag with the dancing cow—the bag had once belonged to Seren's mom—and was back at Seren's side a moment later. Seren had loosened her grip on the table. She straightened now and breathed out.

"Contraction over?"

"That one is." Seren gripped her belly, her face strained. "And, fuck, they hurt. I know everyone says it hurts but…"

"It looks awful."

"Like worst gas pain ever combined with horrible cramps." Seren forced a smile. "I keep telling myself this means we get to finally meet the baby."

"Can't wait." Paige held out her hand and Seren shakily grasped it. "Let's get you to the hospital."

She wanted to ask the interval between the contractions, but by the time Seren was in the car, she was in no condition to talk. Which meant all Paige could do was run through every possible complication. She drove slowly over the pothole-riddled gravel lane, but when they reached the main road she pressed the gas pedal to the mat.

After a minute, she risked a glance at Seren. "You're doing great. Do you want to talk about breathing?"

"Not even a little bit. Only thing I want right now is to not be pregnant anymore."

"Bet you a dollar you won't be pregnant by tomorrow."

"Very funny." Seren stuck out her tongue.

Seren being punchy was a good sign. Paige exhaled, feeling the stress level drop a notch. She focused on the road and checked her speedometer. Pushing it to ninety was risky, but she wanted Seren to be at the hospital an hour ago. Another contraction hit and Seren gripped Paige's leg. This one seemed more intense than the others but was over nearly as fast.

"If this baby comes before we get to the hospital—"

"We're almost there." Not technically true, but Paige knew what Seren was about to say. She'd assisted in deliveries of everything from kittens to llamas, but she had no intention of delivering a baby human. Especially not Seren's. If something went wrong, she'd never forgive herself.

"Tell me you could deliver this baby just in case."

The edge of panic in Seren's voice broke Paige's resolve. "I could. But I won't need to. We'll be there in ten minutes." Ten minutes was pushing it. Fifteen was more likely, and only if the roads stayed clear.

Neither spoke after that. Seren had another two contractions, exactly four minutes apart. She reached for Paige's leg each time, and by the third go, Paige knew her thigh would be bruised with five fingertip-shaped blotches.

When they reached the outskirts of town, Paige slowed to fifty. Still technically speeding but no one was around. At the first traffic stop, she cursed the red light.

"It'll be fine," Seren said. "We're almost there." Whether she was convincing herself or Paige wasn't clear.

"It will be fine," Paige agreed. Sweat beaded at the back of her neck despite the cool October day and the air-conditioning blasting. "And before you know it, you're gonna be holding them in your arms."

"What if—"

"You're gonna rock this and the baby's gonna be fine." She wasn't only saying the words to make Seren feel better. She knew it was true. How exactly she knew, she couldn't say.

Seren nodded and closed her eyes, clearly bracing for another contraction.

\* \* \*

As soon as the hospital came into view, Seren wondered why she hadn't considered a home birth. She answered the question a moment later—because as much as hospitals scared her, the alternative of needing to rush to the hospital if something went wrong was worse. Exponentially worse. But they'd made it past step one.

Paige's words swirled in her head as the pep talk she didn't realize how much she needed: *You're gonna rock this and the baby's gonna be fine.*

She let Paige take care of the check-in process, answering as few of the questions as she had to and holding on to Paige's arm like a lifeline throughout. She'd already pre-registered and there wasn't anything to sign. She reminded herself to breathe and focused on how calm Paige seemed chatting to the receptionist. Then came the nurse's exam in a little room with pale orange curtains and walls the same color.

After the nurse pronounced her five centimeters dilated and in active labor, and went to notify the doctor, Seren looked over at Paige. "I feel like the Landrys talked to whoever decided the decor of this place."

Paige reached for the edge of the curtain and pretended to study it carefully. "Would you call this color mango or peach?"

"Awful is what I'd call it."

Paige laughed. It was so nice to hear the sound that Seren wanted to ask her to laugh again. But then another contraction came. This one was definitely stronger, and Seren felt a wrenching in her back along with the full clench of her lower abdomen. She wanted to vomit, but she'd already done that at the house. Nothing was left in her stomach. Still, bile surged up her throat and she fought to breathe through it.

Paige came to stand next to her, her face full of concern. "Want me to call the nurse?"

Seren shook her head. The contraction ended as abruptly as it started, and she felt almost normal the second the clenching stopped.

"They're getting closer together," Paige said.

"It's like I'm having a baby or something."

Paige laughed again, the sound as soothing as the first time. "I thought you were gonna be more nervous once we got here, but you're cracking jokes."

"Only because you're here. And because I'm gonna rock it and the baby's gonna be fine." Repeating Paige's words aloud buoyed her spirit even more.

"All true."

The nurse reappeared, pushing the curtain aside far enough to stick her head into the room. "Your doctor's on her way. She's asked me to move you to one of the delivery rooms. If you'll follow me—"

Before the nurse could finish, another contraction hit. Too close on the heels of the last. Seren reached for Paige, clinging to her as mind-numbing pain pulsed through her.

"Give us a minute," Paige said.

The nurse nodded.

What if the baby didn't want to wait for the doctor? Seren reminded herself she was only five centimeters dilated. It couldn't come yet. That realization came along with the thought that she had many more contractions to suffer through. "Fuck."

"I can talk to the doctor about pain meds if you'd like," the nurse said, directing the comment to Paige. She continued, "I know the doctor said an epidural wasn't on your wife's birth plan, but there are other options."

"I'd like to hear my options," Seren said. If the most recent contraction was any indication, she might also reconsider an epidural.

The move from the nurse's little mango-colored exam room to the delivery room was a blur. Seren knew Paige helped her stand, but the next thing she remembered she was lying on her back on a bed. The doctor came and went, deciding she wasn't dilated enough and would have to labor longer.

"Labor" was way too polite a word for it. Thank god Paige was at her side every minute. Neither of them mentioned the wife comment, though Seren thought of making a joke about it more than once. The weird part was how not weird it felt. She wondered what Paige would say if she admitted that. But conversations weren't happening. She couldn't even think of any one thing for long. Every contraction built on itself, and all she managed was moving through one to await the next.

Time was impossible to measure. There were no clocks and no windows and only muted light. Seren stripped out of the hospital gown at one point and sweated even naked. She knew she must look like a wild mess, but every time Paige met her eyes, the look on her face was so loving she decided not to worry. They didn't talk much, but whenever she reached out, Paige was there. Between Paige offering sips of water and massaging her back, she murmured "I love you" and she'd never felt it more.

Soon the only thing she thought of at all was how many breaths she took between the contractions. Then there was no break.

Paige seemed to sense the change, reaching for the call button before Seren could say the words. "We need the doctor."

The speaker buzzed: "Tell your wife the doctor's on her way up."

Paige glanced at Seren. "Okay."

The longest ever contraction finally let up, but Seren was glad the doctor was coming. "Well, wife, are you going to tell me or not?" Despite everything, Seren couldn't help smiling. It might have been more of a grimace, but she knew she'd made her point when Paige laughed.

"The doctor's on her way up, honey." Paige met Seren's gaze. "I feel like I should have a ring for you. I mean, the truth is, I'd like to give you a ring if you'd want one from me."

"You know how we both feel about marriage."

"Overrated." Paige nodded. "But still. Rings are nice."

"You can buy me a pretty ring anytime."

Paige glanced down at their hands. Seren had reached for Paige at every contraction, and this time she didn't want to let go.

"Ring or not, you got me for life. If you want me."

Tears sprang to Seren's eyes. Paige's words were simple, but the way she looked at her and how that made her feel was anything but. "Same."

Paige leaned close and kissed her. She pulled back at the sound of the door opening.

Dr. Bueller looked between Seren and Paige. "You two ready to have a baby?"

Seren exhaled. "Please tell me you can magically get this baby out without another contraction."

"That I can't promise." Dr. Bueller gave a wry smile. "Let's see how close you are."

Very close was the answer. Dr. Bueller didn't leave a second time. Instead, she called for a nurse and instructed Seren to lie down. Paige stood at the side of the hospital bed, one hand on the bed rail, the other palm up if Seren needed to grab her hand. And she did. Nothing prepared her for the final push, for the pain or the chaos that followed, but then it was all over.

And then there were no words to describe the feeling of a baby—her baby—on her chest. No words to describe how she felt gazing at the most beautiful human she'd ever seen. No words for how happy she felt despite how drained and weak her body was. She leaned close to kiss the fuzzy blond head and whispered, "I've waited so long to meet you." Tears coursed down her cheeks when the baby gazed up at her.

She looked for Paige then and realized she'd taken a step back from the bed, as if wanting to give her a moment alone with the baby. Seren appreciated the sentiment, would have thought she'd want it, even, but the space between them felt like a wide gulf. A thousand words filled her mind, but the only ones she managed were, "Come here."

Paige stepped forward. She kissed Seren's forehead lightly and then caressed the baby's cheek. "You two are beautiful together. I knew your baby would be perfect."

"Our baby."

Paige studied her as if doubting that she'd understood.

"It's what I want if it's what you want too."

"More than anything in the world." A tear slipped down Paige's cheek. She brushed it away and then touched the baby's tiny open hand. All five fingers immediately gripped Paige's one index finger. "I love you already," Paige murmured.

Love was too simple a word and yet the only one that was needed. Seren leaned against Paige and snuggled the baby closer. Her heart was filled.

Bella Books, Inc.

*Women. Books. Even Better Together.*

P.O. Box 10543
Tallahassee, FL 32302

Phone: 800-729-4992
**www.bellabooks.com**

CPSIA information can be obtained
at www.ICGtesting.com
Printed in the USA
JSHW031937280522
26363JS00001B/1

9 781642 473834